THE LETTER - KITTY'S STORY

(BOOK 1 IN THE LIFE ON THE MOORS SERIES)

ELIZA J SCOTT

This book is dedicated to my wonderful family: My husband for his well-timed supply of Yorkshire tea, ginger biscuits and regular words of support, and my daughters for being so understanding during the chaos of the latter weeks of writing this book. Mention must also be made of our two black Labradors who were my constant companions throughout – I couldn't have done it without you, boys

1

SPRING

KITTY HAD BEEN EXPECTING IT, but its arrival that sunny spring morning still sent a flurry of butterflies racing around her stomach.

She reached down and picked up the envelope; it felt cool and crisp and stiff with formality. Her eyes hovered over the neatly typed rows showing her name and address, the tell-tale frank in the corner. She drew a deep breath as anxiety – that unwelcome old acquaintance – inched its way up inside her.

She swallowed, reminding herself that this was what she wanted. What she needed to silence the niggle in her conscience. But that did little to stop the fresh bunch of worries that jangled away.

As she made her way into the kitchen, Kitty relaxed her shoulders – suddenly aware that they were hunched up around her ears – puffed out her cheeks and slowly released her breath as if exhaling any lingering dregs of negativity. She placed the envelope on the scrubbed pine table; she wasn't ready to open it just yet. She'd have a cup of tea first; calm herself down.

She filled the kettle and set it on the Aga hotplate, then headed over to the mullioned window, pushing it half open. She was relieved to see it had stopped raining, and the tumultuous grey clouds that had hung heavily over the thatched rooftops had been pushed back to reveal a bright expanse of crisp, blue sky. White wisps of cloud now hurried across it, whipped along on a light breeze that made the air smell deliciously fresh. She shivered as the cool air sneaked in, giving the curtains a gentle shake before slipping onto the window sill, brushing over the smiling faces of the daffodils in their squat blue and white jug, and mingling with the warmth of the kitchen.

Kitty's nose tingled as she breathed in the year's first earthy scent of spring, laced with the whiff of wood-smoke from the chimneys of the cottages in the moorland village of Lytell Stangdale. She smiled as a wave of sunshine came pouring into the room, molten and golden, splashing up the uneven lime-washed walls and casting muted, lacy shadows across the age-worn flagstone floor. After a bitingly cold winter – even by North Yorkshire's standards – spring was at last showing its face.

She lifted the kettle off the hotplate, silencing its shrill whistle. Boy, was she ready for a cuppa.

Cradling her mug in her hands, Kitty headed back to the Aga. Leaning against it, she took a sip of tea, sighing as it delivered a wave of warmth across her chest. The school run had been surprisingly chilly – raw, her mum would have called it – and it felt like the cold had crept right into her bones.

The letter loitered in her peripheral vision, setting off a ripple of nerves in her stomach as she contemplated the recent changes in her life. To say the last six months had been eventful would be an understatement. And, not for the first time, she wondered what her parents would have made of things. God, it still hurt how much she missed them, especially her mum. A shadow of sadness crossed her face as painful memories loomed. She took another gulp of tea and briskly flicked the thoughts away. Yes, the numb, slightly dazed feeling she'd had for months was still there, still had a grip on her, but its fingers were, very slowly, being loosened by the stronger fingers of hope. There was light, she told herself, at the end of the tunnel.

The sweet song of a blackbird pulled Kitty back to the window. The leaded casement objected with a groan as she pushed it wide open, before offering up her drawn, pale face to the sun's rays. She took a deep breath of the crisp breeze as it washed over her, shivering as it tingled its way into her soul.

Spring, a time for fresh starts and renewal. How appropriate, she thought, that the letter should arrive today.

The sense that she wasn't alone drew her back into the room. Her heart pumping faster, she set her mug down on the granite worktop, rubbing her arms that were suddenly peppered with goose-bumps. She was the only one in the house; the kids were at school, Humph and Ethel, her loyal black Labradors, were sniffing around the garden and Dan, well…

Nibbling at a hang-nail, she glanced around her, relieved to see that everything seemed as normal, but as she headed towards the door something caught her eye. She looked carefully, squinting, as a small white feather weightlessly zig-zagged its way down from the ceiling, landing silently on the letter.

Kitty stopped worrying her nail as the faint smell of honeysuckle wrapped itself around her. 'Mum,' she said softly, smiling as her eyes prickled and a tear escaped. She swept it away with her fingertips. It wasn't the first time she'd experienced this; there'd been several occasions throughout the bumps and blips of the last six turbulent months. Always appearing at a significant moment, it comforted Kitty to believe that it was a sign from her mum. She'd read about such things, guardian angels sending messages to loved ones from the other side. She liked to think that her mum was watching over her, saying, 'I'm here, looking out for you, my darling. Stay strong, and you'll be fine.'

Taking a deep breath, she picked up the letter. 'If ever there was a time to be strong it's now, Mum,' she whispered. She knew just how easy it would be for a tiny chink in her new-found resolve to grow into a gaping weak-spot. Or for her customary self-doubt to start nibbling holes in it, like a moth nibbling holes in a jumper. The proverbial corner had been turned and the black, miserable days of the last few years were forming an orderly queue, ready to be put firmly and resolutely behind her.

Or they would be if she'd let them.

2

AUTUMN - SIX MONTHS EARLIER

'Is it only me who wants to go on this sodding holiday?' growled Dan as he stormed into the hallway, dragging his fingers through his thick, sandy-blond hair before checking his watch for the umpteenth time. He wasn't a man known for his tolerance, and a deep shade of volcanic red was beginning to creep up his face.

'Two ticks. We're nearly done,' called Kitty from the bathroom upstairs. Her soft North Yorkshire accent sat in stark contrast to her husband's plummy tones. She did her best to sound breezy, but her stomach churned as she helped their six-year-old daughter, Lily, wash her hands. It was always tricky to leave the house on time with young children, and Kitty had struggled to master the art since her two were born. Consequently, she'd anticipated this morning's brewing impatience from her husband when Lily made a last-minute dash to the loo. It could have been worse if, five minutes into the journey, they'd had to stop in the middle of nowhere in search of a toilet. Kitty chewed at the corner of her mouth as the image of how angry that would have made him loomed in her mind. She quickly brushed it away, hoping the children wouldn't pick up on their father's black mood.

'There. All done.' She smiled down at her daughter and turned to hang the towel on the rail.

'Is Daddy cross with you again, Mummy?' asked Lily, a frown crumpling her brow.

Kitty's heart plunged. 'Of course not,' she said with a too

cheerful smile. 'He's just very excited to get on holiday and can't wait to set off. Now, come on, Lily-Loops, let's get you downstairs.' She ruffled her daughter's hair and ushered her out of the bathroom.

Lily had earned her nickname thanks to her tangle of golden curls. The colour was courtesy of her father, and she had her mum to thank for the curls and her large, chocolate brown eyes. She'd also inherited Kitty's easy-going temperament which had already, at her tender age, worked to her detriment since the arrival in the village of Evie Mellison who bullied her mercilessly at school. Lily was no match for the girl and regularly came home in floods of tears. And the last thing Kitty wanted for her daughter this weekend, was to pick up on any negativity from Dan.

There was always so much to do, even for just a long weekend away, and Dan's contribution was to nag, moan and put pressure on everyone else to be ready as soon as he was. They'd had enough experience of it to realise that this approach wasn't conducive to a happy family break, and invariably resulted in him being in a foul mood. Kitty was beginning to wonder if he engineered this sort of tension deliberately; he seemed to thrive on it.

'Sorry, Daddy,' Lily called down from the landing. 'I thought I just needed a wee-wee, but I needed a poop as well. I just need to get Snuggles. I promise I'll be quick.' She scurried off on her tip-toes in the direction of her bedroom, curls bouncing as she went in search of the slightly faded, well-cuddled rabbit.

'Just bring Snuggles, Lils,' Kitty said as she headed downstairs. 'And please try to be quick.' She saw Dan glance up at her as he headed towards the front door. He rolled his eyes before checking his watch again. She knew he hated this kind of toilet information the kids were sometimes overly keen to share.

Once in the oak beamed kitchen she headed to the table where she could have sworn she'd left her handbag. A familiar sense of panic slowly began to prickle its way up her spine. She was sure she'd just popped it off her shoulder and put it on the table next to her keys before she went to hurry Lily along in the bathroom. She scanned the work surfaces, but there was no sign of it. *Oh, God, where is it, where is it?* she thought, gnawing at her bottom lip and tapping her hand anxiously against her thigh. She needed to find it quickly before Dan sussed that she'd forgotten where she'd put it. He used to find her scattiness appealing and quirky, but now it only served to irritate him. This would sour his mood even more. Kitty shuddered at the thought.

Thinking quickly, she tried to retrace her steps, but it was futile, panic was playing havoc with her mind, muddling everything up. In her haste to help Lily, she must have chucked it down on the nearest spot. Her heart rate picked up speed and anxiety formed a tight knot in her chest as a shadow in the doorway told Kitty it was too late: she'd been rumbled.

Glowering, Dan didn't give her chance to speak. 'Why do we always have to have this mess about when we leave the house?' He strode over to the rocking chair that sat in the corner by the Aga. Kitty's eyes followed him until they found the object of her brief, but frantic, search. 'This what you've been looking for?' He picked up the bag from its resting place on the patchwork cushion.

A chill spiked through her as he moved towards her, a familiar cold expression in his eyes. Tauntingly, he dangled the bag in front of her then released his grip on the handle. Kitty reached for it, but she wasn't fast enough, and it fell to the floor with a loud clatter, spewing most of its contents across the flagstones. 'You clumsy cow,' he sneered.

'Oh, er, I'm really sorry, Dan.' Kitty was flummoxed, he was looking for an argument. Her heart tensed a little tighter, and she blinked away tears that had begun to pool in her eyes. She didn't want the children to see her upset. They were looking forward to this weekend away, and she didn't want anything to spoil it for them. She really couldn't understand why Dan always seemed determined to make things unpleasant.

It was at times like this when his moods bothered her the most; when they should be feeling happy and looking forward to spending precious moments of quality family time together. But such days were now regularly tainted by his anger and Kitty had finally given up making excuses for him.

She had sensed her feelings changing towards her husband. It had crept up on her slowly, but she was now conscious that the foundations of her once unconditional love for him had begun to falter. And she knew it would only take a tiny push for it to slip away and disappear into an inky black pool of nothing.

Tears abated, Kitty took a deep breath. She reached down, tucking a stray straggle of straightened, highlighted, blonde hair behind her ear, and scrabbled to push the escaped items back into her bag. But her hands, too riddled with anxiety, were clumsy and sent the contents careering further across the floor. Quickly, she shovelled them back in, but as she went to stand up her mobile phone tumbled out, hitting the floor with an unforgiving crack. Back on her haunches, she looked to see if Dan had noticed. His icy expression said it all.

'Sorry,' she said in a small voice.

'Sodding marvellous,' he snarled. 'I need a break from this crap.' He stormed out of the kitchen, knocking Kitty off balance as he passed.

She gathered herself together and watched from the window as Dan strode out into the garden and headed over to where his new sleek, dark-blue car was parked. He climbed in, leaving the door open and threw his phone onto the dashboard. Even from this distance, Kitty could sense his annoyance as he drummed his fingers impatiently on the steering wheel. Moments later, he snatched up his phone and made a call.

'Are you okay, Mum?' Lucas, Kitty's ten-year-old son, had come in from swinging on the tyre in the back garden.

'Fine thanks, Lukes. Just waiting for Lils to get Snuggles then we're all ready for the off.' She mustered a smile for her mild-mannered boy. He was tall for his age and the mirror image of his father. His temperament, however, couldn't have been more different. Where Dan was volatile and bad-tempered, Lucas was laid back and easy-going. He put her in mind of her older brother, Jimby.

From the kitchen Kitty could hear Dan talking to someone and, judging by his tone, it wasn't anything to do with work.

She was right. At the other end of the conversation was Samantha, the latest object of his adulterous affections. She was a ballsy blonde who gave him a run for his money.

'Hi, Dad.' Lucas's voice startled him, making Dan drop his phone.

'What the bloody hell do you think you're doing, creeping up on people?' He snatched up his phone. 'Hello. Sorry about that. I'll drop the papers off on Monday after I get back, okay? Bye.' He ended the call abruptly.

Lucas tried to hide the expression of hurt in his blue eyes. 'I wasn't, I was just coming to tell you that Mum and Lily are nearly ready.'

'About bloody time,' Dan muttered.

'Who were you talking to?'

'Just one of the clerks from work. I need to drop off a brief on Monday night.'

Lucas wrinkled his freckle-strewn nose. 'So, how come you were talking to them in that funny voice?'

'Look, stop asking so many questions. I'm the adult, not you, okay?'

'Everything alright?' Kitty had joined them outside, her elusive handbag now slung over her shoulder. The bright October sun sat low in the sky, and she shielded her eyes with her hand. It didn't escape her attention that Dan was looking decidedly shifty, and an unwelcome feeling of déjà vu slowly inched its way into her thoughts.

'Yeah, everything's fine. Stop fussing. It's just bloody work; you know what they're like. They can't leave me alone for five minutes. I feel like I can never have any time off. Can you imagine what they'd be like if I called them when they were leaving for a few days away? Anyway, I've agreed to drop the Stanton brief off at Pete Jackson's in Middleton-le-Moors on Monday night after we get back. I've been double-booked, so he's going to cover the PCMH in York Crown Court for me on Tuesday, but it sounds like the lawyer at the CPS is kicking-off about it. It's out of my hands because bloody chambers have organized a conference in Leeds in the Mackenzie murder trial at nine-thirty that day, with a plea in the Davies kidnapping in court two later that afternoon. And I'm duty-bound to deal with the latter two cases.'

He was ranting, and his feathers were ruffled. Kitty knew he wasn't telling her the truth.

'Well, try not to think about chambers. It's family time now, and you work so hard during the week you deserve a few days off. I'll just go and hurry Lily along so we can get going.' She forced a smile.

'Yeah, well, make it quick. If we leave it any later there won't be any point going.'

She turned back to the house where Lily stood in the doorway wearing a heart-melting smile and holding an armful of teddy bears. 'Please can I take them all, Mummy?' she asked. 'I don't want to leave any of them on their own because they'll get lonely.'

Hoping Dan hadn't heard, she ushered her daughter back into the house. 'Oh, Lils. What am I going to do with you?' She smiled, noticing that her daughter's curls were already doing an excellent job of escaping from their bobble.

After a brief negotiation, Kitty agreed to let Lily take just one more toy, quickly locking the large oak door before she could sneak back in and grab any more.

As they reached the car, Lucas began to complain bitterly.

'Aww, that's so crap! Why is she allowed to take another toy? Dad wouldn't let me take anything else.' He threw his arms up in outrage.

Kitty held the door open for Lily; it wasn't like her ten-year-old son to be so bad-tempered, and he wasn't usually so negative about his sister either. But she'd heard Dan snapping at him and, sensing that her son's feelings were still a little sore, put his outburst down to a subconscious need to channel his emotions. Hopefully, it would blow over quickly.

'It's just two teddies, Lucas,' said Lily.

'Well, it's not fair, and they'd better not come on to my side.'

'Come on, Lukes, there's plenty of room in the back, and I'll make sure Lils keeps Snuggles and Pickles on her side of the seat,' Kitty said with a smile.

'Okay,' he mumbled, 'but they'd better not cross this.' He used his finger to draw an invisible line down the middle of the seat.

Pouting sulkily, Lily climbed in and arranged Snuggles and Pickles carefully around her, shooting Lucas a black look.

'Stop looking at me like that, Lily. I haven't done owt.'

Dan's anger was simmering under the surface, gradually swallowing up the air in the car. 'Owt? Owt? Since when did you start speaking like a yokel? Don't they teach you how to speak properly up at that bloody school?'

'Dan!' Kitty felt hurt for her son, but fear of making the situation worse meant she didn't say any more. Instead, she reached behind her seat and gave Lucas's hand a reassuring squeeze.

Dan found this part of family life unbearable. Stifling. To his mind, this sort of situation justified his dalliances with other women. He worked hard and, thus, it followed that he needed time to switch off – something he couldn't do at home where there was too much noise, toys everywhere and, more often than not, Kitty's brother James. And he really couldn't stand James.

Kitty was about to climb into the car but was distracted by the loud tooting of a horn and the sight of her cousin, Molly, whizzing by in her mud-spattered four-wheel drive. She was waving furiously, a slice of limp toast clenched firmly between her teeth. She worked as a district nurse and appeared to be running late, as usual. Waving back, Kitty put on her happy mask – the one she hoped would cover her true feelings; she didn't want Molly catching on to her problems with Dan. Pity was the last thing she needed.

Molly beeped her horn again, this time at one of her sons, Ben or Tom – Kitty couldn't tell which twin it was – who was heading towards her in an old silver banger. Ben or Tom beeped back and slowed down in response to his mother's wagging finger.

With her smile still fixed, she caught Ollie Cartwright's eye as he strolled by taking his lemon cocker spaniel, Mabel, for her morning walk on the moor. 'Morning, Kitty,' he said with a grin that triggered dimples in his cheeks, his aquamarine gaze lingering on her for a moment.

'Hi, Ollie,' she replied shyly as her stomach responded with a flip.

Spotting Ollie, Dan jumped out of the car. Kitty knew that there was only one person in this village her husband hated more than James, and that was Oliver Cartwright. He knew there'd been something between him and Kitty when they were younger, and Dan was convinced he still had designs on her. 'Don't let us keep you,' he said, glowering.

'Morning, Dan,' said Ollie. 'Mind you have a good weekend.' He whistled for Mabel and walked off, hands thrust deep into his pockets.

'Bloody typical,' said Dan. 'We can't set foot outside of the house without seeing that loser or at least one of your sodding relatives.'

Kitty decided now wasn't the best time to remind him that her family were locals and went back generations, so it was inevitable that they would regularly bump into relatives. Dan's family were recent incomers and hadn't had the benefit of decades to merge and blend with other families. As for Ollie, well, they went back a long way.

Before he could get back into the car, Aoife Mellison stopped at the gate. Dan groaned and rolled his eyes, though she didn't appear to notice.

'Morning, Dan. Off somewhere nice?' she asked in an affected tone that jarred with her native Teesside accent — fake posh, Lucas called it. She was walking her lurcher and looked quite giddy at the opportunity to talk with him. As usual, she ignored Kitty.

'Ah, you again! Yes, and we're running late, so we need to get off.' That she was still grinning inanely at him suggested she hadn't detected the sharpness in his voice. Kitty knew he found the woman irritating, and he'd mentioned that there'd been several occasions recently when she seemed to appear out of nowhere, making tedious small-talk. He'd complained that she didn't seem to get the message that she didn't interest him.

Aoife had arrived in the village eighteen months earlier along with her husband, Dave, and their children, Teddy, who was in the same year as Lucas, and Evie, who was in the same year as Lily. Dave, with his arrogant swagger, had quickly gained the reputation of being a layabout. He told people he was an executive landscape gardener, but no one had ever seen any evidence of him lifting a finger. All he appeared to do was bum around the village or prop up the bar at the pub in the next village, Danskelfe. Occasionally, he could be heard making tortuous sounds on his saxophone.

Dan viewed the pair with contempt.

'Rufus and I are off for our daily run,' she announced, shaking the lead in confirmation. 'Hence the stream-lining.' She tapped the luminous yellow nylon cap that was stretched tightly over her head, ending just above her ears, where stumpy bunches of hair made a bid for freedom, sticking out at right-angles.

Dan glared at her.

'Morning, Aoife,' said Kitty; she felt awkward, conscious of Dan's rudeness, and that Aoife seemed only to be aware of his presence.

Scowling, Aoife's eyes flickered over Kitty before settling once more on Dan. An uncomfortable silence hung in the air for several seconds, and Kitty searched her brain for something to say. 'Er, is that a new coat you've got? It's nice and bright.'

'Hmm. Do you like my coat, Dan?' Aoife, apparently still reluctant to acknowledge Kitty's presence, patted the collar of the coat in question and beamed at him.

'What?' Dan's patience was being stretched. Kitty noticed a vein throb at his temple. He looked Aoife up and down, snorting as he took in the luminous pink nylon jacket over which was a neon-yellow, Hi-Vis tabard, edged with flashing LED lights. Rufus appeared to be dressed in a similar outfit. 'Jesus Christ! Every time I turn around you seem to be there! It's beginning to feel like you're stalking me.'

'Dan!' Kitty whispered.

Aoife's grin morphed into the scowl she usually reserved for Kitty. Her eyes bulged angrily as she glared at Dan. Rufus, pulling on his lead to chase Little Mary's cat on the other side of the road, snapped her out of her trance. 'Right! Come on, Rufie. Let's go and find Rosie, see if we can organise a party tea for Abbie and Evie.' She jutted her jaw and flounced off.

'What the hell is she wearing? She looks bloody ridiculous,' Dan muttered under his breath.

'She'll hear you, Dan,' Kitty said quietly.

'I couldn't give a damn. The woman's deluded. Now get in the car before we get held up by any more village idiots.'

THOUGH THEY WERE STILL a little subdued, Lucas and Lily quickly forgot the niggly start to the journey and their quarrel was soon a distant memory. Kitty and Dan barely exchanged words, which was preferable to the alternative and suited Kitty; she was tired of all the drama. The peace of the current cease-fire meant she was allowed head-space to savour the breath-taking scenery. She gazed out of the window as the wild ruggedness of her beloved North Yorkshire moors gave way to the broad sweeping fields of the dales, where large field barns stood in silent solitude, casting their long, looming shadows. The morning mists had cleared, pushed aside by bright strobes of sunshine, leaving the county to glow in all its autumn finery. The fields were still well stocked with animals, and the hedgerows were resplendent with brightly coloured berries. Over-head, a crisp blue sky was splashed with high, whippy clouds. Kitty loved the myriad muted shades bathed in mellow light, and the sense of cosiness that autumn brought.

Dan appreciated the silence, too. It allowed him to listen to the rich purring of his new car. He was enjoying the drive, feeling his anger ebb away as he negotiated the twisting, turning roads, which the car took smoothly and effortlessly. Realising they weren't far from their destination, he'd taken the longer route, keen to eke out the drive. Tapping his fingers on the steering wheel, he flicked on the radio and whistled along to the music. This weekend wasn't going to be too bad after all, he decided, as he felt his mind wandering to his new female pupil in chambers. She was a tasty morsel and, by all accounts, a bit of a tease. And there was nothing he liked better than the thrill of a chase, especially when it involved a hot, self-assured blonde. A smile hovered over his mouth; time to sample her, he thought.

'I feel sick,' Lily piped up from the back. 'Please, can we stop?'

Dan's mood nose-dived, taking with it the atmosphere in the car. Kitty felt her heart plummet when she saw his expression. He clearly had no intention of stopping.

'Maybe some fresh air would help?' She eyed him warily; she was struggling to understand his mentality these days. Surely any half-decent parent would realise that a child suffering from travel sickness needs to get out of the car for a while, she thought.

'Can't she wait? We're almost there,' he said.

'Maybe we could just stop for a quick minute or two?' Kitty tensed, waiting for his response.

'Bloody kids,' he snarled. 'Nothing but a bloody nuisance.'

Kitty winced, wishing he wouldn't speak like that in front of Lily and Lucas.

'I'm going to be sick!' Lily clamped a hand over her mouth.

'Don't worry, little love, we'll…' She was cut off by Lucas.

'Er, Mum, Lily's gone green. Stay over on your side, Lil, don't vom on me.'

Kitty turned to look at her daughter, who was sitting behind Dan. Lucas's description was worryingly accurate; Lily had gone green, and tears were streaming down her cheeks. 'Oh, Lils, don't worry, Daddy'll stop for you.' She turned to him. 'I really think we should pull over and let Lily get some fresh air.'

Dan shook his head in disbelief. 'Lily, you can just bloody well hang on, we're nearly there. Stop fussing, okay?' He pressed his foot down harder on the accelerator, exhaling noisily, ensuring no one was in any doubt about his displeasure. His mind fell on to the offer he'd had from Sam for this weekend. It would have been far more enjoyable than dealing with this crap. With her, he would have been able to unwind, be himself, not the family man he was struggling to be now. The thought of it made his anger surge; he could feel it coursing its well-worn route on auto-pilot around his body. His knuckles blanched white as he increased his grip on the steering wheel, struggling to keep his temper under control. Everyone was only too well-aware it wouldn't take much more for him to lose it.

Kitty cast an anxious glance at him, her heart banging in her chest. His face was getting redder, and he was clenching his teeth.

She couldn't understand why he found it so difficult to put his daughter before his own selfish needs for once.

'Don't look at me like that,' he said, badly negotiating a sharp bend and slamming the brakes on to avoid a head-on collision with a grocery delivery van. 'Stupid tosser,' he yelled at the driver who sounded his horn angrily. Kitty was hurled into Dan, and he shoved her away roughly. 'Drama queen.'

He was high maintenance, and he was exhausting. His spoilt brat behaviour if things didn't go his way was starting to get to her, particularly if it was directed at the children. There wasn't an ounce of empathy in his body.

Lily's travel sickness was gaining pace. She retched a couple of times. Then, with no further warning, she put her head back as her stomach relieved itself of its contents in a projectile tsunami of vomit. It hit Dan's headrest. And the back of his head.

Lucas's mouth formed a wide "O" until the smell assaulted his nostrils. 'Eurghh, man, that's so minging.' He covered his nose with his hands and lurched as far away from Lily as possible.

With his shoulders hunched around his ears, Dan swerved off the road, the car bouncing onto the grass verge, crushing the lanky cow parsley skeletons that swayed idly in the breeze. A clutch of sparrows, pecking at berries in the hedgerow, scattered, twittering angrily as he pulled the vehicle to a whip-lash halt. He sat, motionless, staring straight ahead as warm vomit trickled down his neck, snaking its way down his collar and under his crisp blue shirt. Struggling to find the right words, Kitty watched her husband from the safety of the corner of her eye.

Lucas was the first to shatter the silence. 'How come puke always looks like it's got carrots in it? Lily hasn't had any carrots, have you, Lils?' Lily shook her head forlornly then promptly burst into tears which snapped Dan out of his trance. He threw open the car door, slamming it firmly before storming off.

Ignoring her husband, Kitty turned to Lily, 'Oh, it's okay, sweet pea, don't cry. Let's get you cleaned up, then you'll feel much better.'

Sending a silent prayer heavenwards for having the foresight to pack so many wet-wipes, she had Lily cleaned up and in a fresh set of clothes in no time. Dan's seat proved more of a challenge, but she managed to get rid of any visible trace of vomit, leaving just the smell to contend with. She picked up Snuggles and Pickles, who were surprisingly vomit-free, and pulled an exaggerated astonished face. 'These guys must have super-magical powers if they managed to avoid getting covered in the contents of Lil's tummy, don't you think, kids?'

'Yeah, well, Dad clearly doesn't,' Lucas observed drily. 'He was dripping in it.' Both children giggled and, despite herself, Kitty found herself chuckling, too.

The fresh air had helped make Lily feel better, and a hint of colour had returned to her cheeks. Dan hadn't moved from the bench he'd been sitting on for the last fifteen minutes. Kitty decided to brave things and test his mood.

He pulled his vomit-sodden shirt out of his jeans and surveyed the damage. It wasn't good; he was covered. But worse than that was his hair. He reached a tentative hand up to it, touching the warm, lumpy slime. He pulled it away quickly. Shock, for the time being, appeared to have overwhelmed his anger. That was until he saw Kitty heading towards him.

She sat down beside him. 'I'm really sorry, Dan. It was an accident, poor little Lily couldn't help it. You know what these roads are like. She's feeling better now.' Anxiety had taken hold of her tongue, making her gabble as she tried to placate her husband and salvage their long weekend away. 'We just need to get you cleaned up. I've brought loads of wet-wipes, and I can get you a clean shirt out of the case. Then we can get go…'

'Shut up,' he snarled. 'Don't you realise you ruin everything?' His face was inches away from hers, and she could feel the warmth of his breath. It was laden with the rancid smell of the previous night's over-indulgence of red wine. She struggled to resist the urge to wrinkle her nose.

'Why is it that everything you put your hands on turns to crap? We can't even have a couple of days away without you messing something up.' He shot her a look of loathing that sent chills up her spine.

'Okay,' she replied coolly and, surprising them both, gathered herself together and headed back to the car. For the first time, Dan's words hadn't cut as deeply as they once had. Yes, they stung, but the tears that she regularly fought back had suddenly dried up. Now she simply felt numb.

For today, at least.

Dan watched her walk away, expecting her to turn back and offer more grovelling apologies, giving him the chance to enjoy the power he usually had to crush her with his words. Much as he hated to admit it to himself, he was increasingly getting a kick out of seeing her squirm as she tried to improve his mood. Yes, maybe he did get carried away with himself sometimes, but he was under a lot of pressure with the demands thrown at him by his job as a successful criminal barrister with the busiest practice in his chambers. Yes, it was becoming increasingly difficult to distinguish work from home. But surely Kitty could understand with all her pathetic empathy that, after tearing somebody apart in the witness box, it wasn't easy to switch off as soon as he came home. He needed time to unwind and relax. She should know he didn't *really* mean it, she should just humour him. But even Dan had noticed that he'd been bringing his work persona home with increasing regularity.

Kitty had reached the car, and she still hadn't turned back. Hadn't even looked at him. *What the hell was she playing at?* Here he was, dripping in *her* daughter's vile-smelling puke and all she could do was walk away and get back into the sodding car. Didn't she know she wasn't supposed to do this? There was a drill, and she should bloody well stick to it. It always worked, had done for years. She should grovel, break down into floods of tears, say it was all her fault and promise that it wouldn't happen again. She should tell him that she loved him, say she was lucky to have him. He would buy her a bunch of flowers, and she would thank him, smiling, her eyes red and swollen from hours of crying. That's how it was with them. That was the routine and, once she fell back into line, they'd be able to enjoy their break together. For some reason she wasn't toeing the line.

Momentarily forgetting the state of his hair, Dan ran his fingers through it and grimaced as they made contact with the half-digested contents of Lily's stomach. 'Eurghh. Christ's sake!' He gave his hand a shake before wiping it on the bench.

A chilly gust of air dumped a confetti of vibrant autumn leaves at his feet. He shivered, feeling suddenly cold.

Back at the car, Kitty was saddened to see her children's anxious faces peering through the windscreen. She opened the door and was immediately assaulted by the rancid smell of milky vomit. Keen to lighten the mood, she ignored the heave in her stomach. 'Hey, kids, everything's going to be fine. And you've got some roses back in your cheeks, Lily-Loops. How about a quick story while Dad gets himself sorted out? You choose which one.'

'Yay!' they both cheered.

'What about the one about the stinky man?' suggested Lucas.

How appropriate, thought Kitty, watching Dan from the corner of her eye as peals of laughter from their children filled the air. He was still rooted to his seat, glancing across at them. He wasn't used to being ignored, and he wouldn't like it. *Serves you right, you selfish bully.* Her heart sank when he got to his feet and headed back to the car.

'I need to get cleaned up,' he said expectantly, hands on hips.

'The wet-wipes are in the boot next to the carrier bag for dirty clothes, and there's a clean shirt in the suitcase. When you're done, the wipes can go in the bin over there,' she said with a nod, trying to keep her voice level and neutral for the sake of the children.

Dan froze; thrown by this new Kitty. Usually, she would back down and help him but, instead, she continued to read to the children. For the first time in their relationship, there was a subtle shift of power.

He headed for the boot. 'I think I'm going to need more than wet-wipes to get this out of my hair.'

'There's a bottle of water in the back-pack, and I noticed a sign for a public toilet which was pointing in the general direction of the village the hotel's in. You could always stick your head under the tap in the sink there.' Kitty was surprised at her own composure. She could feel Dan's eyes on her but resisted the urge to look up.

'Christ!' he gasped as he poured two litres of freezing spring water over his head.

Shivering, he fastened up the buttons of a fresh shirt. He looked cold, and he stank. Kitty could sense his anger bubbling beneath the surface; it wasn't like Dan not to lose his rag. He was obviously using his lawyer's instincts and had decided to play it cool.

Once in the car, he turned to Lily and Lucas, doing his best to ignore the smell. 'Listen, kids, when we get to the hotel, and once I'm cleaned up, why don't we go for a swim?' The pool's heated and has palm trees, we can pretend we're on a desert island. Sound good?'

'Really, Daddy?' said Lily.

'Cool.' Lucas beamed at his sister. He loved it when his dad spent time with them.

Dan turned to Kitty and gave her a satisfied smile; the kids were putty in his hands.

3

KITTY FAIRFAX HAD CAUGHT Daniel Bennett's eye when she was seventeen. She was waitressing in the Sunne – the local village pub – with childhood best friend, the aubergine-haired, curvaceous Violet Smith. The pair were saving to go travelling before starting university in York – textiles for Kitty and business studies for Vi. Kitty's cousin, Molly, who was a year older, had planned to join them, but falling pregnant with twins the previous year had scuppered those plans.

The money Kitty earned, together with the tips she shared with Vi and the other staff, was totting up nicely. Other than a couple of package holidays to Spain with her parents, Kitty hadn't seen much of the world. It was the same for Vi, and the pair were itching to get out there and explore.

Dan and his parents, George and Gwyneth (or the Dragon, as she was known by many), had migrated thirty-seven miles north of York to Lytell Stangdale. They'd taken up residence at the Manor House, a magnificent cruck-framed building with a thatched roof and carefully tended formal gardens.

At twenty-three, Dan was almost at the end of his second six months of pupillage as a barrister at the prestigious Minster Gate Chambers, in the mediaeval city of York. After spending three years studying for a law degree at university in Durham, and a further year doing his Bar finals at Bar School in London, he'd begrudgingly returned home to live with his parents. This was out of necessity rather than choice, since the meagre pupillage grant he received from his chambers was barely enough to keep him in his two weak spots: booze and inappropriate women, both of which he indulged in heavily. And, even though he'd much rather have the privacy of his own place to come and go as he pleased, he'd convinced himself he could have the best of both worlds by living at home – which he could do rent free and have the luxury of his mother running around after him. He'd experienced the squalor of student life and was determined never to go there again. He'd put up with his mother for now, but once he started earning decent money, he'd put down a deposit on a house and find a suitable woman to take her place.

A recent nagging from Gwyneth had added a sense of urgency to his plans. And his first impressions of Kitty had got him thinking that, with a bit of moulding, she could fill the role perfectly. She seemed sweet and shy, as well as being naturally pretty. With a few tweaks here and there, she had the potential to be the perfect girl to settle down with. The short crop of tight brown curls gave her an appealing elfin appearance, but he didn't really do brunettes or curls for that matter. He'd suggest she grow her hair, try it a lighter colour and straighten it out. She was a bit on the curvy side for his liking, too, but nothing that a diet couldn't fix. And, even better, living out here in the sticks meant she was far enough out of the way so he wouldn't have to give up his penchant for ballsy blondes. If his father could manage a wife and his bits on the side for over twenty years, there was no reason he couldn't.

'I don't know why you want to be messing about with that common village girl. She's not good enough for you. She's only interested in your money,' Gwyneth said bitterly as Dan was preparing to take Kitty out on a date.

He rolled his eyes. 'She's called Kitty, Mother, and she's not common. And I very much doubt she's after my money. From what I can gather her parents' farm and all the property they own in and around the village is worth a small fortune.'

This rankled with Gwyneth, she didn't like the idea of anyone else in the village being wealthier than the Bennetts. 'Huh! So she tells you, but talk's cheap. She's just trying to snare you, and when she's got a ring on her finger you'll find out the truth: they'll be as poor as church mice and will need you to bail them out. Mark my words.'

Dan looked across at his mother, she was really getting on his nerves. The sooner he got out, the better.

Gwyneth had other ideas. She thought no girl was good enough for her precious son and intended to keep him firmly tethered to her apron strings for some time yet.

As soon as he was old enough, she'd drummed into him that he should have no equity in women – aside from herself, of course – and this eventually became the motto he had lived by, following it to the letter. With her foolish attitude, Gwyneth had created a man who had no respect for women, including her.

GEORGE WAS AFFABLE AND HANDSOME, and the couple were thought by many to be ill-suited.

Gwyneth had practically blackmailed George into marrying her which, he felt, justified his many dalliances. She always found out about them, but if they meant he left her alone in the bedroom, then she was more than happy to turn a blind-eye. It was a small price to pay for living in the biggest house in the village and benefitting from the perks associated with being married to such a revered senior partner at a high-ranking firm of solicitors. If her family in Wales could see her now, they wouldn't believe it.

But the least said about them the better.

George regularly overheard Gwyneth's lectures to her son and was keen for Dan not to fall into the same trap as he had. 'Listen, son, take no heed of your mother,' he'd said after one of her lectures, and when she was well out of earshot. 'If you find a girl who makes you happy, and you want to settle down with her don't, for God's sake, let her slip through your fingers. Live your own life, not the one your mother wants for you, or you could end up regretting it. Forever. And trust me, I know what I'm talking about.'

His father's words were never far from Dan's thoughts, especially when he observed his parents' relationship in action. And it was no coincidence that he'd chosen a girl like Kitty: the polar-opposite of his mother.

Growing up in a chilly atmosphere, with George and Gwyneth as role models, meant he didn't really stand a chance of learning the dynamics of what constituted a happy marriage. Instead, he grew up observing how spite and point-scoring were used as weapons by his mother to deal with his father's sarcastic indifference. Their marriage was toxic.

Dan was a manifestation of each of his parents' worst genes. There was no doubt he'd inherited his mother's manipulative, cruel streak and her startling lack of empathy, but he'd also received a generous splash of his father's wandering eye and philanderer's DNA. Though, luckily for Dan, he'd been blessed with George's good looks, and bore no resemblance to the pinched, mean features of Gwyneth.

A MAN USED to getting his own way, Dan was surprised that Kitty stood firm and resisted his charms. But her reluctance only served to heighten her appeal. He'd have her whatever it took, he mused to himself one evening over a pint of beer in the Sunne, as he watched her busily taking orders and delivering plates piled high with food. He liked her ready smile and the easy, but ever-so-slightly shy manner she had with people. And the way the apples of her cheeks flushed when she was rushing around was beginning to drive him crazy with desire. He had an inkling that there was something going on between her and Oliver Cartwright, which niggled him, but dropping a few hints that things were blossoming between himself and Kitty seemed to have thrown Cartwright off the track. There was nothing like planting a little seed of doubt, then sitting back and watching it grow. Dan felt no guilt over Kitty's confusion when Ollie suddenly started to keep her at arm's length.

But, contrary to what he thought, Kitty hadn't been playing hard to get, she wasn't like that. She was, quite simply, in love with Ollie and, if she was honest, more than a little intimidated by Dan's confidence.

Violet hadn't been fooled by his charm offensive and had proffered liberal warnings.

'That arrogant Dan Bennett seems to be hanging around you a lot these days,' she said. They were in the Sunne, preparing for the evening shift.

'He's actually quite nice when you get talking to him.' Kitty's face flushed as she busied herself folding napkins, conscious of the weight of her friend's gaze on her.

'Really? There's something about him I don't trust. I know he's good-looking and all that, but he knows it and he's cocky.'

'He's not that bad. He's just being friendly; trying to get to know people in the village.'

'Well, if I'm not mistaken, I'm sure I saw him getting very friendly with some woman in the carpark the other night.'

'How do you know it was him? It'll have been dark.' Kitty didn't like the way this was going.

'Well, I'm pretty certain it was him. Anyway, how come Dan isn't trying to make friends with the lads in the village? Jimby and Ollie, for example, or your Molly's brother, Mark?' Vi raised a quizzical eyebrow.

'I don't know.' Kitty shrugged. 'Maybe it's because they've got nothing in common.'

'Maybe it's because Dan's trying to get his claws into you, more like. I saw him talking to Oll the other day and from where I was standing it didn't look very friendly.'

'I think you're wrong. And, anyway, I've hardly seen Ollie recently, he seems to be avoiding me.'

'I wonder why? But, seriously, hun, just watch yourself with Dan. I have a gut feeling about him, and my mum always tells me to trust my gut.'

But Violet's warnings were no match for Dan's well-honed manipulation skills.

He cornered Kitty in the Sunne one evening. 'Look, what harm can it do to go on just one little date?' he asked.

Kitty looked around, hoping to catch someone's eye so they could come and rescue her. 'Er, I er…'

'Just one date, and if you decide you really don't want to go out with me again, I'll leave you alone. I promise.' He gave her such a disarming smile that she found herself reluctantly agreeing to his request, to shut him up, if nothing else.

'Just a quick drink, then,' she said, determined that was all it would be, and hoping it would stop him pestering her.

It took a frighteningly short space of time from their first date to Dan getting himself firmly established in her head. Within weeks, she'd given up her plans to go travelling, which didn't go down well with Violet.

'What do you mean, you can't go travelling? What about all our plans? Mum and Dad have just spent a fortune on a new backpack for me.' Vi and Kitty were washing-up in the kitchen of the pub.

'Please don't be cross, Vi. Dan's booked us a romantic trip to Paris. He did it as a surprise but ended up having to tell me when I mentioned my travel plans with you. He feels really guilty about it.'

'I'll bet.' Vi clattered a plate down on the draining board. 'Can't he cancel it or re-arrange it or something? We've been talking about going travelling for ages. We've been looking forward to it; or I thought we were.'

Kitty knew her friend was annoyed and that her feelings were hurt. But, though part of her felt guilty about this, a bigger part was desperate to go on the trip with Dan. The way he'd described it had made her head swirl. And going to Paris with your best friend was hardly the same as going with your boyfriend.

'Oh, Vi, I can't ask him to cancel it, he's put so much effort into it. And it's not as if we'd actually got around to booking anything ourselves, had we? I know we'd talked about travelling but *talking* about it and *doing* it are two different things.'

'Not as far as I'm concerned, they're not.' Vi's blood was boiling.

'Please don't be like this, Vi.'

'Like what?' Violet turned to face Kitty. 'Disappointed? Upset that my best friend has dumped me for a manipulative bloke who's slowly brainwashing her? You know he's only done this because he can't stand the thought of you going anywhere without him keeping an eye on you?'

'That's not true!'

'Isn't it?'

'You know what I think, Vi? I think you're jealous! Jealous because, just for a change, it's me who's getting the attention.' Kitty threw the tea-towel down and stormed out of the kitchen.

'The next thing we know, you'll be giving up your plans to go to uni,' Vi called after her.

'Yeah, yeah! Whatever.'

Several months had lapsed before the friends made up, but their friendship wasn't the same, and a cool air lingered between them.

Not long after this, Dan bought Plum Tree Cottage and invited Kitty to move in with him.

'What the hell do you want to live with that dick-head for?' asked Jimby. They were sitting at the kitchen table. Kitty was flicking through a magazine. 'You've got a lovely home here, Mum and Dad are great, and you've got an awesome big brother.'

She sighed. 'Look, Jimby, if you can't say anything nice about Dan, don't say anything at all. Anyway, I'm ready to move out, spread my wings and all that.'

'Really? It's not five minutes since you were at school.'

'I've been through all this with Mum and Dad. And it's not as if I wouldn't be moving out when I go to university, is it? I don't see what the difference is.'

'Well, as long as you do go to university.'

'Why wouldn't I?' she asked.

'I think you know why.'

'I don't know why everyone's got it in for Dan. He only wants the best for me. He even said I don't need to stay in grubby student accommodation. Instead, I can commute with him.'

Jimby shook his head. 'How thoughtful. Anyone would think he was wanting to keep you right where he wants you. That's not controlling at all.'

Kitty's chair scraped as she pushed it back and stood up. 'Get lost, James!' She stormed out of the room, slamming the door behind her.

A month later, after she'd finished at sixth-form, Kitty moved in with Dan.

'HIYA, MUM.' Kitty pushed open the garden gate and headed towards Elizabeth Bennett who was weeding a flower border. It had been three weeks since she'd left home, and the first time she'd been back.

'Hello, lovie.' Elizabeth brushed back her hair, her eyes squinting in the bright sunshine while a broad smile lit up her face. She rushed over to her daughter and enveloped her in a hug.

'The garden's looking lovely.' Kitty eased herself out of her mum's embrace.

'It is now I've got these weeds out.' Elizabeth smiled at her daughter. 'Cuppa?'

'Sounds good.' She followed her mum into the house; she still hadn't worked out how she was going to tell her.

Kitty sat quietly while her mum made the tea.

'Everything okay, lovie?' Elizabeth asked.

'Yeah, fine thanks.'

'Dan okay?'

'Mmhmm. Actually, I've come to tell you something.' She paused, biting her lip. 'I've decided to put off going to university for a year. I just don't feel ready for it yet. I've talked it through with Dan, and he thinks it's a good idea, too.'

Elizabeth took a moment to absorb Kitty's words. 'Are you sure? I mean, have you really thought it through? You were so excited about it not that long ago. It was all you could talk about; that and the travelling with Violet.'

'I know what you're thinking, Mum. You blame Dan, but it's my decision. He's got lots of exciting plans for us. We're going to have long weekends away, and he says I can stop working at the pub because he doesn't want me doing a job like that. He told me he can't believe he's lucky enough to have a girl like me to look after him.'

'Really?'

Kitty nodded, beaming.

'Oh, Kitty, love. I really want you to think about this. Trust me, this is the best time to go to university, while you're young, with no responsibilities. Never mind what Dan says. It's alright for him, he's already had the experience, and if he really loved you, he would encourage you to go.' She placed her hand on top of her daughter's and gave it a squeeze.

'Dan does really love me.' Kitty snatched her hand away. 'But I might've known you'd be the same as all the rest. I don't know why you've all got it in for him,' she said, and stormed out of the house.

After that, her family resisted the temptation to lecture her and share their feelings for Dan. They were all too aware that playing into his hands would only serve to alienate her from them. One day she'd need them, and when that day came, they'd be there for her.

James had an almighty struggle on his hands keeping Molly and Violet from confronting her about the situation. And when rumours of Dan cheating on Kitty started to circulate, Molly had threatened to separate Dan from his testicles using sheep castration bands from her parents' farm.

∾

AT THE AGE OF TWENTY-TWO, Kitty married Dan in a low-key ceremony at the registry office in York. Only two guests were present: his parents, who also acted as witnesses. It was a far cry from the wedding day she'd dreamed of, surrounded by her family and friends in St. Thomas's church in the village. But he'd convinced her it was a good idea, saying what a great surprise it would be for everyone when they found out. And, if it was so important to her, they could have a church ceremony at a later date.

The day before the wedding, Dan had been distracted and uncommunicative. He'd disappeared for hours and returned home with a bloodied nose and a bruised cheek. But he'd brushed it off, saying he'd stumbled up the steps to chambers.

The following morning, she was relieved to see his mood was brighter, and the only scowl was on Gwyneth's face.

Two years into the marriage Lucas came along, all ruddy-cheeked and gummy smiles, bringing Kitty untold happiness, and giving Dan an excuse to stay away from home for longer periods – the sound of babies crying, he said, drove him mad.

The promised village wedding never materialised, and it only made him angry if she mentioned it. She eventually gave up asking.

4

THE MONDAY MORNING after their weekend away arrived, blustery and bitterly cold. Kitty made sure that the children were wrapped up in their winter coats before walking them to school. Dan had already arranged to work from home that day. He had a mountain of paperwork with looming deadlines hanging over him, and he could get through piles more working in his study than he could at his desk in chambers with its various distractions. Notably, Astrid Eriksson, his latest pupil, a Nordic blonde with ice-blue eyes and legs that went on forever. She had a penchant for tight-fitting pencil skirts that hugged her pert bottom and made him yearn with lust. He regularly found himself fantasising about sliding his hands slowly up there and sampling the hidden delights. There was nothing like a juicy temptation to take his mind off his work.

Dan licked his lips as he thought of her. *No*, he came to his senses. After the weekend he'd had with Kitty, it would be best to keep Astrid out of his mind today. She was already hinting that she'd do anything to secure a tenancy in chambers. And he was sure he hadn't just imagined that she'd been hitching her naughty, tight skirt a little higher, revealing a sliver of lace stocking top. She'd even once joked to him that she went commando, causing a bolt of lust to surge through him, making his manhood go from nought to sixty in two seconds flat.

He padded into the kitchen where the comforting aroma of toast made his stomach growl. Taking a slice of toast from the rack, he added a quick smear of butter, topped it off with marmalade and took a bite, savouring the sharp citrus tang. Kitty would be back from the school run any time. It was only a short walk unless she was snared by some of the gossipy mothers. It always amazed him how they could talk for so long; usually about a load of old crap.

He finished his toast, wiping the crumbs from his mouth with the back of his hand, then filled the kettle and set it on the hotplate to boil. Leaning against the Aga he folded his arms across his broad chest, enjoying the warmth that seeped up his back. He gazed out of the window, watching the bare branches of the trees sway vigorously back and forth, as his thoughts fell onto the recent change in his wife.

A sudden flash of blue topped with a dark-blond head caught his eye from the other side of the road by the phone box. *It couldn't be*, he thought, striding over to the window, a stab of irritation spiking through him. He looked out to see Dave Mellison leaning against his bike, his lank, greasy ponytail hanging limply down his back. He was having an animated conversation on his mobile phone and blocking Dan's view. *Bloody layabout!* Closer inspection satisfied him that it must have been his imagination confusing one of the local teenagers with the very last person wanted to see in this village.

The shrill whistle of the kettle brought his thoughts to a halt. He winced and lifted it off the hotplate. Setting it down, he reached for the teapot; he was keen to bring Kitty round to his way of thinking again, and surprising her with a cup of tea would be a good start. The sooner things got back to normal, the better; he didn't have time for this crap.

He struggled to remove the lid from the teapot; no matter how hard he tried it just wouldn't budge. There must be a knack to it, he thought and tried again. 'Sodding thing!' Even the bloody teapot was giving him grief. Eventually, after a few twists and turns, the lid obliged, allowing him to throw a couple of teabags into the pot before pouring hot water over them.

The wind, which seemed to be holding the rain at bay, was blustering around the cottages, scooping up coppery leaves and scattering them across the street. The faint aroma of wood-smoke, blown down from squat chimneys, mingled with the smell of cold, damp earth; a warning to the residents of Lytell Stangdale that an early winter was lurking around the corner. Kitty walked briskly back from school, her eyes fixed firmly on her boots and her chin tucked into her scarf, hoping to avoid conversation with anyone. She was steaming ahead as she passed the village shop, when, 'Umphhh!' She crashed into a tall, solid wall of muscle encased in a waxed jacket, the wearer of which appeared to have sturdy, broad shoulders and, judging by the grip that was currently keeping her upright, a strong pair of hands. She looked up to apologise and was met by a pair of heart-stoppingly handsome aquamarine eyes, edged in thick dark blond lashes. Aquamarine eyes that belonged to Oliver Cartwright. 'Oh, er.' Her heart gave an involuntary flip as she hastily removed her hands that had found themselves resting on his chest.

'Oh, God, I'm so sorry, Kitty. Are you okay?' he asked, his eyes full of concern as he looked down at her.

The wind was playing havoc with her hair, and several wayward strands that had escaped from her ponytail were blowing around her face. She tucked the stray wisps behind her ear and nodded, feeling the prickle of a blush stain her cheeks. 'Yes, I'm fine thanks, Ollie. And it's me who should apologise. I wasn't watching where I was going. Couldn't see for my hair.' She gave an embarrassed laugh.

'Well as long as you're alright,' he said gently. He seemed reluctant to let go of her.

Long-hidden feelings swirled in her gut, catching her off-guard, as she felt her care-worn heart begin to race. For years, she'd done her best to avoid him, which hadn't been easy in a small village, and she couldn't remember how long it had been since they'd been this close physically. He appeared to be having the same struggle to break eye contact as she was.

Breaking the spell, Kitty cleared her throat. 'Erm, how's Anoushka? Still dancing?' she asked after his fifteen-year-old daughter.

He ran a hand back and forth over his dark-blond hair. 'She's great, thanks. Still busy with her dance classes. Working hard at school, or so she tells me.' He laughed, there was no mistaking the affection in his voice.

'She gets more beautiful every time I see her. Lily's sure she's a fairy princess.'

Ollie beamed. 'Oh, she'll be chuffed to bits when I tell her that. And how are your two rascals?'

'Oh, you know, just being typical six and ten-year-olds.'

'Ahh, I remember it well. Wait till they hit the teenage years, then it gets interesting,' he said, grinning.

'I'll bet.' Kitty paused for a moment and fiddled with her gloves, unsure of what to say. 'Well, I'd best be getting back home.' She smiled up at him, glancing at his handsome face, his strong, square jaw that was grazed with dark-blonde stubble. Her eyes briefly rested on the mouth that turned up deliciously at the corners. A sudden flash-back to the feeling of those lips on hers made her cheeks burn hotter. She hoped he hadn't noticed.

'Yep, and I'd better get back to work. Nice to see you, Kitts. Mind how you go.' He gave the top of her arm a brief squeeze.

'Bye, Ollie,' she said and hurried off, conscious of his eyes on her as she went.

There was no denying, Ollie Cartwright touched her in a way that Dan never did.

As she headed home, not for the first time, Kitty wondered what type of life she would have had if her fledgling relationship with Ollie hadn't been scuppered all those years ago. He was her brother, Jimby's, best friend and had been a regular at their home for as far back as she could remember. She'd had a crush on him since she was thirteen; his eyes the colour of the Mediterranean Sea, the sun-kissed highlights in his hair and the dimples that appeared every time he smiled had featured regularly in her daydreams. And, oh, how she'd loved his smile, it had made every bit of her turn to jelly. But it wasn't until she was seventeen and he was nineteen, that she realised the feeling was mutual. They were at a Young Farmers' barn dance when he'd told her that she was the most beautiful girl he'd ever seen, and they'd shared their first kiss. Her heart had soared.

A month later Dan Bennett moved into the village, oozing confidence, arrogance and way-too-much testosterone. Soon after, Kitty's budding romance with Ollie mysteriously fizzled out.

Sighing at the memory, she thrust her hands deep into her coat pockets, tucked her chin back inside the warmth of her scarf and hurried on, eyes cast down once more. The wind had picked up, pushing her one way, pulling her another, and ruffling her poker-straight ponytail of highlighted blonde hair. She felt a couple of stinging, icy splashes of rain land on her face. A storm was brewing, there was no doubt about it.

She hurried past the thatched Damson Cottage where craggy-faced local artist, Gerald Ramsbottom, was fighting a losing battle raking up leaves in his garden. 'Morning, Kitty, pet.' His voice was snatched up by the wind and carried off down the street, blowing by Kitty as it went.

'Oh, morning, Gerald, sorry I was miles away.' She took in his latest flamboyant multi-coloured outfit. It clashed alarmingly with his hair and beard which were dyed a mixture of vibrant shades.

'I can see that.' He gave her a gummy grin.

'Eee, Gerry, man, why are you smiling at Kitty without your teeth in?' Big Mary, his wife, bustled out of the house in an outfit that rivalled Gerald's for brightness. It was topped off by a shock of vivid pink hair. 'Morning, pet,' she said to Kitty.

'Morning, and it's fine about the teeth. I didn't notice,' she fibbed.

'Well, he should be getting some wear out of them. Paid good money for them. Come on, young man, where are they?'

Young man? Kitty stifled a laugh, Gerald was eighty if he was a day and Big Mary wasn't far behind.

He rummaged in his trouser pocket and pulled out a set of grubby looking false teeth, spat on them and gave them a cursory wipe with the hem of his jumper before pushing them into his mouth. He beamed broadly at his wife. 'That better, my angel of lovelinesh?'

'Eee, much!' She put her hands on her hips. 'He got them off eBay. Five ninety-nine. His was the only bid, mind. They're a bit of a funny fit, but he'll get used to them *if* he keeps wearing them.' She gave Gerald a stern look, and he returned one of utter adoration.

Kitty could feel a giggle rising but did her best to contain it. 'Oh, wow, er, what a bargain. Well, I hope you get used to them Gerald. Anyway, I'd best get back. See you both later.'

'Bye, pet,' said Big Mary.

'Aye, gan canny, pet,' added Gerald.

As Kitty continued on her way, a succession of ear-splitting squawks were carried down the village on the cold north wind, shattering the peace of the village. She didn't need to hazard a guess as to the owner: James's macho Leghorn cockerel, Reg, had been terrorising the residents of Lytell Stangdale with his over-developed territorial instincts since his ubiquitous arrival six months ago. Kitty sympathised with whoever had found themselves on the wrong side of the bird's humour this morning. An image of accident-prone Jimby chasing Reg a couple of weeks ago triggered a smile. Both had ended up in the village pond.

As she drew closer to Oak Tree Farm and the heavily thatched, whitewashed longhouse that was her home, her smiles peeled away, replaced by a feeling of apprehension when she arrived at the gate.

She paused and took a deep breath before pushing it open. It was the first time she'd been alone with Dan since Friday morning, and she didn't know what to expect.

Dan had just set the teapot onto the wicker mat when he heard the familiar sound of the gate creaking open, announcing Kitty's return. He peered out of the window, trying to assess his wife. He wondered if it was the Kitty he knew or the unfamiliar doppelganger who'd taken her place over the weekend. Pursing his lips, he was disappointed to see that her expression gave nothing away. He took two mugs down from the dresser, noticing the one she seemed to like, for some daft reason, had a chip on its rim near the handle.

Hesitantly, Kitty pressed down on the latch, pushing open the heavy oak door. The hallway exhaled a breath of warm air, recoiling as the chilly wind that had followed her home sneaked in, spitting out a flurry of leaves on the coir doormat. She quickly closed the door behind her, leaning against it for a couple of seconds.

She pulled off her gloves and stuffed them into her coat pockets before hanging it up on the peg by the door. With no enthusiastic black Labradors to welcome her home – they were still along at James's – the house felt uncharacteristically quiet, though, she thought she could hear Dan busying himself with something in the kitchen. She rubbed her cold hands briskly together before heeling off her boots.

Coming in from the cold always made her nose run. She sniffed – something else that annoyed Dan – and took a tissue from her jeans pocket, wiping her nose.

For a moment, Kitty hovered in the hallway, wary of facing her husband. Then she puffed out her cheeks, shoved her hands into the back pockets of her jeans and headed into the kitchen where she was caught off guard by the sight of him making a pot of tea. She wasn't even aware he knew how, but there he was, doing it right before her eyes. Her stomach flipped, he looked so handsome. As fed-up as she was of him, he could still melt her heart a little. And he knew it. He was looking relaxed in a pair of faded blue jeans and a grey marl t-shirt clinging to his well-defined abs, a blue checked shirt slung casually over it – a stark contrast to his dark, formal three-piece work suits. His sandy-blond hair was ruffled, and his pale blue eyes were emphasised by the remnants of the golden tan the Italian sun had kissed onto his skin the previous August. Glimpses of him like this were how Kitty liked him best, and not so very long ago she would have been taken in. But something inside her had shifted, and she knew she was looking at a wolf in sheep's clothing.

Dan turned to face her and mustered his most charming smile, the one with the proven track record for melting female hearts. He handed her a mug. 'There you go, Kitts. I've made you a nice cup of tea. Good and strong, just how you like it. In your favourite mug, too. Though I notice it's got a chip in it, so I'll buy you a new one. A better one.' He was trying to sound magnanimous, and it grated on her.

Kitty took the tea, grateful for its warmth against her cold hands. 'Thanks,' she said, 'but I don't want a better mug. I like this one, it's special. Mum bought it for me just before she died, and the chip doesn't bother me.'

'Since when do we keep chipped mugs?' He narrowed his eyes. 'Only joking, I understand why you'd want to hang onto that one. Sentimental reasons and all that.' He flashed a disingenuous smile. Kitty knew Dan didn't trouble himself with sentiment.

She stood in silence, focusing her attention on the steaming tea in her mug, the chip in its rim. She could feel Dan watching her. He'd be keen to start a conversation, get things back to normal, so he could get on with his usual routine.

The silence was clearly testing his patience. 'Look, Kitty, it's time we got this sorted out. I've got a shed-load of work to do. I've got Bar Two forms coming out of my ears – all marked urgent – and a great pile of charging advices to write up. I don't have the time to be pratting about like this.'

She took a sip of her tea and glanced across at him just in time to see him roll his eyes. But, instead of feeling anxious or scared as she usually would, she felt bold and strong. 'Something's changed, Dan. I've changed,' she said, holding his gaze.

'Too bloody right.'

'For years you've treated me like I'm a worthless nobody and made me feel like I'm nothing but a nuisance to you, and I really don't understand why. Half the time you talk to me like you despise me, and that hurts.' Her stomach clenched, but she was on a roll; there was no way she was going to stop now. 'Everything I do seems to make you angry. I don't know how I manage it, it just seems to happen. But you know what? I really don't care anymore. And I actually don't think the problem is with me, as you've been telling me for years. I think it's you.' She could feel herself shaking, and it was a struggle to keep her voice under control, but she was determined to stay strong. She'd got this far; no way was she going to weaken and cry.

'Don't be so ridiculous. If that's what you think you've obviously got a screw loose. Don't you realise how lucky you are?'

'Lucky! You think I'm lucky to have a husband who seems to hate the sight of me? I honestly think if you could point the finger of blame at me for everything that goes wrong in the world, then you would. And half the time when I'm talking to you, you just walk away without even acknowledging what I've said. I end up speaking to the back of your head.'

'Well, if you had anything interesting to say, something worth listening to, then I'd answer you. But you don't. You just talk mindless, boring crap. What you need is something to worry about. All you do, each and every day, is sit on your fat arse and do nothing while I'm working my backside off in court. You don't do anything to contribute to this house. Oh no, that's all down to me. Don't you realise how much pressure I'm under constantly, while all you have to do is worry about how many cups of sodding tea to have?' His face was inches away from hers, and the look in his eyes told her he was getting a real kick out of this.

Outside, the wind had whipped up. It rumbled down the chimney and made the Yorkshire sliding sash windows rattle in their frames. But Kitty didn't notice. Her heart was galloping. Anxiety had a hold of her, making her breathing shallow, but she mustered all her strength and swallowed hard; she didn't want anything to stop her words in their bid for freedom. She placed her mug on the worktop and, much as it made her feel uncomfortable, she held eye contact with Dan. 'This weekend has made me realise that the way you've treated me over the years has worn away any last shred of love or respect I ever had for you. All I feel for you now is emptiness. I … I don't love you anymore, Dan.' She didn't know where the words were coming from, but she continued, her voice low and calm. 'I'm sorry, but it's your doing. You've pushed me away, and I've no intention of staying in a marriage with someone who makes me feel like such a worthless human being. I'm thirty-four; I've still got a life to live, but not like this. And I'm not just doing it for myself. I'm also doing it because I don't think our marriage sets a very good example to Lucas and Lily.'

Dan was uncharacteristically silent, his face ashen as his eyes searched hers, marshalling his thoughts. Court-room battles were a doddle, but here at home, with Kitty fighting back, this was new territory.

Feeling herself begin to shake, she clenched her jaw and sat down heavily on a chair at the table. A buttery toast crumb caught her eye. She rolled it around under her forefinger. A welcome distraction, it became the focus of her attention as she struggled with the tears that threatened.

Dan wiped his hand across his face. Never in all the years they'd been together had Kitty spoken like that. She was so convincing, he almost thought she meant it. But he'd let her speak, let her have her little moment, and now it was his turn. Now it was time for him to take back control. Using his courtroom tactics, he pulled himself up to his full six feet and puffed out his chest as his eyes bored into Kitty's. He was going to break her down into little pieces and put her back together, bit by tiny bit, in a form that suited him. Years of experience had taught him exactly how to do it.

'Finished? Well, now you can listen to me, you pathetic little nothing. You need me. You're nothing without me. And I don't give a damn what you think.' He could feel the familiar buzz of adrenalin surging through his body. He was back in his comfort zone.

His words stung. 'What a horrible thing to say, but if that's what you feel, then I think it says more about you than it does about me.' She knew he'd be expecting the apology and the tears and she could tell he was taken off guard by her uncharacteristic response. It made her all the more determined to sustain an outward appearance of control. But the reality was that she was terrified, and her heart was pounding so hard she was sure Dan would be able to see it as it hurled itself against her chest.

'You're being ridiculous! What's the problem, is it your time of the month or something? You women and your sodding hormones make everyone's life a misery. Just pull yourself together and start behaving normally.'

Kitty stopped fiddling with the toast crumb and looked up at Dan who was now towering over her. Fear was creeping its way up inside her, but she was determined to carry on. 'Any time things don't go your way it's always my fault. I can see it coming when you walk through the door from work. If you have that look in your eyes, I know I'm in for it later. And you know what? I've had enough.'

'It's your fault if I'm irritable at home; the way you witter on.'

'I should've known.' She shook her head. 'It has nothing, whatso-ever, to do with the fact that you're a bully.'

'Me, a bully? You don't know the meaning of the word. And I'm not leaving. If you want out of this marriage, then you leave. And don't even think about taking the kids. I'll make sure I get custody of them; my mother will be more than happy to look after them when I'm at work. You won't even get to see them if I have anything to do with it. Judges don't look kindly on unfit mothers. So, you'd better make bloody sure you have a good solicitor because I'm going to wipe the floor with you.'

Kitty's heart beat faster, and a whooshing sound filled her ears. She hung her head and struggled in vain to stem the salty tears that had been dammed up by her bravado. They broke free and were now pouring down her cheeks in rivulets, running off her chin and splashing onto the table. Her children were her ultimate weakness. And he knew it.

'I can't be bothered with this crap. I'm going to chambers to get my work done, and when I come back, I expect you to have pulled yourself together and tidied yourself up. My mother's calling round to see the kids tonight, and you can just behave yourself in front of her. She always said you weren't good enough. Please don't prove her right.'

Kitty wiped her tears away with the back of her hand and looked up at him. He was glowering at her, hands on hips, and breathing heavily. Her feeling of fear had been replaced by repulsion that he thought it was acceptable for him to behave like a prosecution barris-ter, treating her like a defendant in the witness box. She got to her feet, the chair scraping angrily against the flags as she pushed it back. 'I can't do this anymore. I'm your wife, Dan, but you talk to me like you despise me. Why is it so difficult to be civil to me or treat me with any form of kindness? I've never treated you badly and I never would because I'm not cruel like you, but I've had enough.'

Dan laughed scornfully. 'You don't know you're born, you little fool. You're nothing but a simple local yokel who doesn't realise how lucky she is.'

'Everything alright?' came a familiar, deep voice from the hall. Kitty and Dan froze. 'Am I interrupting something?' The tone was grave and they both turned to see her brother, James's six-foot-two frame filling the doorway.

5

THE WIND that was noisily whistling around the cottage and the fact that Kitty and Dan had been so engrossed in their argument meant that they hadn't heard the low rumble of James's old Landie as it pulled up outside. Nor had they heard him knock at the door before he came in.

'That's all I need! Since when has it been okay for you to just walk into my house as if you own it?' asked Dan.

'Dan!' said Kitty.

'Er, I did knock. A couple of times, actually, but I couldn't get you to hear me, so I tried the door, found it open and here I am. No offence intended.' Though James was apologising, there was a note of warning in his voice.

'It's good to see you, Jimby,' said Kitty, using his family nickname. 'Come in, let me get you a cup of tea.' She felt relief at seeing her brother's friendly face.

Dan shook his head in disbelief. 'I'm off. The last thing I need is a sodding Fairfax family convention.'

In the hallway, he snatched his keys that were hanging from an old meat hook on one of the beams, grabbed his waxed jacket and stormed out, slamming the door behind him.

Kitty flinched. Chewing on her bottom lip, she glanced at her brother. She didn't know how much he'd heard.

'That was quite an exit your husband made just there.'

'You could say that.' She gave a watery smile.

'You okay, sis?' James ran a hand over his short, dark curls, an expression of concern troubling his features. He looked at his sister intently. Her heart-shaped face looked drained, and purple circles hung wearily below her tired-looking eyes. She seemed to have lost quite a bit of weight recently, too, which she could little afford as she was already stick thin and looked smaller than her petite five-feet-four inches. 'Come and give your old brother a hug, Kitts.' He hung his waxed jacket on the back of a dining chair and walked over to her, enveloping the shadow that remained of his sister in his bear-like arms.

The kindness and concern in Jimby's voice was too much for her, and the adrenalin that had scaffolded her while she stood up to Dan suddenly leached away. She felt herself crumple as she buried her head into her brother's chest and let the tears flow.

EVENTUALLY, Kitty stopped crying, leaving her head thumping and her eyes swollen and puffy. James loosened his hug and regarded the tear-sodden image before him with the same round brown eyes as his sister. 'Hey, snotbag, I think I'd better get you a hankie, I don't think my jumper can soak up any more tears.' He made a joke of trying to wring it out then rummaged in his jeans pocket, producing two clean, but crumpled tissues. 'There you go, once a boy scout, always a boy scout,' he said with a cheeky grin.

'Thanks.' She smiled back weakly and blew her nose into one of the tissues. 'You were only in the boy scouts five minutes, Jimby. I seem to recall you were kicked out.'

He shrugged. 'I think you'll find it was the cubs I was kicked out of, actually. High spirits, Mrs Muggins said. Miserable old bugger. Anyway, enough about me and my misspent youth. How about you? Want to talk?'

With a weary sigh, Kitty flopped onto a dining chair. 'I'd love to talk, but the last thing I want is to get you involved, and all wound up. I've been so stupid, and it's taken me a long time to open my eyes properly and be honest with myself about the situation I'm in. I feel partly to blame because I've allowed myself to become a victim and that's something I really don't want to be.'

James let out a low whistle. 'Wow. That sounds pretty serious. I think you don't have any other choice but to tell me. I'm your brother, and we're all we've got since Mum and Dad died. I know you've got the kids, but you know what I mean. You've only got me to look out for you and vice versa,' he said.

She looked down at her hands, her thin fingers, with nails bitten right down to the quick, were busy twiddling and twisting the soggy tissues. She felt a desperate sadness deep in the pit of her stomach, but she knew she wasn't going to cry anymore. Not today at least; her supply, for now, was depleted. 'Have you got time for this? I know you've got a load of work on and I...'

James raised his hands, 'Don't you go worrying about me. I've got no one to answer to. Apart from Jerry and Jarvis, of course,' he said, referring to his spaniels. 'That's the beauty of being your own boss.' James was the local blacksmith, like their father who'd trained him. He'd taken over the business after their parents died.

'If you're sure?'

'Absolutely. I was only going to call in on Ollie, I've got a few things I'd like to run by him, but we can always do that later over a beer. And there's nothing so urgent I can't have a chat with my little sister.' A low bark emanating from James's Landie interrupted him. 'Ahh, yes. My reason for calling round was to drop off those two wayward Labradors of yours.'

'Wayward? That sounds ominous, what have they been up to?' Kitty wiped her nose, feeling slightly awkward at the mention of Ollie's name.

'Well, Ethel's been as good as gold, but Humphrey's been an old tart again. Usual stuff, flirting outrageously with anything in a sequinned collar. And now he's in the dog-house with his missus. Ethel's giving him the silent treatment.'

'Oh, poor old Humph. When's he going to realise at twelve he's too old to be a womaniser?' Kitty giggled. 'It's very undignified behaviour for a gentleman of his advanced years. No wonder Eth isn't speaking to him.'

'Hey, it's not his fault he's irresistible to the ladies, it's his animal magnetism. You should've seen the latest bit of hot stuff who caught his eye; the one who's caused all the trouble. A right little floozie she was. Honestly, Kitts, Humph's got no taste. She was that fluffy the only way you could tell her head from her arse was because she was wearing a bright pink top covered in those sparkly diamond things. Very tight it was too – in all the wrong places.'

'Oh, Humph.'

'It gets worse. He made an arthritic attempt at humping the furball's head and ended up falling on top of her. Blamed it on his cataracts. Her owner wasn't impressed, but don't worry, it wasn't anyone we know.'

Humphrey gave another bark and James headed for the door. 'Sounds like someone's keen to see his mum – if you're willing to take him back after hearing that, of course.' He gave one of his trademark wide grins.

'I'm always keen to have them back, the house isn't the same without them.'

Kitty followed her brother to the front door and watched as he opened the rear of the Landie. Ethel leapt out first but, due to his arthritic legs, Humph had to be lifted down, and judging by the expression on Jimby's face, it wasn't an easy task.

'Christ Humph, you solid old bugger, I think you've got heavier since I lifted you in there.' Humphrey responded by licking James's face, covering it with slobber. 'Mmm, just what I need. Come on, let's go and see your mum.' He set the elderly Labrador down, wiped his face with the sleeve of his jumper and rolled his eyes good-naturedly.

Ethel charged down the path, tail wagging at the sight of Kitty. 'Hiya, Eth.' The Labrador stopped for a quick ruffle of her ears before running into the house to check her bowl for biscuits. Humph tried a trot, which wasn't much faster than his walk. He was in raptures, a wide smile on his grey muzzle, his otter-like tail wagging so hard it made the generous proportions of his rear wiggle. 'Hiya, handsome. I hear you've been hell-raising with the ladies again.'

Back in the kitchen, she flopped into the rocking chair while Humph sat on the floor beside her, resting his head in her lap and enjoying her gentle, rhythmic pulling of his velvety ears. Soon sleep got the better of him and, with a harrumph, he eased himself down, laying his head on Kitty's feet, and before long the kitchen was filled with the rumble of his snores.

James, who'd been sitting at the table opposite Kitty, jumped to his feet when the shrill whistle of the kettle sounded. 'You look like you're slightly indisposed, with Humph sleeping on your socks, so I'll make the tea while you tell me what's been happening. If you're still up to it?'

With a sigh, she leaned back in her chair. 'Oh, bugger, Jimby, it's all such a mess.' She looked up at the low-beamed ceiling as if searching for answers.

'Well, you know you can always talk to me, sis. And you can always tell me to stop being nosy, too, if you like.'

'I just feel so stupid, sitting here in the cold light of day, I can see what a bloody fool I've been. But I've had time to think about things over the weekend, and I also feel really clear about what I have to do – in the short-term at least.'

'Right,' said James. 'The last part of that sentence sounded good, but why do you think you've been stupid and a fool? You're neither of those, by the way, but I'm interested to hear why you think you are.'

Kitty pressed her lips together and looked over at her brother. The kindness in his eyes, so like their mum's, was too much. If she wanted to tell him, and she did, then she'd have to find something else to look at. The wind rattled one of the windows opportunely, and she turned her gaze to it.

'Thanks, Jimby,' she said, taking a mug of tea from him. She paused for a moment, puffed out her cheeks and exhaled noisily. 'Well, if I'm completely honest, then I'd say that the warning signs were there pretty early on, only I chose to ignore them. I was so taken up with how good-looking Dan was and how much fun we had when he was in a good mood. He had a brilliant sense of humour and could be very charming.'

'Sounds like a deadly combination to me. Anyone's head would've been turned by it.'

'Before I go any further, I just want you to know that by me telling you all of this I'm not wanting you to pity me or feel sorry for me. I would hate that. And I don't want you to think badly of Dan either; we're equally to blame for the mess that's our marriage, but for different reasons.'

'I'll do my best not to judge, but it won't be easy. I've just seen you sobbing your heart out and heard him speaking to you like crap. But,' he shrugged, 'I'll just sit here quiet as a mouse and listen.'

Thanks, Jimby.' She sighed and carried on. 'From the moment I first started to go out with Dan he didn't hide his moods, so it's not like they're something new, it's just that there are more of them now. A lot more. In fact, I'd go so far as to say, when he's at home he's always in a mood with me, and that's what I don't understand. It's not like something happens which could, maybe, explain or justify it. It's as if as soon as he sees me, he's cross. It's almost like it's become a habit, and that's how he is automatically, without him actually needing a reason. Does that make sense?'

James nodded. 'It makes a lot of sense, and I think you've probably hit the nail on the head. His moods sound like they've become a habit, or the 'norm' if you like. Plus, the fact that you've allowed him to get away with such bad behaviour for so long has given him the green light to carry on and push things even further. But it still doesn't excuse it. He makes you feel worthless, and no one has the right to make another person feel like that – sorry, I couldn't help over-hearing.'

Kitty's cheeks flushed. 'I'm not surprised you over-heard; we were going for it.'

James listened as his sister explained how she couldn't remember when things had soured between her and Dan, it just seemed to have crept up on them and become part of their daily life. 'What I do know is that I don't want my life to be like this anymore,' she said firmly. 'I have to set an example to Lucas and Lily, and what kind would it be if I carried on with things as they are? It would just rubber-stamp their father's behaviour. As their mum, I have a duty to them, and I need to take control now.'

There was a strength in Kitty's voice that made James smile. 'That's my girl. But don't be so hard on yourself; you're a fantastic mother and role-model to the kids, and they adore you. The reason you've found yourself like this is because Dan has such a strong personality and is used to getting his own way, or he throws a tantrum. From where I'm standing, it's Dan who's setting a bad example to the kids, not you.'

'That's a very neat way to sum things up.' She reached down to stroke Humph who was still sleeping on her feet. His eyes flickered for a second, and his tail gave a couple of wags. 'But I'm sure as hell not going to take the role of victim or the hard-done-by little woman. That would be embarrassing. It's time for me to be strong, especially for the kids. I know I've got a hell of a battle in front of me, and the second I start to look weak, Dan will be in there like a shot.'

Her head was still pounding; she took a long sip of her tea then slumped back into the rocking chair with a sigh. 'Bloody hell, I'm knackered.'

The phone in the hallway trilled. Kitty sat bolt upright and froze, her heart racing. She looked at her brother for reassurance.

'Shall I get that for you?'

'Would you mind?' She extricated herself from Humph and followed James out of the kitchen.

'Hello, Kitty Bennett's phone.' He paused for a few seconds. 'Hello? Hello? Hello?' He replaced the handset and scratched his head, turning to face his sister, who was chewing anxiously at her fingernails. 'No one there. It was probably just one of those automated calls where no one was available to speak to you. Everyone gets them these days.'

Kitty wasn't convinced.

'Listen, I'm starving. How about we go and get a bite to eat from the tea room? My treat and I'm not taking no for an answer.'

She was about to decline but thought better of it; getting out of the house would stop her from stewing. 'Are my eyes puffy? Do I look like I've been crying?'

'Nope, you look absolutely fine.' James wasn't being completely truthful. 'Come on, it'll do you good.'

'Yeah, why not? I haven't been to the tea shop for ages. Isn't it in the process of being sold to Lucy and Freddie?'

'Yep, they've got big plans for it. They're going to keep it as a tearoom but extend the deli part of their shop into it, too. They've got some great ideas.'

Kitty pulled on her boots, threw on her coat and grabbed her keys. 'Come on then, what are you waiting for?' She forced a smile as she re-tied her ponytail.

Pulling the door closed, she couldn't help but think how different her life had become here in her childhood home. She and Jimby had enjoyed a blissful childhood, filled with an endless supply of unconditional love, happiness and seemingly never-ending sunny days.

She locked the door and pushed the key into her pocket, smiling to herself as she recalled how Jimby had managed to get himself stuck in the old apple tree. Caught by the seat of his trousers, he'd had to wait for an age, suspended in mid-air, before their father was able to get him down. Typical Jimby. It felt like only yesterday, yet now her own children were running in their footsteps. Although, it saddened her to think, not quite so carefree or happily.

❧

OAK TREE FARM had been in the Fairfax family for generations, and the cottage attached to it was, like the other properties in Lytell

Stangdale, a chocolate-box pretty, vernacular longhouse with a low, but steeply-pitched thatched roof and thick, lime-washed walls. The byre-end that had originally housed animals had long-since been converted to form part of the dwelling-house, creating a roomy four-bedroomed home. It sat quietly at the far end of the village; a gateway to the twenty-six acres of land attached to it. Kitty couldn't remember a time when the fields weren't teeming with an eclectic mix of sheep, goats and clucking hens. Her favourite time was spring, when orphaned new-born lambs, swaddled in old towels and snuggled up in a cardboard box, were kept warm by the Aga in the Fairfax kitchen.

As she headed down the path behind Jimby, her eyes landed on the broad flower borders, filled with autumnal hues. A gust of wind had set it swaying in a Mexican wave; the burst of colour on such a grey day was a heart-warming sight. Elizabeth, their mother, had planted them. She was nearly always a permanent fixture in the garden, busily setting out broad borders of blowsy country cottage flowers. Kitty had promised herself she'd do her best to tend it with the same love and attention, keeping her lovely mum's memory alive.

With broad, sweeping lawns at the left and rear of the cottage, the garden had also been a wonderful playground for herself and Jimby. They had been limited only by their imaginations, which had run riot. The well-established trees had afforded them perfect hiding places in their endless games of hide and seek. And the two tree-houses, built by their father, and linked by a wooden walkway had echoed with their laughter. Dan had had the treehouses demolished almost as soon as he'd taken up residence at Oak Tree Farm, not bothering to hide the glimmer of enjoyment in his eyes when he told Kitty what he'd done. It was his way of putting his stamp, very firmly, on her home.

Oak Tree Farm had been a happy home once; a place filled with love and laughter. It stood in stark contrast to the house she now shared with Dan, whose moods had permeated the very fibre of the building. But Kitty was determined to turn things around. Deter-mined to sweep away the negativity and gloom, especially for the sake of her children.

6

DAN SLAMMED the front door behind him and strode to the gates of the drive, angrily flinging them open. He was livid with Kitty and her annoying git of a brother but, more than anything, he felt annoyed that James had heard the way he had been talking to his wife. Image was everything to Dan, and he liked to portray himself as a dutiful husband and father. One who worked hard and lavished expensive gifts on his family, treating them to expensive holidays in the finest hotels. What right did James have to turn up like that, uninvited, only getting half the story?

In the confines of his car, Dan channelled his aggression into the accelerator. He got a thrill out of speed and, as the country roads were quiet, he put his foot down. He didn't know where he was going, he just needed to get out of the house and drive somewhere. Anywhere.

Soon his thoughts turned to his pupil, and Dan found himself following the road that led to chambers.

He pulled into his personal parking space behind the imposing Georgian building that was Minster Gate Chambers. It housed twenty-six of the best legal brains in the north of England, having won the accolade of best chambers in Yorkshire four years on the trot and, more recently, best chambers in the whole of the north. It was true to say that the most high-profile cases in the area usually found themselves being dealt with by this set. It had spawned sixteen judges, eight recorders and a multitude of Queen's Counsel. Securing a pupillage in this cut-throat profession was tough at the best of times but securing one in Minster Gate Chambers was nigh on impossible. The Pupillage Committee interviewed prospective candidates annually, and the standard was sky-high – only the very best ever dared to apply. An invitation to be interviewed by this daunting group of legal brains was hugely flattering, but the tiniest hint that an applicant couldn't cut the mustard meant that they immediately took up residence on the rejects' pile. Minster Gate Chambers had a reputation for getting the job done to a very high standard, and there was no room for anything less than perfect.

As he climbed out of his car, Dan's attention was drawn to one of the first-floor windows. He wasn't disappointed by what he saw. Sucking on a pen was Astrid, looking back at him, tantalizingly holding his gaze.

He smiled and headed inside to the familiar smell of wood polish hovering in the air, while the printer, spewing out sheets of A4, hummed away industriously in the background. He strode across the plush carpet, stopping at the desk of the newly-recruited office junior. 'Morning Laura, where's Frances?' he asked after the senior clerk to chambers, giving a lopsided smile.

Blushing, Laura said, 'Erm, Miss Delaney's still in a meeting with the head of chambers, sir. She shouldn't be long, though. Can I pass on a message?' She was shy and struggled to meet his gaze. Dan found it very appealing; she reminded him of Kitty when he'd first met her. And it hadn't escaped his attention that she was pretty, with her long blonde ponytail that swung playfully from side to side when she walked. She was a bit on the curvy side for his taste, but it still wouldn't put him off trying to find out what delights were hidden beneath that austere little trouser suit. And he wouldn't mind getting a feel of those plump, full lips either. He'd leave her on the backburner for now, but she was definitely a possible conquest for the future. The chambers Christmas party sprang to mind.

He looked at her intently, smiling as her blush intensified. 'No, thanks, Laura. I'll catch her later.' He turned to walk away. 'Oh, and by the way, it's Dan, not sir.'

She gazed after him, watching him disappear through the door.

'Anyone else hear that ping?' asked Alfie, one of the junior clerks to the civil team.

'What ping?' Laura looked puzzled as the other clerks sniggered.

'Leave her alone,' said Pete, the head civil clerk.

'The ping of your knicker elastic going when Dirty Dan gave you one of his killer smiles. But careful how you go, my girl. He has a certain reputation, if you get my drift. And if Miss Delaney hears you calling him anything less than Mr Fairfax-Bennett she'll have your guts for garters,' warned Alfie.

Laura looked flustered. 'Well, you don't have to worry about me, I've got a boyfriend.'

'Just be careful, that's all I'm saying.'

'I don't know what you mean,' she replied, as she busied herself with a collection of papers on her desk, which suddenly took on a life of their own and fluttered to the floor around her.

Alfie raised a knowing eyebrow.

7

OLLIE HAD SEEN Dan race out of the village, tyres screeching and music blaring. Not for the first time he thought how mismatched Kitty and Dan were. And not for the first time he wished he'd fought for her way back when that loser had first got his claws into her.

Only James knew how devastated Ollie had been when she married Dan. His hopes and dreams were quashed before they ever got started. So, one summer, when the circus came to Middleton-le-Moors, and a pretty, young Russian performer started paying him attention, he thought he had nothing to lose and buried his broken heart, and the pain it brought, as deeply as he was able.

Nataliya Shishkin was a half Romany, half Russian trapeze artist. Strikingly beautiful, she had razor-sharp cheekbones and piercing ice-blue Slavic eyes, set off by a glossy curtain of platinum blonde hair. An expert manipulator, she'd taken a shine to Ollie when they'd got talking in a pub in town and, very quickly, managed to worm her way into his life.

To the young penniless Nataliya, who was bored of travelling with the circus, Ollie was an appealing prospect. That he was tall, good-looking and conveniently vulnerable made the task of winning him over an easy pleasure.

The cogs of her mind had started whirring when he'd told her how his boss, Woody Woodhead, with whom he'd served his joinery apprenticeship, had retired, passing on the business to Ollie. And how he'd been working all hours and had managed to save enough money to put down a deposit on Rose Cottage, one of the tiny two-up, two-down weavers' cottages on Church Street in Lytell Stangdale. In need of modernisation, it had been going cheap, and Ollie had snapped it up with big plans for renovating it.

His words had set Nataliya thinking...

The circus's stay in Middleton-le-Moors had come to an end. Ollie hadn't seen Nataliya for a couple of days and had assumed she'd moved on. Even though their relationship had been pretty casual, he was surprised she hadn't said goodbye. But, as a sultry summer dusk was settling over the village, he found Nataliya, and her suitcase, on his doorstep. The circus may have gone, but she had stayed behind, citing love for him as the reason. When she said she had nowhere else to go, he took pity on her and invited her to stay with him until she managed to get her own place. In the blink of an eye, she'd manoeuvred her feet firmly under his table. Within a month, she'd found herself pregnant.

At the age of twenty-one, Ollie's life had changed forever.

Two months after giving birth to their daughter, Anoushka, an angelic baby girl blessed with bright blue eyes, a shock of golden curls and an easy temperament, Ollie returned home from work to find Nataliya gone, and a sobbing Anoushka alone in the house. The only trace of Nataliya was a short note left on the kitchen table saying that she wasn't cut out to be a mother. She was leaving, and Ollie wasn't to try to find her.

And so began his life as a single parent.

8

DAN CLIMBED the wide stairs leading to his private room in chambers, the thick, red runner soft beneath his feet. He relished this space with its dark oak panelling, leather chairs and fabrics in thick, muted tweeds. Everything about it exuded masculine elegance, from the legal prints that shared wall space with hunting prints, to the vast leather-topped partner's desk.

He'd earned it through sheer hard work, elbowing his way to the privilege of having a senior tenant's room in no time. A dazzling advocate, his reputation attracted much work to chambers. And it wasn't unknown for fellow members of the Bar to take a seat in the public gallery to view his cross-examination of an unwitting defendant in his latest high-profile case. They would watch, with morbid fascination, as he wormed his way into the defendant's mind before savagely tearing them down.

Unfortunately, such viciousness was proving difficult for Dan to shake off with the removal of his wig and gown in the robing room. Which was why he was still riddled with it when he returned home.

He walked over to his desk, stroking the worn green leather where he'd spent hours poring over complicated briefs, inhaling the scent of beeswax polish that pervaded the air. Here was where he felt truly at home.

A silver-framed black and white photo caught his eye, and he picked it up. It was of Kitty and the children, all three of them sat amongst the heather, laughing. Kitty was in the middle, an arm around each child, with Humphrey – wearing one of his customary grins – and Ethel at their feet. Dan had taken it in happier times, high up on Great Stangdale moor above their village. He couldn't remember when he'd last seen them all looking so carefree. He quickly flicked away a twinge of unease before it could take root.

A tapping at his door broke his train of thought. 'Come in.'

Astrid appeared in the doorway, sashayed across to his desk, and all thoughts of his family were obliterated. He was pleased to see that she was wearing a tight-fitting black suit with a short skirt. Her crisp, white blouse was buttoned low and struggled to restrain her generous breasts that jiggled with every step. The outfit was hardly appropriate for the Bar, and she was the talk of the robing room, but to Dan she was a welcome distraction. He savoured the vision as she teetered on her dangerously high heels. 'Miss Eriksson, how can I help you?' he said with a wolfish smile.

'Well, Mr Fairfax-Bennett.'

'Dan.'

'Well, *Dan*, I've prepared all the documents you need for tomorrow's conference in Bewley and Travis and I've chased the CPS for the forensic report in Davies, so I was wondering if there's anything else I could do for you?' She smiled suggestively as her gaze fell to Dan's mouth.

'Oh, you do, do you?' His eyes moved from her lips to her chest. 'Well, I haven't got anything to give you at the moment, but I'm going to be working here quite late tonight, long after everyone else has gone, so if you want to pop back then, I'm sure I'll have thought of something.'

Astrid popped her pen back into her mouth, rolled her tongue around the end, then sucked it gently. 'Sounds good.'

It certainly does, he thought, watching her bottom wiggle as she walked away.

9

As Kitty and James headed down the path of her windswept garden, her attention was drawn to the boy standing by the old red phone box – his usual place. He was, she guessed, about fifteen or sixteen and looked vaguely familiar.

'Don't look now,' she whispered to James who was holding the gate open, 'but there's a boy over the road, dark-blond hair, wearing a navy puffa jacket. He's been hanging around there a lot recently.'

James turned to look at the boy in question.

'Jimby! I said don't look, not cop yourself a blatant eyeful!'

He pulled an apologetic face. 'Sorry, Kitts. Couldn't help myself. You know what it's like when you're told not to look at someone, you get an irresistible urge to do it. Don't worry, I'm sure he didn't notice.' He closed the gate, making sure the sneck was fastened. Bill Campion's hefted sheep were roaming the village, and James didn't want them getting in and demolishing Kitty's carefully tended garden.

'I'll tell you more about it when we're out of earshot but, if you can, try to get a bit of a look at him. *Discreetly*, please.'

James pressed his lips together and nodded. 'Message understood. Discreet is my new middle name.' He smiled at his sister, scanning her face. The light outside was much more revealing and unforgiving to her appearance than the dim light of her home. She looked as though she'd had every last drop of energy sapped out of her. The dark shadows that hung heavily under her once smiling brown eyes took on a deeper appearance, and her skin was dull and sallow.

As they walked by on the opposite side of the road, James cast a furtive glance over at the young lad, who quickly averted his eyes before he turned to walk away.

Brother and sister walked briskly along the trod, battling the strong autumn wind as it swirled around them, blowing leaves across their path.

'Morning, you two,' Little Mary trilled as she hurried towards them on her way to the shop. 'Blustery day again.' She pressed her hat down onto her rows of neatly permed white curls. As usual, she was carrying a shopping bag that was almost as big as her. One of the village's most well-loved characters, she was a sprightly scrap of a woman in her late seventies, with small bird-like features and kind eyes.

'Morning, Mary.' Kitty smiled.

'Morning, Mary, don't get blown away,' called Jimby.

'I'll do my best, young Jimby,' she chuckled.

When the teashop was about a hundred yards away, James stopped, placing a hand in the crook of Kitty's elbow. She looked up to find a pair of mischievous eyes twinkling back at her. She'd seen that look many times before. 'Fancy a game?'

'A game?'

'Yep, Last One Stinks.'

She rolled her eyes, smiling. 'Honestly, Jimby.'

'Hey, don't knock the old classics. Come on, last one to the cake shop stinks.' He nudged her and bolted off.

Hampered by the element of surprise, Kitty was resigned to the fact that she was never going to catch up with him. She laughed, stuffed her hands in her pockets and trotted after him.

But her luck was about to change as her brother badly negotiated old Mr Jowsey's feisty Jack Russell, Spud, who'd run into his path, barking and snarling. Jimby went to leap over the terrier's snapping jaws, but Spud lunged at him, his jaws clamping down onto the right leg of his jeans, making him lose his balance and slip on a patch of decomposing leaves.

James fought hard to stay upright. 'Arghhh!' he yelled. Kitty pressed her lips together, struggling not to laugh.

'Look out, James!' called Lycra Len, whizzing by on his racing bike, skilfully dodging the calamity that was unfolding on the road.

Spud clamped his jaws ever tighter on the leg of James's jeans, growling as he gave it a shake.

Kitty pressed a hand to her mouth and winced as her brother landed, with a thud, at the feet of Freda Easton, one of the village "characters" whose grubby appearance and pungent body odour left no one in any doubt that she never troubled soap and water. Spud scampered off to his owner.

The old lady gave James a couple of prods with her grimy walking stick. 'Now then, lad. What are you doing down on the floor? Have you fallen for me?'

Jimby scrambled to his feet, his face burning. He'd never been in such close-proximity to Freda before, and the smell that was assaulting his nostrils was so vile he was forced to hold his breath. She stuck a pointy tongue between her pink gums, pulling her mouth into a toothless smile, but he couldn't take his eyes off a crop of spiky grey whiskers that protruded from her chin. Only when she let out a grating cackle, spraying thick, foul-smelling spittle across his face, did he manage to avert them.

Mumbling an apology, James rubbed his hands together in a futile attempt to remove the mud and rotting leaves that were stuck to them. They, together with his knees, had taken the brunt of the fall but he was thankful that embarrassment served to numb the pain.

He made his way over to Kitty who had been laughing so hard there were tears pouring down her cheeks. 'Are you okay, Jimby?' She stifled more laughter.

'Oh, great thanks. Never been better.' He wiped Freda's spit off his face with the sleeve of his jacket. 'Remind me never to challenge you to a game of Last One Stinks again. And as for that bloody dog...'

'Poor old Spud?'

'Yeah, he wants a kick in the bloody spuds.' James wiped his still dirty hands down the front of his jacket and grinned at Kitty, whose tired eyes still danced with mirth.

A car horn tooted and a mud-spattered four-wheel drive pulled-up beside them. 'Doesn't get any better, does he?' said Molly, who'd witnessed the debacle and was barely able to contain her laughter. There was no getting away from the family resemblance – all three shared the same large, brown eyes. Molly and James still had rich chocolate curls, though Molly's were loose, and Jimby's were cut close to his head. It had been a long time since Kitty's curls or natural colour had seen the light of day since Dan had got his hands on her. The same could be said of the gentle curves that had once adorned her petite frame, but still graced Molly's.

'Got any injuries that need attending to, Jimby?' Molly grinned. 'Scrubbed knees, bloodied knuckles? It's like talking to a six-year-old, isn't it?'

'It is,' Kitty agreed, laughing.

'Haha, you're both hilarious,' said James as he held up his skinned palms to Molly.

'Ouch! I bet they sting like bugger.' She rummaged in her glove-compartment 'Here. Clean 'em up with these.' She flung a handful of wound wipes at him. 'Well, I'd best get cracking. I'm running late, and I've got to pop and see Granny Aggie before I start work. She sent me a bonkers text about needing my help to get the vicar out of her bed. God forbid.' Molly rolled her eyes, and James's ensuing laughter quickly morphed into a wince as he cleaned his grazed hands with the wipes.

'Ahh, I'm guessing you still haven't told her that predictive text is a bad idea for her?' asked Kitty.

Molly slipped her car into gear and shook her head. 'Nope, gives Pip and me way too much pleasure trying to guess what the bloody hell she's on about. Anyway, see you later, folks. Oh, and, Jimby, try not to throw yourself about anymore.'

'Bugger off to work, Florence bloody Nightingale,' he replied.

'Don't worry, I'm going. See ya.' She released the handbrake and drove off just as Violet Smith flew by in her little purple city car, waving enthusiastically.

Vi hadn't seen Kitty for ages, so she swung her car around, pulling into Molly's recently vacated parking place. She wound down the window and a heady cloud of perfume spilled out. 'Hiya, Kitts. How's things? Hi, Jimbo.'

'Well, here's a sight for sore eyes. Hiya, Violent.' James's eyes twinkled as he used the nickname he'd coined for her at school when she'd punched him in the goolies after he'd tried to kiss her in the playground when she was seven and he was nine.

'Hi, Vi, you're looking as glam as ever.' Kitty smiled, taking in her friend's trademark glossy, deep aubergine-purple hair, immaculate make-up and sumptuous moss-green velvet coat. She always thought Violet could pass for a fifties Hollywood starlet. 'I hear you've bought old Mavis Thacker's cottage.' She hoped her still puffy eyes didn't give away that she'd been crying.

'Yes, I'm now officially the new owner of Sunshine Cottage. In fact, I'm seriously thinking about moving back to the village and commuting to York from here. But listen, I'm in a bit of a rush and can't really stop. We'll have to sort out a girls' night out, have a bit of a catch-up and celebrate my new house purchase. No excuses, Kitts, it's been ages.'

Kitty nodded. 'Sounds good.'

After her plans for travelling were scuppered, Vi had left the village to go to university in York and never moved back, only returning to visit her parents or catch-up with Molly and Kitty. Driven to succeed, she'd set up Purple Diamond, a highly-successful PR company which, together with her passion for burlesque dancing, demanded a generous portion of her time, to the detriment of any potential romance, which was exactly why her relationship with accountant, Nick Carter, was on the rocks. Well, it was one of the reasons.

Violet looked from Kitty to Jimby, it was obvious she knew something was amiss. 'Kids and Dan alright?'

'They're fine, thanks.' Kitty nodded as James was shaking his head behind her, mouthing something about Dan being a prat, and making call me gestures with his hand.

'Oh, right, well.' Violet was doing her best to process Jimby's non-verbals. 'I'll send you a text the next time I'm here, and we can sort out a drink with Moll, but I must dash now, I've got a meeting back at the office. See ya, Jimby, and you look after yourself, Kitts.'

Watching Vi's car disappearing out of the village Kitty turned to her brother. 'You've still got the hots for Violet, haven't you?'

'Oh, yes.' James gave a face-splitting smile.

'So, you're not heart-broken that you and Amanda split up?'

'Nope. It was an amicable break-up, and we're still friends,' he said with a shrug.

'As long as you're okay. I'd hate to think I'm dumping all my troubles on you if you're nursing a broken heart.' Kitty looked up at her brother's face, trying to read his expression.

'Trust me, Kitts, no hearts were broken, neither hers nor mine. Though, I can't deny it would be nice to find "the one". At thirty-six, I'm not getting any younger.' He looked in the direction of Violet's car. 'I wonder if Vi still does her burlesque dancing…'

Kitty rolled her eyes.

THE BRASS BELL tinkled as Kitty pushed open the door of Ye Olde Tea Shoppe. 'Mmm, what a lovely smell.' Her stomach rumbled in response to the aroma of freshly baked scones. An open fire crackled busily in the inglenook fireplace making the room warm and inviting. 'Where shall we sit?'

'Over there looks good to me.' James nodded in the direction of an empty table for two by the fire.

'I wonder what Lucy and Freddie's plans are for this place – apart from extending the deli into here.' Kitty scanned the room, closer inspection showing up the tired décor and dirty tables set with dog-eared menus.

'From what I gather they're going to gut it, get new furniture in, you know comfy leather sofas, chunky oak tables and they're going to completely revamp the menu. Should be good; they've got flair those two.'

Kitty nodded. Her stomach rumbled again; she hadn't eaten properly for longer than she cared to remember.

The waitress, Sophie, a teenager from the village, came over to their table. She was wearing a grubby white blouse that was at least two sizes too small. 'Yeah, what can I get yer?' she asked as she chewed vigorously on a vibrant piece of pink bubble-gum, before popping a noisy bubble through her teeth.

James glanced at Kitty who was struggling to suppress a smirk. 'Er, two scones with jam and cream and…'

'Make that just one with cream, thanks, Sophie,' said Kitty.

'OK, one with and one without. And a pot of tea for two, please.'

'Owt else?' Sophie's tone suggested she'd rather be anywhere else than there.

Once they were alone, James rested his hands on the table, wove his fingers together and leaned in. 'She needs a good kick up the backside.'

'Mmm.' Kitty's gaze followed the waitress as she sauntered into the kitchen and repeated their order in a monotone voice.

'So, are you going to enlighten me about this mysterious lad by the phone box?'

'Well, it's a bit weird really. As I said before, I first noticed him a few weeks ago, hanging around by the phone box, always on his own. I didn't think anything of it at first, but then I realised that he always seemed to be looking over at the house. He'd disappear into the phone box, then our landline would ring, but no one would answer when I picked it up.'

'Hmm. It does sound a bit funny, but he's probably just a bored kid, and, like I said, the calls are probably computer generated. I'm sure there's nothing in it at all.'

Kitty frowned. 'I thought that, but he's always in the phone box when I get those calls. And I know they're not computer-generated because I've heard background noises like cars going by, dogs barking or something that sounds suspiciously like Reg squawking. And before you ask, I've checked the number, and it's always with-held. But the weirdest thing is, although I'm pretty sure I've never seen the lad before he started hanging around, he looks weirdly familiar.' Her shoulders slumped. 'I sound like I'm losing my marbles, don't I?'

'No, Kitts, you don't. You just sound like you've been having a really stressful time recently and you could do with a break from it all.'

She wasn't convinced. 'I've just got a really funny feeling about it.'

10

By the time Kitty had returned home, she was relieved to see there was no sign of the boy by the phone box. She was also relieved that there was no sign of Dan.

She loaded the washing machine and tidied the breakfast things away, mulling over their earlier argument, wondering where he'd driven off to in his rage. Feeling a new wave of tension begin to rise, she glanced across at Humphrey and Ethel; they'd been watching her, sensing something was wrong. 'Fancy a walk, you two?' She unhooked their leads, and they leapt to attention, trotting behind her down the hall, wagging tails bashing enthusiastically against the furniture. A walk would do them all good, she thought. And she could do with having her worries blown away.

As Kitty made her way along the path, she spotted Ollie in the doorway of his workshop. 'Hi, Kitty,' he said, rubbing his chin and looking thoughtful.

'Oh, hi, Ollie.' She smiled and carried on walking. There was that feeling again, and it was making her face flush.

As she headed out of the village, Kitty passed Hugh Danks, a retired farmer of indeterminate age (he'd always looked ancient to her). Another of Lytell Stangdale's "characters", he'd been known locally as Hugh Heifer for as long as anyone could remember, on account of his herd of prize-winning English Longhorns. Since his retirement, and his son, John, had taken over the running of Tinkel Top Farm, Hugh had always kept a heifer – always called Daisy – for showing in the country fairs and was regularly seen taking his latest pride and joy for a daily stroll through the village.

'Morning, Hugh.' Kitty nodded at him.

'Morning, young 'un,' he replied in his broad moorland accent. He was wearing the same shabby old checked raincoat he'd worn for the past twenty odd years with a grubby length of baler twine tied around his middle serving as a belt. On his feet were his latest pair of worn out old wellington boots, with ill-fitting soles from another old pair glued to the bottom, that made him walk with an awkward gait. His rustic ensemble was topped off by a threadbare flat cap, its greasy peak set at a jaunty angle.

'Hello, again.'

Kitty turned to see Ollie smiling down at her. 'Oh, hi, Ollie.' She smiled back, sweeping her hair off her face, hoping he couldn't tell she'd been crying earlier. Her heart leapt as they made eye contact and she looked away shyly.

'Mind if I join you? Thought I'd get the dog walk out of the way before it starts to chuck it down.' He bent down to unfasten Mabel's lead, and she shot off after Ethel who'd disappeared into the hedgerow in pursuit of an irresistible scent. His tail wagging, Humph sniffed Ollie's jeans with interest.

'I'm not sure I'll be much company, Ollie, but you're very welcome to join us, isn't he, Humph?' Humphrey looked up with rheumy eyes and barked. 'I think that's a yes.' She laughed. 'I'm heading up onto the rigg. Need the cobwebs blowing out. It's a slow process with Humph and his old legs, but he loves it.'

Ollie bent down and ruffled the Labrador's head. 'That's alright, isn't it, old fella? Mabel and me don't mind a steady wander.'

Making small-talk about the weather, they continued along the road before turning into Fower Yatts Lane, a gated road which led onto a well-worn trod that would take them up Oakley Bank and high onto Great Stangdale rigg. It was a steep climb, but they took it slowly for Humphrey, pausing regularly to give him a rest and to catch their breath. At the lane end of Oakley Side Farm, declaring herself warm, Kitty undid her coat and unfurled her scarf from around her neck. Beads of perspiration peppered Ollie's brow, and he removed his jacket, slinging it over his shoulder, while Humphrey sat beside them, panting. Kitty glanced surreptitiously at Ollie; she'd forgotten how lovely it was to spend time with him, and how his handsome face had the power to turn her knees to jelly. He looked across at her and smiled, making her blush and look away.

The cry of a buzzard circling high above resounded around the dale but was soon drowned out by the plaintive bleating of the sheep enclosed in a large, boulder-strewn field where old Harry Cornforth was fixing a dry-stone wall, hefting the lumps of sandstone around as if they were light as air. His sheepdog, Tip, came bounding over, barking vociferously, disturbing a pheasant whose rattling call caught the attention of Mabel and Ethel. 'Now then,' called Harry in a North Yorkshire greeting before giving a shrill whistle, calling for Tip who obeyed in a flash.

They ploughed on in companionable silence, both lost in their own thoughts until they finally reached the top of the rigg. 'Phew! That was quite a pull, but the breeze is so refreshing.' Kitty sucked in a lungful of earthy moorland air, as strands of hair that had broken-free from her ponytail blew around her face.

'Yeah, and just look at that view.'

Kitty swept her hair out of her eyes and put her hands on her hips. 'Mmm. I never tire of looking at it.'

'Same here,' he replied, looking at Kitty.

They drank in the panoramic vista of the dale. On a clear day you could see for miles, but today the view was muffled by low-hanging cloud. Further along on the right, voluminous black storm clouds gathered, awaiting their orders to march down and deposit large spots of rain. But they did nothing to detract from the rugged beauty. The moor was wearing its autumn coat in sumptuous shades of copper, russet and gold. It was hard to believe that only a couple of months earlier it had been swathed in a thick eiderdown of sweetly scented heather that jostled for supremacy with the bullying bracken fronds. Kitty loved that every season brought its own unique beauty.

A cacophony of countryside sounds filled the air; Bill Campion's milkers bayed noisily on the other side of the dale, Tom Storr's old tractor thrummed in the fields below, while a parliament of rooks was in session in Oak Acre Field to the left of them. The soundtrack to rural life. And Kitty didn't want to listen to any other.

Her gaze settled on Lytell Stangdale, nestled half-way down the sweeping glacial dale of Great Stangdale. Further along, sandstone farmhouses dotted the landscape, set in plush fields that lined the base and sides that had been set out in the same patchwork patterns during the enclosures some two hundred years earlier. The moorland winters could be biting and cruel, but the residents of the dale were offered some protection by the two vertiginous ridges, or riggs as they were known locally, that loomed protectively either side of the village. On the one side lay Danskelfe Dale that sheltered the village of Danskelfe and on the other, Arkleby Dale where the hamlet of Arkleby nestled.

As much as Kitty wanted to get away from Dan, she couldn't contemplate living anywhere else. These moors were in her blood, ingrained in her very being and Lytell Stangdale was where she belonged. She could trace her family back to this small, ten-mile radius for generations. Yeomen farmers was how the Fairfaxes were described, and there was even a rumour that they had a connection to the grand Hammondely family (pronounced Hamley) who were the landed gentry of the mediaeval Danskelfe Castle – or the big house as it was known locally, albeit, supposedly, on the wrong side of the bedclothes. Kitty was related directly or indirectly to many of the locals in the village – and some neighbouring ones, too. Dan and his mother took great pleasure in describing her as 'in-bred'. But that's how it was in these moorland villages, and everyone looked out for each other. It was the same for Ollie, and neither of them would change it for the world.

'Look,' said Ollie, pointing towards their village. 'You can see Hugh Heifer and Daisy at the top end.'

Kitty squinted. 'Oh, yes. Let's hope Reg doesn't venture out.'

'Mmm. Hugh's threatened to neck him if he goes for him or Daisy again.'

'Well, he's had it coming, but I'm not sure how Jimby would feel about it. I think he's strangely attached to that bird.'

'Sounds about right; Jimby being strangely attached to a bird,' said Ollie, making Kitty giggle.

Even from this distance, Lytell Stangdale looked achingly pretty, with its low, heavily thatched lime-washed cottages that appeared to spring from the ground like mushrooms, their stone mullioned windows peering out shyly onto neatly tended country cottage gardens. Most could claim their origins in the seventeenth century, some even further back. Their age was evident in their cruck-frames, original oak panelling, salt and spice cupboards and a variety of apotropaic marks. There was even an old priest hole in The Sunne, which also boasted a witch post adjoining the settle by the inglenook fireplace, and a Richard III connection.

Further along the dale, despite the low-hanging cloud, the ancient walls of Danskelfe Castle, perched precipitously on a sandstone crag were still visible, its pock-marked crenellations looming eerily through the mist.

As she walked on, Kitty was enjoying the distance, both physical and mental, from her home. It created a clear, subjective vantage point from which to view her situation, allowing her to put her thoughts into perspective – even with Ollie there. He was a low-maintenance companion, one who didn't invade and dominate her thoughts and, so far, they'd spent most of the walk in an easy silence.

As she made her way along the stony path, she tried to marshal her thoughts, hoping to gain some clarity. She had to consider every aspect before she made her decision, especially how things would affect Lucas and Lily. But it wasn't easy. She puffed out her cheeks and released a noisy breath.

'You okay?' Ollie turned to look at her, holding back a long bramble briar, so it didn't spring back at her. 'Watch yourself on that.'

'Thanks.' Kitty eased by Ollie, not daring to look him in the eye. 'I'm fine, don't worry about me.'

An awkward moment hovered between them but was broken by Mabel who had trotted back to Ollie, wagging her tail furiously. Pleased with herself, she deposited something at his feet before running off again. 'Hmm. A dried-out, dead frog. Not sure what she expects me to do with that.'

Kitty smiled. 'Not much you can do really.'

'Hey, do you remember that time Jimby took a frog to school and put it in the teacher's drawer?'

'Oh, heavens, yes. It was old Mrs Hill, wasn't it? I was always really scared of her, she was so strict. I'm amazed he was brave enough to do it.'

'Everyone was scared of her, she had an evil streak and a liking for locking kids in dark cupboards.' He shuddered at the thought. 'I remember when Jim did it, it was the last day of the summer term and we were moving up to secondary school in the September. It was his way of saying thank you for all the years of torture she'd inflicted on us. She just about screamed the place down when she opened her drawer and it jumped out at her.'

'I know, I was doing PE in the playground at the time. We thought someone had been murdered.'

'She threatened to keep the whole class back until six o'clock unless the culprit owned up. Though, I think she knew it was James; it had all his hallmarks.'

'It did, and everyone knew only Jimby would be daft enough to do it. He was in so much trouble with Mum when she found out. She made him weed the garden for a week as punishment, but that didn't really bother him because he found loads of worms to add to his collection. Dad couldn't keep a straight face; it was just the sort of thing he would've done when he was that age.'

'Hah! I can believe that. And James went up to secondary school with a kind of super-hero status. Me and some of the other lads hoped it would rub off onto us by association.' He smiled at the memory.

The pair continued their walk until they reached Aud Bob, an ancient stone marker that indicated a crossroads. It slumped wearily into the heather, leaning against the prevailing south-westerly winds, where it had stood for hundreds of years. Words carved in North Yorkshire dialect were now barely visible, worn smooth with age and covered with lichen. Going right was a quick way back down to the village, left would take them over the rigg to the neighbouring dale of Arkleby, and straight on followed the path that looped right around the rigg, leading back to the path at Oakley Bank.

'Which way?' asked Ollie.

Kitty checked her watch, it was almost one thirty. 'Hmm. I have to pick the kids up at quarter past three, so I'd better take the quicker route.'

'Yep, and I'd better think about getting back to work. Mind you, looking at the state of those clouds I don't think we've got much longer before the heavens open.'

'Hmm, I think you're right,' said Kitty, taking in the swell of the bruised sky and the encroaching charcoal-grey clouds.

Whistling for their dogs, they set off down the track, reaching the road three-quarters of a mile from the village before the rain began to fall in an unforgiving torrent. They sought shelter in a derelict shepherd's barn that nestled behind a straggly hawthorn hedge. For a while, they stood in silence watching the rain blow along the dale in a broad, horizontal band. A drenched-looking grey squirrel sprang along a dry-stone wall before scampering up the mossy trunk of an old oak tree, disappearing into a cluster of gnarled branches.

Ollie sniffed the air. 'There's nothing like the smell of wet

Labrador, is there?' he said, wrinkling his nose at Humphrey who sat at Kitty's feet, steam rising steadily from him.

She laughed and looked up to see Ollie grinning down at her, dimples punctuating his cheeks. Her heart responded with a flutter. 'Nope, there's definitely nothing like it. It has a pungency all of its own, and Humphrey is particularly ripe.'

Ollie's eyes drank in her small, elfin features. 'Listen, Kitty, if you ever need anything; to talk, or just somewhere to go for a bit of peace and quiet, you know where I am. I know you've got Jimby, but if he's not around, I want you to know you can come to me. Any time, day or night. And Noushka won't mind; she thinks the world of you.'

Feeling her face flush, Kitty looked at the floor, not daring to catch his eye. 'Thanks, Ollie, that's good to know.' His breathing had become deeper, and she was suddenly aware of his closeness, the citrusy smell of his cologne. There was an electricity in the air, sparking between them, and she knew he could feel it too.

'I mean it.' He took her hand. But she shook her head, fighting back the sting of tears that threatened, and he knew not to push it any further.

He exhaled noisily as he leaned against the uneven surface of the barn wall, rubbing the back of his neck with his hand. 'I don't know how many times I've wished I could turn the clock back, Kitts. If I'd only had the balls…'

'Ollie, don't,' she whispered.

'Okay. Sorry.' He sighed. 'Just know I'm here for you. I always have been, and I always will be.'

The moment was shattered by a succession of ear-splitting squawks from the road. The pair hurriedly fastened leads to their dogs and peered out of the doorway. The rain had all but stopped, and wisps of mist drifted along the valley. They watched in silence as a coast-to-coast walker came hurtling down the road, his bright yellow cagoule billowing out behind him. He was hotly pursued by James's errant cockerel, Reg, who looked terrifying with his wings flapping and spurs brandished. Humphrey barked which made Mabel spin around in excitable circles, while Ethel watched intently.

The walker had committed the sin of whistling as he walked by Jimby's gate where Reg was on patrol, trying to out-crow the other cockerels in the village. He didn't cope well with competition, and the walker's whistling was tantamount to the throwing down of a gauntlet.

Hearing the sound of fresh footsteps stampeding down the road, Kitty and Ollie turned to see Jimby, his face flushed, teeth firmly clenched together, bearing down on Reg. 'Come here, you feathery little sod.'

Reg flew at James, who tackled him to the ground and, in a matter of seconds, he had the rooster under control. He struggled to his feet, holding Reg by his scraggy yellow ankles, an expression of satisfied victory on his face.

Kitty clamped a hand over her mouth, hoping to contain the laughter that was rising in her chest.

'Well caught, Jimbo,' said Ollie as Kitty's giggles escaped in a splutter through her fingers.

Until now James had been unaware that he had an audience, and his face broke into a wide grin. 'Chicken pie, anyone? Reg 'n' Veg, Coq Au bloody Vin?' he said as Reg squawked and flapped his wings in protest.

'Sorry,' he called after the walker who was still running but managed to find the breath to throw a series of expletives James's way. 'Charming. Hurry back.'

'How come it always happens to you, Jimby?' asked Kitty.

James shrugged and grinned, glancing from his sister to his friend. He was clearly wondering why they were looking so cosy in the sheep shed. 'I'm fine, by the way, thanks for the concern, you two. I could be seriously injured, and you're both just stood there laughing at me.'

'You're always alright, Jimby,' Kitty said affectionately. And it was true, James always was fine. His glass wasn't just half-full, it was brimming over; he had the happy knack of seeing the positive in everything. Though he would be the first to admit he struggled to find anything good in Dan.

'Ollie and I bumped into each other when we were taking the dogs for a walk.' She thought she'd better offer her brother some kind of explanation.

Jimby nodded and smiled.

As the three headed back towards the village Kitty's mind was in turmoil about the state of her marriage and about the feelings she clearly still had for Ollie. They'd never gone away, she'd just buried them deep for the past however many years. But why were they being resurrected now? She rubbed her brow with her fingers.

'Actually, I was going to give you a bell, Oll. I've got something I want to run by you and wondered if you fancied doing it over a pint in the Sunne tonight if that's any good?' said James.

'Yep, sounds good to me. Usual time, sevenish?'

'Spot on.' James nodded.

AS THEY STROLLED by the pub on the village green, Pip Pennock was dropping off several colourful braces of pheasants to landlord, Jonty Latimer. Pip was the local game-keeper and Molly's husband. 'Now then, gents,' called Ollie. 'I'm looking forward to tasting what Bea's got in mind for those little beauties.'

'Now then, you lot,' said Pip. He was resplendent in his full shooting regalia.

'Afternoon, all. The blighters will need hanging for a while, but I dare say it'll be game pie and pheasant casserole galore,' replied Jonty in his plummy accent.

'Sounds great. And, by the way, if Bea's ever short of a rather wayward cockerel for any of her recipes tell her to let me know. This one doesn't know how close he is to getting the chop.' He held aloft a complaining Reg.

11

'Do you have time for a quick word?' Kitty was standing by herself at the school gates when she was approached by Rosie Webster, the softly spoken mum of Abbie, Lily's best-friend. Concern troubled her pretty features. 'Sit, Truffle,' Rosie said to the chocolate brown Labrador she had on a lead. Truffle obeyed and was rewarded with a quick ruffle of the ears.

'Of course, is everything okay?'

Rosie lowered her voice and began to fiddle with Truffle's lead. 'Well, it's a bit awkward really. I've spent ages mulling over whether or not I should say something, but I'd feel bad if I didn't.'

'Blimey, that sounds ominous.'

'It's about Lily.' She paused. 'And Evie Mellison.'

That girl, Kitty groaned inwardly. 'Oh?'

'Abbie says Evie is horrid to Lily and won't let her sit with anyone in class or join in with their games. Apparently, she's even tried to start a club against Lil.'

Kitty's stomach twisted. It would explain why Lily had been coming home with bruises on her shins, rips in her clothes and why some of her things had been going missing. She ran a hand across her face; could things possibly get any worse?

'I'm really sorry I've had to tell you this, Kitty. I feel like I'm a right tittle-tattle, but I'd feel bad just sitting back; I'd like to think someone would do the same for Abbie. Evie has such a domineering nature, with a right temper on her. I don't like the way she's trying to drag the other children in, particularly Abbie.' Rosie gave a sympathetic smile.

'Honestly, Rosie, you don't sound like a tittle-tattle, and I really appreciate you telling me. Evie's name has been cropping up a bit at home, and Lily's been reluctant to go to school. But what reason could Evie have for disliking Lil?'

'I think it's a case of the green-eyed monster: Lily's popular and Evie isn't. And, from what Abbie's saying, Lily's doing better than Evie at school. And we all know how competitive and pushy Aoife is; her kids always have to be the best at everything. She's probably piling the pressure on at home, which is manifesting itself at school, and with Lily being so good-natured, she's an easy target for a strong character like Evie.' She paused. 'And a few people are under the impression that Aoife is rather, er, *fond* of Dan.'

'Oh.' Kitty cast her mind back to when they were leaving for their break and Dan's blatant rudeness to the woman. 'Are you sure? About Aoife, I mean?'

'Well, er, she does talk about him a lot. And she keeps saying that she's got an intellectual connection with him.' She placed a hand on Kitty's arm. 'Sorry, Kitty, this must be awful for you. I didn't mean to say this much.'

'Look, don't worry about it; I'm pretty certain he won't have done anything to encourage it, he's actually quite rude to her. But thanks for letting me know about Lily. I'll ask her a few discreet questions, see what I can find out – I won't mention any names.' Kitty was biting back rage at the thought of Lily being bullied.

'Sorry again, Kitty. If it's any consolation, I'm feeling a bit pushed into a corner by Aoife. It's like she's decided that Abbie has got to be Evie's best friend and that I've got to be hers. We can't do anything without them. It's all a bit controlling and manipulative, and I'm concerned about Abbie having too much to do with Evie in case she gets dragged into anything. I can't even take Truffle for a peaceful walk after the school drop off on a morning without Aoife shouting after me so she can join us with that daft dog of hers. Honestly, it's stifling.'

A tap on her shoulder made Rosie jump. She turned to see Aoife looming behind her. 'Hi, Rosie, we've got to go now.' She ignored Kitty. 'But Evie wanted me to ask if Abbie could come to ours for tea tomorrow after school?'

'Er, I'm afraid she's been invited to Lily's for tea tomorrow,' replied Rosie, her face flushed.

'Well, she might change her mind when she finds out we're having a party tea and Dave's setting up his disco lights, so they can have a boogie. Evie's invited a few of the other girls, too.' She gave a smug smile.

'I think it'll have to be another time, Aoife.'

'Right, fine.' She set her mouth in a grim line before glaring at Kitty and walking off.

How Kitty wished for the return of happier times for her daughter, to the days before the Mellisons arrived.

They'd moved to the village from Teesside a year and a half ago, and the equilibrium at school had changed immediately. Six-year-old Evie's personality dominated the infant classroom, and her older brother, Teddy, hadn't wasted any time in putting his manipulation skills to good use in the junior classroom or lashing out at anyone who annoyed him.

Under the illusion they'd injected some much-needed intellect and sophistication into the village, the family had put people's backs up as soon as they'd arrived. The father, Dave, had a severe case of small-man syndrome and spent his days bragging to anyone within earshot about his cycling victories and his days in a band. People were too polite to tell him they weren't interested, but it rankled with those working all hours to make a living while he just idled his days away sipping pints at the Fox in Danskelfe.

Already, Aoife was proving to be a spiteful, vindictive piece of work. With her superior attitude and self-proclaimed high level of intelligence, she looked down her nose at everyone. A part-timer at the local council, she liked to tell people she was "high up" in her department.

Evie and Teddy had inherited their mother's spiteful nature. And, just like her, they acquired friends through manipulation, which caused an uneasy air to linger over the mums in the playground.

Kitty wasn't the only parent who wished they would go back to Teesside. Despite the anger that was currently raging inside her, feeling hurt for Lily, she resisted the urge to storm into school and share what Rosie had just told her. She'd calm down first, speak to Lily and Lucas, then think about what to do. *Poor Lil, as if there isn't enough going on in her little life.*

On the way home, they stopped off at the shop, had a quick

catch-up about their plans for extension into the teashop with Lucy and Freddie, and picked up a couple of bags of pre-made sweetie mix-up for the kids. Kitty also grabbed a loaf of yesterday's bread so they could feed the ducks at the pond on the village green.

By the time they were heading home, it was quarter past four, an hour since school had finished.

A heavy mizzle now hung in the air as Lucas and Lily were running along the stone trod that lead to Oak Tree Farm. 'Uh oh,' said Lucas, stopping in his tracks. He turned around to Kitty and whispered loudly, 'Groaning Granny's here.'

Oh, Lord, not more confrontation. Kitty rubbed her forehead. With everything that had been going on she'd forgotten that Gwyneth was calling round. She came to a halt behind her children. 'Sshhh. Careful what you say, Lukes, she might hear you.' She wasn't going to be accused of influencing how the children thought of their grand-mother, no matter what the circumstances were between herself and Dan. She didn't want to have them dragged into it.

As they reached the garden gate, they saw Gwyneth's pinched features framed in one of the mullioned windows, distorted by the panes of Georgian glass. There was no sign of Dan's car, so she'd obviously let herself in again. The realisation that she'd have to face her mother-in-law on her own sat like a heavy weight on Kitty's shoulders.

'Granny's cross with you again, Mummy,' said Lily. 'Look at her angry face. I don't want to go in now.'

'It's alright, Lils. Come on, it'll be fine.' She put a supportive arm around her daughter. Usually, when she saw Gwyneth looking displeased it made Kitty's heart sink, and she would go into over-drive, gabbling in an attempt to appease her and bring her round. But today she felt different.

The gate gave its usual creak as Kitty pushed it open, her children close behind. 'I don't want to see grumpy old Granny.' Lucas kicked a pile of fallen leaves angrily.

'Me neither.' Lily scrunched up her face.

'Come on, it'll be fine. You can tell her all about your day,' Kitty whispered.

'Bummer,' said Lucas just as the door flew open and Gwyneth's sour face looked out. 'Where on earth have you been? I almost rang Daniel to find out where you were. You knew I was calling round.'

Hello would've been nice. Kitty waited for her mother-in-law to step aside so they could get in out of the cold. She bit her tongue and mentally counted to ten. The children eyed their grandmother warily. She remained rooted in the doorway glaring back, her skinny arms folded defensively across her chest, a confrontational glint in her eyes. She was making it very clear that Kitty would have to wait until *she* was ready to let her into the cottage.

The mizzle quickly turned into long, icy slices of rain and Gwyneth was showing no signs of budging. But Kitty wasn't in the mood for games. 'Hello, Gwyneth.' Her voice was deliberately laced with irritation. 'I see you let yourself in again, but I'm afraid you're going to have to move out of the way for the kids and me to get through the door. We're getting soaked, as you can see. Come on, kids.' Surprising herself as much as she surprised Gwyneth, Kitty pushed past her, closely followed by Lucas and Lily.

'Why didn't you let us in, Granny? It's cold and rainy, and you just stood there.' Disgruntled, Lucas hung his mizzle-soaked coat on a hook and kicked off his school shoes.

'Silly Granny.' Lily shook her head as she struggled to unbutton the toggles of her new duffle coat.

Gwyneth pursed her lips. 'How rude. Are you going to allow your children to speak to me in that way?'

Here we go. Kitty's heart was pounding in her chest, and she tried to busy herself, helping Lily undo her coat and ease off her boots. 'Well, they do have a point actually, and I don't think they meant to be rude.'

'What? You think it's alright for your daughter to call me silly?'

'That's not what I meant. I was referring to Lucas saying you stood...Oh, never mind.' She'd had a gut-full today, and her tolerance levels were at saturation point. 'Look, Gwyneth, I've had quite a day, and I really don't want any trouble. I'm sorry we were late back, but I've got a lot on my mind. So, if you've got nothing nice to say I'd be grateful if you could go home and come back another day. Maybe even when Dan's here, whenever that might be. And, in future, I'd also be grateful if you didn't just let yourself in.' She'd never stood up to Gwyneth before, she was on unfamiliar ground. She braced herself for her mother-in-law's response.

'How dare you speak to me like that? Just who do you think you are?' Gwyneth was livid, her eyes bulging. 'And, yes, I did let myself in, I've got every right. This is my son's house, bought with his hard-earned money, and don't you forget that. And you, you've contributed absolutely nothing. And that's exactly what you'd have without him. Nothing! You ungrateful little nobody.'

'Granny!' gasped Lily.

'Don't you talk to my mum like that.' Lucas stood protectively in front of Kitty, pulling himself up to his full height. Gwyneth pinched her lips together and glared at him.

'It's okay, Lucas, you just take Lily into the kitchen for me.' Kitty didn't want her children to witness this, but Lucas stood firm. She placed her hands on his shoulders and gently guided him into the direction of the kitchen, kissing the top of his head as he went. 'Go on Lukes,' she said, and he did as he was bid, albeit reluctantly.

She looked at Gwyneth and took a deep breath. 'Actually, Gwyneth, you've spoken to me like I'm dirt for years and I've put up with it, but I'm tired of it now. And for your information, this house is not Dan's; he didn't buy it. When he sold Plum Tree Cottage he kept every penny of the equity to himself.'

They'd lived in the tiny house for a few years after they were first married, until Kitty's parents had suggested they move into the cottage at Oak Tree Farm, while they moved into a smaller cottage they owned in the village. 'This house actually belongs to James and me as part of the trust my parents put the whole farm into. And the money for repairs, the extension, everything, comes from the trust fund attached to the farm. Dan has contributed absolutely nothing to it. But you won't know that because your precious son didn't want anyone to know that; it would hurt his arrogant pride. He made up some story about buying it off my parents and paying through the nose for it, but it's a load of rubbish.' Unused to standing up to her mother-in-law, Kitty was shaking.

Outrage danced in Gwyneth's eyes. 'I don't believe you. It's all lies. You're nasty and spiteful and you don't deserve my son!' Before Kitty had time to answer, she turned on her heel and left the house, slamming the door behind her.

Kitty hurriedly bolted it, then covered her face with her hands and sighed. *Christ, what a bloody day.*

Lucas popped his head around the kitchen door. 'Mum, you were awesome!'

She raised her eyebrows and, with a shrug of her shoulders, gave a sheepish smile. She was still reeling from the encounter but thought to herself that, yes, she was rather awesome.

12

Six thirty arrived, and Dan and Astrid found themselves the only people working late in chambers. With a cursory knock on her pupil supervisor's door, she pushed it open and stalked her way to his desk. Dan was leaning back in his leather chair, his hands clasped behind his head, a lopsided smile playing on his lips. 'Ahh, Miss Eriksson, I've been putting a lot of thought into our earlier conversation.'

'Oh, I like that you've been thinking about me,' she replied, her Nordic heritage barely discernible in her accent. She'd removed her jacket, and Dan's gaze was drawn to the struggle that her blouse was having to rein-in her generous breasts, its fabric pulled taught over nipples that stood erect like a couple of sentries on duty.

He gave her a wolfish smile as he put his mobile phone on silent mode. *This is going to be interesting.* She sashayed around to his side of the desk and sat astride his lap. She'd read his signals, loud and clear.

∾

Thirty minutes later, Dan was zipping up his flies. He pulled on his jacket and grabbed his keys; he wanted Astrid out of here now. He checked his phone; he'd had two missed calls from his mother on top of the ones he'd ignored earlier. He'd better call her back, even though he wasn't in the mood for her wittering on at him but leaving it any longer would only make her worse. He'd get it over and done with, then head off to Sam's. He was looking forward to seeing *her*; she was low maintenance and dirty. Just the sort of woman he liked. And it would serve Kitty right if he stayed out all night. In fact, he would have done exactly that if he'd come to chambers in his suit instead of his civvies. Bloody Kitty, it was her fault he'd had to storm out of the house this morning. And that sodding, irritating brother of hers.

Dan sat back in his chair and called his mother's number, bracing himself for the impending torrent of bile.

'Daniel! Where on earth have you been? I've been trying to get hold of you for hours!'

At forty years of age, Dan didn't think he had to explain his whereabouts to her. 'Work, Mother, that's where I've been.'

'Well, you knew I was calling round to visit you and the children, and it's very rude of you not to be there. You've obviously been with that Fairfax girl for too long. Her rough manners have rubbed off on to you. And I really don't know what's got into *her*, but she was extremely rude to me, as were the children. You need to speak to her. She was coming out with all sorts of lies; she needs sorting out!'

Damn, he'd forgotten she was calling round. He slapped a hand to his head. *Ughh*! Her shrill voice was grating on him and, regardless of what he thought about Kitty, he didn't like to hear his mother bad-mouthing her. 'Look, I'm sorry, Mother, but I had some last minute, urgent work to attend to — you know how the job is. And I'm sure Kitty didn't mean to appear rude, or the children for that matter.'

'Oh, that's right. Take her side. Put her before me.' Her words jabbed accusingly at him.

'Look, calm down. I'll talk to her, but I've got a load of work to do now, and I need to get back to it. I'll speak to you later, okay?' Dan cut the call before she could yell anymore. His father would get it in the neck tonight, for sure but he wasn't going to let that bother him; he needed to get to Sam's.

At Oak Tree Farm Lily and Lucas, fresh from their bubble bath, were sitting in front of a roaring fire in the living room enjoying a supper of cinnamon toast and hot chocolate. Kitty was tidying round the kitchen when there was a knock at the door. She'd kept it bolted fearing a return visit from Gwyneth and wondered if it was Dan; he'd be annoyed that the door hadn't yielded to him immediately. Humph, tired from his walk, gave a half-hearted bark but didn't budge from his bed, unlike Ethel who trotted inquisitively to the door, peering around Kitty's legs as she opened it warily, to find Violet and Molly standing on her doorstep.

'Surprise!' they said grinning, their breath hanging in plumes in the chilly night air.

Kitty couldn't remember the last time they'd called on her like this. Certainly not since she'd lived here with Dan.

'Don't just stand there with your cake-hole hanging open, let us in. We're freezing our nuts off out here.'

'Speak for yourself, Moll,' said Violet.

Kitty opened the door wide, and both women stepped in, each giving a shiver. 'Well, this is a lovely surprise. Come on in, if you can get past Ethel, that is. Dan's not here.' Kitty closed the door on the chilly night.

'We can tell; you're smiling,' said Molly, who received a nudge in the ribs from Violet.

'Auntie Molly! Violet!' Lily came running out of the lounge, chocolate smudged at the corners of her mouth.

'Hiya, Lils,' said Molly.

'Hi, sweetie.' Violet smiled affectionately at her god-daughter and held her arms out for a cuddle.

'We've had yummy hot chocolate.' Lily wiped her face on her pyjama sleeve before scuttling over to Violet. Kitty, rolled her eyes, smiling.

'Hi.' Lucas peered round the door-frame.

'Hello, trouble,' said Molly.

'Hi, Lukes. Goodness, you've got tall, and you're looking more and more like your Uncle Jimby,' said Vi.

Lucas beamed with pride; his Uncle James was his hero.

'He says he wants to be just like Jimby when he grows up.' Kitty tried to ruffle her son's hair, but he ducked out of her reach.

'What, when Jimby grows-up?' Molly said with a smirk.

'Moll, that's never going to happen,' quipped Violet.

'True.' Molly sniggered before turning to Lucas and Lily. 'Anyway, the reason we're here, kids, is to take your gorgeous mum out for a quick drink and a chinwag at the pub. And before you use having no babysitter as an excuse, Kitts, we've got my mum – Auntie Annie – lined up for the job. She just needs the word from you.' Everyone looked expectantly at Kitty. 'Oh, and I should point out that we're not leaving until you come out with us.'

'Oh, er…' Kitty trawled her mind for excuses.

'Come on, Kitts, you haven't been out for ages, and I can't remember the last time we had a catch-up.' Vi set her aubergine designer handbag on the floor and pulled off her plum leather driving gloves finger-by-finger.

'But I'm scruffy, look at me.' Kitty glanced down at her boot-cut jeans and chunky blue jumper, then across to Molly in her new coat, her freshly-washed curls peeking from beneath her bobble hat and Violet, glamorous as ever, looking like a fifties movie star.

'Yeah, well, Vi could've made an effort for a change,' Molly said jokingly. 'And you look great, Kitts, but if you want ten minutes to get changed, slap a bit of lippy on, then that's fine, we're happy to wait. No escaping out of the bathroom window, mind.'

'Go on, Mum,' Lucas and Lily pleaded. They loved the few occasions they'd had Noushka or Auntie Annie babysit for them. They were heaps nicer than sour-faced, grumpy Granny.

'All it'll take is a quick phone call, and my mum'll be over here by the time you've got yourself ready.' Molly waved her mobile phone.

'Oh, go on then.' The words tumbled out before Kitty could stop them. She'd had a rotten day and was still feeling more than a little punch-drunk from earlier events. The prospect of fretting over them while she waited for Dan to come home wasn't appealing. No, a quick drink at the pub with her friends would do her good. She struggled to remember the last time that had happened; certainly not since the pub had been refurbished six months ago. And probably a good couple of years before that.

'Yay!' Lucas and Lily grinned at each other.

'Though, I think it's probably best if I don't stay out too late because, well…you know…' Kitty didn't want to say too much within earshot of the children, but she thought it wouldn't go down well with Dan if he came home and found her out late.

'No probs, I'll ring Mum straightaway. Now you go and get yourself ready. You've got ten minutes, tops.'

～

SHORTLY AFTER ANNIE ARRIVED, Kitty popped her head around the living room door. She'd replaced her jumper with a moss-green paisley print tunic-top and had draped a soft cotton scarf of contrasting sludgy greens and raspberry reds around her neck. She'd also freed her hair from its pony-tail and spritzed it so it fell in loose waves on her shoulders. The finishing touch was a smudge of peachy blusher which added some much-needed colour to her cheeks. 'Hi, Auntie Annie, thanks for this. It's good of you to pop over at such short notice.'

'Hello, Kitty, lovie. You're welcome, I've been looking forward to it, I haven't seen the three of you for ages. And you've got the place lovely, so cosy and warm.'

'Thank you.' She glanced around the room; it did look cosy with the wall-lights casting a soft glow against the yellow-ochre lime-washed walls, a lively fire dancing in the stove.

'Wowzers, you scrub up well, Kitts.' Molly beamed at her.

'Yes, you look lovely, petal.' Auntie Annie nodded, smoothing down her bob of loose, brown waves.

'Oh, Kitty, your hair looks gorgeous with its natural curls,' said Violet.

'Thanks,' she replied shyly.

'Right, let's get going before this one changes her mind.' Molly had previous experience of last-minute changes of heart from her cousin.

Kitty reached for her coat. 'Help yourself to anything, Auntie Annie; Lucas and Lily will show you where the tea and coffee stuff is. And I've left a message on Dan's voicemail – I've no idea what his plans are, but I doubt I'll be out late and…'

'You just go out and have yourself a nice time and don't worry, everything will be fine.' Auntie Annie touched her gently on the arm.

The three friends headed out of the door, chatting away ten-to-the-dozen. A thick frost had already started to creep over the old flagstone path making it sparkle in the bright moonlight. 'Bloody hell, it's freezing, lasses,' said Molly as the cool, crisp air nipped at their cheeks.

'Yep, best foot forward to the Sunne, ladies. Could be tricky; though, the path's pretty icy.' Vi was beginning to regret wearing her beautiful, but impractical four-inch heels.

Kitty shivered and glanced down at her friend's feet taking in the delicate floral tattoo that curled its way out of her left shoe and wrapped itself around her ankle, wondering if it hurt to have it done. 'Hmm, I'm beginning to wonder if I should've left that chunky jumper on.'

'Well, I'm nice and toasty in my new coat,' said Molly of her navy-blue jumbo cord parka, as she linked arms with her friends. 'Ahem. Just saying.'

'It's lovely, Moll,' said Kitty. 'I noticed it when we were in the house.'

'Thanks, it's a birthday present from Pip. He's finally redeemed himself after so many years buying absolutely crap presents. Though, to tell the truth, I'd dropped so many hints, leaving the catalogue open on the appropriate page with a great big red circle around the picture and the size underlined several times. I think the twins got so sick of seeing it they made sure he noticed it. He bought these, too.' She wiggled her fingers, showing off a pair of Fair Isle gloves. 'And the hat and scarf. They were already paired with the coat in the photo, so I can't give Pip the credit he says he deserves for his amazing fashion skills, but I'm not letting on.'

'Lord, no. If keeping quiet means getting great pressies, then keep schtum. The last thing you want is to go back to the days of getting a new hoover for your birthday. Oops!' Violet slipped on the ice and gripped tighter on to Molly's arm.

'I'd forgotten about that one.' Kitty laughed.

'Yeah, Pip really excelled himself that year; a hoover for my birthday and a steam cleaner for Christmas.'

'Bloody hell, Molls. I know where I'd like to steam clean if I got something like that as a gift from a man!' said Vi.

'Trust me, he came dangerously close.'

'Ouch. Poor Pip' Kitty giggled; seeing her two closest friends bounce-off each other, just like the old days was making her feel better already.

13

—————

'EY UP, ME AUD MUCKER.' Ollie gave James a friendly pat on the back; he'd just arrived at the pub and joined his friend at the bar.

'Now then, Oll, mate. Grab yourself a gob-full of this; it's bloody gorgeous.' James slid a freshly-poured pint of beer towards him.

'Cheers. So, how's things?' Ollie asked, taking a sip.

James peered over his glass. 'I'm a bit worried about our Kitty, actually. And I don't know what to do or how to help without her withdrawing; you know how loyal she is to that dick-head she's married to.'

'What do you mean you're worried about her?'

'It's that prat of a husband of hers. I called round this morning and overheard him speaking to her like dirt. She was in a right state, really upset. The last time I saw her cry so much was when we found out Mum and Dad had died,' James said, referring to a collision with a lorry that had killed their parents outright. 'It was awful seeing her like that again.'

'Why was he speaking to her like dirt? And why does she put up with it?' Ollie clenched his fists.

'He speaks to her like dirt because he speaks to everyone round here like dirt. I just can't get my head around it. The way he treats her you'd think she was the enemy, not his wife; the mother of his children. And I know I'm biased, but she's a sweet, kind lass who'd do anything for anyone. She doesn't deserve his nastiness. I honestly struggled not to punch his lights out this morning. I had to force my hands as far into my coat pockets as they'd go to resist the temptation. And it was bloody hard, I can tell you.' He reached for his beer. 'What do I do? I just don't know what the bloody hell to do.'

'What a monster.' Ollie shook his head. 'Maybe all you can do at the moment is just give Kitty and the kids all the support they need, and make sure she at least understands that it's not right for a man to treat his wife like that.'

'It's easier said than done, mate. You know how he's isolated her from just about everyone; he clearly doesn't like her having anything to do with anyone other than him and his old witch of a mother. He's brainwashed her; the man's a bloody control freak.'

'Christ, I wish I could turn the clock back.' Ollie said with a sigh.

James patted his friend's arm. 'Me too, mate. Me, too' He paused for a few moments. 'Anyway, I rang our Molly this afternoon and gave her the low-down – I know Kitty wouldn't like it if she knew, but Moll won't let on we've been talking about her, and I didn't think there was anything to lose. She's been worried too, said she's going to try to get Kitty over here for a drink when Vi's next back in the village. Sooner, rather than later, I hope.'

Ollie ran a hand back and forth over the stubble on his chin, remembering the spark he'd felt between himself and Kitty that morning — he knew she'd felt it too. All he could think about was his feelings for her. But as he listened to James, his mind wrestled with the thought that he should quash his fledgling hopes. She was a married woman, albeit married to the wrong man, and he didn't want to add to her problems.

AS THE THREE women arrived at the Sunne, an image of Dan flashed through Kitty's mind making her stomach clench. She knew he wouldn't be happy about her coming here and would, without doubt, kick off about it. But it already felt good to be out with her friends, and she wasn't doing anything wrong. The new, bolder Kitty shrugged off her concerns and turned to Molly who'd pulled off her hat, releasing a bounce of springy curls. 'Your hair's looking good, Moll. Is that Stefan's handiwork?'

'Ta.' Molly ran a hand through her hair. 'Yep, he's the only one who can tame this mane.'

'Same here,' said Kitty, putting a hand up to her own curls that were gradually re-emerging.

'Ooh, talking of gorgeous hair, I saw Anoushka today. Hasn't she just blossomed? I drove past her this morning and had to do a double-take at this tall girl with a model's figure and long, golden hair to die for who was waving at me. At first, I hadn't got a clue who it was, but then those amazing Slavic eyes gave it away; just like her mother's,' said Vi.

'Ahh, she's a lovely girl. Ollie's done a good job with her. Can't be easy being both father and mother to a teenage girl,' said Molly.

'Lord, no,' agreed Vi, raising a dark purple eyebrow.

Kitty felt her face flush at the mention of Ollie's name and was pleased that her two friends didn't seem to notice. A flurry of butter-flies took flight in her stomach. What if he was there? She was sure he would be, hadn't Jimby said something about meeting up with him tonight? *Oh, heck!*

Molly was still fiddling with her hair which was now full of static thanks to her raking her fingers through it. 'Oh, bloody hell, I can feel my hair sticking out all over. I bet I look like a sodding dandelion clock.'

'Right, that's enough fussing about your hair, Mrs Potty-Mouth, we're freezing our proverbials off out here. Your hair looks fine, or it will do in a minute if you leave it alone.' Violet gave Molly a gentle nudge towards the entrance.

'Vi's right, Moll, if you stop touching it, it will calm down.'

Unconvinced, Molly pushed open the pub door, and the three friends were instantly enveloped in a heart-warming tang of wood-smoke courtesy of the large open fire that crackled busily in the inglenook. It curled around the mouth-watering aroma of Boozy Beef that inched its way out of the kitchen. Kitty followed close behind her friends, her anxieties instantly erased by the easy atmosphere that tinkled with the sound of laughter and the hum of conversation. It was good to see that at seven-thirty the pub was already full of friends and neighbours. The new-style Sunne, basking in its renais-sance, appeared to sit back and wrap its ancient, wonky walls around this new generation of customers.

'Oh, wow!' said Kitty. 'I'd never have recognised the place. It looks amazing.' Her eyes wide, she scanned the room, taking in the heavy tweed fabric of the curtains, cushions and seating in rich, moorland colours. Their sumptuous shades complemented the soft ochre of the freshly lime-washed uneven walls and age-darkened oak cruck frame. Polished brass pumps and foot-rests gleamed in the subdued lighting along the thick, oak bar. Kitty smiled at the sight of Nomad and Scruff, the Latimer's two rescue dogs of indeterminate breed, who were slowly baking themselves in front of the roaring fire, their old lives of hardship and neglect apparently forgotten.

Once they'd reached the bar, the three women spotted James and Ollie deep in conversation at the other end. 'Looks serious.' Molly nodded in their direction just as the butterflies in Kitty's stomach started to flutter again.

'Mmm. Most unlike those two,' said Vi. 'I can't remember the last time I saw James without a mischievous smile plastered across his face.'

Kitty glanced across at the pair but was distracted by her cousin. 'Right, what can I get you, ladies? Gin and tonic, Vi?' Molly reached inside her bag and pulled out her purse.

'Perfect. Thanks, Moll.'

'How about you, Kitts?'

'Ooh, erm. I quite fancy a dry white wine, thanks. Or what's that on the bar?' Kitty spotted a silver hammered bucket filled with ice cubes and a slender-necked bottle.

'That would be a rather cheeky little Prosecco.' Jonty's smile was warm. 'And it comes highly recommended by my darling wife.'

'Well, in that case, I think I'll have a cheeky little glass of Prosecco.'

'Coming up.' Jonty poured the fizz with an expert hand and passed the glass to Kitty. 'There you go, m'dear. Enjoy.'

It was getting crowded around the bar. James and Ollie decided to move to the large table by the fire to free up some space. They'd also notice a tiddly Lady Carolyn Hammondely working her way through some of the men, flirting shamelessly. They decided it would be best to get out of the danger zone. Jimby had clocked his sister standing at the bar with her friends. He caught Molly's eye; she gave him a collaborative wink as she turned back to Kitty and Violet. 'Right, it looks as though those two have got their serious chat out of the way. Why don't we go and join them?' she suggested, triggering a wave of nerves in Kitty's stomach again.

'Sounds like a good plan,' agreed Vi.

'So, what's the goss, you two.' Molly pulled out a chair, followed by Violet. Kitty found herself sitting on the banquette beside Ollie, hoping the soft lighting would hide the blush she could feel warming her cheeks.

'Hello, ladies, it's nice to see you out and about like the old days.' Ollie smiled and sat back, folding his arms across his broad chest, his half-finished beer in one hand. Kitty could feel the warmth of his gaze lingering on her, but she resisted the pull to return it.

'I've just been telling Oll about my spare barn. He needs to find somewhere new for his workshop, and I need to find some use for the barn now I've got all that junk out of it. It's all rigged up with electric, has good parking for wood deliveries. Makes perfect sense if he moves in,' said James with a shrug before he drained the last dregs of his beer.

'Yep, I'm going around to have a look at it tomorrow, and if it's suitable, which from what Jim says I think it will be, I'll get moved in straight away.'

James got to his feet. 'Right, my round. Same again, Oll? And can I get you lovely ladies another drink?'

'Cheers, mate.' Ollie drained his glass and handed it to James.

'Violent, another gin and tonic?' Jimby grinned mischievously as he dodged a whack from her. 'Anyone fancy giving me a hand?'

Violet stood up to unbutton her coat which she hung on the back of her seat. 'We all know you can't be trusted with a tray after the last time you held one.' She nudged James in the general direction of the bar.

He grimaced. 'Oh, don't remind me. I'm surprised I'm still allowed in here.' He shuddered at the memory of carrying a trayful of drinks to a table, tripping over Scruff and tipping half a dozen glasses and their contents over Kitty's father-in-law, George, who'd taken it surprisingly well. Unlike his poisonous wife, who'd presented James with a hefty dry-cleaning bill.

Thanks to the Prosecco and the cosy ambience of the pub, Kitty was beginning to feel herself relax. For a brief moment, she wondered why she hadn't done this more often, then she remembered that Dan usually managed to talk her out of it. That, or if she did venture out with Molly and Vi, he'd be in such a foul mood when she returned that she'd stopped bothering to do it at all; the consequences had been getting increasingly unpleasant. But the new, stronger Kitty resolved not to leave it so long before the next time.

'I saw Noushka earlier today, Oll.' Violet placed a fresh glass of

Prosecco on a coaster in front of Kitty, before setting her gin and tonic down. 'I hardly recognised her, she's grown so tall.'

Ollie turned to Violet, his eyes filled with pride. 'Yeah, she's definitely shot up over the last six months, grown out of all her clothes, she tells me. Though I reckon it's a convenient excuse to hit the shops in York with her friends. Which, I have to say, suits me down to the ground; I'm rubbish with that sort of thing. Luckily, she's had my mother to help out, but now she's older it's nice for her to go with people her own age. Mind you, some of the things she's brought back home have resulted in a few heated words between us.' He rolled his eyes good-naturedly.

'Well, I think you've done a great job with her. She's always so polite and friendly, she's definitely inherited your temperament,' said Molly before downing a large mouthful of her Chardonnay.

'She's gorgeous, too,' said Vi.

'Well, she certainly didn't bloody-well inherit that from Oll!' quipped James.

Their conversation was brought to a halt by a series of shrieks. They turned to see Pat Allison dragging Lady Carolyn Hammondely out of the pub by the hair. Apparently, when her husband hadn't arrived home for his dinner, Pat had come looking for him, and found Lady Carolyn wrapped around him like a boa constrictor.

'Wowzers!' Vi turned back to her drink. 'Who says it's quiet in the countryside?'

'Don't worry, that sort of thing doesn't usually happen.' James said to Kitty who looked at him askance.

'No, it doesn't, but I'm afraid to say Carolyn's had it coming for a while. She's been getting worse and doesn't seem to realise how bad she makes herself look,' said Ollie.

'Aye, you're right there.' Jimby nodded. 'She'll try it on with any man. She's not fussy, though she does seem to prefer it if he's got a girlfriend.'

'Or if he's wearing a wedding ring,' chipped in Molly, recalling the time Carolyn had made a play for Pip, telling him she liked the idea of being Lady Chatterley. He'd returned home wild-eyed and terrified.

'I can't help but feel sorry for her, though. Since her brother died she's been a bit of a lost soul, what with her father going to pieces the way he did. And as for her mother, well, Lady Davinia's a real cold fish. Carolyn won't get much TLC from her.'

'I s'pose.' Violet looked thoughtful. 'I wonder if there's any truth in the rumour about her getting pregnant by someone inappropriate when she was younger? If what they say is true, she got no support then, from the father or her family.'

James caught Ollie's eye. 'Right. Time for another drink, me thinks. Who's for another one?' *And time to steer the conversation away from that particular story.*

KITTY HAD FINISHED her drink and began pulling her coat on. 'Right, I think I'd better be getting back. I promised Auntie Annie and the kids I wouldn't be long.' She'd enjoyed herself and was reluctant to leave, but the prospect of Dan arriving home and finding her out had started to creep into the forefront of her mind, slowly erasing the relaxed feeling she'd been enjoying.

'Yep, I'd better be heading back myself.' Ollie checked his watch before draining his glass. 'I'll walk you back, Kitts.'

From the corner of her eye, Kitty noticed James and Vi exchange a quick glance. 'Oh, it's okay, you don't have to, Ollie. I'll be fine.' She pulled her gloves from her pockets and put them on. It wasn't Jimby and Vi that bothered her, but if Dan saw her walking back with Ollie, he'd go ballistic.

'Well, at least let me walk you back as far as my house then?' Ollie had shrugged his jacket on and was zipping it up. As it was on the way to her own home, Kitty felt she couldn't argue with that.

14

AT JUST GONE seven-thirty Dan's car pulled up outside Sam's small Georgian terraced house on the outskirts of York. He rapped impatiently at her front door. Several seconds later she answered, wearing a flirtatious smile and a flimsy black lace kimono. Arching an eyebrow, she took a sip of claret from the bulbous wine glass she had cupped in her hand. 'You're late.' She opened the door wide, allowing him to step out of the inky-black night and into her neat hallway.

'Don't nag.' He took a slug from her glass and followed her into the warmth of the softly-lit lounge, where scented candles flickered in glass tea-lights. He fell into his usual soft leather chair, adjusting the collection of cushions – *what is it with bloody women and cushions?* – and exhaled noisily through his mouth.

'Rough day?' Sam curled-up on the matching sofa opposite; it hadn't escaped her attention that distraction loitered at the back of his eyes.

'You could say.' Dan took a slow sip of the wine, swirling its rich flavours around his mouth before allowing it to trickle in a warm rivulet down his throat. It soothed instantly, combining with the warmth thrown out by the log-burner, and soon he could feel himself begin to relax as he melted into the soft curves of the chair.

Allowing himself another gulp of claret, he cast an eye around the room. Minimalist would sum it up. Masculine almost – if it wasn't for the candles and cushions. It couldn't be more different from the cottage at Oak Tree Farm with its reminders of children everywhere. You couldn't bloody-well get away from them. Lily's brightly coloured paintings were plastered all over the fridge, held in place by garish magnets. And Lucas's gargantuan models of spacecraft and rockets occupied the kitchen window sills where other, more tasteful, things belonged. Luckily, it was a room he didn't spend much time in, but Kitty did, and he didn't know how she could stand it. And don't mention the bathroom, with those bloody awful plastic toys everywhere. Sometimes it felt like the floor was sodding booby-trapped, with agonising little plastic objects and their nasty sharp edges just waiting for you to unwittingly place your bare foot on them. He was glad to get away from all of that crap. There was nothing like it here. Here it was all clean lines and immaculate; infused with an air of calm.

Sam eased herself onto his knee. 'Poor baby. I know just the thing to help you relax.' She slipped between his legs and opened the zip on his jeans. Dan rested his head back and let out a low groan.

'YOU'RE A DIRTY GIRL.' Dan glanced at his watch then threw his arm around the back of his neck, shooting Sam a lop-sided grin. They'd migrated to her bedroom where they'd spent the last hour and a half in a sweaty tangle, their antics hanging heavy in the air. 'But I'm going to have to love you and leave you.' Much as he disliked the idea, he should really head off home soon.

Sam propped herself up on her elbows. 'Hey, don't ever think you can just call here and treat me like some sort of whore. What we've got going on,' she waved a finger between the two of them, 'is a mutually-beneficial, uncomplicated two-way thing and not just for you to come and get your rocks off whenever it suits you.'

'Trust me, Sam, I don't think that for a second. You're one hell of a ballsy woman with the same attitude to sex as a man. No one could ever treat you like a whore.'

'Hmm. And don't you forget it.' She threw the Egyptian cotton sheet back and straddled him. He responded by massaging her generous breasts, their mutual arousal evident. 'A quick one in my favourite position before you go.' She smirked as he put his hand behind her head, pulling her to his lips.

'Oh, I forgot to mention this earlier, but I overheard a woman from the next office talking about you last week.' Sam was watching Dan who was sitting on the edge of the bed, buttoning-up his shirt. Frowning, he turned to her and noted her playful grin. 'Odd looking woman – not your usual type – she must be knocking on for six foot, has a large, masculine jaw and badly dyed hair. Sound familiar?'

The furrows of Dan's frown deepened. 'Er, no.'

'Daft stubby bunches?'

'Nope.'

'She has an inordinately high opinion of herself and talks in the most annoying affected accent which drives everyone mad. And – this is the interesting part – she claims to have an intellectual connection with you.'

'Me?'

'Yes, you.'

'I haven't a cl…oh, shit.' Realisation dawned on Dan, and he clapped a hand to his forehead, curling his lip in disgust. 'Daft stubby bunches, masculine jaw…the only woman who fits that description is Aoife Mellison, who's an irritating, silly cow. And I can assure you I do not have any kind of connection with her, intellectual or otherwise.'

'You sure? Me think the gentleman doth protest too much.' Sam tipped her head to one side and raised her eyebrows mischievously.

'Christ, Sam. Give me some credit.'

'Well, she's known as *Evelyn* Mellison at work, Eve for short. Though, out of the blue, she started to sign herself as "Aoife", wittering on about her Irish heritage.' Sam hooked finger quotes around the last two words. 'And what we don't know about her Celtic colouring, isn't worth knowing.'

Dan bristled. 'Ughh! She's a bloody nightmare of a woman, always creeping up behind me, trying to make the most ridiculous, inane conversation. She even asked me if I liked her new coat the other day, like I would even notice what the hell she's wearing. Trust me, if she was the last woman on earth, that's all she'd be; I wouldn't go anywhere near her. The human race would die out. And as for that layabout she's married to, he needs to get his finger out of his arse and do a day's work for a change. All he does is swagger around the village with an arrogant expression on his face or play his sodding saxophone. And I use the word *play* very loosely.'

'Ouch. So, you're not the Mellisons' biggest fan then?'

'You noticed? And they've bred the most horrible kids.'

'Eugh. The bloody nerve of it.' Sam pulled a face; she was the first to admit she didn't have a maternal bone in her body; the mere thought of children was enough to bring her out in hives.

Dan stood up and rested his hands on his hips. 'Right, I'd better head back.' He loitered for a moment. 'You didn't mention anything about us, did you?'

'Don't be ridiculous. What I do with my private life is exactly that, private. And anyway, I can hardly bring myself to speak to the woman, she gets my back up just looking at her.'

What Sam hadn't shared with Dan was that while Aoife had been boasting about their, so-called, intellectual connection, she'd been slating Kitty and saying she wasn't good enough for Dan. It had made Sam's blood boil.

She may be having no-strings sex with Dan, but Sam had no intention of making a claim on him. She valued her freedom and didn't want him for herself. Rather bizarrely, when she'd heard Aoife speaking unkindly about Kitty she'd felt an unlikely kind of loyalty to Dan's wife. And her dislike for Aoife Mellison intensified.

In the hallway, Dan pulled on his jacket and turned to her. 'I'll try to pop over sometime this weekend. If that's okay, of course?' he asked, fishing his keys out of his pocket.

She was leaning against the wall, examining the ends of a lock of hair. 'I've got plans for Friday, but if you're around you're welcome to join me. Could be fun,' she said mysteriously.

15

KITTY AND OLLIE left the pub, stopping when they reached the gate to his cottage. 'Sure I can't see you properly home? It's dark down your end of the village.' His breath curled out in front of him, suspended in the cold night air. He was pleased to see she was looking brighter, with a bit of colour in her cheeks and a hint of happiness in her eyes.

'I'll be fine thanks, Ollie, it'll only take me a couple of minutes to get home.' She shivered and rubbed her hands together; the thick, hoar frost had tightened its grip on the village, making it sparkle in the pale moonlight. She glanced up at him smiling shyly. 'I've really enjoyed tonight.'

'Me, too.' He smiled back at her.

Silence hung between them for a moment. 'Well, I'd best head off.' She turned away from him.

'Oh, er, yeah. Bye, Kitty.' He watched her make her way carefully along the trod. She still had something of the startled deer caught in the headlights about her, but she'd joined in with their laughter, relaxing more as the evening went on. He hoped it wouldn't be too long before she joined them again.

~

THERE WAS STILL no sign of Dan when Kitty returned home, which settled on her in an uncomfortable mix of relief and apprehension. Once Auntie Annie had left, she checked on Lucas and Lily who were tucked up snugly in bed. Feeling overwhelmed with love for them, she dropped gentle kisses on their cheeks, savouring their warm, comforting scent.

Downstairs, the old farmhouse felt cosy as soft lighting sat harmoniously with the low, heavily beamed ceilings and thick, uneven walls. No one would've guessed at the unhappy scenes they'd witnessed earlier that day.

Kitty headed into the kitchen to make a cup of tea, ruffling the heads of Humph and Ethel who were curled up in their shared basket, pleased to have her home.

Clutching her mug, she made her way into the living room where the wood-burner sat at the far wall, spewing out a gentle warmth. She curled herself up on the sofa and flicked on the television, but she struggled to concentrate on the drama that played out on the screen. Instead, her mind wandered over the events of the evening. She'd been surprised at how much she'd enjoyed herself, how the earlier tensions of the day had easily slipped away. Molly and Vi had listened patiently as she'd shared the details of her unpleasant encounter with Gwyneth, offering words of support and humour. 'She's a silly wizened old bag,' said Molly, and Violet had readily agreed. It had made Kitty realise how much better it felt to share her bad times with friends, rather than keeping them to herself, incubating the pain, allowing it to grow and feed off her like some greedy parasite.

Her thoughts drifted on to Ollie. Gentle, kind Ollie. She hadn't spent so much time in his company for as long as she could remember. Her stomach flipped as she admitted to herself how good it felt. She'd done all she could to avoid him since she'd started to date Dan. It must've hurt him; he hadn't deserved that. A shard of guilt spiked through her conscience. She could barely face the memory as she recalled the look on his face when he first saw her with Dan, hurt writ large across his handsome features, sadness clouding his usually vibrant eyes. She'd never really acknowledged it until now and, Lord, it made her feel lousy.

An image of Dan, arrogant and angry, pushed its way into her thoughts, making her feel guilty for thinking of Ollie. She sipped on her tea, her spirits plummeting as she recalled how he'd stormed out of the house that morning. But that was nothing new; the feelings of apprehension and general unhappiness that pervaded when she was around him had become the norm. She began to nibble on what was left of her fingernails as the other stressful events of the day started to creep into her mind; the spite-riddled words that Gwyneth had thrown at her, and what Rosie Webster had told her about Evie Mellison. It had definitely been a day of highs and lows.

Kitty sighed and stretched out her legs, resting her feet on the oak coffee table that sat in front of the sofa. She changed channel on the television, settling on a wildlife documentary, thinking how Lucas would have enjoyed watching it; she'd seek it out for him after school tomorrow.

But she couldn't concentrate on the narrator's voice. Instead her mind drifted back to Ollie. She knew she'd hidden her feelings for him for years, wrapped them up and buried them deep. They were precious and needed handling carefully. It had been a while since she'd dusted them down and allowed her mind's eye to linger over them. Though her recollection of his clean scent of soap and citrus, warmed with a hint of sandalwood had always been just out of reach, until she'd bumped into him this morning, that is. And it had triggered an unexpected yearning deep inside her.

Kitty allowed her thoughts to roam over her most precious memories. The feel of her hand in Ollie's, which was big and rough from work, and how she'd felt safe and warm when he'd wrapped his strong arms around her. Her eyes smiled as she re-lived that magical first kiss and how she'd sworn to Molly and Vi she'd felt fireworks; something she'd never felt with Dan.

Reality hit her like a bolt of lightning. She was still in love with Oliver Cartwright. She'd never stopped loving him, she'd only told herself she had.

How did I get myself into this mess?

HER MIND STEADIED, she flicked off the television, and took a sip of her tea, pulling a face: it had gone cold. She threw a log onto the fire, watching as it crackled and spluttered, then headed into the kitchen to make a fresh pot of tea. Humphrey was flat on his back, legs splayed and fast asleep, a pneumatic snoring emanating from his rotund body. Ethel lay beside him wearing a weary expression. Seeing Kitty, she pulled herself up and made her way to the Aga, settling down beside it with a "hmphh". Kitty chuckled as she gave her a pat. 'Oh, poor you, Eth. Can't you sleep for noisy old Humph's snoring?' Ethel responded with a wag of her tail.

Kitty filled the kettle, wondering at Dan's whereabouts and what sort of mood he'd come home in. If, indeed, he did come home tonight. Her musings were interrupted by the feeling she wasn't alone. Her nostrils tingled as the familiar scent of honeysuckle curled around her nose. Setting the kettle down she turned and scanned the kitchen, but the room was giving nothing away. The only difference was a small, pure-white feather that appeared to fall from nowhere right in front of her eyes. She watched, transfixed, as it slowly zig-zagged its way silently to the floor. A rash of goose-bumps erupted over her body, and her heart started to thump in her chest. That comfortingly familiar smell could only belong to one person. 'Mum!' Kitty pressed her hand to her mouth. The word was out before she'd had the chance to apply any kind of logic to her thoughts. She glanced around the kitchen, half of her expecting to see her mother, the other half telling herself to stop being so ridiculous.

With her legs like jelly, Kitty dropped into the nearest chair and glanced over at Humph and Ethel. They were both fully awake and looking around, as though troubled by something. Humph let out a long whine and Ethel gave a whimper. 'Did you sense it too?' she asked. 'I can't have imagined it if it woke you from that deep sleep, eh, Humph?' The chair creaked as she leaned back into it. Kitty was suddenly overwhelmed by a feeling of reassurance, and in that moment, she knew her life was going to get better.

THE GRANDFATHER CLOCK in the hallway struck ten-thirty as Kitty, armed with a fresh mug of tea, returned to her place on the sofa in the living room, and to her thoughts of earlier that day. As she was jostling with new feelings of confusion and guilt – after all, she was a married woman – she heard the rattle of Dan's key in the door and her body tensed.

Sensing his presence in the doorway she looked up, curling her feet more tightly beneath her. He looked tired, his hair was ruffled, and four-day-old stubble covered his chin. Kitty scanned his face, trying to assess his mood, searching for something to say that wouldn't antagonise him. But it was Dan who broke the silence. 'Look, about before, I think we should just forget about it. I'm not sure what's got into you, you seem very different, but I'm prepared to ignore it and I'm...'

'Dan, please don't.' Despite the fear rising in her gut she wasn't prepared to go back to being a doormat. 'Please don't try that, it won't work anymore. And I don't want to forget about it; I can't. I'm sorry. I feel so unhappy about the mess we're in, and I don't want to carry on like this anymore. It's not fair on the kids. You're back home so late you didn't even get chance to see them before they went to bed. They think you don't care.' She braced herself.

Dan didn't like what he heard, but years at the Bar had equipped him well with an array of advocacy skills to deal with whatever was thrown at him. 'Look, Kitts, darling. You know I adore you, but I'm under an enormous amount of pressure at the moment. Ask anyone in chambers, I'm absolutely snowed under with work, I've got the CPS and solicitors constantly hounding me for this and that; everything's always urgent to them. I feel like I'm perpetually juggling to keep my practice running smoothly. You've no idea. The upshot is that I barely get a minute to myself, never mind you and the kids.'

Kitty, surprised he hadn't erupted with anger, listened impassively. 'And I gather you've had a bit of a run-in with my mother, but you of all people should know what she's like when she gets a bee in her bonnet. I'm happy to brush the whole thing under the carpet and forget about it. Just pop in to see her, sweeten her up with a bunch of flowers, say you're sorry, and it'll all be forgotten about.' He walked across the room and sat beside her on the sofa, nudging her shoulder with his.

His last words made her blood boil. She lifted her gaze from the floor and faced him. 'What you've just said proves you have no respect or regard for me and my feelings. And over the years I've become used to that, though it doesn't make it right. But what I think is far worse is that you don't seem to give a damn about seeing our children. You can't even get home to see them for a mere half hour before bedtime. You have no idea what message that sends to them, do you?'

Dan was visibly shocked. 'Look, calm down. This isn't like you at all.' His voice was uncharacteristically quiet. 'As I said, work's just gone crazy, I can hardly move in my office for briefs, and I've just been assigned a new pupil, who's a bit of a handful, to be honest. I'm not sure she's got what it takes to hack the cut and thrust of the Bar.' He pushed away an image of his earlier encounter with Astrid and leaned across, taking hold of Kitty's hand. She snatched it away; the touch of his skin now repulsed her. And there it was again. Lingering, taunting and thumbing its nose at her: another woman's perfume flirtatiously entwined around the threads of his clothes, still running its fingers through his tousled hair.

Kitty inched away from him. 'I wonder what she would be good at? What did you say she's called? Astrid? Is that her perfume you reek of?' Adrenalin charged through her petite body, making her feel the size of a lion.

Feigning exasperation, Dan sat back in the sofa. 'You're being irrational now, blowing everything out of proportion. Adding two and two together and getting a bloody dozen. The reason my coat smells of perfume is because Frances, *my clerk,* hung her coat next to it. And the reason I'm late is because I've been working my backside off in chambers, trying to play catch-up because I took my family away for a long weekend.' His chest swelled with misplaced sanctimony.

But Kitty wasn't fooled. 'I don't believe you, but do you know what? I don't care anymore. I've had enough, and I don't want a life like this for the kids and me. We're worth more than that, even though you don't think so. I'm not saying I'm perfect, far from it, but you could at least treat us with a little bit of respect.' From the corner of her eye, she saw Dan rub his forehead; his body language seemed different, less intimidating. She swallowed and carried on. 'I partly blame myself for putting up with things for so long, the way you talk to me, the way you let your mother treat me. I was stupid to let it happen, and it's taken me a long time to get to this point, even though there were plenty of times when I should've taken notice. And in doing so, I've set a bad example to our children.' Kitty felt her bottom lip wobble and clenched her teeth, holding back tears that threatened.

Dan's impatience was growing. 'Come on then, name some occasions when you think I haven't shown you respect? Everyone knows I spoil you rotten, give you anything you want. They only have to look at the expensive clothes you wear, this house we live in. You and the kids have the best of everything. You get taken away on nice holidays to the best hotels.' He knew she couldn't argue with that. 'So, go ahead. Name the times you've been hard done by.'

She held his gaze. 'Do I really have to itemise them, Dan?' she asked, slipping over to the door and closing it gently; she didn't want the children to hear even a whisper of this. 'How about all of the horrible names you call me? Or the constant put-downs that make me feel like I'm dirt on your shoe? You make me feel like I'm a criminal in the witness box.'

'You know I don't mean it; I'm just the sort of man who says things in the heat of the moment. And it's definitely not worth getting this upset about.'

'Really? How about when I lost my parents? You have no idea what a shock that was, and you gave the kids and me no support whatsoever. You even made me feel guilty for crying because I wasn't focussing my attention on you.'

Dan pinched the top of his nose. 'Why do you always have to drag up the past? It hasn't been all bad, but you have to focus on the negatives.'

Kitty gave a weak laugh and leaned back into the sofa, feeling utterly washed out. 'I really wish you could hear yourself, Dan.'

Detecting weariness in her voice, he seized the chance to work on her softer side. 'I do respect you, Kitts, more than you know.' He tilted her face towards his. 'I may not show it, but I adore you. You're everything to me, you and the kids. I'd be lost without you.' His voice cracked, and he put on a convincing act of fighting back tears. 'It's just the pressure of work really gets to me sometimes. It's hard to switch off, and it's heavy stuff I'm dealing with, none of this shop-lifting trivial stuff like Henry Wilkinson deals with day in, day out. The stuff I do really takes its toll, and I can't just leave it at the robing room door like he can. He can swan off home without a care in the world. But not me, my work really matters to me. I genuinely care about getting the right result for the punters. You, of all people, know that.' Dan could see his words were beginning to chip away at Kitty's defences.

He edged closer to her on the sofa and stroked her hair. Feeling herself bristle, she inched away from him. 'You don't need to belittle what Henry does to make yourself look better; he's supposed to be your best friend. I know you work hard, but there's that thing called a work/life balance that other people seem to manage. And I don't think it's asking too much of you to come home early a couple of nights a week so you can see the kids before they go to bed.'

Dan sighed. 'Look, how about a couple of times a week I try to get home early enough to put the kids to bed and read them a story?' He regretted saying it as soon as the words had left his mouth, but he knew it was what Kitty needed to hear to get things back on track. 'It's going to be tricky, but if it's what you want…'

His words hung in the air. Kitty gnawed on her bottom lip, mulling them over. Could he be the father that told bed-time stories? The father who snuggled down with his children until they fell asleep? While a niggling doubt vied for her attention, a deep hope that he could be – and might even find himself enjoying it – won the day. She had to give him a chance, if only for the sake of their two children, who had so much love for him that was just waiting to be tapped into. It was the deal-maker that meant the most to her, and Dan knew it.

She took a deep breath and turned to him. 'That would mean the world to the kids. I don't think you have any idea just how much, so please don't let them down.'

And, once again, he'd reeled her in.

16

The following morning, it came as no surprise to Kitty that Dan had left for work before she and the children had opened their eyes, but she still couldn't help feeling a pang of disappointment. She told herself that it was his usual routine – and, in fairness, he hadn't made promises to hang around until they were all up – but it always felt as though he couldn't wait to get away from them, to be around them as little as possible. After last night, she thought this morning might be different.

Stalked by disappointment, she padded into the kitchen and was pleasantly surprised to see that he'd left a scrawled note on the table saying he'd be back for six o' clock, which would give him plenty of time to do the things he'd promised.

Hearing movement upstairs, Kitty quickly crumpled-up the note and pushed it into her dressing-gown pocket. As much as she was desperate to tell the children, Dan's track record meant that she decided to keep it to herself – just in case. *Don't let them down Dan.*

Lucas appeared in the doorway, yawning widely, his hair ruffled and his eyes still heavy with sleep. 'Morning, Mum,' he said through a yawn, rubbing his eyes.

'Morning, Lukes.' She smiled at him. 'Sleep well?'

'Mmmhmm.' He dragged out one of the chairs at the table, frowning as it scraped noisily along the flagstone, then flopped onto it. 'Lil says to tell you she doesn't want any breakfast, she doesn't feel very well, and she's staying in bed.' His words were distorted by another wide yawn.

'Oh. Any ideas what's up with her?' Kitty placed a glass of milk on the table in front of him.

He scooped it up and took a couple of noisy gulps, wiping his mouth with the back of his hand when was done. 'I think it's something to do with Evil Smellison. She's been saying horrible things.' Lucas appeared reluctant to make eye contact with her. Something told her he knew more than he was letting on.

'Right, I'll pop up and have a word with her.' As she headed for the door, Lucas released a loud belch that even had Humph's ears twitching.

'Lucas! That's why I tell you not to rush your drinks down.'

'Soz, Mum.' He grinned at her, and she shook her head in affectionate despair.

Upstairs, Lily was still in her bed. She pulled the duvet over her head when Kitty opened her bedroom door.

'Morning, little love.' Kitty gently pulled the duvet back revealing her daughter curled up in a tight ball, attempting to make herself invisible. 'Don't you want to come down for breakfast? I was going to do you some yummy dippy eggs with lots of buttery soldiers.' She brushed Lily's curls off her face and saw that it was wet with tears.

'Oh, sweetheart, don't cry.' Kitty scooped her onto her lap.

Lily flung her arms around her mum's neck and buried her face in her chest. 'I don't want to go to school because I've got a really bad tummy ache, Mummy.'

Kitty kissed the top of her head and rubbed her back in soothing swirls. 'Oh dear. Has something happened that might give you a tummy ache, do you think? You know you can tell me anything because I'm your mummy and mummies can always help put things right.'

Lily nestled into her and shook her head.

'Is it anything to do with Evie Mellison?'

After a moment, Lily nodded. 'She's been so mean to me, Mummy. She won't let me play with anyone, or sit next to anyone in class, and if I do she makes fun of my work and tries to make my friends laugh at it, too. And she calls me horrible names.' The words fell out in a tumble. 'And she says… she says Daddy's got a girlfriend.'

'She says what?' Kitty's breath caught in her throat as icy fingers closed around her heart.

'She says Daddy's got a girlfriend. Her mummy told her, and she says it's true because her mummy's seen him with her. She said there's lots of things you don't know about.' Lily's eyes were fixed on her fingers that were fiddling with Snuggles.

Kitty could hear her pulse thrumming in her ears. Keen to remain calm for Lily's sake, she took a deep breath and gave her daughter a squeeze. 'Listen to me, Lils. I don't want you to take any notice of what that girl says. She's nasty, and she shouldn't be going around saying things like that about anybody. She could get herself into a lot of trouble for it.' It took all of her strength to keep her voice calm.

What Kitty didn't know, nor Dan for that matter, was that Aoife's sister, Trish, had recently moved next door to a woman called Karen; a woman whom Dan had called upon regularly for many years. On a recent visit there, Aoife's curiosity had been aroused when she spotted Dan's car at the neighbour's. It was piqued even more-so when she was informed that he was a frequent visitor there.

AFTER MUCH GENTLE coaxing Kitty managed to get Lily into her uniform and agreeing to give school a try for the morning. As they made their way up the path, Aoife was heading towards them, on her way down from school. Lily shrank behind her mum, and Aoife appeared to cross the road to avoid them. Kitty was bombarded by a mixture of emotions but, for the sake of the children, kept her usual demeanour, bidding the woman good morning. It stuck in her throat, especially when her greeting wasn't reciprocated, and was instead met with one of Aoife's customary scowls.

Kitty had been puzzling over the best way to handle what she'd learned that morning; she didn't want to make matters worse for Lily. But seeing Lil's teacher on duty in the playground had helped make her decision. Mrs Prudom, as well as being the infant class teacher was also head of Lytell Stangdale Primary. She listened carefully as Kitty explained Lily's reluctance to come to school, and what Rosie had told her yesterday, though she couldn't bring herself to share what Evie had said about Dan.

'Don't worry, Mrs Bennett, I'll keep a close eye on things and have a word with you at the end of today.' She pushed her spectacles up her nose and held out her hand to Lily, smiling as she did so. 'Come on, Lily, you can be on playground duty with me this morning.' Lily took her hand, and they walked across to the Buddy Bench where a forlorn looking Tommy Yoxall from Year One was sat picking his nose, waiting for someone to be his friend.

Content that Lily was in good hands, Kitty wove her way across the playground, dodging a game of hopscotch, a handful of girls skipping and a group of boys – including Lucas – playing a noisy game involving cards, the same games she and Jimby had played when they had been students at this very school. She gave her son a small wave; he'd reached the age of being too cool to acknowledge a parent in front of his friends. He gave a barely-discernible nod and continued with his game.

As Kitty got to the gate, she sensed she was being watched and turned to see Evie Mellison's deep-set gaze boring into her. She hurried out of the playground with a feeling of unease.

As she made her way down the path an unforgiving wind, loaded with the promise of a bitterly cold winter, whipped up, rocking the naked branches of the trees, tearing off any remaining leaves before scattering them around the village. Kitty quickened her pace as it sliced at her exposed face and nipped at her ears; she regretted not wearing a hat.

A jumble of thoughts were wrestling around inside her head. *Bloody Dan!* What if there was some truth in what Lily had told her? The rumours lurked like spectres; Kitty had always had suspicions tucked away at the back of her mind. *Like father like son* was an expression she'd heard whispered many times in reference to George and Dan but, on the rare occasions she'd dared to mention it to her husband, he'd always skilfully managed to bat it away. But then again, it could just be that Aoife really did fancy Dan and was doing her best to undermine their relationship by making Kitty feel suspicious. After all, Rosie did say that a few people thought Aoife had the hots for him. And it could just be that she'd seen Dan with a female member of chambers, or his pupil, and jumped to the wrong conclusion. Kitty continued this argument in her head as she headed past the village shop.

'Ey up, Kitts. How are you diddlin',' said James as he crossed the road towards her.

'Hiya, Jimby.' Though her smile didn't reach her eyes, Kitty was still pleased to see him.

'Got time for a cuppa? I've got the biccies.' He waved a packet of custard creams at her.

'Sounds like a plan. Come on.'

KITTY PLACED a wicker mat on the kitchen table and set the teapot on it. 'There, it just needs a couple of minutes to mash.' She sat down and began to wipe away imaginary crumbs.

Not wanting her to think he was prying, James decided to wait for his sister to instigate the conversation.

He didn't have long to wait.

She sighed noisily. Humphrey, sensing her sadness had plonked himself heavily on the floor beside her and placed his head in her lap, his tail wagging hopefully. 'Oh, Humph. What am I going to do?' She rubbed his smooth black head that was speckled with grey.

'That good, eh?' James set his mug down.

'Oh, shit, Jimby. It's all such a mess.' She noticed his eyes widen at her uncharacteristic use of an expletive. 'Just when I think we're making progress, something or someone comes along and throws in a massive hand-grenade to stuff things up again. Talk about one step forward and twenty-five back.'

'Right. Has something else happened since yesterday – if you don't mind me asking?'

'Look, before I go any further, I'm very conscious that I'm heading into the realms of becoming a serial whinge-bag who's constantly throwing pity-parties. And I'm concerned that all I seem to do when I see you now is blub and moan, but I promise it'll stop soon.' She glanced across at him.

'Hey, no worries, sis. You've every right to have a grumble the way things have been for you. You've kept your troubles to yourself for so long, you've got a shed-load of catching up to do, so whinge away.'

He listened quietly as Kitty repeated the conversation she'd had with Dan the previous night and, though he didn't share his thoughts with her, he felt more than a little sceptical about Dan's promises. He was more concerned when he heard what Lily had said. There'd always been rumours about Dan's philandering, but Kitty had never let on that she knew anything, and James didn't feel it was his place to interfere with his sister's marriage; to do so could potentially risk Dan alienating her further from the rest of her family. But now that Lily was involved, it changed things.

'Look, Kitts, I don't want to appear out of order, but for how long can you keep putting up with this crap?' James's voice simmered with anger. 'It's been bad enough to just sit back and watch this happening to you but, for God's sake, your kids are involved now, and that's wrong. Plain bloody wrong!' He slammed his clenched fist down on the table, making Kitty jump and Ethel bark. He lowered his voice. 'Sorry, I didn't mean to shock you. It's just been so frustrating to have to sit back and not be able to do anything.'

Kitty had been picking at what was left of her fingernails; she stopped and regarded him. 'What do you mean, sit back and watch what's been happening to me?' She'd always thought she'd managed to keep the troubles in her marriage well hidden, wearing her mask of fake happiness and making endless excuses for Dan. In fact, she'd become so adept at making excuses for him, she'd even begun to believe them herself.

James, feeling he'd said too much, was scouring his brain for something less controversial to say when he caught sight of Violet heading down the path. 'Oh, look, here's Vi.'

They both watched as Violet teetered across the icy flagstones in a pair of her trademark heels. 'How the hell can she do that in those when I'm on my arse in these?' He lifted a foot encased in a chunky boot.

There was a light knock at the door followed by a cheery, 'Hiya, Kitts, s'just me,' as Violet peered around the door, breaking into a wide smile. It dropped as she glanced from Kitty to James. 'Oh heck, you both look serious. I'm not interrupting anything, am I?' The faint aroma of toast that had been lingering in the kitchen was quickly shooed away by the sweet scent of her perfume that wafted in. It didn't go unnoticed that Jimby struggled to take his eyes off her.

'Hi, Vi, no of course not, come in. It's great to see you again.' Kitty pulled her friend into a warm hug.

'Earth to Jimby. Earth to Jimby.' Violet was clicking her fingers under his nose, her eyes dancing mischievously. 'You didn't hear any of that, did you?'

'Er, were you saying something about your new cottage?' It was worth a guess, he'd been half aware of hearing Kitty refer to it.

'Well done, Jimbo. Spot on.'

He sat back down at the table and grinned. 'Actually, can you imagine the washing line, strung with all of Vi's burlesque gear? All those nipple tassels, corsets and lacy knickers will be enough to give all the old guys a heart attack.'

Kitty tutted and rolled her eyes. 'Don't take any notice of him, you know what he's like.'

Vi delivered a sharp back-hander to his forearm. 'Thank you. I won't be hanging anything on the washing line, actually. Never use the things but trust you to lower the tone.' She raised an eyebrow at him which James mirrored, before leaning across the table and scooping up a handful of peanuts from the small bowl. He threw one of the nuts up in the air and caught it in his mouth.

'See, still haven't lost it,' he said, crunching the peanut. 'Mmm. These are really nice, got an unusual, creamy flavour. Where d'you get them from, Kitts?' He repeated his nut catching trick a further three times.

'It's like watching a seal being thrown a fish,' observed Vi.

Jimby pulled a face at her before throwing another nut higher into the air and catching it.

'Show off.' Vi pulled a chair out from under the table and sat down opposite him.

Kitty looked on in horror. 'Erm, Jimby. I'm not sure it's such a good idea to eat those nuts.'

'Why not? Taste alright to me. What's up with 'em?' He grabbed another handful and funnelled them into his mouth.

As she was working out how to tell him, the phone started ringing in the hallway. 'Let's just say they're not the, erm, freshest.' Her voice tailed off as she disappeared to answer it.

'You women worry too much about sell-by dates. I always follow the rule of sniff it and see: if it smells alright, it'll taste alright. And I apply the same rule to women.' Amused at his own joke, he chuckled.

'S'just as well I know you don't mean to sound like a sexist pig,' said Vi as she tried to kick him under the table.

Kitty walked back into the kitchen, pulling her coat on. 'That was school; Lil's still got tummy ache, and they want me to go and get her,' she said, winding a brightly coloured scarf around her neck.

Concern clouded James's face. 'Oh dear, poor old Lily-Loops.'

Kitty tugged her gloves out of her coat pockets and slipped them on. 'Mmm. I'm not so sure just how poorly she is, but I'll pop up in the car just in case. One of you stick the kettle on, will you? I feel the need for more tea coming on.'

Kitty jumped into her four-wheel drive, turned the key in the ignition and whacked the heat up to the maximum. The sky had taken on an unforgiving wintry hue, and the flecks of sleet that had collected on the windscreen were being rhythmically pushed to one side by the wipers. She waited a moment, allowing the windows to clear of condensation. It wasn't far to walk to the school from here, but if Lily really was poorly it wouldn't be fair to make her walk back down in this nithering cold; it got right into your bones.

An image of Aoife popped into her mind as she remembered what Lily had told her earlier that morning. That family had a lot to answer for, she thought as she put the car into gear and headed off up the road.

Arriving at the school door, Kitty could see Lily sitting with Mrs Marr, the school secretary, who was reading her a story. Her daughter was smiling and, as far as she could see, didn't look particularly unwell. It was more like the poor little thing was feeling unsettled and needed some time with her mum. She pushed the buzzer and waited to be let in.

Mrs Marr looked up and smiled before hurrying to the door. 'Hello there, Kitty, come on in. Look, Lily, your mummy's here for you,' she said in her soft Scottish lilt. 'You go and pop your coat on while I have a quick word with her.' She stepped into her office and beckoned Kitty to follow her.

Smiling kindly at Kitty, she picked up the head-teacher's diary. 'Mrs Prudom is teaching just now, but she wondered if you could pop in and have a word with her? She said you mustn't worry, and that it can be easily sorted out, but she'd just like to have a wee chat with you, if that's okay?'

Kitty's heart sank. As much as she didn't want Lily to be ill, it was preferable to her being so upset she had to be brought home from school. 'Oh, yes, of course. When would Mrs Prudom like me to call in?' Her mind was racing and, hesitating for a moment, she asked, 'Erm, I don't want to put you on the spot, but did she mention if it was anything to do with the Mellison children?'

'She did, yes. But please don't worry about it; we're keeping an eye on things. Oh, do excuse me.' The phone had started to ring, Mrs Marr leaned reached across her desk to answer it.

Ella Welford, one of the school's teaching assistants, and a relation of Kitty's on her dad's side, caught the tail-end of the conversation. She leaned in to Kitty and whispered, 'That family. They think they're so perfect and expect everyone else to think the same. The way the mother looks down her nose at everyone, I don't know who she thinks she is. And those kids have always got to be the best at everything. Talk about putting pressure on them.'

'Tell me about it.' Kitty rolled her eyes.

'Evie in particular. She has a very dominant character on her that one. Likes to form little gangs, exclude individual children and rope other kids in to pick on them. Nasty piece of work. But her mother thinks she's a little angel,' added Ella.

Mrs. Marr had finished her phone call. 'So, is tomorrow morning at nine o'clock, just after drop-off, any good? Don't worry, if Lily's still unwell we can always rearrange.'

Seeing Lily heading down the short corridor, her coat on and reading book bag in her hand, she nodded a quick agreement. 'Yep, that's fine.'

'THAT WAS GOOD TIMING.' James poured a fresh cup of tea for Kitty. 'And how's my favourite niece then?' He pulled a sympathetic face at Lily. 'I gather you're a poorly girl.'

She nodded, sad brown eyes dominating her small face.

'Fancy one of Uncle Jimby's special cure-all bear-hugs?'

'Yes, please.' Lily gave a small smile.

He scooped her up, sat her on his knee and wrapped his arms tightly around her, then growled like a bear. 'There you go, I bet that feels better already.'

'Yep.' She giggled, peering into the empty bowl beside James's mug that had once contained the peanuts. A frown creased her brow. 'Uncle Jimby, where have all those nuts gone?'

He patted his stomach. 'They're in here, in my tummy. They were a bit moreish, I'm afraid. Once I started to eat them, I couldn't stop. I'm worse than Humph. In fact, I think I'm going to pop!' He puffed out his cheeks, and Lily jabbed her fingers into them, forcing out the air in a sharp rasping sound making her giggle again.

'See, Mummy, the nuts didn't go to waste. Uncle Jimby's eaten them all for me. Oh, Uncle Jimby, you're the bestest.' She took his face in her small hands and planted a kiss on his cheek, rubbing it in for good measure.

Kitty looked from the bowl to Jimby and back again.

'Am I missing something here?' he asked, a look of concern creeping over his face. 'There was something wrong with those peanuts, wasn't there? Has that snorty pig Humphrey gozzed on them or something?'

Violet sniggered, and he flashed her a look of outrage.

'Don't be silly. Mummy wouldn't let Humph do anything like that.' Lily covered her mouth with a plump hand and threw her head back against her uncle's shoulder, laughing.

'Phew! That's a relief,' he said, brushing aside Lily's curls that were tickling his nose.

'They *were* chocolate peanuts, Uncle Jimby,' she placed a generous amount of emphasis on "were". 'But I sucked all the chocolate off them and put them back in the bowl. Mummy said it was a waste, but now you've eaten them all, so it wasn't.' She beamed up at him.

A look of horror inched its way across his face as realisation dawned.

'Your face,' said Kitty as she and Violet had collapsed into a helpless heap of laughter.

Vi was struggling with her mouthful of tea which, thanks to her mirth, was now stuck in her throat and impossible to swallow without the risk of choking. She waved her hand in front of her face, but James's incredulous expression was too much, and she spluttered, spraying tea all over Ethel who'd been sitting beside the table, hoping that a stray biscuit from tin would find its way to her. She looked daggers at Violet then flounced off to the other end of the kitchen where she observed the goings on with an unimpressed air. This added fuel to their giggles, and soon tears were pouring down their cheeks, leaving James torn between feeling slightly nauseous at eating second-hand peanuts, and happy that Kitty was laughing more than he'd seen her laugh for a very long time.

'Oh, please stop. My face is aching,' said Vi, rubbing her cheeks.

'Oh, mine, too.' Kitty sighed.

'Never mind that. What about my guts? I'm the one who's been scoffing down second-hand, sucked peanut cast-offs.' James rubbed his stomach and pulled a face of mock disgust.

Lily flung her arms around her uncle's neck. 'Oh, Uncle Jimby, never mind. It's only my spit, and I haven't really got tummy ache.'

'Ah, well, thank goodness for that, eh, Lily-Loops?' He smiled, ruffling her curls.

'And what was that you were saying about not really having tummy ache?' asked Kitty, raising her eyebrows.

'Oops!' Her eyes wide, Lily's hands shot up to her mouth.

Once the hilarity had subsided Violet cleared her throat and spoke. 'Anyway, Kitts, the reason I've popped in is to see if you fancy meeting at the pub again on Friday night?' She and James looked expectantly at her, awaiting her answer.

17

D an had left for chambers early that morning. Despite his flaws as
a father and husband, he was a dedicated barrister. Solicitors, independent and CPS alike, were confident that when they briefed Dan
Fairfax-Bennett, they were getting the best. He was thorough, effi-
cient and absolutely merciless in the courtroom, earning him the
nickname "The Assassin". His opponents both respected and feared
him in equal measure. God forbid any poorly-prepped lawyer who
tried to blag their way through court proceedings when Dan was
acting for the other side. He would rip them apart. Friend or foe, he
didn't discriminate. He had no patience or respect for anyone who
didn't take the job seriously – as far as he was concerned they gave
the Bar a bad name. Dan was all about getting the job done and
getting it done well. His natural competitive streak meant that he
had to excel at everything, and his job was no exception; he wouldn't
rest until he was at the very top of his game.

As he drove the winding country lanes to York, the previous
evening's conversation with Kitty was still ringing in his ears. This
recent shift in their relationship had started to jostle for headspace
previously taken up by work.

He was oblivious to the fact that as the years had inched forward,
he had become two distinct people. In his work environment he was
the highly respected, successful barrister. He was charming and
friendly to the court staff, using his skills of manipulation to great

effect whenever he needed to get his case brought higher up a list, some photocopying done, or a coffee from the canteen.

Chambers, too, benefitted from his beguiling charm; there it helped if he needed to jump the typing queue or talk the clerks into negotiating better brief fees. Though his clerk, Frances, knew there was a very different side to Dan. She'd witnessed one of his spectacular tantrums in the early days when he was just out of pupillage, and she didn't fancy going there again. Dan was still rather ashamed of himself for showing that side of his character at work and eased his conscience by regular deliveries to chambers of luxury cakes and biscuits.

He was nicely in control of his professional life and until recently, had thought the same of his personal life.

DAN WAS the first to arrive in chambers, closely followed by his friend and fellow tenant, Henry Wilkinson. While it could be argued Henry was as dedicated as Dan, he didn't quite match up in the ruthlessness stakes. They'd been called to the Bar in the same year, but Henry's practice hadn't enjoyed the stratospheric rise that Dan's had, nor did he have the back catalogue of high-profile cases under his belt.

Dan's patience was being tested by the newly installed all-singing-all-dancing coffee machine when Henry lurched through the front door on an icy blast of air, juggling a bulky brief.

For crying out loud! All I want is a sodding, straight-forward cup of coffee!' Dan threw the pod of coffee on the tray. Henry was one of the few members of chambers from whom he didn't hide his temper. 'You need a flaming degree in how to use these things. Exactly whose idea was it to get this useless lump of machinery?' He glared at his friend, who was struggling to resist a smirk. Henry was well acquainted with Dan's hatred of technology, no matter how basic.

'What have you done so far?' Henry rested his brief down on one of the junior clerks' desks, slid his red bag containing his tools of trade – wig tin and robes – off his shoulder and onto the floor beside it. He headed over to Dan, pulling off his gloves as he went.

'How the hell should I know?'

Henry picked up the discarded pod, slotted it into place, pressed a button and, in an instant, the machine hissed into action. 'There you go.'

Dan grunted as Henry handed him the steaming cup. 'Smells good.' He took a sip. 'Mmm. Tastes good, too.'

'You're welcome.' Henry's sarcasm was wasted on Dan, who, he noted, was looking uncharacteristically ruffled. 'I haven't had chance to ask you about your weekend away in the Dales. How did it go? Did the hotel live up to expectations?'

'It was alright.' Dan narrowed his eyes, and a muscle twitched in his cheek.

'That good, eh?' Henry paused for a moment. 'Kitty and the children alright?'

'The hotel was fabulous. But Kitty's been a bloody nag. Whinging about me not being home to tell the kids a sodding bedtime story, would you believe? Like I haven't got anything better to do. So I've got to report home early tonight, or I'll be in the crap. It's as bad as living at home with my mother.'

'That's not so bad, is it? Your family are lovely.'

'That's alright for you to say, you've got no kids making noise and mess, no nagging bloody wife who doesn't even try to understand the pressure you're under. And trust me, Kitty can be a self-centred pain in the backside with her demands. Nothing's good enough for her at the minute.' His face twisted into a snarl.

Henry was taken aback; he'd known Kitty for years, and this description didn't fit the easy-going, mild-mannered woman he knew. He'd always suspected she had a tough time of it with Dan, but she was loyal to the core, and he'd never heard her complain. In fact, he'd never heard her say a bad word about anyone and, from their first conversation, he'd secretly harboured a soft-spot for her. 'I suppose she's been through quite a bit over the last few years, what with losing her parents and the baby so close together.'

Dan rolled his eyes and huffed. 'You always did see her as some kind of perfect little angel, but trust me, the reality is very different.' He stomped out of the clerks' room and up the stairs to his office.

Frances, the senior clerk, arrived in time to catch the tail-end of this exchange, stepping back as Dan pushed past her. She looked at Henry askance.

'Argument with the coffee machine.'

'Ahh.' Frances nodded as she placed her handbag on her desk. 'Coffee?'

'Please. So, you think I should wait to tell him that his opponent in tomorrow's case of Brettle and Others is now being prosecuted by Connor O'Dowd from King's Crescent chambers in Newcastle?'

'Dowdzilla versus The Assassin. Ouch! They really don't like each other. He's as ferocious in court as Dan; it'll be a bloodthirsty battle that one. The poor jury won't know what's hit them.' Henry winced. 'Yep, it might be wise to keep that under wraps for now.'

~

AFTER THE REVELATION of her non-existent tummy ache, Lily had discreetly sloped off to her bedroom – just in case her mum decided to take her back to school.

'Right. I'd better get cracking.' Violet pushed her seat back and stood up. 'I've got a meeting in York this afternoon, and I've got to pop into the flat first. But, as I say, I'll be back on Friday night if you fancy venturing out to the pub to celebrate.'

'Sounds like a plan,' said James, rubbing his hands together. 'And I reckon the others'll be up for it, too.'

'How about you, Kitts? D'you fancy helping me celebrate the purchase of Sunshine Cottage?'

'Erm, I'm not sure. I don't have a babysitter, and I don't like to ask Auntie Annie again. And Dan likes to go for a pint with his dad on a Friday night after his heavy week at work.' The reality was, Kitty was concerned about how Dan would react to her going out twice in one week. She didn't want to rock the boat, especially if Dan was going to make an effort to get home to spend more time with the kids.

'Well, I've spoken to Moll, and she says her mum really won't mind babysitting again. You know she thinks the world of your two, and Molly said it's nice for her mum to get away from her dad and his talk of ewes, tups and tractors for a bit. And if he wanted to, Dan could even join us.' Vi uttered the last sentence through gritted teeth.

'C'mon, sis. You've got to be part of the celebrations for Vi coming back to the village.' James nudged her with his shoulder.

Kitty thought for a few seconds. 'Oh, alright then. When you put it like that, I'd love to join you.'

'Yay!' Vi grinned, clapping her gloved hands together before pulling her friend into a fragrant squeeze. 'I'll text you about time and everything, and Molly and me can co…' Her words were brought to an abrupt end as Humphrey, who was sleeping by the Aga, broke wind thunderously. Vi glared at him in disgust. 'Oh. My. God.'

'Stylish, Humph.' James sniggered as Kitty shook her head.

Ethel looked as outraged as Vi. And it had been so loud, it had even registered in Humphrey's age-ravaged ears, rousing him from a deep slumber. He looked around with rheumy, squinting eyes and settled his gaze accusingly on James. 'Don't look at me as if I did it, you farty old bugger. It was your backside that shook the founda-tions, not mine, so take ownership, Humphrey Fairfax-Bennett.' Humph's ears twitched as he held James's gaze. 'What the hell have you been feeding him on, Kitty?'

'It's just that new food for older dogs, "Fitter". It's good for his geriatric joints and is actually supposed to reduce wind.' She started to giggle as Violet pulled a face of utter mortification.

'Well, it doesn't bloody work. Quite the opposite. You should write to the company that makes it and tell them they should call it "Farter", not "Fitter."' James snorted at his own joke, and Humph responded with another resounding trump.

Unable to control her mirth, Kitty lay her arms on the table and rested her head on them while her body shook with laughter. Violet, too, had succumbed and tears were now pouring down her cheeks.

'Oh, God,' said Kitty as she raised her head, brushing her hair back. 'I haven't laughed so much in ages.'

'Good old Farty Pants. Eth doesn't look very impressed, does she? And it's just as well as our Moll's not here, she'd probably have wet herself.' James chuckled.

'Well, on that note I'm definitely going.' Vi smoothed her glossy hair. 'Right, I'll see you Friday,' she said, picking up her bag before hugging Kitty and delivering a playful punch to James's solid bicep.

'Can I tempt you to a hot chocolate, Jimby?' Kitty was pouring milk into a pan. 'I'm going to make one for Lil. I know she doesn't really have tummy ache, but I think she's feeling a bit fragile.'

'Eh? I, er.' James's voice tailed off as something caught his eye out of the window.

'So, would you like one?' Kitty turned her attention from the pan onto her brother, who was craning his neck out of the window.

'Like one what?'

'A hot chocolate.' She had the milk bottle poised over the pan, ready to pour.

'Erm…' he turned his head slightly, but his eyes were still glued to the glass.

'Is that a yes, or a no?'

'Erm…'

'Jimby!'

'What?'

She walked over to him, following his gaze to see what had captured his attention. Her eyes alighted on Violet who was clickety-clacking her way along the road towards her car, avoiding the slippery flags of the trod. Kitty rolled her eyes and grinned. 'Would you like a hot chocolate? To make up for the chocolate you lost out on with the peanuts.'

James frowned at the reminder. 'Er, no thanks, sis. I'm afraid I'm going to have to head off now. I promised Oll I'd meet him at ten and I'm already five minutes late.' He drained the luke-warm dregs of tea from his mug before rinsing it under the tap and leaving it in the sink.

Kitty spooned the chocolate powder into the milk and began whisking as she looked over at her brother. A gaping hole at the elbow of his dark-blue Arran jumper caught her eye. 'Oh, Jimby, look at your sweater. If I'd known about it, I'd have fixed it for you.' She smiled. Repairs like that would have been swiftly taken care of by their mother when she was still here.

James's hand felt for the hole. 'Ey up, it seems to have grown since this morning.'

'What you need is the love of a good woman; someone to look after you.'

'No, what I need is the love of a *bad* woman.' His eyes twinkled mischievously. 'A *very bad* woman.' He was staring out of the window again, watching Violet in her car. She'd slowed down to let a handful of Bill Campion's hefted sheep pass and glanced across to see James looking at her. She blew him a kiss and winked.

'I hope you know what you're getting yourself into there, Jimby. Much as I love Vi to bits, she can be a very driven career woman. She's got the potential to eat you for breakfast, suck the meat of your very bones and spit them out by lunchtime.' Kitty poured the frothy chocolate milk into Lily's favourite unicorn mug.

'Sounds bloody good to me. She can suck my bones anytime.' James gave a cheeky grin.

'Jimby! Please, no more talk like that. You're my brother, she's one of my best friends, and I'd rather not think of either of you in that context if you don't mind.'

'All I'm saying is…'

Kitty pushed her fingers into her ears and squeezed her eyes together. 'Lalalalalalalala. Can't hear you.'

James laughed. 'Okay, okay. I get the message.' He patted Kitty's arm and gestured for her to pull her fingers out of her ears. 'I promise, no more dirty talk about Vi.'

18

Bryn Bennett was shivering at the bus stop in the market town of Middleton-le-Moors. The bus that would pass through Lytell Stangdale was already ten minutes late, and he was freezing cold. He breathed heavily into his gloved hands, briskly rubbing them together before shoving them into the pockets of his puffa jacket. He sighed, exhaling noisily, his breath curling off like a wispy white cloud in the chilly autumn air. He repeated it, attempting to make smoke rings. Anything to relieve the boredom and take his mind off the cold. He could have cheered when, five minutes later, he saw the bus trundling its way towards him.

When the bus eventually arrived at Lytell Stangdale, Bryn climbed off at the stop directly outside the post office and headed in the direction of Oak Tree Farm. He knew he was going to have to do something about the situation soon, he couldn't keep standing outside the house all the time, that would be weird. And he had a feeling that Dan's wife was starting to get suspicious, worried even, and the last thing he wanted to do was scare her. He'd even thought about saying something to her; she had a friendly face, looked kind. But how on earth did you throw *that* into the conversation with someone you didn't even know? 'Hi. Oh, and, by the way, I'm your…' Nope, his mother's warnings rang in his ears. He would have to think long and hard about this one.

As Bryn approached the cottage, he spotted a glamorous looking lady heading out of the gate. She put him in mind of a Hollywood movie star from the old films his grandmother liked to watch. She glanced across at him a couple of times, and he slowed his pace as he crossed the road and headed towards the old red phone box where he watched as she walked carefully on the frosty road across to a cute little city car.

He prized open the heavy door and inhaled the distinctive phone-box whiff of stale cigarettes, even staler urine and years of damp dust. He wondered if the spiders' webs that were draped around like mini Christmas decorations actually absorbed the smell, hanging onto it as it intensified with age.

He was disappointed to find that the phone box offered no protection from the biting cold and, despite being inside, his breath still hovered in front of his face. It was already beginning to steam up the small glass panes. With his gloved fingers, he wiped one of the panes at eye level and peered across at the cottage. The lights were on in one of the downstairs rooms, and smoke curled out of the chimneys. It looked cosy and welcoming, and he longed to knock on the front door. In his imaginings, he would be welcomed in with open arms. Dan would hug him and ruffle his hair, then introduce him to his family. He would be guided to a comfy seat by the fire, and the family would bombard him with a million questions, eager to hear his story. Before the night was out, he would be one of them. He would belong.

But deep down, Bryn knew that the cold, stark reality would be very different. He couldn't do it now, he couldn't shatter their peace. So, with a heavy heart, he pushed open the door and headed back to the bus stop. He cut a solitary figure as he walked away, his head and shoulders slumped.

He'd only known the truth for a couple of weeks. He'd needed his birth certificate so he could apply for a new passport and go on the school skiing trip. His mother, Karen, had made up a million and one excuses for not letting him have a look at it, saying she'd sort it out. But her protestations had aroused his suspicions, and he knew it had something to do with the identity of his father; something she'd never revealed to him. In the end, Bryn called her bluff, saying that he'd just have to go to the registry office and obtain a new copy himself.

Realising that her son was going to find out sooner or later, Karen had tentatively handed over the original and waited for her son's reaction.

Bryn had stared at the limp piece of paper, his eyes fixed on the words naming his father. He read it aloud, 'Father: Daniel George Bennett. Occupation: Barrister-at-Law'. His expression had morphed from confusion to disbelief. It was too much of a coincidence. 'Daniel George Bennett. Shit, Mum. Why didn't you tell me?'

Of course, his mother had tried to wriggle out of it, telling him that there was more than one Daniel Bennett in the world. It was, after all, a very common name. But Bryn was having none of it. After years of secrecy, he felt he was owed the truth. He couldn't hold back the tears any longer, and his mum couldn't bear to see the pain she'd caused her son. She'd wrapped her arms around him gently, stroking his thick, sandy-blond hair as her fifteen-year-old boy wept into her shoulder. The day she'd been dreading had finally arrived.

It was time to tell him the truth.

Bryn had sat in stunned silence, watching his mother intently, his eyes the very same pale blue as his father's, as she'd explained how she'd met Dan when she was working as a junior court clerk in the crown court at York. He'd started paying her lots of attention and, being five years his senior, she'd felt flattered that he'd ignored the younger girls in favour of her. He'd asked her out, and she'd happily agreed, unaware that he had a live-in girlfriend back at home.

They'd been dating for six months when she'd fallen pregnant. Dan was furious, accusing her of tricking him into fatherhood when she'd refused to get rid of the baby. Angrily, he'd told her no one must know he was the father; he wasn't going to risk the scandal harming his career. He'd insisted she leave her job, making her agree only to resume work when the child had started school. He would support them both financially until the child reached eighteen, and he would be generous. But it had been delivered with a stark warning that, if she let his identity slip to anyone, the money would stop immediately. Bizarrely, he'd insisted that he was named as the child's father on the birth certificate before he'd coldly informed her that their relationship was over.

Karen had bowed down to all of Dan's demands, and whenever Bryn had quizzed her about his father, she'd just brushed it away, saying he was some bum who'd left the country before he was born and she hadn't heard from him since.

⁓

It had been a lonely few years for Karen in her little cottage in Middleton-le-Moors, but one Saturday morning she answered a knock at her door and was surprised to find the newly married – and newly hyphenated – Dan Fairfax-Bennett on her doorstep, hiding behind a huge, fragrant bouquet of flowers and a disarming smile. He'd come equipped with all he would need to charm his way back into her life, and into her bed. And before long his golden, velvety words wrapped themselves around her, hovering over her skin like gentle caresses until she was, once more, putty in his hands.

Dan was struggling with married life and felt the need to provide himself with a convenient bolt hole, where he could be fed and watered, and have on-demand sex whenever he chose. Karen, dazzled by him once more, happily offered that place.

And so began a bizarre and one-sided relationship.

Karen had never married, nor had the inclination for a serious relationship with another man. She'd always secretly hoped that Dan would one day decide to stay with her permanently. But she was to be disappointed as, over the years, his visits, which were mostly when Bryn wasn't around, all but petered out. Until recently when, out-of-the-blue, they'd increased, his presence explained to her son as an old work colleague.

Karen finished telling her story and looked tentatively at her son. Throughout, his expression had veered between disbelief and sadness. She took his hands in hers. 'Please don't be angry with me, Bryn, love. I had to keep it secret, so I could look after you and give you a good life. The arrangement with Dan meant that you had the best of everything and wanted for nothing. I couldn't have afforded to send you to a school like Middleton Hall or pay for the expensive school trips. I just don't have that sort of money. But my silence meant that you've always had the best money can buy, and it's Dan whose paid for it all.' She searched her son's face, so similar to his father's; she was always amazed that nobody had guessed.

Bryn shook his head. 'Don't you see, Mum? It's not all about money and having the best of everything. It's about having a dad. Maybe even brothers and sisters. And by keeping secrets, you've both deprived me of all that for fifteen years.' He swallowed the lump of sadness that was clogging his throat as a solitary tear sprang from his eye and rolled down his cheek. Karen reached across and wiped it away, inwardly relieved that her son didn't recoil at her touch.

'I understand why you're sad and angry, love. But, even if you find it hard to believe now, everything I did was truly done with your best interests at heart. I love you more than anything else in the world, and I've always wanted what was best for you. Wanted to give you a good life. Nothing I did was done for selfish reasons, or to hurt you, and I hope, in time, you'll see that.'

'So, what happens now?'

Karen flopped back into her chair and sighed. 'Well, I think we need to tread very carefully. There are several people involved who'll be affected by what you've just learned, so we need to take things slowly before we decide what's best to do.'

'Okay,' he said with a sniff.

'You know who your father is now, and you can ask me anything you want. It's better that things are out in the open. No more secrets between us.'

Mother and son had talked into the early hours, and when Bryn went to bed that night, sleep was pulled out of reach as thoughts swirled around his mind. By the time he'd drifted off, he'd felt secretly thrilled at having a half-brother and half-sister.

And he'd made up his mind that he wanted to meet them.

19

WITH HIS HANDS THRUST deep into his pockets, whistling a nameless tune, James was heading back home when he noticed a tall lad waiting at the bus stop. He wasn't a local, he mused, but he did look vaguely familiar; and absolutely nithered by the frosty air that loomed over the village. He'd have a long wait, he thought. The next bus wasn't due for hours.

As James drew closer, it didn't escape his attention that the lad seemed to deliberately turn his face away, averting his eyes. But he'd caught enough of a glimpse of him to trigger a flash of memory. James remembered where he'd seen him before.

'Morning.' Like everyone else in the village, James always said hello to locals and visitors alike.

'Morning.' Rubbing the sole of his shoe over a loose stone, the lad still appeared reluctant to make eye contact.

'You might be better off going for the train. The next bus is hours off.'

'Oh, er, thanks. But I don't think the train's running, something to do with a tree on the line. I don't mind waiting.' He shrugged, looking flummoxed, his cheeks flushing bright red in the cold.

'Aye. Right, well it was pretty windy last night, I suppose.' James paused. 'Shouldn't you be at school anyway?'

'We were given the day off. The boiler's broken. Has been all week and they say it's too cold for us to work. We've had a few days off because of it.'

'Bet you were gutted about that.' He grinned, he had never been a fan of secondary school. 'But you'll catch hypothermia if you stand there waiting for it. You'd be better off going to a friend's house, kill time there.'

'Er, it's a bit difficult to do that. I, er don't really know anyone here.' Bryn gave a small shrug and an awkward smile before burrowing his chin into the collar of his jacket. He knew James had some sort of connection to Dan; he'd seen him leaving the house a few times. And, perversely, part of him wanted James to ask more questions and discover the truth. But another, bigger, part of him was terrified and wanted him to leave him alone so he could wait for the bus in peace. Even if it wasn't due for hours.

But James's interest was piqued. 'Oh, we're a bit out of the way here, so I thought you were visiting a relative or friend. I think I've seen you in the village before.' He blew on his bare fingers which were seizing up with cold.

'Er, no. Not really. I, er. I erm…'

James grasped the nettle. 'Actually, I think I've seen you standing near the phone box just opposite my sister's, Oak Tree Farm. Just down the road there.' He nodded in the general direction of the house and smiled to demonstrate he wasn't being hostile.

Bryn felt his face burn; he didn't want anyone to think he was some sort of stalker weirdo. A stodgy lump wedged itself in his throat. He tried to gulp it down and gave a small cough before he spoke. 'Oh, yeah. I know the one. I had no mobile signal, so I was trying to ring my mum.'

'Yeah, mobile signal, Wi-Fi, they're both pretty unpredictable round here, I'm afraid.'

'Isn't that the house where Dan Fairfax-Bennett lives?' Bryn felt a surge of courage and the words had tumbled out of his mouth before he'd had chance to think. He hoped Jimby couldn't hear his heart thudding.

'That's right. He's married to my sister, Kitty. Know him, do you? I'm James, by the way. Sorry, I didn't catch your name.'

'Yeah, I do know him, you could say.' Bryn tried to gulp down the lump that had found its way up to his throat again. He was talking to Dan's brother-in-law and, right out of the blue, he felt a sudden overwhelming desire to unburden his secret onto him. He needed to get rid of the pressure this secret was building up inside him. He seemed friendly and smiled a lot. 'And I'm Bryn. Bryn Bennett.'

'Bennett, eh? And Bryn's an unusual name. Sounds kind of Welsh, if I'm not mistaken, like Gwyneth. So, I'm guessing you're related to Dan's family then?'

'Yeah.' Bryn's face prickled with worry, but it was too late to backtrack now. And now he'd come this far, he didn't want to keep his secret in any longer. 'Erm. There's no easy way of saying this, but, er, Dan's my father.' His heart fluttered as adrenalin surged through his veins. How strange it felt to utter those words to someone. *Dan's my father.* He released the breath he'd been holding onto as the words echoed in his mind and a weight lifted from his chest.

Shock had frozen James's expression as he stood before Bryn, his mouth gaping. A few moments passed before he was able to speak again. 'What? You're telling me that Dan Bennett's your father? My sister, Kitty's, husband?'

Bryn nodded, shadows of worry hovering in his eyes. James dragged a hand across his face, shaking his head in disbelief. 'Right, well, I think we need to talk about this, but the middle of the village isn't the place. We'd better go to my house – if you're okay with that? And I need to contact my mate who was supposed to be meeting me at my workshop fifteen minutes ago.' He rummaged in his pocket for his mobile and checked signal strength. One measly bar, but that was enough. He fired off a quick text to Ollie and put off their meeting until later that afternoon.

AT FORGE COTTAGE JAMES led Bryn into the cosy, but slightly messy kitchen where last night's pots rubbed shoulders with this morning's breakfast dishes in the white Belfast sink. Jerry and Jarvis jumped up out of their beds, their tails wagging enthusiastically, a warm welcome for their dad and his new guest. Jarvis dropped the remnants of a stuffed toy pheasant at Bryn's feet, hinting for a game of fetch. Bryn obliged and chucked it across the kitchen. In a flash, the young spaniel was back, and the toy was deposited at his feet again but was quickly snatched away by the bigger Jerry which resulted in much barking and growling between the two dogs.

'Right, you two. Outside!' said James, and the pair scampered after him as he opened the back door and let them out into the garden. 'I'm afraid fetch is their favourite game. You'd be at it all day, but they can get a bit competitive – as you just witnessed.' He pulled a chair out from under the small pine kitchen table. 'There you go, make yourself at home. Can I get you a drink of anything, tea, coffee, coke?'

'I'll have whatever you're having, thanks.'

'Tea it is then. Seems it's the answer to everything, eh?' James gave a hollow laugh as he filled the kettle. 'I wish…'

An awkward silence hung in the air and Bryn fiddled nervously with the sleeve of his coat, racking his brains for the right thing to say. But only one word came to mind. 'Sorry.' He couldn't look at James.

'What for? You've got nothing to be sorry about.'

'My mum's going to kill me. She told me not to say anything.' He paused for a moment. 'I'm so sorry I shocked you, but I've only just recently found out who my dad is myself and it's all…well, confusing.'

'Sounds like you've had a shock too then, eh?' James took a couple of mugs from the rack and threw a teabag in each one.

'Yeah. A total shock.' Bryn sighed, wondering what to say next. He was relieved when James helped him out.

'Why don't you tell me everything from scratch? Go right back to the beginning and don't miss anything out.' The kettle had boiled. 'Milk? Sugar?'

Bryn nodded. 'Yes, please. And, er, three sugars.' He pulled an apologetic face.

'Bloody hell. The sugar police'll be after you.' He spooned the sugar into Bryn's tea, smiling as he passed it to him, instantly regretting his choice of mug. 'Oh, and, er, sorry about the mug. It's nothing personal.'

Bryn turned the mug to see the word "TWAT" printed on it in large, black letters. 'Oh.'

'Blame my best mate. He has a very warped sense of humour, same as me. We've got this challenge thing going on where we try to find the rudest, most offensive mug to give each other for Christmas or birthdays. I think he's winning at the moment. I'd better have a look at what I've given myself.' He pulled out a chair opposite Bryn, turning the mug so the writing faced him. The design was in the style of a pub sign. 'Cock o' The North,' he read aloud. 'Could've been worse I s'pose.'

Bryn looked across at the mug rack and saw a collection that was distinctly blokey.

'Sнiт!' James ran a hand back and forth through his hair as Bryn finished his story. 'And you really had no idea before then?'

'Nope. Not a clue. My mum's clearly very good at keeping secrets.'

'She's not the only one.' James frowned. 'You poor kid. And poor Kitty, too. What a bloody mess. Dan's stuffed up big this time, and I don't know how the hell we're going to sort it out.'

Bryn's face reddened again. 'I'm really sorry. I should've listened to my mum and not said anything. I should've stayed away and left everyone alone. I've scared your sister, and I really didn't want to do that. From what I've seen she seems really nice and so do you. I'm so sorry. My mum's going to go ballistic. Look, I'll go, and we can forget everything I've told you. I promise I'll leave your sister alone and never come back to the village again.' Gripped by a mix of panic and regret, Bryn stood up to leave.

'Hey, lad, calm your jets and sit yourself back down. I didn't mean that you shouldn't have said anything. You have every right to know about your father. All I meant was that Dan has gone and done it again. It's been one thing after another, and Kitty hasn't had an easy time of it being married to him. All I know is that I haven't got a clue how to deal with this. Or how to break it to Kitty, because she's got every right to know about this, too.'

Bryn felt bad, but he also felt relieved that he'd shared this with James, who seemed like a decent person. He felt sure that whatever he decided to do, James would do it with everyone's best interests at heart.

'Right then. Here's what we do.' James sat forward in his chair. 'As I said before, Kitty definitely needs to know about this, and I think it's going to have to be me who tells her. I'd rather she heard it from someone who cares about her than from some gossip, or worse still, Dan. But I'm going to have to think long and hard about how I'm going to do it so, for now, I need you to promise that you won't breathe a word to anyone else about what you just told me.'

'Okay. Yes, I'll do whatever you say.' Bryn nodded.

'I don't even want you to tell your mother we've had this conversation in case she says something to Dan, and he gets to Kitty first.'

'I promise I won't say a word. My mum doesn't even know I've been coming here,' he said sheepishly.

James looked at his watch. 'Bloody hell, is that the time? Listen, it's still a while till the next bus, so I'll run you back to Middleton-le-Moors.' Bryn went to protest, feeling he'd already put James out enough. 'No arguments. Come on, grab your coat while I send Oll another text.'

20

DAN HAD SURPRISED Kitty and been true to his word. Much as it had pained him, twice this week he'd been home early as promised, reading bedtime stories to the children. He'd even taken Kitty and the kids to Gino's, the popular Italian restaurant in Middleton-le-Moors. It meant more to Kitty than Dan could ever know. To see the excitement of their children as they'd watched their pizzas being made in front of them, their eyes wide as double-sized portions of the sumptuous Italian ice-cream were heaped into bowls for them by Gino. He'd bestowed a god-like status upon Dan since he'd prosecuted a thug who'd beaten Gino's son, Pepe, half to death in a dark snickelway in York. He'd been particularly savage in his cross-examination, securing a conviction and a lengthy prison sentence for the defendant. And ever since, Gino had been more than generous in showing his appreciation. At their latest visit, he'd allowed Lucas and Lily to have a go at twirling their own pizza bases, which had them in fits of giggles. Dan seemed to be enjoying himself, too, Kitty noticed, even if he was distracted by his phone every now and then.

She'd decided against confronting him about the latest rumours and put them down to Aoife's infatuation with him. It was the easy option; she didn't want to risk further upset for the children. Though, it didn't stop a hazy doubt from lingering at the back of her consciousness, gnawing at her peace of mind. But, for the sake of Lucas and Lily, she quashed it down, pushing it out of reach, hoping it would take the hint and leave her alone. Which, with so much practice behind her, she managed to do with ease. The hardest part was seeing the look in Jimby's eyes which swung between concern and disappointment and seemed to be manifesting itself in a slight awkwardness between the two of them.

Determined to look towards a future with Dan, Kitty clung onto the hope that he'd changed, that he would spend time with their children and show that he was enjoying it, rather than doing it under sufferance. She knew it would be an uphill struggle to get her marriage back on track, but for the sake of the kids she would stick with it. Her resurfacing feelings for Ollie would have to be placed out of reach once more.

≈

KITTY HAD GIVEN Dan several gentle reminders of her planned evening out – even extending the invitation to him, knowing full well he'd turn it down; he'd never got on with her friends or her brother. So, when seven o'clock on Friday evening arrived, and there was still no sign of him, she wasn't completely surprised. She'd tried to call him on his mobile phone, but it had gone straight to voicemail, and the couple of texts she'd sent remained ignored. Reluctant to send any more for fear of being accused of stalking him, and deep-down knowing he had no intention of turning up on time, she called Auntie Annie – her back-up babysitter – and arranged for her to come around. She knew, despite his efforts with the kids this week, Dan would be angry that she'd planned to go out. He always had to be in control of what she was doing, and if she was doing something that didn't meet with his approval, he would have to ruin it for her. But, tonight, Kitty was determined to celebrate with her friends.

Unlike her earlier visit to the pub, she'd thought long and hard about what to wear. She didn't just want to go in jeans but, on the other hand, she didn't want to look too formal. And, tonight, she wanted to feel like herself, rather than the person Dan thought she should be. After rummaging through her wardrobe, she'd found a dress she'd bought years ago from a bohemian clothes shop in York. It was empire line with three-quarter sleeves that just skimmed the shoulders, the skirt finishing mid-calf. Kitty loved its sumptuous shade of rich, raspberry red. She'd embellished it herself, sewing beads in muted shades around the neckline and cuffs, giving it the

Bo-Ho vibe she used to love to wear so much. But it was a style that Dan hated and had successfully steered her away from, until tonight.

BY THE TIME the grandfather clock chimed seven-thirty, Kitty was beginning to feel on edge. It was so typical of Dan; he wasn't even here, yet he still managed to get her full attention. Her mouth was dry, and she could feel her pulse race as she wondered at his reaction if he arrived home to find Auntie Annie in her place. She checked her phone for missed messages, but there were none. And there it was again, that familiar tight feeling in her chest as stress wrapped its fingers around her lungs, squeezing them tight and making her breathing short and shallow.

'Try not to look so worried, lovie.' Auntie Annie, who'd arrived fifteen minutes earlier, rubbed Kitty's arm and smiled. 'Just concentrate on having a nice time with everyone tonight. When Dan gets back he can join you all at the pub, or he can stay here, and I'll get back to your Uncle Jack's scintillating conversation about ewes and tups.'

Kitty gave a small laugh and glanced at the clock again. Chewing on the side of her mouth, she decided to try Dan one last time. 'No reply,' she said with a sigh, tucking the phone into the inside pocket of her bag.

'Not to worry. It's hi…'

Auntie Annie was cut off by a brisk knock at the door. 'Hiya, Kitty! Are you ready to come out and play?'

'Hi, Vi, come in. And yes, I'm ready to come out and play,' she called from the living-room as her frown slid from her face.

Immaculate in an amethyst moleskin coat that cinched in at the waist before flaring out into a full skirt, Vi breezed into the room in a waft of floral perfume. She was immediately pounced on by Lily. 'Auntie Vi, Auntie Vi, look at my nails. They're just like yours.' She waggled tiny, shell-pink painted nails under Vi's nose.

'Hi, Lily-Loops. Let's see.' Vi bent down, taking Lily's hands in her own. 'Oooh. They're gorgeous. Did Mummy do them for you?'

'Yep.' Lily held her hands in front of her, gazing at her fingernails.

'Hiya, Auntie Vi.' Lucas swung around the doorframe.

'Hiya, Lukes, how's school?'

'School's pants, 'cept for football. I'm on the football team, and I scored a hat-trick at our match against Dankselfe on Wednesday,' he said proudly.

'Hey, well done you.'

'You're just like your Uncle Jimby,' Auntie Annie said proudly, making him beam with pride.

'Right then, let's get you over to the pub, missus. Moll and Pip are meeting us there, and I'm a woman desperately in need of a G and T.' Vi looked around her. 'No Dan?'

'No Dan.' Kitty shook her head, not noticing Auntie Annie roll her eyes heavenwards.

But Vi did, and wanted to get her friend out of the house in case he turned up. 'Grab your coat and let's get cracking.'

21

AT SEVEN FORTY-FIVE Dan was chewing on a pen as he sat at his desk in chambers. He knew he'd promised Kitty that he'd try to work at their marriage, but he was seething that she was going out with *that* crowd tonight. And it was such a joke that he'd been invited too. He wouldn't go, and they all knew it. Even so, he assumed that Kitty would revert to her usual routine of turning them down. But her string of calls and texts appeared to suggest otherwise. He scowled as he read her last text saying she'd meet him at the pub if he got back in time. She was still acting out of character, and the feeling of unease and the change of dynamics in their relationship sat heavy in his gut. He wasn't accustomed to bowing down to accommodate anyone's feelings, and he definitely didn't like the feeling that he was no longer in charge of their relationship.

It had never been his intention to go to the pub with that bunch of in-bred losers, and it was up to her if she did, though he failed to see why she needed them when she had him. He should be enough. But if Kitty was so desperate to spend time with them, then she could bloody well get on and do it. Without him. And she was more stupid than he thought if she assumed he was going to waste his Friday night babysitting when he could be savouring a glass of claret some-where. No, he wasn't going to jump through her hoops. It was bad enough he'd been dragged into the tedious bedtime routine twice a week without her dictating how he could spend his spare time.

Dan leaned back in his leather chair, clicking his pen. He was bored. There was no one else left in chambers, even the dedicated Frances had gone home to her family. He'd been killing time trying to get to grips with a murder brief that had arrived from the CPS that morning, the papers of which were strewn chaotically across his desk. It was another high-profile case that had made the national press; another professional feather in his cap. But now his mind wasn't on it. Now he had an itch that needed scratching: he was feeling horny. Astrid had turned him down, she was going to the pub with Toby Smythe-Waterman, the new pupil from Lord Mayor's Walk chambers. Dan found himself having to bat away a prickle of jealousy at the thought; he hadn't finished with her yet.

Snatching up his mobile phone he scrolled through his contacts. Karen was out, but Sam had mentioned something about tonight the last time he'd seen her. It had piqued his interest; she was always good for a bit of no-strings fun. And she would know just how to scratch his itch.

'CHRIST, I NEEDED THAT,' Dan gasped. He was lying in a crumple of sheets in Sam's bed. He rolled onto his back, throwing one arm above his head, the other resting across his taut abdomen.

'I could tell.' Lying beside him, Sam propped herself up on her elbow and ran a long crimson fingernail across the dark-blond hair on his chest. 'Did you manage to get rid of some of that pent-up tension?'

He wiped the sweat from his brow with the back of his hand and sighed. 'Yeah.' As far as he was concerned, loveless, no strings-sex was a necessity. And one that left no imprint of guilt on his conscience.

Sam reached for her kimono and slipped it on. 'Time for a little drinkie before I take you out, I think.'

'Take me out?' Dan lifted his head from the pillow, looking puzzled.

'Yep. I told you on Monday, remember?' She disappeared through the doorway before he had chance to ask further.

Sitting in the soft lighting of Sam's living room, wearing his suit trousers and court shirt with the day collar removed, Dan drained the last dregs of claret from his glass. He was about to pour some more when Sam appeared in the doorway wearing an indecently short trench-coat. Smiling mysteriously, she said, 'Come on. Time to go. You can have some more wine when we get back.' She turned and headed for the front door, grabbing her car keys from the bowl on the hall table as she passed.

Dan followed, reaching under her arse-skimming coat to find that she wasn't wearing underwear. 'Mmm. You do realise you're going to catch your death out there? Want me to warm you up?' He smiled wolfishly.

'Naughty boy. Come on, we'll be late.' Sam pushed him out of the door, delivering a slap to his backside as she followed him.

'So, are you going to tell me where we're going?' He shrugged on his heavy winter coat.

'You'll see soon enough.' She aimed the key fob at her little black city car and pressed the button. 'Now climb aboard.'

'It's not the first time I've heard you say that tonight,' he said with a smirk.

THEY HEADED south of York and, after a twenty-minute drive, turned off into what looked like an old tractor track which was riven with suspension-challenging pot-holes. As the little car lurched and lunged along, Dan's head bumped against the passenger window. Anger flashed through him, and he shot an irritated look at Sam, but she continued to negotiate the road, apparently unfazed; she'd clearly driven down here before.

The inky black of the night wrapped itself more tightly around them as they drove through a wood of tall, looming conifers of increasing density. The car continued along the narrow track, bouncing and jarring over a succession of dips and bumps. Dan raked his fingers through his hair; his patience was beginning to fray.

'Here we are,' said Sam as the car nosed its way into a small clearing where a cluster of other cars were huddled together. She flicked off the lights, plunging them into a pool of darkness and rendering the other vehicles invisible. A thick wad of clouds moved across the moon, and Dan squinted into the shadows. 'So, are you going to enlighten me?' He turned to Sam whose eyes, bright with excitement, twinkled back at him.

'Are you serious?' Realisation slowly dawned on Dan as panic inched up his spine.

'Oh, come on. You're not going to go all goody-goody on me, are you? Don't tell me you haven't been tempted.'

Before he had chance to answer, they heard the thud of a car door shutting and watched as a man wearing a pair of leather chaps hurried his way from a scruffy looking truck that was tucked well back into a dark space between the trees. Glancing furtively around him, he headed over to a four-wheel drive that was parked under the shadow of a large Scots pine.

As they watched, the clouds parted sending pale shafts of moonlight through the gaps in trees. 'Bloody hell, I've seen it all now,' said Dan as the luminous white bottom of the man in the chaps bobbed back and forth at the rear of the vehicle, glowing in the iridescent moonlight. He was soon joined by an audience of voyeurs who appeared to be enjoying the al-fresco performance.

'Come on, get your coat off – it'll only get in the way.' She gave Dan a nudge. 'Time to let your hair down. And don't worry, no one will have a clue who the hell you are, or care, for that matter.'

Dan couldn't deny it, he'd been curious about the practice of dogging – he'd even had a tantalising glimpse of it on the occasions it had featured in his trials – but it had all the hallmarks of being a career-wrecker for a lawyer, and he'd been reluctant to take the plunge.

'Scaredy cat.'

'Bollocks!'

'Well, here's your chance. Go for it.' They watched as a tall, skinny woman wearing a pair of tipsy-looking bunny ears and a Venetian mask slipped out of an estate car and walked round to the boot. She flicked her hair flirtatiously and slipped off her coat to reveal a skimpy dress, before jumping into the back of the vehicle.

Dan could feel arousal mix and merge with apprehension as he opened the door and headed over to the car.

As Sam watched him go, a rotund male climbed into the passenger seat and slipped his hand inside her coat.

Dan was doing his best to ignore the overwhelming stench of wet dog that pervaded the messy car. It was beginning to jar with the owner's sharp perfume that was now irritating his nostrils. And he couldn't shake the feeling that there was something unsettlingly familiar about this woman. She began to groan, making him wish she would just be quiet. 'Oh, do that again,' the voice moaned. He froze as realisation slapped him in the face.

Carolyn Hammondely? 'No! It can't be!' He rolled off her and grappled for his trousers.

'What's wrong?' she asked, just as the dark sky was suddenly illuminated by a flashing blue light.

'Police. Nobody move,' a voice boomed out in the stillness of the night.

'Shit!' Dan grabbed what he hoped were the rest of his clothes and shoes, slipped out of the car and raced into the woods as if his life depended upon it. He could hear voices shouting and the low rumble of a car engine behind him, but he didn't dare look back. Instead, he carried on running, zig-zagging his way through the dense wood in what he hoped was the general direction of the road that led back to Sam's.

HE'D PUT some considerable distance between himself and the clearing when he stumbled over a mossy tree stump and landed face first in a boggy patch of ground, skinning his shin in the process. Still not wanting to risk looking back, he crawled behind the nearest tree, resting against it while he caught his breath. He was drenched in sweat, gasping for breath and his injured leg was throbbing painfully. His heart was beating so loudly in his chest he was sure it would be heard by any police officers searching nearby.

Dan rummaged for his mobile phone that was vibrating in the muddy bundle of clothing he was holding. 'Jesus Christ, Sam!' he whispered angrily. 'Where the bloody hell are you?'

'You managed to get away then?' she laughed. When the police arrived, she'd escaped, sloping off down a narrow track that led a convoluted, but discrete way back to the main lane.

The amusement in her voice irritated him. 'Yes, but it's the last time I get involved in one of your bloody stupid ideas.'

'Oh, just relax. Anyway, where are you?'

'How the bloody hell should I know? And I don't know how the hell I'm supposed to relax when I'm stuck in the middle of some wood with my balls hanging out, wearing only my socks and no idea of how the hell to get out.' He shivered as a line of cold sweat trickled down his back, finding its way into the nick of his bare backside.

Sam did her best to stifle a giggle. She'd grown up in the area and knew the wood well and, after Dan had given her a rough idea of the direction he'd run in, she gave him instructions on how to get to the picnic area. 'And can I recommend that you get your kit back on before you walk any further, or you'll risk arrest for being a flasher instead of a dogger.' She made no effort to hide her amusement.

'Just make sure you're waiting for me when I get there. I'm freezing my balls off and don't want to wait around until you decide to turn up.'

22

As Kitty headed along the road with Violet, she was beginning to wonder about going to the pub without waiting for Dan to get home. The feeling that there would be unpleasant consequences was beginning to take up headspace. Sensing this, Violet linked her friend's arm, giving it a squeeze. 'Hey, Kitts, I'm so chuffed you could come out tonight; it means a lot. And you look absolutely gorge in that dress.'

'Thanks, Vi, I've been looking forward to it. I just wish Dan had managed to get back before I left the house. I've no idea where he's got to, and he's not answering my calls or texts.' Despite her recent vow to be stronger, the prospect of being on the receiving end of Dan's disapproval sat like a malevolent spectre lurking in the shadows of her mind, ready to pounce just as soon as she started to relax.

Violet pursed her lips. 'Look, I don't want to speak out of turn or anything, but it's kind of typical of Dan to do this. So, I think you should just put that right out of your mind and concentrate on enjoying yourself with the rest of us. You deserve it, and you're not doing anything wrong.'

Vi's words resonated. Tonight was about Vi, not Dan, and Kitty was determined that she wasn't going to play into his hands again. It wasn't a crime to go to the pub for a drink with friends. 'You know what? You're right.' She smiled, pushing an image of Ollie and his heart-melting smile to the back of her mind.

'Yay, that's my girl. Come on, it's bloody freezing. Best foot forward.' Which was easier said than done with icy paths and Vi's less than practical footwear. The early winter that had taken a tight hold of Lytell Stangdale showed no sign of releasing its grip.

The pair were still chatting away when they entered the warmth of the Sunne. It pulled them in as if greeting old friends. Kitty felt her worries melt away as she followed Vi to the bar where the others had gathered. Ollie smiled broadly when he saw Kitty walk towards them, his eyes never leaving her.

Molly, sitting next to Pip, jumped down from her stool. 'Well done, Vi, mission accomplished,' she said, before planting a kiss on her cousin's cheek. 'Great to see you, Kitts. Ready to celebrate?'

Kitty laughed. 'You know what? I think I am.' Already buoyed by the pub's friendly atmosphere, she couldn't ignore the lightness in her heart or the flush to her cheeks caused by the warmth of Ollie's gaze. Feeling self-conscious, she smoothed her hand over her hair.

'Now then, sis. Now then Violent.' James's eyes glinted mischievously at Vi, which she reciprocated with a prod.

'Hiya, ladies, what can I get you?' asked Ollie, reluctantly pulling his eyes away from Kitty, as he took the freshly poured glass of Pinot Grigio proffered by Jonty. 'Thanks.' He smiled at the landlord. 'There you go, Molly, you look like you could do with another one of these.'

'Ooh, cheers, Ollie. After the day I've had I need a glass of wine or two. District nursing isn't what you'd call a glamorous job. It's been nothing but wall-to-wall leg ulcers and haemorrhoids. Oh, and a really grumpy bloke with a twisted testicle.'

The men winced, and Pip shook his head. 'Thanks for sharing that with us, Moll.'

'No wonder he was grumpy,' said Ollie, wearing a pained expression as he turned to order Kitty a Prosecco and Vi her usual.

Molly gulped down a mouthful of wine. 'S'alright for you lot, you don't have to stare them in the face three days a week. And on top of all that I've had to decipher one of Grannie Aggie's bonkers text messages telling me she wants to Brazilian the vicar's nuts for his birthday. Honestly, Rev Nev would be mortified if he knew.' She giggled. 'What she actually meant was, she wants to give him some Brazil nuts for his birthday.'

'Well, we hope it is,' said Pip.

Jonty, who was pulling a fresh pint for James, snorted and almost lost the glasses that were perched on the end of his nose. 'Your frank-ness is certainly refreshing, Molly.'

Vi had scrunched up her face. 'Right, that's it. Any more talk of testicles, other intimate body parts, bodily functions or intimate procedures and I'm outta here. And I'm being deadly serious, Molly.'

'Vi's right, it's making my toes curl. And I think it's time we turned off the predictive text on Granny Aggie's phone. It's causing all sorts of rumours to fly around the village.' Despite himself, Pip couldn't help but laugh. Only last week his grandmother had sent a text to her equally antiquarian friend, Nellie, informing her that she'd seen her son, Mike, and Rev Nev in the village shop comparing penises. The communication had caused considerable outrage, followed by a flurry of hastily gathered explanations. The truth was harmless in contrast: she'd seen the pair in the village shop buying *pens*. There hadn't been a penis in sight. 'She's going to be slammed with an ASBO if she isn't careful,' warned Pip.

'Mmm. You do have a point, though it's not going to go down well. But as she's your grandmother, you can have the jolly job of telling her,' she said, grinning at him.

'See what you've been missing? It's like being part of a live comedy show.' Ollie turned to Kitty who was negotiating a mouthful of Prosecco and a fit of the giggles. She had her hand clamped over her mouth and nodded. She'd taken her coat off and his eyes skimmed over the rich fabric of her dress; he remembered it from years ago, though it seemed to hang a little looser on her now. But she looked more like the Kitty he knew before Dan got his claws in her, or at least a fragile version. And she still looked beautiful.

THE GROUP MOVED to a long table beside the warming glow of the fire, which was currently being soaked up by Nomad and Scruff, who were stretched out in front of it. Neither looked up from their slumber.

Kitty slipped onto the banquette, shuffling up and making space for another. Ollie slid in beside her, sitting so close she could feel the heat from his body. She hoped Dan wouldn't turn up; he'd be furious if he saw them.

Vi held up her glass. 'Right, I think it's time to propose a toast.'

'Good idea, Vi,' said Pip, who was still in his tweeds, having arrived at the pub straight from work. Molly's threats of what she'd do to him if he was late meant he hadn't had time to go home and get changed.

'To Violent's new home.' James gave a cheeky grin, which was quickly followed by an 'ouch' when Vi nudged him in the ribs.

'To my new home and, more importantly, to friends,' she added.

'To friends,' they chorused, clinking glasses.

'I hope you all remembered to hold eye contact with the person you were chinking glasses with, or you'll be cursed with a lifetime of bad sex,' said James, wearing a grave expression.

Ollie patted him on the arm and laughed. 'Good old Jimbo, he can always be relied upon to lower the tone.'

'That's where we've been going wrong all these years, Moll,' joked Pip.

'I think Jimby said *bad* sex, not *no* sex,' she retorted.

James leaned towards Ollie and muttered, 'Don't know about you, mate, but I reckon bad sex is better than no bloody sex at all, which is pretty much what I'm getting at the moment.'

Ollie laughed quietly and nodded in Vi's direction. 'Not for much longer I reckon.'

Grinning, James raised his pint to his friend, speaking quietly so only the two of them could hear. 'I'll toast to that. We just need to find someone for you before you forget what to do.' Their sniggering was cut short by Violet.

'Anyway, Jimbo,' Vi gave the ice-cubes in her G&T a swirl around the glass and arched an eyebrow, 'what's this I've been hearing about you having a wayward cock?'

'Oh, my word,' said Bea, who was whizzing by with a fragrant plate of chicken curry in her hands, her eyes wide. Pip spluttered into his pint.

Everyone turned to look at James. He'd been about to take a drink of his beer but was rendered speechless, his pint hand suspended half-way to his mouth which was now hanging open.

'In his dreams,' said Molly. 'Anyway, I thought you'd banned us from talking about body parts.'

Vi glanced around at the bemused expressions at the table. 'I was referring to a cockerel, actually. Called Roger, or something like that.'

Jimby placed his glass on the table and folded his arms across his chest. 'Ahhh. You mean Reg?'

'Bloody hell, I wondered where that was going,' said Pip.

'You lot have got dirty minds,' said Vi, as snorts of laughter rang out from the table, causing other customers to turn and look at them. 'Don't worry, Kitts, we don't always have such high-brow conversations when we get together.'

'Not much,' said Molly.

CONVERSATION FLOWED SEAMLESSLY, and Kitty soon relaxed, blending in with her friends like old times. She could feel the warmth of Ollie's leg as it rested against hers; it felt good, and comfortable, and right. Tonight, the distance of the lost years between them seemed to shrink into nothing. He still smelled the same: soap, fresh air and a hint of sandalwood from his cologne. She took a deep breath, savouring every tiny molecule. As he reached for his pint, she sneaked a look at his forearm. The sleeves of his blue and white checked shirt were rolled back, and she felt the sudden urge to run her fingers over the silky hairs that shone golden in the soft lighting. Shocked at her own thoughts, Kitty sat on her hands. *Best keep them out of mischief.*

'Room for a little one?' Bea arrived at the table sporting a large white bowl of slow-roasted sweet potato wedges in one hand and a tray of freshly made dips in the other. She squeezed herself into the gap between Ollie and Bill Campion – he was busy giving Dave Mellison a piece of his mind about something, so didn't notice Bea. 'Thought you good folks might like a little fortification in exchange for letting me join you for a chinwag.' She smiled, pushing her tortoiseshell glasses up onto her head.

The friends made various sounds of approval as they dived in. 'Oh man, these are good, Bea,' James enthused through a mouthful of steaming sweet potato.

'Mmm. How on earth do you manage to make a simple sweet potato taste like this?' Molly savoured the flavour, her eyes tightly closed.

Bea tapped her nose and smiled. 'Ah, trade secrets, darlings.'

'Well, I'm more than happy to try any food you send my way, secret or not.' Ollie dipped another potato wedge into a creamy garlic dip and popped it into his mouth.

'Same here. I don't care what's in them, I could eat them all day.' James plunged his potato wedge into a sweetcorn and red pepper dip. 'And those Yorkshire puds you did the other night were to die for. You missed out on a right treat while you were out lamping on that freezing moor top, Pip, mate. Yorkie puds with the most amazing filling. Mwahh.' Jimby kissed his fingers, savouring his gastronomic flashback.

'You're very sweet. But, in all seriousness, I genuinely value your opinions on my new recipe ideas. I can't rely on Jonty, he'll eat anything. His mother's cooking was diabolical. I could serve up burnt pan scrubber doused in drain water, and he'd declare it was delicious. But he still likes me to ask his opinion, and I don't like to hurt his feelings.'

'Well, we're more than happy to be your guinea-pigs,' said Jimby.

'Yep, it's a hard job, but someone's got to do it.' Ollie nodded in agreement.

'Our Jimby is the human equivalent of a Labrador when it comes to food. Always thinking about his stomach.' Kitty giggled, reaching for another sweet potato wedge. The tempting smell of the snacks had made her stomach rumble. Feeling anxious about not being able to get hold of Dan had quashed her appetite earlier, and she'd only managed a couple of slices of toast since lunchtime.

'Too right. Actually, I heard all about how you enjoyed an unusual bowl of peanuts earlier this week,' Molly said with a smile.

James pulled a face and reached for another potato. 'I'm so traumatised by that experience, my mind is trying to erase all memory of it.'

'Doesn't appear to have affected your appetite, Jimbo.' Ollie's observation was met with a broad grin and a shrug of the shoulders from his mate.

Bea glanced around at the friends, clasping her hands together. 'Now, folks, I want to put an idea to you. Jonty and I are very keen to start some sort of regular music thing going here in the bar. Tasteful stuff – most definitely not karaoke or anything horrific like that. Anyway, we'd heard on the grapevine that some of you quite enjoy a good old sing-song and wondered if you'd be interested in starting Music Night at the Sunne? Say, every first Thursday of the month. What do you think?'

Bea's suggestion was met with a variety of nods and sounds of approval. 'Mind you, you do realise that by objecting to karaoke you're depriving Pip's public of the chance to hear him sing again.'

Ollie struggled to resist the smirk that tugged at the corners of his mouth.

Pip clapped a hand across his forehead. 'Please don't go there; I swore I'd never do karaoke again.'

'No, please don't go there. My lug 'oles still haven't recovered,' said James with a laugh.

'Neither has Granny Aggie's pot rhododendron after Pip threw-up in it on the way back home. She still blames next-door's cat for it,' said Molly.

Kitty smiled as she listened to the banter. She and Dan had been invited to the party but, as with everything to do with the village, he'd said it wasn't his type of thing so they couldn't go. But hearing her friends and family talk and laugh about this shared time highlighted her loneliness and made her long to be part of village life once more. To be part of a community, where people look out for one another, her mum used to say, was the backbone of the countryside; it held villages together. And tonight, thought Kitty, proved she was right.

≈

As the night progressed, the friends slipped easily back into the camaraderie they'd enjoyed before marriage and children had come along, altering the dynamics of their relationships. None more so than Kitty's marriage to Dan.

The warmth of the fire, regularly stoked by Jonty, and the three glasses of Prosecco that had slipped down with surprising ease, had helped Kitty feel more relaxed than she'd felt for a long time. She sighed and flopped back onto the banquette, resting against Ollie's arm that was stretched out behind her. His body heat radiated through her shoulders, rekindling those feelings she'd assumed had withered away years ago. She found herself gazing at him, admiring his strong profile.

Sensing her watching him, Ollie turned to her, his gentle eyes twinkling as the fire-light danced in them. They crinkled at the corners as he gave her an easy smile, and her heart responded with a flutter.

She'd forgotten how easy it was to be around Ollie. He was the polar-opposite of Dan. Kitty constantly felt that she had to be on high alert when she was around her husband, which was draining. But with Ollie, she could relax and be herself. She was glad she'd ignored her doubts and taken the plunge to come to the pub without waiting for Dan to get home. In fact, she was quite pleased that he hadn't come home at all. She took a sip of her Prosecco, scrunching her nose as the bubbles tickled their way up it.

'You okay?' Ollie smiled, bringing his arm forward it brushed against hers, sending a delicious tingle right through her.

'Ooh. Sorry.' She moved slightly, force of habit making her apologise. She looked up at him, and her heart leapt as the intensity of his gaze took her by surprise. She felt her face prickle with the heat of a blush as electricity sparked between them with such force, Kitty felt sure the others must be able to feel it. And, judging by the look in his eyes, she knew Ollie could too.

'It's fine, you don't need to apologise. I was the one who moved, and you and me go a long way back for things like that to be alright, Kitty,' he said softly.

Oh, God. His voice, those words. Her heart melted into a puddle and the ever-present flurry of butterflies tumbled around her stomach.

A knowing look flashed between James and Vi; the vibes flickering away opposite hadn't gone unnoticed.

23

THE LARGE WALNUT grandfather clock stood stoically, just as it had for generations, in the chilly drawing room of Danskelfe Castle. Wearily, it chimed the hour of ten as Lady Carolyn Hammondely gulped down her fifth – or was it her sixth? – gin and tonic of the evening. Chunks of ice rattled against her teeth as she tipped her head back, allowing the watery remnants to trickle onto her eager, outstretched tongue. Obligingly, an alcohol-soaked ice-cube plopped into her mouth, its frozen delivery setting her teeth on edge. She wrapped her tongue around it and pushed it into the side of her cheek as the sound of a door slamming down the draughty hall heralded the return of her mother. Carolyn shivered, partly because of the coolness of the ice, but mostly at the thought of her mother.

The door flew open and, on a chilly waft of air, in blew Countess Davinia Hammondely, wife of Jeremiah Archibald Devereux Hammondely, the sixth Earl of Lockwood and owner of the rambling Danskelfe estate. She flounced into the room, draped in her customary garish colours, her bright-blue over-sized handbag swinging in the crook of her arm. A pair of well-tailored trousers in vivid tangerine were teamed with a white chiffon blouse covered in wild swirls of blues, pinks, oranges and yellows. Caro blinked several times, her tear-stained eyes aching as she tried to focus; the gin must have been stronger than she thought.

The countess lurched across the antique kilim rug on feet of canoe proportions, her turquoise blue shoes, trimmed with a large fuchsia-pink bow coming to an abrupt halt in front of her daughter. Narrowing her eyes, she glanced over at Caro who had curled herself up at one end of the antique red and gold sofa, empty crystal glass in hand, and a box of well-thumbed photographs on the floor beside her.

Davinia struggled to arch a recently botoxed eyebrow. 'Stewed again, I see,' she sneered through a vivid pink slash. 'You really ought to find something better to do than pore over the past. What happened was in the best interests of everyone concerned, and you'd move on if you knew what was good for you, my girl. Lord knows, you've had long enough. And I was way too young for all of that granny nonsense.' She dumped her bag and waved a manicured hand dismissively at her daughter, stalking across to the large gilt mirror that hung above the black marble fireplace.

Caro sighed and smiled weakly at her faithful golden Labrador, Mr Tubbs, who was sitting on the sofa beside her.

Pursing her thin lips, her mother sniffed disapprovingly. 'And you shouldn't allow that bloody animal on the furniture. Your father would have an absolute fit if he could see. You don't seem to appreciate that Queen Victoria is supposed to have sat on that sofa. And on the very spot that smelly creature is licking his unmentionables.' She screwed up her face and teased her stiffly lacquered hair with her fingers, watching her daughter's reaction reflected in the mirror, oblivious to the fact that she'd lost a couple of bright orange fake fingernails in her over-processed bird's nest.

'Hello, Mother, it's lovely to see you, too.' Caro heaved herself up from the sofa, gathering up the photographs. 'Come on, Mr Tubbs, you come with me. We'll find ourselves another perch. One where things are less chilly.' She tapped her thigh and, with a grunt, the portly Labrador eased himself off the sofa and followed her.

24

TWELVE YEARS EARLIER

IT WAS A STILL and balmy Thursday afternoon in June; the afternoon before Kitty's marriage to Dan. She was sitting in the sun-filled kitchen of her parents' home at Oak Tree Farm. Birdsong poured in through the open windows as she enjoyed a long-overdue catch-up with her mum, Elizabeth, over a pot of tea.

Dan had booked himself out of court for the day, telling Kitty he had a backlog of paperwork to catch up on. But later that morning, he'd appeared in the kitchen, grabbed his car keys and muttered something about how he had to go out. Her question, asking if he'd be back in time for dinner, fell unanswered on the ground behind him.

Feeling the need to escape the cottage and to get away from intrusive thoughts, Kitty found herself heading up the road towards her parents' home. She hadn't seen them in a while; Dan wasn't keen on them visiting and would make them feel unwelcome without uttering a word. He didn't like Kitty to spend too much time at her parents' house either and would accuse her of spreading her attention too thinly, of not loving him enough. He couldn't see why she would need anyone else when she had him.

She'd been living with him for just over a year, and Elizabeth was glad her daughter hadn't gone straight down the marriage route, hoping that living with him would open her eyes and show him in a different light. The light they could all see him in. But she was to be disappointed and, instead, there ensued a transformation in Kitty which had been swift and dramatic. From a change of hair colour to the disappearance of her curls, he'd even encouraged her to wear blue contact lenses so she would look like his latest celebrity crush, but they'd left her eyes red and watering. And she'd lost an alarming amount of weight along with the happiness in her eyes. But, more worrying, was the change in her demeanour. Always on the quiet side, Kitty was now timid and subdued. And if any questions were asked, she jumped to Dan's defence, leaving Elizabeth fearful of pushing her daughter away by saying the wrong thing. Instead, she skirted around the delicate issues, dropping subtle hints, reminding her that they were there for her if ever she needed them.

'There you go, flower. You look like you could do with a nice strong cuppa.' Elizabeth handed Kitty a mug of freshly poured tea.

'Thanks, Mum.' She took the mug, cradling it in her hands. 'You've caught the sun, you look really well, doesn't she, Dad?' She turned to her father who was draining the lukewarm dregs of tea from a mug that boasted the words "Babe Magnet" – a Fathers' Day gift from Jimby.

'Aye, she's every bit as bonny as the day I met her, this one.' John walked over to his wife, wrapped his arms tightly around her and gave her a squeeze, planting a noisy kiss on her cheek.

Elizabeth giggled. 'Give over, you daft beggar.'

At that, the door flew open, and James fell in, tripping over Fly, the sheepdog who pushed his way out past him, ready to get back to work. 'Don't mind me, Fly.' He glanced at his parents and grinned. 'Er, could you two get a room? But before you do, you can pour me a cuppa.'

'Take no notice, Jimby. It's just your dad larking about as usual.' Elizabeth pulled at the tea towel draped over her shoulder and flicked it at John who dodged it nimbly, winking at Kitty.

'Listen, lad, when you find the woman of your dreams, you'll be just the same, mark my words,' he said good-naturedly. Elizabeth shook her head, smiling while Jimby mimed making himself sick and Kitty giggled into her mug.

Her parents were a textbook example of a happy marriage, based on mutual respect and deep affection. She couldn't remember a time when the Fairfax family home wasn't filled to the rafters with love and laughter. It stood in stark contrast to her own set-up with Dan, which couldn't have been more different. But she wasn't ready to admit that to herself just yet, never mind anyone else.

Jimby joined his mum and sister for a cup of tea in a "Young Farmers Do It Better" mug, before getting back to help his father with the sheep. It had been a while since he'd last had a conversation with Kitty that lasted longer than five minutes. Today, she was clearly distracted, but her mum and her brother kept their concerns to themselves.

Over their chat, there were several times when Kitty came close to telling her parents and Jimby about the wedding. She'd love more than anything for them to be there. Keeping it quiet made her feel deceitful, and she didn't like it. But Dan had made her swear not to say anything, and the consequences of breaking that promise were far worse than not having her family with her tomorrow.

AT PLUM TREE Cottage the air was filled with the mouth-watering aroma of Dan's favourite homemade lasagne. Kitty had prepared it, hoping it would improve his strange mood.

By seven thirty there was still no sign of him, and he wasn't answering his mobile phone. Unable to settle herself to the book she was reading, Kitty paced the floor. Running to the window whenever her ears were alerted to the sound of a car engine, looking out, hoping to see Dan's sports car pulling up. And being disappointed when it wasn't him.

Why did he have to do this? She hovered on the edge of the sofa, chewing on her fingernails as paranoia slowly ate its way into her.

IT WAS A GLORIOUS EVENING, and the land was still throwing back the heat of the sun. Ollie, Jimby and Pip had decided to walk across the dale to the Fox and Hounds at Dankselfe, finishing off at the Sunne later in the evening. It was as they were winding their way back along the lane to Lytell Stangdale, just past the sandstone packhorse bridge that arched over the river Swang, that they saw Dan climb out of a familiar dark-blue estate car. A dark-blue estate car that belonged to Lady Carolyn Hammondely. His hair was dishevelled, and he was pulling up his flies as he headed over to a track that led into a wooded area. There they saw his sports car, secreted in a dark corner.

Without time to think, a surge of anger propelled James along the path. 'Had a slight detour on your way home, have you, you twat?' He stormed towards Dan.

Dan looked startled for a second, but quickly composed himself. 'Er, it's really not what it looks like. I was just coming back from chambers when Caro called and asked if I could give her some legal advice. It's private, and she didn't want to do it up at the big house, so I told her I'd meet up with her en-route to home.' He fished his keys out of his jeans pocket, pressing the key fob, the car beeping as it unlocked.

Carolyn jumped out of the car, lipstick and panic smeared across her face. 'Yes, er, that's right. It was something I didn't want Mummy or Daddy to find out about. It's jolly decent of Dan to help me out.' She gave a nervous laugh and smoothed down the tiny scrap of body-con black lycra she was almost wearing.

'I'll bet.' Scorn dripped off Ollie's words.

'So how does that explain why you've got what looks like a massive love bite on your neck, eh, Dan?' James seethed.

'And you might want to put your tits away.' Pip shook his head at Caro, who gasped and hoicked her dress up.

Dan's hand flew to his neck, running over the condemning mark. 'You stupid cow!'

Her eyes filled with tears. 'I'm sorry, Dan. I didn't mean to. I was just, well…'

Before James realised what he was doing, he found his fist flying towards Dan, making contact with his left cheek and glancing off his nose. 'You bastard,' he yelled as he watched him stagger backwards, before falling to the floor. Breathing heavily, James loomed over him, teeth gritted, fists clenched into tight balls.

Carolyn shrieked, flapping her arms in panic as Ollie and Pip lunged towards James, hooking their arms under his, easing him back. 'Come on, mate, leave it. He isn't worth it.' Ollie shot Dan a look of disdain.

Dazed, Dan eased himself up onto his elbows, blood trickling from his throbbing nose. 'What the hell was that for? You do realise I could sue the arse off you, you pathetic inbred moron.'

James stepped forward, only to be pulled back again by Ollie and Pip. 'Yeah, but you won't, will you? You'll go home and very nicely break up with my sister. She doesn't deserve to be with a piece of scum like you.'

Dan got to his feet, pulling out a handkerchief from his pocket to stem the flow of blood from his nose. 'Well, that's where you're wrong,' he said disdainfully. 'Kitty absolutely adores me; she'll do anything I want just to please me. And if you say anything to her, I'll simply tell her you're lying. That you're jealous. All of you. You've always wanted to break us up, and she knows it. Especially you, you loser.' The last comment he threw in Ollie's direction as he headed towards his car, opening the door. 'Do you really want to be responsible for alienating your sister from her whole family? Oh, and one last thing, lay a finger on me again and I'll unleash the big guns. And I can assure you, you won't know what the hell's hit you.'

'Dan, wait! Are you okay?' Caro ran over to him, her face streaked with mascara; she gripped onto the driver's door.

'Don't touch me! Don't you think you've done enough damage?' The door was snatched out of her fingers as he slammed it shut. She was forced to jump back as he reversed past her and roared off down the road to Lytell Stangdale.

'Forget him, Caro. Just get yourself home.' She cut a pathetic figure, and Ollie couldn't help but feel sorry for her. He turned to James. 'Listen, I think we should head back to my house for a bit, let things simmer down, then you can think about what would be best to do for Kitty.'

'Oll's right,' said Pip. 'We need to calm down before anything gets said that might come back and bite us on the arse later.'

James rubbed his hand, suddenly aware of the throbbing in his knuckles. 'Yeah, you're right. Come on, let's head back.'

AFTER RELIEVING Ollie's mother of babysitting duties, and several cups of coffee later, the three men agreed that it would be best, for now, to keep things under wraps. Such was Dan's hold over Kitty, they knew that if they said anything she'd take his side, and they'd run the risk of her probably never speaking to them again. It was something they weren't prepared to do.

SIX MISERABLE WEEKS had passed since Carolyn Hammondely's last encounter with Dan, and she'd heard nothing from him. A feeling of nausea, combined with indescribable tiredness and sudden dashes to the loo had warranted a trip to a chemist in York.

She locked herself in her draughty en-suite bathroom at Danskelfe Castle. 'Oh, no,' she whispered as proof stared up at her accusingly. A hollow loneliness descended upon her.

25

DAN SANK into the armchair in Sam's living-room and sipped his claret, half watching the local news that was flickering across the TV screen. They'd been back in the warmth of her house for an hour and, in that time, he'd showered and changed into the sweat pants and t-shirt he kept in his sports bag in the boot of his car.

'Feeling more relaxed now?' She topped up his glass with what was left of the bottle. She'd changed into pale pink cashmere lounge-wear and had tied her long, blonde hair into a mermaid plait that snaked over her right shoulder.

Dan rested his head back. 'Too bloody right. I don't think I've ever run so fast in my life as I did through that wood.'

She gave a throaty laugh. 'Oh, that would've been worth seeing. You, tearing through the woods knack-naked.'

'It wasn't funny.' He frowned, swirling the wine around his glass.

'It was from where I was standing. Anyway, if you're sure you're going to stay the night, we might as well have another one of these.' She waved the empty wine bottle at him.

He opened his mouth to reply, but his words were snatched away as his attention was drawn to the unfolding events on the TV screen. Sam followed his gaze to see the local news reporter, Dermot Jones, standing in the clearing of the wood they'd been in earlier. Dermot's fingers were pressed to his ear as he listened to his ear-piece.

Grabbing the TV remote, Dan pressed the volume button impa-tiently, a black cloud descending over his face as the TV anchor in the studio spoke. 'We're just receiving details of several arrests made at a notorious site known locally to be a favourite dogging haunt. Dermot, what can you tell us about these arrests?' she asked, struggling to keep a straight face. Dermot, too, was wrestling with a smirk. He pinched his lips together and took a deep breath.

'Well, Emma, we understand that police responded to a tip-off from a member of the public, suggesting that there was a dogging session taking place here at Dog Daisy Wood, now known more commonly as Dogging Wood. And that several well-known, high-profile individuals were involved, including the actor Adam Appleby from the popular TV soap, The Moors. Other names have yet to be revealed.' He nodded at the camera, awaiting a response from the studio.

The laugh Emma was trying to contain escaped but was quickly disguised as a cough. She patted her chest. 'Oh, dear. Do excuse me.'

'What? It can't be!' Dan froze, drink in hand, as colour leached from his face.

'That was a lucky escape,' said Sam, slinking back into the kitchen in search of more wine.

'What the bloody hell are you, mistress of the understatement?' Small beads of sweat had begun to spring from his brow. He wiped them away impatiently. 'Don't ever suggest anything like that to me again. If I'd been caught my career would've been wrecked. Years of hard work gone, like that.' He snapped his fingers together.

'Oh, don't be so dramatic. You weren't caught, nobody has the foggiest idea who you are, and your career isn't ruined. Just chill, will you?' She rolled her eyes before dropping a champagne truffle into her mouth, licking the sugar off her fingers. Dan was high maintenance sometimes.

He took a mouthful of wine, rolling it around his mouth as he marshalled the concerns now stampeding around his mind. Sam's laid-back approach to life was starting to annoy him. He was beginning to feel irritated again. There was no room in his life for a woman with an attitude like that. If it carried on, she'd be destined for the scrap-heap. But not tonight. Tonight, she was useful to him. He needed somewhere to sleep; he couldn't go home in this state.

His thoughts shifted to Kitty. He wondered if she'd had the nerve to go out with her friends, or done what she knew he'd prefer, and stay in, waiting for him. That thought gave him a kick; the power he had over her. *Had*, the word loomed back at him. She knew he wouldn't go out with her friends. They'd known her longer than he had, and he'd made no secret of the fact he couldn't stand them – especially Ollie bloody Cartwright; that man made his blood boil. Dan never felt like he belonged in that stifling little circle of half-wits, not that he ever wanted to. And Kitty was just a selfish cow if she expected him to give up one of his precious Friday nights to go out with that lot. Didn't she realise just how hard he worked? How it made him value his favourite night of the week? She needed a reminder. And him not going home tonight would do just that.

'RIGHT THEN, THAT'S ME DONE.' James drained the final dregs of beer from his glass. 'If any of you lovely ladies need escorting back to your respective homes, I'd be very happy to oblige. Except you, of course, Moll.'

'Are you trying to say I'm not a lady, Jimbo?' His cousin cocked an eyebrow as she contemplated the last mouthful of wine in her glass.

'Well, if the cap fits…' said Pip, earning him a dig in the ribs from his wife.

'This is a tiny village in the middle of the North Yorkshire Moors at quarter to ten on a Friday night, what do you think's going to happen to us?' Vi wore a look of incredulity.

'Well, a lot could happen, actually.' Jimby flashed a mischievous grin as they made their way to the door.

Ollie pulled the door open, 'Brrr! Bloody hell, it's freezing!' he said as an icy blast rushed at him.

Outside the temperature had plummeted and a thick, hoar frost had crept over the paths that now glittered in the moonlight. Saying their goodnights, the others headed off home, leaving just Kitty and Ollie, whose cottages were at the other end of the village. She pushed her hands into her coat pockets; standing in the fresh air the relaxed feeling she'd had in the pub had suddenly cranked up to slightly tipsy. She looked up at the clear night sky and smiled, admiring the swathe of stars that was splashed across it, silently twinkling down on them. 'I've had such a lovely night, I don't want it to end.' She sighed, the warmth of her breath hitting the cold air in a cloud of vapour. *And I don't want to leave you yet, Ollie.*

Dan couldn't have been further from her thoughts if he'd tried.

Ollie wasn't ready to let her slip through his fingers. 'How about a coffee or night-cap back at mine?' His breath furled with hers. 'Noushka's on a sleep-over at one of her dance friends.' He wasn't sure why he'd added that but, for some reason, he thought it would make a difference.

Their eyes locked and they stood in silence for a moment. From nowhere a dart of lust shot through Kitty's body as she was suddenly overwhelmed with a yearning for the feel of Ollie's mouth on hers, of his naked body pressed against her, his hands caressing her. She swallowed, 'Mmm. That would be nice. A night-cap, that is.'

'Good.' He smiled, his eyes twinkling as he offered her his arm. She smiled back, linking him as they walked the short way to his house.

KITTY KICKED off her boots in the hallway and followed Ollie into his small, neat living-room, unbuttoning her coat as she went. He opened the door of the wood-burner, threw a log in and opened the spin wheels. In an instant, flames leapt into action, filling the room with a cosy glow and the delicious smell of wood-smoke. He turned to her, smiling. 'Right, what can I get you? Tea, coffee? Or are you feeling daring enough to try some of my killer home-made rhubarb wine?'

'Ooh, since you put it like that, I think it's got to be the killer rhubarb wine.' She giggled, ignoring the vague tap-tap-tapping of her conscience, vying for her attention; she wasn't doing anything wrong, she was just having a drink with an old friend.

The light of the flames danced in her eyes, and Ollie longed to kiss her. 'Wine it is.' He smiled. 'Here, I'll take that.' He took her coat and hung it up on the peg next to his just by the front door, where it looked like it belonged.

It had been years since Kitty was last in this room. It hadn't changed much, except for the addition of photographs of Anoushka, along with her dancing trophies. In pride of place on the sideboard was a large photo of her being presented with an award by her idol, prima ballerina Jacinda Bell-Mackintosh. Evidence of Ollie being a proud dad; it warmed Kitty's heart. 'I can't believe how grown up Noushka is, she's so beautiful,' she said as he came back into the room holding two glasses and a kilner bottle containing a dusky-pink liquid. 'You've done such a great job of bringing her up, Ollie.'

His face beamed with pride as he placed the glasses on the sideboard and poured the wine into them. 'She's a good kid, just like your two.' He handed her one of the glasses.

'Thanks.'

'Cheers,' he said, clinking his glass against hers. A comfortable silence fell as they each took a sip. 'And she's not the only one who's beautiful.' He looked intently at Kitty; the expression in his eyes had changed to something very different to pride.

Kitty felt her cheeks flame. 'Mmm. This is delicious,' she said, looking into her glass, not knowing what else to say. She wasn't used to receiving compliments these days and didn't really know how to deal with them.

'I mean it, Kit. You're the most beautiful woman I've ever seen, and…' Emboldened by the beer he'd drunk earlier, the words came tumbling out before he'd had time to think, '…and I'm still in love with you. Always have been, just ask James, he knows. I can't love anyone else. I've never been able to love anyone else because my heart…well…my heart only knows how to love you.' There, he'd said it. Released his feelings. His heart that he'd just been talking about was now racing, and he took a sip of wine as relief and embarrassment flooded him in equal measure. 'Only you, Kitty.'

'Oh, Ollie.' She placed a hand on her chest where she could feel her heart thudding against it. An unstoppable tidal wave of happiness surged through her, its strength taking her by surprise. She looked up at him, holding eye contact, as she searched for the right words to say.

He took her wine glass from her and placed it, together with his, on the sideboard. Turning back, he took her delicate face in his large, work-roughened hands, his thumbs rubbing circles against her cheeks. He looked deep into her eyes, drinking in their expression before his gaze moved down to the full, plump lips he'd longed to kiss for as long as he could remember. As if reading his thoughts, Kitty swallowed nervously. He was so close now, she could feel the warmth of his breath on her face. 'Kitty,' he whispered as he surrendered to the urge and pressed his lips against hers, kissing her tenderly. Without a second thought, she kissed him back, feeling her legs turn to jelly as butterflies took flight in her stomach. He ran a hand over the small curve of her breast as years of pent-up passion made a bid for freedom, released in kisses that burned with an urgency that took Kitty's breath away.

When they pulled apart, drunk on lust, Ollie took Kitty's hand and slowly led her upstairs. Pausing at his bedroom door, he kissed her again. 'You okay with this?' He pressed his forehead against hers.

'Yes,' she whispered. All thoughts of anything but the here and now had left her mind.

He pushed open the door, and she followed him in.

Cupping her face in his hands, Ollie tenderly kissed her eyelids, moving down to her mouth, then her neck. She could feel his eager arousal against her belly as he began to undo the buttons on her dress. A moan escaped her lips as she tugged his shirt out of his jeans and ran her hands over his muscular body, desire flooding her tiny frame.

'God, I want you, Kitty,' he groaned as he pressed his mouth against hers.

She froze as, without warning, an image of Dan, angry and seething forced its way into her mind, calling a halt to everything. It was as if a bucket of ice cold water had been thrown over her. Their moment was irreversibly broken. It had crashed to the ground around them, shattering into a million tiny shards.

'I'm sorry, Ollie. I can't do this.' Kitty pulled away, dragging her hands across her face. 'It's wrong, I'm married, and I'm behaving no better than Dan. It's not fair on you. I'm so sorry, Ollie. I really am.'

He raked his fingers through his tousled hair. 'No, it's me who should apologise, Kitty. I was out of order, and I let myself get carried away.' His hands came to rest at the back of his neck as he released a breath of frustration.

She rushed downstairs, fumbling to fasten her buttons. In the hallway, she hurriedly pulled on her coat before pushing her feet into her boots.

'At least let me see you back.' Ollie had followed her downstairs, tucking his shirt into his jeans.

She shook her head, avoiding eye-contact. 'It's okay, I'll be fine. I'm just so sorry.' She pulled open the front door and ran out before he had time to say anything else.

Negotiating the slippery path, Kitty hurried home, the way illu-minated by a pale iridescent moonlight. The familiar cry of tawny owls shattered the frozen silence of the village, their hoots and shrieks carried across the dale on a frosty air. As she approached her cottage, slumbering silently against the night sky, a plume of smoke curling upwards from the chimney pot, it was no surprise to see a vacant space on the drive where Dan's car normally stood. She slowed her pace and heaved a sigh of relief as panic ebbed away. His good intentions hadn't lasted a week. Although she was glad of it tonight, she shuddered at the impending confrontation, whenever that would be, hoping the kids wouldn't witness it.

As she pressed down the latch to her front door, Kitty wondered if guilt would be written across her face, exposing her sins to Auntie Annie. She was a jumble of emotions but, thanks to years of practice, she'd got pretending that everything was okay when it wasn't, down to a fine art.

If she did suspect something, Auntie Annie wasn't letting on. She did, however, seem reluctant to leave, insisting her niece have a glass of Uncle Jack's home-made sloe gin. 'You know what he's like, he'll want me to report back on what you thought about it.' Kitty's heart sank, she'd already drunk more than she was used to, and didn't even like sloe gin at the best of times. Her dad used to say it was like rocket fuel. With an inward groan, she smiled and thanked Auntie Annie when she handed her a generous measure, refusing to leave until it was gone. 'It'll help you sleep and thicken your blood for winter, chick. That's what my old mum used to say anyway.'

AN HOUR LATER, and the dregs of the twice-topped-up sloe gin drained from Kitty's glass, Annie declared it was time to go home. She didn't seem to notice that such a potent liquor wasn't sitting well with the alcohol Kitty had consumed earlier. Unsure of how she was going to get to her feet, she was relieved when Annie insisted on seeing herself out.

With the room spinning around her, Kitty crawled her way up the stairs to bed.

26

THE WARMTH of Lily's body snuggling into her gradually roused Kitty from her slumber. Thanks to the thick curtains refusing admittance to even a sliver of light, the room was still swamped in darkness. Pushing her hair off her face, she squinted at the alarm clock on the bedside table and groaned; it was nearly nine-thirty. She couldn't remember when she'd last slept so late. 'Is it school today, Mummy?' came a small voice from the depths of the duvet. Kitty moved to kiss the top of her daughter's head, wincing as the movement sent stabbing pains through her skull.

'Ohhh,' she groaned. Her head even hurt as she tried to recall what day of the week it was. 'Er, I don't think so, Lils.' Her voice came out in a feeble croak; her mouth felt as dry as sand-paper. She cleared her throat. 'It's Saturday, and you don't have to go to school on a Saturday.'

'Hooray!' Lily threw back the duvet, a smile lighting up her heart-shaped face. 'Come on, Mummy, me and Snuggles want our break-fast. We're *starving* aren't we, Snuggles?' Lily launched herself off the bed and proceeded to drag the heavy goose-feather duvet off Kitty and onto the floor.

'Okay, okay, Lils. I get the picture. I'm up.' Her voice came out in a rasp. As she rubbed her aching eyes with the balls of her hands, a niggle began to inch its way into her mind, making her feel uneasy, and she didn't know why.

She pushed herself up onto her elbows, once more triggering the intense throbbing in her head. 'Eurgh.' Realisation was beginning to dawn as a vague memory of Uncle Jack's sloe gin surfaced. Her stomach lurched; she never wanted to touch the evil stuff again.

With each movement being rewarded by a painful thud inside her head, she gingerly eased her legs around to the side of the bed, placing her feet on the thick, cream carpet. The tangle of last night's clothes in a messy pile in the corner caught her eye.

Just as she was bracing herself to stand up, Lucas bounded through the door with the enthusiasm of a Labrador puppy. 'Hey, Mum, you're awake!' Usually, his exuberance was one of the things Kitty loved most about him, but this morning she would have preferred it if he came with a volume control. 'You've got to come downstairs quick. Uncle Jimby's here, and he's going to do us a great big fry-up. He say's you've got a hangover, and it's the best cure. He's doing runny eggs, sausages, fried bread and everything!' He threw himself onto the duvet.

The thought of runny eggs made Kitty's stomach hurtle up towards the back of her throat. She pressed a hand to her mouth as an unwelcome image of a plate piled high with a fried breakfast, swimming in a puddle of grease, took up prime position in her mind.

'You okay, Mum?' Lucas gave her a quizzical look. He'd never seen her like this before.

'Mmm. Just a bit tired.'

In the kitchen, James had just finished swirling teabags around the teapot and was about to pour Kitty a mug of tea. He looked up to see a crumpled version of his sister in the doorway, creases of the bed sheets imprinted into her face. She was sporting a pair of over-sized, badly done-up, purple dotty pyjamas, the legs of which were tucked into a fluffy pair of multi-coloured welly socks. The look was topped-off by an explosion of corkscrew curls, which were matted in places. 'Morning, Kitts, if you knock your breakfast back quickly, you'll still be able to make that 10k charity run you promised you'd do this morning.'

Kitty's face dropped. 'What? No! Tell me you're joking!' A grin crept across his face, and he burst out laughing. 'That was cruel.' She trudged across the floor, unable to find the energy to lift her feet, flopped into the nearest dining chair and pressed her forehead against the table with a groan. 'Never make me drink alcohol again.'

'That good, eh?' He put a steaming mug of tea in front of her and a glass of freshly-squeezed orange juice beside it. Pushing up the sleeves of his jumper, he rested his hands on his hips. 'Go on, get that down you, you'll feel better for it.'

Another groan came from the mass of curls on the table. 'Can't face anything, sorry, Jimby. Auntie Annie made me drink some of Uncle Jack's sloe gin.'

'Ouch! That's rocket fuel, no wonder you're feeling as rough as a badger's bum.'

In truth, Annie had called him earlier that morning, expressing concern for Kitty, saying, in retrospect, that making her niece down such a large measure of sloe gin was probably not the best idea, especially as she wasn't much of a drinker. Insisting her intentions were good, she'd hoped a tot of it would give Kitty a night of restful sleep, what with Dan not coming home and all. James had reassured her by saying he'd pop in on his sister and, if there was no sign of Dan, make sure she had a decent breakfast.

Kitty looked up, folded her arms on the table and rested her head against them. It was more comfortable than the hard wood which was starting to press into her skull. 'I feel like I've got a pneumatic drill hammering against my forehead and it won't stop.'

Lucas and Lily looked on concerned. Their mum was hardly ever ill. 'Are you okay, Mum?' Lucas wrinkled his freckly nose.

'Here, this'll make you feel better. It always helps when you do it to me.' Lily began rubbing Kitty's back in huge, exaggerated swirls. 'Is it working?' She leaned forward and scraped a handful of curls off her mum's face.

'Mmm, yes. I'm feeling loads better.' She didn't have the heart to say it was having the opposite effect.

'She's fine, kids. Your mum had a couple of glasses of wine last night, and she's not used to drinking, so she's suffering for it this morning. But after one of these…' James placed a glass containing a fizzing concoction in front of her, '…drink that up quick, Kitts…one of my legendary fry-ups and some fresh air, she'll be right as rain.'

'Thanks, Jimby.' It hurt her head to speak much above a whisper. 'I'll try anything as long as it works.' She reached for the glass, which took every ounce of energy she had. And there it was again, that niggle, that fuzzy memory. She hoped she hadn't said something silly or offended anyone inadvertently last night. Pushing the doubt

away, she gulped down the fizzy potion, its bubbles burning the back
of her throat.

'Yay! Well done, Mummy. Woohoo!' Lily punched the air.

James rubbed his hands together. 'Right, come on kids. Why
don't you watch some Saturday morning telly while I get breakfast
ready?' The suggestion went down well, and the pair ran off into the
living room, arguing about what to watch. James fished around in his
bag of tricks for his apron. Once found he gave it a quick shake out,
grinning to himself as he looped it over his head.

Setting a large cast-iron frying pan on the Aga hotplate, he
dropped a fat dollop of butter into it, whistling as he set to work.

In no time the kitchen was filled with the sounds and scrump-
tious smells of James's "full Yorkshire". Humphrey and Ethel
watched on appreciatively as he pricked the plump, locally made
pork sausages, and cracked open eggs with sunny yellow yolks,
courtesy of his own free-range hens.

Food was one of Humph's great passions in life and before long,
gloopy ribbons of drool hung from his jowls like a pair of swaying
fangs. 'That's a good look you've got going on there, Humph?' James
padded to the sink.

The dryness in Kitty's mouth finally got the better of her, and she
mustered all available strength to raise her head and take a slug of
tea. 'Mmm. S'good,' she murmured.

Up until that point Humph had been watching the food prepara-
tion so closely he hadn't noticed Kitty's presence in the kitchen.
When she'd come downstairs, he'd been in a deep, comatose sleep
and awoke when the smell of butter sizzling in the pan tickled his
nostrils. There was only one thing that could distract him from his
stomach, and that was his mum. He heaved his ancient bones off the
floor and waddled over to her. With every step, the thick columns of
drool – now so long they were just millimetres from touching the
floor – swayed back and forth, eventually sticking together in one
thick length of slime. Reaching Kitty, he pushed his square head onto
her lap, his wagging tail thudding against the leg of the table.

'Hiya, handsome.' She smiled into the pair of rheumy eyes that
gazed up at her adoringly. She hadn't noticed Humph's Pavlovian
offerings but, as she fondled his ears, she could feel the warm saliva
seeping into the fabric of her pyjamas. 'Oh, Humph. You gozzy old
boy,' she groaned. But her words only served as encouragement, and

he nudged her hand with his nose, hinting for the stroking to continue. Despite her pounding head, she didn't have the heart to push him away. 'Oh well, it's too late to worry about it now that you've wiped all of that drool on my jammies. How come Uncle Jimby isn't treated to any of this?'

'Uncle Jimby is in the process of creating a culinary masterpiece, that's why.' James grinned, wiping his hands on a tea towel before throwing it across his shoulder. 'And, more importantly, I'm not you. Fancy a top-up?' He nodded to her mug.

Kitty glanced up at her brother, an expression of horror on her face that quickly morphed into one of confusion. What on earth was he doing wearing ladies' underwear? She blinked quickly before the power of speech returned. 'Jimby, what…erm…why? Oh, my God.' Realisation dawned. 'Ooh, that looks so realistic.' Her brother was wearing an apron with a life-sized photo of a scantily-clad woman's body printed on it, proportioned in such a way it created the optical illusion that the wearer was sporting risqué, lacy underwear complete with suspenders. 'For a split-second, I was almost very jealous of your figure,' she said with a giggle.

'Birthday present from Oll. And if you think this is bad, you should see the mug he bought me.'

She grimaced and raised her palms to him. 'Spare me the details.' The mention of Ollie's name triggered a prickle of concern and a hazy collection of images from the previous evening eased their way into her mind. She tried to grab at them as they swirled around, but they remained elusive.

THE MEDICINAL PROPERTIES of the fizzy drink had kicked-in surprisingly quickly, and Kitty had managed to devour a full plate of breakfast. It was delicious, and she couldn't remember the last time she'd eaten so much. She was feeling more awake, and the pounding in her head had practically disappeared. She pulled herself up to help James, who was loading the dishwasher. 'Nope, you finish your tea. I'm nearly done.' He guided her back to the table.

'Sure?'

'Yup. Park your bum, it's not every day my little sis suffers from a hangover.'

She gave him a sheepish look. 'Oh, don't remind me.'

'Fancy a walk later? It's a lovely day, would be a shame to waste it. We could head off up to the crag, let the kids run off a bit of steam?' He turned to face her. Dan clearly hadn't come home last night, and it was now gone eleven, with no sign of a text or call from him.

'Sounds great.' Kitty looked up at him and smiled, tucking a wayward curl behind her ear. It sprang straight back out. 'I could take a flask of hot chocolate and pick up some of Lucy's chocolate flapjack on the way – it's the kids' favourite. But I think I should tackle this before I face the world.' She scooped up a handful of messy hair.

'Not sure there are enough hours left in the day for you to sort that out.'

'Yep, that could definitely take some time, Kitts.' Vi appeared in the doorway followed by a cloud of floral perfume. 'Any more tea in that po…' Her smile dropped. 'Jimby, what the bloody hell are you wearing?'

'Ah, you're referring to this rather fetching offering from my best mate who has absolutely no taste. You're thinking sex kitten, aren't you?' He placed a finger on his mouth and pouted.

'More like a ropy old hooker with a bad case of trout-pout.' Vi smirked.

'That's a bit harsh.' James feigned hurt feelings.

'Harsh, but true. Anyway, I've just got time for a quick cuppa before I head off back to York.' She turned to Kitty. 'It's good to see you up and about, chick.'

'Don't tell me, you've already heard about my sloe gin experience,' she said with a groan.

'Afraid so, flower. News travels fast around these parts. Your Auntie Annie was on the phone to my mum at the crack of a sparrow's fart, filling her in on all the details.' Vi pulled out the chair opposite her and sat down. 'Though I must admit, you look better than I was expecting – except for the bird's nest on top of your head.' She scrutinized Kitty's curls, giving them a prod.

'You should've seen me an hour and a half ago. It was a very different story. I still feel a bit jiggered, but thanks to one of Jimby's breakfasts I'm feeling a bit more human again. I wouldn't have needed it if it wasn't for that bloomin' sloe gin, though.' She shuddered at the thought of it.

'Hmm. A large sloe gin on top of four glasses of Prosecco when you don't normally drink would hit you like a sledge-hammer,' mused Vi. 'And what did you have at Ollie's?'

Kitty could feel what little colour she had drain away from her face as a vague recollection of being at Ollie's began to grow.

27

It was agreed that Kitty would call at Jimby's an hour later, armed with kids, dogs, hot-chocolate and flapjacks. What hadn't been factored into the equation was the return of Dan, who'd arrived back home when she was in the shower. And he had other plans for her.

Driving back had given him time to think. Judging by the sound of the texts and phone messages she'd left on his mobile last night, Kitty had still planned to go to the pub with her moronic friends, despite knowing he didn't like the idea. She needed reminding of her place, and that's exactly what he intended to do this morning. His lucky escape from Dog Daisy Wood the previous evening had left a bad taste in his mouth, and he needed to channel his annoyance somewhere. He'd drop the kids off at his mother's for a couple of hours, and then he'd set to work.

But his plans had been scuppered when he'd returned home and spotted James's Landie and the car that belonged to that purple-haired woman parked outside. He didn't know who they thought they were, parking there liked they owned the bloody place, blocking the driveway.

He'd driven around until the coast was clear and sneaked in with his mud-encrusted suit stuffed into a carrier bag. He was pushing it into a cupboard in his study when Lucas appeared in the doorway. 'Hi, Dad. I didn't hear you come in. Where've you been? Are you going for a run?'

Dan jumped up, bristling at almost being caught out. 'Since when did I have to explain myself to you?'

Lucas looked crestfallen. 'Sorry, Dad.' He loved his father, but he had the knack of making him feel like he was in trouble all the time. He hung his head and left the room.

A rare surge of guilt prodded Dan's, usually numb, conscience. He followed his son down the hall and into the kitchen, placing his hand on his shoulder. 'Listen, Lukes, I didn't mean to snap. It's just the pressure of work.'

'It's okay.' He gave a small smile. His dad hardly ever called him "Lukes", but he loved it when he did.

The news that they'd planned a walk with James infuriated Dan. He decided to throw a spanner in the works. 'Fancy going for a quick bike ride, just you and me? We can take the dogs and grab a pasty or something from the village shop on the way back. What do you think?'

Lucas beamed. 'Really, Dad? Just us two and the dogs?'

'Yep.'

'Cool!'

'Right, you go and get our cycle helmets while I get the bikes out of the shed. Meet me outside with the dogs. Go on, quick as you can. And don't forget their leads.'

Lucas was unable to hide his joy at doing something with his dad. He bolted up the stairs; the excitement of the bike ride had wiped away all thoughts of the walk with his mum and Uncle Jimby.

He was standing at the foot of the stairs, fastening his cycle helmet when Lily appeared from her bedroom, frowning when she spotted her brother. 'Lucas, how come you're putting that on? We're only going for a walk.'

'Because I just am, that's why,' he answered quickly, feeling his face redden as he remembered the walk. He snatched up the leads and his dad's cycle helmet he'd hung over the bannister and rushed out of the door, whistling for the dogs to follow him.

Lily ran into her parents' room and over to the low mullioned window, watching as her brother clipped the dogs' leads to their collars. She could hear muffled voices, one of which sounded like it belonged to their daddy. She leaned across the deep window sill, craning her neck to get a better view, to see Lucas wheel his bike down the path before climbing onto it and following their father down the road, the dogs trotting beside them.

'Mummy,' she yelled, scampering to the bathroom.

WITH LILY PLACATED by the promise of her favourite chocolate flap-jack and having her mum and Uncle Jimby to herself, the three set off on their walk. James and Kitty were admiring the clear blue sky — a welcome sight after weeks of dark, angry clouds — but the flapjack was torturing Lily, and had been since its purchase. Half an hour in, when they'd reached the wooden bench on the crag, Kitty could bear Lily's badgering no longer. She slipped off her backpack and declared it time for them to have their snack.

Lily perched on a lichen-covered rock, silent but for the occa-sional "nyom-nyom" sound as she tucked into her flapjack. 'There you go, Jimby'. Kitty handed him a melamine mug of hot chocolate.

'Mmm. Thanks. Looks good.' He had an infamous sweet-tooth. 'And you two can get stuffed, you're not getting any of this,' he said to Jarvis and Jerry, whose eyes were boring into him.

'I really appreciate all this, you know.' Kitty cradled her mug, a plume of chocolatey steam curling its way up in front of her. 'You spending time with me and the kids, helping me get my head straight.' Though, she thought, she hadn't had time to get her head around what had happened last night with Ollie. For that, she'd need some time to herself to piece together the hazy memories that were randomly making an appearance.

'No probs, sis. It's such a hardship eating cakes and drinking hot chocolate while looking at that view.' He flashed one of his customary grins. 'And anyway, you're actually doing me a favour. I needed some time away from thinking about an awkward design for an even more awkward customer.'

'Oh?'

'Dave Mellison and his delightful wife, to be precise. They're wanting me to make a gate that fastens in such a way that isn't phys-ically possible. She's already explained to me how a lot of people struggle with their superior level of intelligence, so she's going to draw some pictures of the mechanism. Apparently, even *I'll* be able to understand it.' He rolled his eyes and dunked his flapjack into his hot chocolate.

'How considerate of her.'

Lily ran across for a top-up of her hot chocolate when James noticed someone running up the track. They appeared to be waving their arms and shouting. Squinting, he leaned forward. 'Who's that down there?' he said, through a sticky mouthful of cherries and oats.

Kitty followed his gaze. 'Oh, I'm not sure, it's hard to make out from here. But it looks like they're calling us.'

'It does.'

'It's Lucas, Mummy! It's Lucas!' Lily jumped to her feet and shouted to her brother, 'Lucas, we're having hot chocolate and chocolatey dippy flapjack!' The spaniels jumped to attention, barking at the approaching figure.

'Hi, Lukes, there's plenty for you,' Kitty called, she didn't want him to think she was annoyed with him for going with his dad without telling her.

But as he got closer, it became clear that he was in distress. Her heart twisted as she realised he was crying. Setting her mug down on the arm of the bench, she scurried down the track towards him, losing her footing several times in her haste. She'd almost reached him when he stopped and bent over, resting his hands on his thighs. 'Mum…you've…got to…come…quick…It's…it's…' He sobbed, unable to get his words out, gasping for breath.

She rushed over to her son, throwing her arms around him and kissing his tear-stained face. 'Lukes, shhh, come on, sweetheart. It's okay. Take a deep breath.' It was a long time since she'd seen him this upset; she was sure it had something to do with Dan.

'Lukes, what the hell's the matter?' Concerned, James hurtled down the track towards them.

Lucas's words were still stifled by sobs. He looked from his mum to his uncle, heartbreak in his eyes.

'S'alright, buddy, come on.' James guided him to the seat, and Kitty sat beside him, pulling him close and stroking his hair which was damp with sweat. Sensing his distress, Jarvis and Jerry sat at his feet, looking up at him, concerned.

'I…don't…want…to sit…down,' he cried, jumping up. 'I c-c-can't. We…h-h-have…t-t-to g-g-g-go!' Sobbing, he pointed back down the track. 'P-p-please…c-c-come on. He was becoming hysterical, his words more incoherent. He grabbed hold of Kitty's arms, pulling her towards the track. Lily began to cry, and James scooped her up. 'It's okay, chick, Lukes'll be alright in a minute.'

Lucas turned to Kitty, snatching tears away from his eyes. 'M-m-mum…it's…H-h-humph. H-h-he's…h-he's.' He put his head on her shoulder and wept. 'I'm s-s-sorry…'

'What's the matter with Humph? He seemed fine first thing.' Her heart began to thump in her chest as she cast her mind back to breakfast.

'Hmm. The only thing that could be the matter with him was the consumption of too many sausages – not that he'd agree with me.' James pressed his lips together.

Lucas managed to control his tears for long enough to tell them about his dad's suggestion of the bike ride, explaining how Dan, who was riding ahead, had taken charge of Humphrey, leaving Lucas with Ethel. Ethel had managed the pace easily, but Humph had started to flag. Eventually, it had become too much for him, and he'd collapsed, pulling Dan off his bike. 'Oh, shit!' There had been no hiding Dan's shock when he'd realised what had happened. He'd run over to where the Labrador lay. 'Come on, Humphrey, get up,' he'd said. Humphrey had been panting heavily and had responded with a whimper.

Lucas had dumped his bike by the side of the road and run over to his father. 'What's the matter with Humph? Is he okay? This is your fault, Dad, he'd cried, pushing Dan away.

'Don't speak to me like that! It's not my fault, though, no doubt, you mother will blame me for it. You need to go and get help. Now!' He'd snatched up his bike and zoomed off down the road. Ethel had barked after him before turning her attention to Humph, licking his face and whining.

Knowing that Kitty was out with James, Lucas had run to Ollie's for help. He'd offered to stay with Humph, while Lucas tried to find his mum – he'd tried calling Jimby's mobile, but it had gone straight to voicemail.

Lucas wiped his runny nose with the palm of his hand, momentarily distracted by the smear of snot which he then wiped down the front of his jacket, leaving a shiny slug-trail. 'There's a boy down there with him, too. Called Bryn. He's been really kind. We've seen him in the village before, Mum.'

'Oh, bugger,' said James under his breath. He paused for a moment. 'Right, 'I'll run on ahead and see you back at your place. Okay?' He glanced at Kitty who was comforting a tearful Lily. She nodded, looking stunned.

He gathered up Jerry and Jarvis, and the three tore down the track at break-neck speed. He was determined to get to Bryn first.

Once back in the village, James raced to his house, sweat glistening on his brow, soaking into his short crop of curls. Thinking quickly, he fastened the spaniels in their run in the yard and grabbed a padded cushion from one of the dog beds in the kitchen, along with the keys for his Landie.

Throwing the cushion into the rear of the vehicle, James followed Lucas's directions out of the village.

One look at Humphrey lying in the roadside, panting heavily, he feared the worst. 'Oh, Humph, what's happened to you?' He sat on his haunches next to Ollie.

'We can't let Kitty and the kids see him like this,' Ollie said quietly as he smoothed Humph's head. 'I think we should get him back to the house and make him comfortable, poor old lad.'

James nodded. 'I agree.' His voice wavered with emotion. He looked across at Bryn who was wearing an anxious expression. He willed him not to let anything slip.

'S'alright, lass. We'll do what we can for him.' Ollie patted Ethel's head, she was standing beside Humphrey, looking confused.

The three carefully transferred Humph onto the cushion, into the back of the Landie and back to Oak Tree Farm. There, James rooted out the spare key, hidden under an ammonite in a moss-covered plant pot. Once inside, they eased Humph down beside the warmth of the Aga. They'd only been there a matter of minutes when they heard the creak of the gate announcing Kitty's return. James rubbed his brow, then turned to Bryn. 'Look, there hasn't been the right moment to speak to our Kitty yet. So, I'm asking you not to say anything until I have, okay? I swear to you I will talk to her, but just let's deal with this first.'

Bryn nodded. 'Of course.'

Confused, Ollie looked between the two of them.

'I'll explain later, mate,' James whispered as Kitty and the kids tumbled into the kitchen.

'Oh, Humph.' Kitty's hand flew to her mouth as she rushed over to where he lay, kneeling on the floor beside him, tears spilling down her cheeks. 'Has anyone called the vet?' her voice faltered.

Ollie swallowed, 'Yeah. Chris is on his way over from Dankselfe. Said he'd come straightaway.'

'Thank you,' she whispered, before kissing Humph's soft head, inhaling his distinctive smell. He whimpered, and his tail twitched as he attempted a wag for his mum, the sound of his heavy panting filling the room. 'Oh, Humph. I'm so sorry this has happened to you,' she sobbed into his fur.

Ethel whined, nudging Humphrey's head before laying down on the floor beside him.

James, struggling to fight back tears, had an arm around Lucas and Lily, hugging them close as they wept uncontrollably. 'This is all Dad's fault. I hate him!' cried Lucas through angry tears.

'I want Humphrey to get better,' snuffled Lily, hiding her face in Jimby.

Ollie pushed any potential awkwardness between himself and Kitty to the back of his mind as he rushed to her side. Kneeling on the floor, he placed his arm protectively around her small shoulders. 'Chris'll be here soon,' he whispered. She put her head on his shoulder as tears rolled down her cheeks.

'Can anyone tell me what the bloody hell is going on?' An angry voice cut through the sadness.

Everyone turned to see Dan standing in the doorway. No one had heard him throw his bike down on to the gravel drive and storm in. But now all eyes were upon him. 'And you can get your sodding hands off my wife.' He looked at Ollie, his eyes blazing. Ollie pulled Kitty closer.

Dan glanced around at the faces in the kitchen. He froze as his eyes alighted on Bryn. 'You? What the hell are you doing here? 'Get out! Get out of my house!' Feeling the weight of everyone's gaze upon him, he lunged towards the boy, intending to drag him out.

'Stop it! Stop it! Stop it!' Lucas flew at his father, fists clenched. Hot tears scorched their way down his cheeks as he rained heavy blows onto Dan's chest. 'Leave him alone. He's nice. And kind. He helped us with Humphrey. Humphrey's poorly because of you. I hate you! I hate you!'

'Control yourself, you little bloody fool. It wasn't my fault; I was only taking the dogs for a walk.' Dan was struggling to catch hold of Lucas's fists when a punch landed on the side of his nose. His head shot back with the force and, for a split second, he was dazed. Lucas's fists stilled, and everyone looked on in silence, mouths gaping as a trickle of blood slowly meandered from Dan's left nostril.

His nose was throbbing, his eyes were watering, and he could feel the warm crimson liquid reach his top lip. Pulling a tissue from his pocket, he dabbed at the blood and glared furiously at his son. 'You stupid little brat. Don't you ever do that to me again.'

'Daddy's scaring me,' cried Lily, huddling into Jimby.

Dan glowered at Kitty. 'You're to blame for this, you evil bitch. Turning the kids against me.' Again, he dabbed at his nose with the blood-sodden hankie. Looking across at Bryn, he said, 'And why the hell are you still here? I thought I told you to get out.'

Before Bryn could answer, Kitty jumped to her feet, snatching her tears away with her fingers. 'I'm not trying to turn the children against you, I'm afraid that's all your own handiwork. And you'd realise that if you could see yourself the way we see you. Your tantrums and the vile way you treat people.'

'You're making yourself look ridiculous,' he said disdainfully.

'Really? It's bad enough you didn't come home last night, without a phone call to explain where you were. But I wasn't surprised, it's what I've come to expect from you. No, what's worse is what you've done to Humphrey. It's cruel and unforgivable. He's old, Dan. Too old to keep up with you on your bike. You should've known that. You're nasty, and you're cruel.' Her voice wavered as fresh tears threatened.

'You're pathetic! I knew you'd twist things, just like you usually do. And you always did care about that bloody dog more than me,' he said with a snarl.

'Don't talk to Kitty like that. And especially not in front of Lucas and Lily.' Ollie's bubble of anger burst.

'And what business is it of yours? You shouldn't be in my house either. So, I suggest you get out and take that other idiot with you before I call the police and have you both removed.' Dan looked from Ollie to Bryn.

'Why are you being so horrible to him?' Kitty gestured at Bryn. 'He's been kind, he helped with Humphrey, and he didn't have to. He's done nothing to deserve your rudeness.'

'He's nobody. This is none of his business, and he's got no right to come here to my house. Go on, get out of my house, Nobody,' he shouted.

Bryn looked stunned; he was clearly fighting back tears. 'I'm not nobody. I'm…'

'I'm warning you.' Dan glowered at him.

I'm your son!'

A stunned silence filled the air; all eyes were on Bryn whose words stood in the room like unexpected guests.

28

A WEEK HAD PASSED since Dan had packed his bags and moved into a flat in York. After a thorough check-over by Chris the vet and an over-night stay at the surgery, Humph made a full recovery, with instructions to take it easy.

Kitty was sharing a pot of tea with Molly who'd called in after her last house visit in the village. 'So, how's things, missus?' she asked, pushing the sleeves of her navy work cardigan up to her elbows.

What had happened with Ollie that night after their drinks at the pub had gradually crept its way back into Kitty's memory, and she blushed every time she thought of it. She hadn't shared what had happened with anyone. It was their secret, and she wanted to keep it that way for now. She'd hug it close and keep it safe until she was ready to confront her feelings for him. But there was too much going on for that just now.

'Good.' Kitty nodded. 'Better than I expected actually, especially now Humph's recovered.'

'Fab! And the kids?'

'I'm surprised at how well they've been coping since Dan left. It's weird, but they seem more settled and relaxed, but I suppose Dan was hardly ever here for them to miss anyway.' She shrugged her shoulders and took a gulp of her tea.

Molly smiled. 'Well, it just goes to show you made the right decision. Maybe, because you were on the inside looking out, you

couldn't see just how bad things were, or how unhealthy the situation was. Unlike the rest of us, who could see things crystal clearly
and had been worried about you for yonks. And they always say
staying together for the kids is the wrong thing to do.'

Kitty nodded and leaned back in her seat, hugging her mug to
her chest. 'It sounds odd, but it feels like I've had a huge weight
lifted off my shoulders and, instead of feeling absolutely gutted, I'm
feeling pretty optimistic. Deep down, I think I'd known things were
wrong with Dan and me for years, maybe even from the start. But
my parents had such a rock-solid marriage, and Mum always said
that it was something that had to be worked at. So, I tried to work at
ours, but the foundations just weren't strong enough.' She gave a
wry smile.

'Your parents would be a hard act for anyone to follow. But, to be
honest, Kitts, it would've been a sodding up-hill struggle for you
with that knob-head, and a lot of pressure to heap onto yourself. It
takes two to make a marriage work, and you did all you could. It
obviously wasn't meant to be.' Molly paused, suddenly aware that
she was beginning to sound like a string of clichés playing on a loop.
'But you've got two gorgeous kids as well as friends and family who
love you to bits, so it's a win-win situation.' She grinned.

'Oh, Moll. What would I do without you?' Kitty laughed at her
cousin, who was rummaging around in the pocket of her jacket that
was hanging on the back of her chair.

'Here, I almost forgot. Get your gob round one of these bad boys.'
She pushed a packet of custard creams across the table.

The pair spent the next hour dunking biscuits and discussing
Kitty's future. Conscious that she didn't want her cousin to feel like
she was being pushed into anything, Molly gently suggested a visit
to a solicitor to start divorce proceedings, before Dan tried to
wheedle his way back into her affections.

CLIMBING INTO HER FOUR-WHEEL DRIVE, Kitty threw her brown leather
messenger bag into the passenger footwell. She'd just dropped the
kids off at school, having dodged the increasingly dark scowls of
Aoife Mellison, who was making her presence felt in the playground.
The last thing she needed this morning was that woman in her head.
She was just about to flick the engine on when she heard the ping of

a text message delivery from the depths of her bag. After a quick rummage, she managed to retrieve her phone to see she'd received a text each from Molly and Violet, both wishing her luck. She read them and smiled; Molly's was decorated with a scattering of celebratory emojis and Vi's came with a picture of a floral tattoo she thought would be great for the three of them to get to mark the event. Kitty wasn't so sure about that!

She was still scrutinizing the image when the feeling that she was being watched crept over her, making the hairs on the back of her neck bristle. She looked up to see Gwyneth's icy glare boring into her as she stomped towards the car. 'That's all I need,' she said to herself as she threw her phone onto the passenger seat and, fumblingly, started the engine. Gwyneth was nearly upon her when Kitty slipped the car into gear and went to drive off. Her heart was pounding and she stalled the car in her haste. 'Bugger!' she swore quietly as it jolted to a halt. Taking a deep breath, she tried again. This time luck was on her side, and she pulled away smoothly, conscious of Gwyneth glaring at her 'Phew! That was close,' she said, brushing a wayward curl off her face.

Kitty hadn't slept much the previous night. As soon as her head had hit the pillow, her mind had taken off, exploring a maze of dark avenues. And she'd risen early, eager to get the day moving. After much deliberation, she'd set out her clothes the night before, wondering what was deemed appropriate clothing for a woman who had an appointment with a solicitor to file for divorce from her errant husband. Sober colours, she thought, and rooted through her wardrobe, pulling out a long navy-blue jersey tunic top splashed with small cream polka dots, navy knitted tights and a matching cotton scarf scattered with tiny silver butterflies. As it was forecast to be bright but chilly, Kitty brushed down her indigo moleskin coat and polished her dark tan boots. That would do, she thought.

Keen to set the wheels in motion – and while she was still feeling brave enough – she'd confided in Molly and Violet about her appointment with Letitia Tickell, a divorce lawyer at Tickell, Whisker, Hoare and Tibbs.

'Her name always puts me in mind of a German side-order,' said Vi. 'The sort of thing you should order with wiener schnitzel.'

Kitty laughed. 'I think it sounds like a tongue-twister.'

'I think it sounds more like a sneeze. I have to stop myself from saying "bless you" whenever I hear it. Well, either a sneeze or the word testicle – if you say it quickly enough, that is. But testicles always remind me of work, so I prefer to go with the sneeze option.' Molly rubbed her nose briskly. 'Anyone got any custard creams? I'm famished.'

Violet rolled her eyes. 'Please spare us the details of why the word testicles reminds you of work. And, I'm fresh out of custard creams. Actually, what is it with you and those bloody biscuits at the moment? You're obsessed.'

Once at Middleton-le-Moors, Kitty found a parking space in the old market square within handy walking distance of the solicitors' office. She thought arriving fifteen minutes early for her appointment would give her chance to flick through a magazine which would, hopefully, settle her nerves. A good idea in theory, but in practice, it didn't seem to be working. Her stomach was performing somersaults and waves of nausea kept sweeping over her. She couldn't believe that she, Kitty Bennett, was sitting here in a solicitors' office, waiting for her appointment to speak to a hard-nosed matrimonial lawyer about divorcing her husband. She was the only one of her peers to do it, the only mum at school to do it, and the first in her family to do it. And she wasn't sure which of those three was worse.

Her thoughts were interrupted by the trill of a phone on the desk of the pretty young receptionist. After a brief exchange of words, she replaced the handset and looked over at Kitty. 'Mrs Bennett, Ms Tickell will see you now. It's just up the stairs, first on the right. Watch out for the step down into her room.'

'Thank you.' Kitty smiled nervously and got to her feet. Her heart was racing with such force she could feel it thrumming in her ears.

Arriving at the large dark wooden door with its brightly polished brass name-plate, Kitty paused. She closed her eyes and took a deep breath. *This is it.* Before she could change her mind, she knocked on the door, reminding herself of the step down into the room.

'Come in,' boomed a low, plummy voice.

Letitia Tickell, known by all as 'Tish', was a non-nonsense, fifth-generation solicitor at the family firm. A huge galleon of a woman, she had a shock of steely grey hair and a broad bosom that rested on her knees as she sat in her leather swivel chair. Tish was in her late fifties and resolutely single — years of dealing with acrimonious divorces had seen to that. 'Well, I wouldn't want to arm-wrestle her,' James had said when Kitty had told him of her appointment with Ms Tickell. 'But, from what I've heard she's shit-hot. And she's supposed to have a great sense of humour, too. Which, I suppose is handy in her line of work.'

'Mrs Bennett, good to meet you.' Kitty found herself on the receiving end of a firm handshake.

The appointment had been half an hour's worth of reassuring straight-talk and had scurried away any remaining doubts that prodded her conscience. 'The man's a bastard, m'dear. And no one should be married to a bastard. If I'd been married to him, I'd have strung him up by the balls and hung him out to dry long before now. Your patience is commendable, but enough's enough.'

Kitty stifled a giggle. *It's Molly with a posh voice.*

Ms Tickell's office had been hot and stuffy and, as Kitty stepped out into the street, she could feel the squeeze of a stress headache pressing against her temples. The cool fresh air offered welcome relief, and she took a deep breath. The morning which had begun with a sharp frost had given way to a fine early winter's day. The sun, now shining brightly, had banished ice from the footpaths, with only the stubborn, shady patches holding on to any remaining frost.

Kitty checked her watch; there was a good forty-five minutes before her appointment at the hairdressers. It gave her time to browse in the quaint, bow-fronted shops that lined the edges of the market square.

She was admiring the Christmas display in the florist's window when her thoughts were interrupted. 'Erm, hello, Mrs Bennett,' said a quiet voice.

She turned to see a young man with eyes like Dan's looking at her. They were tinged with apprehension. Kitty was shocked for a second before she realised that this pair of eyes were friendly and crinkled pleasantly as their owner smiled. 'Oh, hello, Bryn, lovie. How are you? And please call me Kitty.'

'I'm fine, thank you, how are you?' She detected genuine concern in his voice.

'I'm, er, good, thanks. I'm doing okay, actually,' she said. 'What are you doing here? No school?'

'My school's here, but we've been given the day off. Faulty boiler, so there's no heating, and it's too cold for us to work.'

'Oh, of course, you go to Middleton Hall, don't you? Silly me.'

Jimby had briefly filled her in on what he knew about the lad, but, at the time, she hadn't wanted to know any more; her brain felt like it was on overload. 'Dodgy boiler, eh? I bet you're gutted about that?' She smiled at him. Although he resembled his father, he had a kindness to his features that had eluded Dan. And despite the painful facts that linked them, Kitty thought there was something very likeable about this boy. The situation wasn't his fault, he was another person hurt by Dan's selfish actions. Something about him reminded her of Lucas too. 'Look, I've got an appointment at half eleven –and you can say no if you want, I'll totally understand – but how do you fancy a hot chocolate and a sticky cake at the tea shop over there?' She wrinkled her nose, hoping he wouldn't think she was weird for suggesting it.

Bryn beamed. 'Yeah, I'd really like that.'

'Me, too.' She smiled back at him. 'Come on.'

THE BELL on the door jangled excitedly as Kitty pushed it open. The tea shop, poised for the lunch-time rush, was quiet save for a young waitress in a crisp white blouse and straight black skirt. Having their pick of the tables, they chose the one tucked away in the corner by a bulky column radiator that quietly belched out heat. Kitty placed their order at the counter while Bryn wove his way through the tables.

'So that's two hot chocolate specials with all the trimmings and two slices of chocolate cake. Anything else?' asked the waitress.

'That's it, thanks.'

'Okay, I'll bring them over to you.'

Kitty joined Bryn at the table and was hanging her coat on the back of her chair when he spoke. 'How's Humphrey?'

'Much better, thanks,' she said with a smile.

'I'm really sorry about what I said. I shouldn't have said anything. It wasn't my place, and I really didn't mean to, it's just… I'm sorry.' His words came out in a torrent. He looked up, searching Kitty's face, trying to assess her reaction.

She could see he looked genuinely concerned and couldn't help but feel sorry for him. From what Jimby had said, Bryn hadn't known the truth much longer than she had. It must have been a lot for him to take on board. 'You don't have anything to be sorry about.

If anyone should be, it's Dan, but the only thing he's sorry about is being found out. You're as much of a – and I hate to use this word – "victim" in all of this as the rest of us.' She paused for a moment, pressing her lips together before letting them melt into a smile. 'Which is why I want to ask you something…'

'RIGHT, doll, what are we doing with this mad bird's nest?' Flicking his hips in time to the bass line of the background music, Stefan buried his fingers into Kitty's curls, fluffing them out until they resembled an electrocuted pom-pom. She covered her mouth with her hand, giggling at her reflection.

Kitty's second appointment of the day was with Stefan, executive style director and owner of The Salon in Middleton-le-Moors. It was all clean lines, funky playlists and beautiful stylists, with emphasis on client satisfaction.

Like the rest of his staff, Stefan wore black skinny jeans, a black t-shirt that hung off one shoulder, with the "The Salon" emblazoned in silver across the back, and a black leather accessories holster-belt slung over his hips, housing his tools of the trade. The look was topped off by the obligatory funky haircut. Today Stefan was rocking a post-punk style, his raven black hair shot through with bold flashes of electric blue and gelled into a gravity-defying faux-hican.

Kitty had been a regular at The Salon since it first opened its doors when she was sixteen. A couple of years older than her, Stefan was a newly qualified stylist, and she remembered him from secondary school when he was still known as Stephen. Ten years later, he bought out the owner and gave the salon a funky re-brand.

'I want to go back to my natural colour. I want to be a brunette again.' She paused, holding eye contact with him in the mirror. 'And I want it all off.'

His mouth fell open, and the hair fluffing ceased. 'All off?' She'd just asked him to do what he'd been trying to get her to do for years. He'd never understood her husband's encouragement of the poker straight blonde look. It only served to make her complexion appear sallow and swamped her pretty, elfin features.

'Yep, all off, how I used to have it years ago. As short as you like. Exactly what you've been itching to do for years.' She giggled at his expression.

He rested his hands on her shoulders and leaned in. 'Right, doll, in my experience there's only one reason a woman wants her long hair cutting off. And that reason is usually a man. A man who's been a complete and utter prat.'

A shadow of sadness clouded her face, and she nodded, casting her eyes down. Stefan gave her shoulders an affectionate squeeze. 'Right, babes, first things first, I'll fetch Amber to get you gowned-up and shampooed. Then we'll sit you back down with a nice strong cuppa, and I'll get to work.' He made a scissor-cutting action with his fingers before sashaying over to Amber, a petite girl with a mussed-up, dusky-pink bob.

SEVERAL CUPS of tea and much snipping later, Stefan allowed Kitty to look at her reflection. 'Right, doll. Moment of truth time.' With a flourish, he whipped off the gown he'd used to cover the mirror. 'Tadah!'

Struggling to recognise herself, she peered shyly at the young woman who was looking back at her. A young woman who had a crop of glossy, short, dark curls that emphasised her large, brown eyes and high cheekbones. She pressed her hands to her cheeks, blushing. 'Oh, Stefan, thank you. I love it. I feel like me again,' she said, her eyes sparkling.

'You're very welcome, babes. Bet you wish you'd listened to me years ago.' He smiled admiringly at his handy-work.

'I can't believe how different you look. Don't ever go back to long blonde hair again, will you?' Amber grinned, unfastening the Velcro of Kitty's gown.

Kitty left the salon with a spring in her step; today had felt like she was shaking off the final chains that kept her shackled to Dan. And it felt bloody good.

29

THURSDAY ARRIVED and with it the first music night at the Sunne — or Songs at the Sunne as Jonty had christened it. Kitty had been sporting her new haircut for two days and still wasn't used to it, particularly the cold feeling around her newly-bare neck. Not comfortable with being the centre of attention, she'd hidden it under a hat when she embarked on the school run.

Throughout the day, her mobile phone had pinged and flashed with a variety of texts from Jimby, Molly and Violet, all keeping her up-to-date with the evolving plans for their evening out. They'd be at the pub for seven thirty-ish but, as usual, Pip would be working on the moor till late, which, Molly joked, would give him less opportunity to sing. Bea was laying on nibbles – which would be heavenly – so she wasn't to have too much for dinner. Would she be up for a quick sing-song? *Most definitely not*! The final text was from Noushka, who was babysitting and doubling-checking what time to arrive. She threw in that her dad would be walking down with her. Kitty's heart fluttered like a butterfly caught in a jar at the thought of Ollie. Her hand went up to her hair, suddenly conscious of its new style, realising that it mattered to her that he should like it.

KITTY WAS APPLYING a slick of lip-gloss in the hall mirror when there was a knock at the door. Lucas and Lily, elbowing each other out of the way, stampeded past her with a barking Humph and Ethel in tow. 'Just be careful you two, you make more commotion than a herd of wildebeest.' She popped the lip-gloss into her bag.

'Hiya, kids.' Anoushka stood in the dim light of the doorway, smiling. Clutched to her chest was a ring-binder file, covered in stickers and doodles. She had a navy pompom hat pulled down over her flaxen hair that hung in waves across her shoulders. 'Where's your mum?' she asked as she stepped into the warmth of the hall, eyeing the elfin stranger with short dark hair.

Ollie followed her, rubbing his hands together. 'Brrr. It's parky out there.' He locked eyes with Kitty, and a couple of beats fell before he spoke. 'Oh, wow! Kitts, you look beautiful,' he said softly and blushed as he realised he'd processed his thoughts into words. Words that had triggered a surge of happiness through her.

Anoushka looked from her dad to Kitty. 'OMG! Kitty, I, like, totally didn't recognise you! You look so gorgeous.' Usually reserved like her father, Kitty's new look had made the teenager uncharacteristically animated. She clapped a hand over her mouth. 'Oops, I, er, totally didn't mean you don't always look gorgeous, because you do. But you look, literally, extra gorgeous now.'

Kitty giggled. 'Thanks, Noushka.'

'Noushka, my mummy looks like a princess.' Lily beamed up at her, twirling Snuggles by the ears.

'She does, Lils, and so do you.' Anoushka scooped her up, planting a kiss on her cheek.

'And so do you, Noushka. Everyone says so, don't they, Mummy?'

'Yes, they do, Lils. Noushka is very beautiful.'

'Eurghh! Women!' Lucas threw his arms up in exasperation. 'Can't we talk about something else. I'm sick of hearing about fairy princesses. Even Ethel has to be a bloomin' fairy princess.' He loped off into the living room.

Ollie cocked an amused eyebrow at Kitty. 'I think he's feeling a little bit outnumbered being the only male in the house now - apart from Humph,' she explained.

'Ah.' He nodded.

'Hey, Lukes, I've been looking forward to hearing all about your footballing skills. I've just joined the girls' football team at school, and I need to pick up some tips from an expert like you,' Anoushka called after him.

KITTY WAS CLOSING the door behind her when Ollie spoke. 'Can I just check, are we okay? You know, after the other night?' She looked up at him, the outside light casting soft shadows over his handsome face. They hadn't spoken properly since she'd fled his house.

'Ollie, we're absolutely fine. I'm sorry for what I did. The last thing I want is to have awkwardness between us.'

'Good, same here.' A smile dimpled his cheeks, making her heart flutter.

A chilly wind picked up as they headed down the path and onto the trod, wrapping itself around Kitty's neck and nipping at her ears. She shivered, and Ollie looked across at her. 'Which part are you apologising for? The fact that we kissed and nearly…well…or for running off – not that you should feel you have to be sorry for any of that, by the way.'

'I'm sorry I ran off, without explaining. It was just… well…you know.'

'Yeah, I know.' They crossed the road, passing under the gentle glow of the Victorian street lamps. Ollie sneaked another look at her new haircut. 'I meant what I said in the house, Kitts. You look beautiful. You look like you used to years ago when we first started to…' He bit his lip and cursed inwardly. 'Sorry, that didn't come out quite how I wanted it to. I didn't mean that you didn't look nice before, I just meant that you really suit it short and natural like you have it now. You look like you again.'

'Thank you, Ollie. I'm still not properly used to it yet.' She smoothed the nape of her neck. As her hand dropped to her side, she felt the warmth of his fingers wrap around it, giving it a gentle squeeze. 'Tell me if this isn't okay.' He looked across at her.

She glanced up at him and smiled. Moonlight glinted off the golden stubble that peppered his strong jaw-line. She was still feeling raw after Dan, but something about Ollie instilled a feeling of security and calm deep within her. 'It's okay, Oll. Actually, it's very okay.'

'Well, that's alright then.' He smiled down at her, and the flutter in her heart cranked up to a full-on somersault.

NEWS OF SONGS at the Sunne had spread like wildfire on the rural telegraph that linked the neighbouring villages. Locals were always keen for something different to do in the dark winter evenings and jumped at the chance to support it. So, when Kitty and Ollie arrived at the pub, it was already bulging at the seams. 'Just as well the others said they'd save us a seat,' Ollie shouted above the chatter as they squeezed their way towards their usual table by the fire.

Violet was taking a sip of her gin and tonic when she spotted Kitty. Her eyes widened as she quickly swallowed her mouthful. 'Wowzers, check out our new-look friend.'

Molly followed her gaze and gave a shrill wolf-whistle which turned a few inquisitive heads. 'Wow! You look amazing, Kitts! Is that Stefan's handiwork?'

Kitty felt her face burn crimson. She tugged at her hair as if to make it longer. 'Thank you. Yes, I got it done on Tuesday. Stefan was surprised, too. He thought I was just going for my usual.'

'Ooh, he'll have been in his element, he loves a challenge,' said Molly as her face stretched into a long yawn. 'Sorry, I'm knackered.'

'Been working too hard?' Kitty noticed the dark circles that hung under her cousin's eyes.

'Something like that.'

'Evening, ladies. Where's Jimbo?'

'Hiya, Oll. He's just gone to get the drinks in.' Vi nodded in the direction of the bar where James was being served.

'Righto, I'll go and give him a hand.'

WITH SO MANY locals keen to give their vocal talents an airing, the evening offered little opportunity for in-depth conversation. Instead, the friends joined in heartily with the choruses, snatching snippets of chat between performances.

Feeling happy and relaxed, Kitty had found herself sitting next to Ollie on the banquette – as usual. 'So, you're not tempted to get up there and give us a song?' He nudged her with his shoulder, sending a waft of his citrussy cologne her way.

'Have you ever heard me sing?'

'Er, good point. I think it's probably better for everyone if you don't.'

'Cheeky!' She giggled, nudging him back. 'But you do have a point. Jimby got my share of singing ability, I'm afraid. How about you? Are you going to have a warble?' She already knew the answer to that.

'Have you ever heard *me* sing?'

'Er, 'fraid so. We couldn't sing a decent tune between us, could we?' They laughed, unaware of the knowing smiles that passed between their friends.

Reaching for the guitar he'd brought with him, James headed over to the designated singer's seat. He cleared his throat and strummed the first chords of a popular slow song. A hush fell over the room which he filled with his rich, smoky voice.

Tables were banged, and shouts for more rang out once he'd finished. 'Right, Violet, get yourself over here and keep me company.' He patted the seat beside him. Vi squeezed her way over and wriggled onto the stool. After a brief discussion about what to sing Jimby twanged a couple of guitar strings and Vi launched into a smouldering rendition of a forties classic.

The pair were a hard act to follow, but old Tom Storr, who was up next, was given rapturous applause after his surprisingly impressive efforts. While Lianne, who was new to the village, managed to earn herself some new-found respect with her powerful vocals.

After a short break for people to replenish their drinks, proceedings were picked up by Gerald and Big Mary whose humorous and heartfelt singing added an entertaining flavour. The pair didn't take themselves too seriously, and all agreed that what they lacked in talent they more than compensated for in enthusiasm. 'Encore,' shouted Ollie and James, and the pair obliged, adding some dubious dance moves which went down a storm.

Dave Mellison was the only contributor to the evening's entertainment who wasn't met with enthusiasm. 'Guess who's brought along his saxophone?' James didn't look impressed.

'Uh oh, brace yourselves, looks like it's time for our ears to get a bashing.' Ollie pulled a face.

'Eh?' Vi wrinkled her nose.

'He only knows one tune, but he absolutely slaughters it,' Ollie explained.

'Oh, fabulous!' Vi giggled.

Molly grinned, craning her neck to get a better view. 'Yep, this should be good for all the wrong reasons.' She leaned towards Vi. 'This is the arrogant tosser who's married to that snotty cow, the one who fancies Dan – more fool her. She's not in tonight, must be looking after their horrible little brats.'

'Ahh,' said Vi. 'Sound like a lovely family.'

Dave perched himself on the stool, flicked his ponytail over his shoulder and proceeded to perform a series of exaggerated mouth exercises. He placed his saxophone to his lips, puffed out his cheeks and blew hard. A piercing squeal forced its way out of the instrument, making the audience jump. Ollie and James snorted into their beer and Molly gasped. 'Bloody hell! I nearly wet my knickers!' She pressed a hand to her chest, her heart thudding against it.

'I thought you said it would be good, Moll,' giggled Kitty.

'Sounds like Reg has got competition in the squawk department, Jimby,' Vi said with a snigger.

Dave continued, oblivious to the stifled snorts of laughter. For nearly five minutes he dragged out a painful noise that vaguely resembled a tune. When he'd done, the audience cheered and he took several deep bows, a supercilious expression on his face, unaware that he was being mocked.

'Thank God he can only play one tune,' James said, taking a swig of his beer and licking away the froth with his tongue.

'What the chuffin' hell was that?' Lycra Len – still in his cycling gear – was never one to keep his opinions to himself. He was treated to an icy glare from Dave.

Keen to dispel any awkwardness, Jonty leapt to his feet, clasping his hands together. 'Thank you very much for your, er, alternative rendition, Dave. I'm not sure how we'd follow that, so I think now would be as good a time as any for a break. Please feel free to tuck into the buffet that Bea's set up in the dining room. Enjoy, and we'll pick things up in, say, half-an-hour.'

Ollie and James headed to the bar to get the drinks in. As they waited to be served they overheard a conversation between Dave Mellison and John Carroll, an older member of the community who regularly shook his head about Dave's laziness. 'Thought you'd 'ave done better than that, the amount of time you spend doing nowt, lad.'

'I don't know what you mean.' Dave bristled.

'Well, from what I hear, you're always propping up the bar at the

Fox and Hounds when you should be grafting. And what you just churned out on that saxophone was a load of rubbish.'

A crimson flush spread up Dave's neck. It travelled across his shiny, bald pate and came to a halt at the start of his scrawny pony-tail. 'I'll have you know I was in a band in my youth, and we had a record out, almost got a recording contract we were so good. And I don't know who told you the rubbish about me propping up the bar at the Fox. I'm rushed off my feet with landscaping contracts. I'm only taking time out of my busy schedule to help the landlords make tonight a success. I should be at home working on my backlog of paperwork.' Fuming, he pushed past Ollie and James, picked up his saxophone, and stormed out of the pub.

Just arriving, Pip was pulling open the pub door when Dave barged through it, pushing him out of the way. 'Don't mind me,' said Pip.

Reeking of burnt heather and looking slightly charred around the edges, he headed over to their usual table. 'Cheers, mate,' he said to Ollie, who passed him his own untouched pint.

'Your need's greater than mine.' Ollie grinned and headed back to the bar to buy himself another one.

Pip leaned over to give Molly a peck on the cheek. 'Now then, love.'

'Christ, you stink!' She grimaced, leaning away from him. He rolled his eyes good-naturedly at the others. The acrid smell of her husband's clothing had caused Molly's stomach to lurch up to her throat. She clamped her hand over her mouth and clenched her abdominal muscles. 'I won't be a minute. Just need to go to the loo.'

THE CLOCK on the mantelpiece struck ten thirty, and customers were beginning to trickle away. Kitty picked up her coat. 'I think it's time I was heading back.' The others nodded, they should be getting home, too.

'Yep, Vi's in danger of turning into a pumpkin if she doesn't get moving.' Sporting a cheeky grin James gathered up the empty glasses, putting them onto the tray.

'Watch it, buster.' She gave him a sidelong look under her eyelashes.

'That's quite a way you've got with the ladies there, Jimby.' Ollie was helping Kitty on with her coat.

'Never fails, Oll.'

'And you wonder why his girlfriends never last more than two minutes,' Molly added wryly.

As they were leaving, Kitty felt a light tap on her shoulder and turned to see her father-in-law smiling sheepishly at her. His cheeks were ruddy and, judging by the fumes on his breath, he'd had more than a couple of whiskies – she couldn't blame him; he was going back to Gwyneth. 'Hello, my dear. How are you keeping? How are the children?' He was immaculate as ever, his crisp shirt collar peering neatly from beneath a pullover.

'Oh, hello, George. I didn't know you were here. We're fine thanks. How about you?' She groaned inwardly. *How awkward is this*?

'Fine, fine, erm, er.' He cleared his throat. 'I almost didn't recognise you at first, what with your smart new haircut. It really suits you.'

'Oh, thank you.' She touched her hair with her fingertips.

'Ahem, look, m'dear, I, er just wanted to say how sorry I am about this dreadful business with Daniel. I don't know what's got into him recently. Though, I do blame his mother for spoiling him rotten when he was growing up.' His eyes, which had thus far remained fixed on his highly polished brown brogues, now looked directly at her. 'And I think you've absolutely done the right thing for yourself and the children. You all deserve to be treated better. I know I've hardly been a saint, but it's not been without good reason – not that I'm making excuses for myself. Life with Gwyneth hasn't exactly been easy. But Dan should've appreciated what he had and cherished you. Instead…well…the bullying…I'm ashamed of him.'

Kitty hadn't been expecting that. 'Thank you, George; it can't have been easy for you to say that, but I appreciate your understanding. I tried hard to make things work, but there were too many problems, and it wasn't fair on the children.' Conscious of other people milling around them, she kept her voice low.

'I understand, my dear.' He paused and stood to one side to allow Lianne's boyfriend, Jeff, take a clutch of empty glasses to the bar.

'Ta, mate,' said Jeff.

When Jeff was out of earshot George leaned towards her, his voice just above a whisper. 'And if I'd been half as brave as you, I would've divorced the Dragon years ago.'

'Oh.' Kitty didn't know what else to say.

'Well, I'll let you go. Take care, dear.' He patted her arm.

'You too, George.' She watched him walk back to his whisky.

Ollie had observed the conversation and was waiting for her by the door. 'You okay?'

She nodded and smiled. 'That was weird, but, yes, I'm okay.'

30

'MRS MARR SAYS you've got to send in the signed permission slip for the pantomime tomorrow.' Lily chomped on a mouthful of home-made chicken pie, spraying crumbs of pastry as she spoke. Kitty and the children were sitting around the kitchen table. 'Everybody else has paid 'cept for me and Rory Davison-Butler.'

Frowning, Kitty swallowed her mouthful of food. 'But I signed it and put it in the front pocket of your school bag for you to hand in like I normally do. It was ages ago, d'you remember, you were there when I did it?' She pushed a piece of chicken onto her fork. 'Lucas, please stop wolfing your food down like that, you'll get indigestion.' She turned to her son who was shovelling his food into his mouth as though his life depended upon it.

He shrugged and pushed his half-chewed food into the corner of his cheek, hamster-like. 'I'm not wolfing, I'm just eating quickly because I'm starving.' He continued his vigorous assault on the plate in front of him.

'And what have I told you two kids about talking with your mouth full? It's like watching a couple of washing machines on spin cycle.' Her gaze rested on Lucas. She remembered thinking his school trousers looked a little short on him the other day; he must be having a growing spurt. She smiled and leaned across with the inten-tion of ruffling his hair, but he ducked out of reach.

'Not the quiff, Mum.'

'Nope,' said Lily, shaking her head.

'Nope, what, Lils?' asked Kitty.

'Nope, I didn't forget to hand it in. I put it in the basket on Mrs Prudom's desk where we have to put everything like that. I remember. I think it's got lost at school. Can you send another one or I won't be able to go, and I really want to?' Lily nibbled on a piece of carrot.

Kitty smiled. 'I'll sort it out, don't you go worrying about it. Just enjoy the rest of your dinner; there's homemade apple pie and custard for afters.' She thought it was odd that the envelope should go missing, especially as it contained the ten-pound voluntary contribution which she'd clipped to the permission slip. She always labelled everything clearly, stating what the envelopes contained. It niggled her that it wasn't the first thing of Lil's to go missing recently.

Lily brushed a spring of curls off her face with the palm of her hand. 'Evie Mellison says I can't go and if I do, that I can't sit next to anyone on the bus, especially not Abbie, and she knows me and Abbie are best friends.'

There was that girl's name again. Kitty felt a shot of anger spike through her. 'Don't take any notice of her, it's not up to her who can go or who people can sit next to. I'll go and sign another form first thing in the morning and give it to Mrs Prudom myself.' She smoothed a hand over Lily's curls.

'I hate that Evil Smellison. And her brother, Teddy. They're nothing but a pair of nasty mingers.'

'Lucas, please. No name-calling, it makes you as bad as them.'

'Well, it's true. Stupid Teddy said his mum told him Dad's too good for us and that's why he left.' He plunged his fork into his mashed potato.

'Mummy!' Lily's eyes began to fill with tears.

Kitty was seething. 'This has got to stop. Don't worry, Lils, I'll get it sorted out for you. But in the meantime, just ignore anything those horrible children have to say.'

Later, while Lily was enjoying a bubble bath, Kitty had a surreptitious rummage through her daughter's school backpack. Before she said anything at school, she wanted to make sure that the missing envelope wasn't lurking under the detritus at the bottom of her bag. Looking at the state of it, that's exactly where she expected to find it, hidden amongst dirty socks, various half-eaten food items – one of which had the potential to be of serious interest to medical research – and scraps of paper. But it wasn't there.

'HOW'S THE SITUATION WITH EVIE?' asked Mrs Prudom the following morning when Kitty popped into her office to explain about the form and sign a new one.

'Not good, I'm afraid,' she replied and went on to share the conversation she'd had with Lily the previous evening.

'Leave it with me. I'll get to the bottom of it,' the head said, firmly.

Feeling reassured, Kitty left the office and headed across the playground, aware of the weight of Evie's eyes on her. As she looked up, the child stuck out her tongue and smirked. But her expression soon changed when Mrs Prudom, who'd witnessed it, marched across and guided Evie into her office.

'HELLO. ANYONE HOME?' Kitty was in the utility room feeding clothes into the washing machine when Molly's head appeared around the door. Ethel gave a cursory bark from her bed.

'Shush, Eth, it's only Molly,' said Kitty. 'Hiya, Molls, this is a nice surprise. I'll just set this washing away then I'll stick the kettle on. You've got time for a cuppa?' she asked, taking in her cousin's work uniform.

Molly rubbed her fingertips against her brow. 'Erm, not so sure I could manage any tea, but a cup of boiled water and a chinwag would be good. I thought I'd sneak a quick break between patients. And I've just had to have a word with Granny Aggie about a text she'd sent the vicar asking if he liked S and M because she'd like to whip him. Poor man was terrified. Anyway, turns out she was telling him she'd bought some whipped cream from M&S for the scones she was making for the church coffee morning.' Molly shook her head, rolling her eyes heavenwards.

'Ah, the dreaded predictive text,' Kitty said with a laugh.

'Yep. She's on her last warning. Any more dodgy messages and the phone gets it. I know her arthritis is shocking, and it's difficult for her to text, but we keep turning her predictive text off yet whenever we check her phone it's miraculously switched itself back on. There's mischief at work there; she's not the innocent little old lady she likes to make out she is.'

'Oh dear.' Kitty scanned Molly's face which, despite her smiles, was pale, and the dark circles she'd noticed the other night were still in residence under her eyes. Something wasn't right.

Molly flopped down onto a chair and sighed.

'You alright?' Kitty set the kettle down on the Aga hotplate before chucking teabags into the teapot.

'Nope, not really. In fact, I'm about as far from sodding alright as I possibly could be.'

'Oh dear, what's happened?'

'Well, for starters, Mum and Dad are giving up the farm early. Dad's Parkinson's has got too bad. He's been struggling for a while, but it's taken a sudden nose-dive, and Mum's finally convinced him it's time to hand it over to me and Pip.'

'Ah, Moll, I'm sorry to hear about Uncle Jack, but isn't it what you want, you and Pip? Running the farm, I mean? I always thought that was the plan.' Kitty went to pour the tea.

'Er, just a mug of boiled water for me thanks, Kitts,' Molly reminded her cousin. 'I don't think I could face tea, especially the strength you make it.'

'Oh, okay. On a pre-Christmas detox, are we? Or was it too much of the devil's brew last night?'

'Not quite.'

'Oh?'

'Oh bugger, more like.' Molly took a deep breath. 'I'm pregnant.'

Kitty stood silent for a moment. 'How?'

'That, dear cousin, is a good question. As far as I'm aware, it must've been an immaculate bloody conception. I'm as gob-smacked as you are that it's happened. I've no idea when it did. I never manage to tear Pip away from his usual bedtime reading of country pursuits magazines, or whatever other game-keeping rubbish he reads, long enough for a peck on the cheek, never mind any of the jiggy-jiggy stuff.'

Kitty chuckled, pulling out the chair opposite Molly. She sat down, cradling her mug of tea in her hands.

Molly took a sip of water. She was on a roll. 'Mind you, he hardly comes to bed dressed for a night of passion. The other night he excelled himself when he rocked up in a skin-tight tiger-print onesie the twins had bought for him for his birthday – as a joke I hasten to add, but Pip insists on wearing it. And you might imagine he couldn't look any more ridiculous, but you'd be wrong. What he hadn't realised was that there was a massive hole in the crotch area and his family jewels, in all their glory, were hanging loose and free. And I can promise you this, gravity has been no friend to Pip in that department.'

Kitty's eyes widened, and she held up her hands in a "stop now" gesture. 'Whoah! Please, no more. That's gone beyond way too much information. And where on earth did the boys get that onesie from?'

'They bought it online. It was meant to be a joke, but Pip's decided he likes it. Not sure how he managed to put a hole in it though. Probably too much fiddling. I sometimes wonder if he's got a magnet in that region that pulls his hand down; he's always subconsciously having a rummage of his balls, says it helps him think.'

'Oh, poor Pip.' Kitty rested her head in her hand, giggles shaking her shoulders. He'd be absolutely mortified if he knew that Molly was sharing such intimate details.

'And to complete the look, he was wearing a pair of fluffy bed socks, pulled up to just below his knees with the legs of the onesie tucked right in. Then he climbed into bed, grabbed a magazine and read till he fell asleep and it fell on his face! Who said romance is dead?' She shrugged.

'Oh, bless him. What does he think about the baby? I bet he's thrilled, is he?'

Molly pursed her lips and looked across at Kitty. 'Haven't told him yet. You're the only one who knows.'

'Okay.'

'Don't know how to tell him really. But, most of all, I'm dreading telling the boys. Can you imagine how much it's going to freak them out, the thought of their parents having sex? It's bad enough it freaks me out – the baby, not the sex – although it is pretty freaky. And to cap it all, Pip's raring to go with the farm. He's brimming with ideas of how we can diversify. You know, get a campsite going. He's been talking of nothing else. How we can build camping pods, do up old VW camper vans, old gypsy caravans. And he even came home with an original nineteen thirties train carriage yesterday, with plans to turn that into accommodation. Don't get me wrong, I love all of his ideas, but my mind's all over the place at the minute.' She puffed a stray curl out of her face.

Kitty leaned across the table and squeezed her cousin's hand. 'Listen, Moll. You've never been one to back away from a challenge. In fact, I'd say you positively thrive on them. Just look at how you were when you fell pregnant with the twins. I think a challenge actually brings out the best in you. And we both know the campsite is a fantastic idea; this area's crying out for one, and you and Pip are the best people to do it with all of your amazing ideas. Granted, some might say the timing is a bit, er…

'Crap?'

'Well, to some people it could be described as that, but would you let it stop you from doing something you'd set your heart on? I don't think you would. You've been saying how ready you both are for a new adventure, or challenge, and you've been fed up of your job for as long as I can remember. I think you should go for it! I'll help out with the baby whenever I can, and the twins already love helping on the farm as it is. And with your plans for diversification, it's created ready-made jobs for them when they leave school. I'd say the timing was pretty good there, wouldn't you?' Kitty could see the sparkle creeping back into her cousin's eyes.

Molly mulled over her cousin's words. 'I hadn't thought of it like that. But we're talking about a couple of challenges all at once. And pretty big ones at that. Oh, bugger, I need a wee again. It's all I seem to do at the moment, well, that or puke,' she called behind her as she ran off to the loo.

MRS PRUDOM HAD FOUND Lily's missing envelope in Evie Mellison's drawer, together with a pair of Lily's PE shorts. 'I think we need to have a word with your parents,' she'd said to Evie, whose already pale complexion turned translucent.

Only Aoife Mellison was available for an appointment that afternoon at the end of the school day. Her husband's mobile phone had gone straight to voicemail. 'Well, I s'pose there's no signal in the Fox and Hounds up at Danskelfe,' Ella had said sarcastically as she handed Mrs Prudom a cup of tea.

The meeting hadn't gone well, with Aoife refusing to accept what

Mrs Prudom told her, saying that somebody else must have put the things in Evie's draw, before going on to accuse Kitty of having it in for her daughter.

'The problem always harks back to the parents.' The head had observed to the other staff later.

31

AFTER THE LATEST MELLISON DRAMA, Kitty was looking forward to having a quiet evening with just herself and the kids. It had saddened her to think that little Lily had been having to deal with being bullied at school on top of coping with the drama of her father moving out. But the resilience of both her children impressed her more than she could say. Admittedly, Dan hadn't been much of a presence in their lives; always finding an excuse not to be around, either by staying back late at work, locking himself in his study or simply having to go out. And when he was around, he usually filled the house with tension, sniping at the kids and belittling her. She figured they'd subconsciously recognised that life was simply more peaceful when their father wasn't around, which appeared to make the break-up easier for them to cope with.

They were good kids, she thought to herself, as she stirred home-made custard in a pan. They deserved a treat, something nice to look forward to. Lucas had suggested ice-skating at the designer outlet; that sounded like fun. And Lily had mentioned the latest animated film that had just been released. They could combine both and grab a bite to eat somewhere – it would be pizza no doubt; both kids loved pizza.

Her thoughts were interrupted by a knock at the door. 'Lucas, can you get that please?' she called, not wanting to leave the custard in case the eggs in it scrambled.

'Can't Lily do it? I'm busy,' his voice wafted down from his bedroom.

'I asked you. And if I leave this custard, it'll be ruined, so there'll be nothing to pour over the chocolate puds we're having for tea.'

The threat was enough. 'I'm there!' He flew out of his bedroom and slid down the bannister, arriving at the door just as there was another, more insistent knock. 'Tada!' he said, followed by, 'Oh.'

Whisking busily, Kitty turned to see Henry Wilkinson in the doorway of the kitchen.

'Hi, Kitty.' He smiled. 'How are you?'

'Oh, Henry. This is a surprise. Sorry, I can't leave this, or it'll spoil,' she nodded towards the pan and, feeling slightly awkward, carried on with her whisking. *Why on earth is Henry here?*

'Oh, er, yes. I do apologise, I should've rung to see if it was convenient to call, but it was a spur of the moment thing really, and I was just passing.' He gulped. 'Er, Dan told me what happened. Well, bits really. Said you'd, er, separated and I've, er, been worried about you. Couldn't get you off my mind actually. And I, er, I thought you might like these.' He thrust a large bouquet of blowsy, pink roses interspersed with frilly clouds of gypsophila towards her.

'Oh, thank you.' She slid the pan off the hotplate and took the flowers. Kitty took in the name written in swirly gold letters on the cellophane of the bouquet. "Bloomz", York's most expensive florists; they would have cost a fortune. Somehow, Kitty doubted Henry's visit was spur of the moment.

Feeling confused and uncomfortable, she thanked him and busied herself putting the flowers in a jug of cold water. Awkwardness filled the kitchen. It made Kitty gabble while Henry simply nodded, conversation apparently eluding him. She didn't want to appear rude, but she really wished he would just go home. Good manners, however, got the better of her and, as it was obvious that Henry was in no rush to leave, she felt obliged to invite him to join her and the children for dinner. He accepted wholeheartedly, much to her dismay.

HENRY WILKINSON WAS A SHORT, slightly rotund man who, at the age of thirty- two, was blighted by premature balding and excessively ruddy cheeks. But, as if to compensate, nature had bestowed upon him a pair of striking cornflower-blue eyes, rimmed with thick, dark lashes that sat beneath a pair of luxurious black eyebrows. No one could deny there was something handsome about him. He was also incredibly kind-hearted and, much to his annoyance, had been described as sweet on more than one occasion. 'What man wants a woman to think he's sweet?' he'd asked Dan, who'd sniggered in response.

Henry also held a torch for Kitty. One that had been burning away quietly. Until now…

'Have you heard from Dan?'

Kitty shook her head. 'No, nothing.'

'Ah. That's probably because he's taken himself off on holiday for a few weeks with an old adversary from his university days.'

'Oh, I didn't know that.' She looked puzzled; Dan clearly wouldn't be visiting the children this weekend as he'd promised.

'Er, it's a male friend,' Henry clarified hastily.

'Well, he's free to do as he pleases now.' She began to set the table. Henry lifted his elbows, so she could place a table mat in front of him.

'Anything I can do to help?' he asked eagerly.

'Er, no thanks. Everything's taken care of.'

Sitting around the table, the children eyed him suspiciously as they ate. They'd only met Henry a handful of times – usually in chambers – and couldn't work out why he was here, having dinner with them.

'I think your mummy looks extremely lovely with her new haircut, don't you?' He beamed at Kitty while Lucas and Lily nodded, chomping on mouthfuls of beef stew.

'Thank you.' Blushing, she self-consciously touched the nape of her neck. 'I'm still getting used to it.' Lord, how she hated this; she wished time would speed up, and Henry would leave so she and the children could feel comfortable in their own home.

Throughout the meal, Henry showered her with countless unwanted compliments that chipped away at her patience. The evening meal which, since Dan's departure, had become a place of catch-up and lively chatter, was eaten in an atmosphere of stilted awkwardness, punctuated by little scraps of small-talk.

The kids seized the first opportunity to leave the room, leaving Kitty and Henry alone in the kitchen. 'Can I get you a tea or coffee before you go?' She was clearing the plates from the table, aware that her hint may be a little unsubtle. She was willing him to say no and just go home; this all felt way too uncomfortable.

'Coffee would be lovely, thanks.' He smiled, and she felt her heart sink. 'That was a delicious meal, you really are a wonderful cook.' He stretched out his dumpy legs and rubbed his stomach, his shirt pulled taut across it, putting the buttons under considerable strain. Kitty expected them to start pinging off around the room at any minute.

She made the coffee as quickly as she could and busied herself with little jobs around the kitchen, hoping Henry would get the hint and announce his departure. She felt a tiny prickle of guilt; he was a decent man, full of good intentions. But she just wished he'd direct them somewhere else.

'Aren't you going to come and sit down and drink your coffee? You deserve a rest after cooking such a spectacular meal.'

She groaned inwardly. Unable to think of a suitable excuse she sat down opposite him and began fiddling with her nails. He seized the moment. Pulling himself up straight he cleared his throat. 'Erm, look, I, erm. I'm, erm, not very good at this sort of thing and I, erm, don't really know how to say this, but here goes anyway.' He cleared his throat again and directed his full attention towards her. 'I think Dan's crazy for what he's done. Everyone in chambers thinks so, too. All of those other women have nothing on you. Absolutely nothing. He's a total fool to leave you and the children.'

Kitty's heart began to gallop; this was awful on so many levels.

He took a sip of his coffee and continued, clearing his throat once more. 'Kitty, dearest Kitty. I know it's early days for you, but I was wondering if you could ever think of me…'

Oh. My. God. I can't be hearing this. Please stop. Please Stop! Panic clawed its way up inside her. 'Gosh, is that the time? I really must…' Henry cut her off, reaching for her hand.

'Please let me finish, Kitty, darling.'

Darling? Oh, no! 'Henry, I…'

'Kitty, I think an awful lot about you and I want you to know that I'm here for you. And your adorable children, too. If there's anything, anything at all, I can do to help I'd be delighted if you'd allow me that honour.' His bright blue eyes were boring into hers like laser beams, rendering her speechless. 'And I'd like to think that, in time, when you're ready, of course, you could look at us being more than friends and allow our relationship to graduate to the next level?' He pressed her hand to his lips.

The next level? Panic plundered Kitty's mind. She needed to get herself out of this situation, and Henry out of her house.

'Look, Henry, that's very kind of you, but I've never thought of you in that way. And, even if I did, I'm not ready for a relationship. And I won't be for quite some time.' She tried to wriggle her hand out of his, but his grip was surprisingly tight and was beginning to hurt. She was momentarily distracted by voices in the hall.

Undeterred, he cleared his throat again. 'I'm prepared to wait for you for as long as it takes. You're a woman worth waiting for, Kitty, and I know we're perfect for each other.' As he placed another wet kiss onto the back of her hand, his eyes were drawn to the doorway. 'Who are you?' he said with a scowl.

Kitty turned, relief washing over her as she saw Ollie's frame filling the doorway. 'Ollie.'

'Who's Ollie? You never mentioned an Ollie.' Henry, still clinging onto her hand, was visibly annoyed.

Ollie misread Kitty's expression of discomfort for one of disappointment that he'd turned up unannounced. He didn't notice that she was struggling to release her hand from Henry's grip.

'Sorry to interrupt. I didn't know you were entertaining anyone. I'll catch you later. It wasn't important.' Seeing her having what was obviously an intimate conversation with another man was like a body-blow. Wondering whether this stranger was the reason she hadn't wanted to take things further the other night, he about-turned and made to leave.

Kitty jumped up, snatching her hand out of Henry's. 'Ollie, wait!' she cried. But it was too late; by the time she got to the door she could hear the roar of his pick-up as he drove off down the road. Frustrated, she ran her fingers through her short curls then turned to Henry who'd followed her into the hall. 'I don't mean to be rude, Henry, but I think you'd probably better leave now.'

This was her home, and she needed to start as she meant to go on, by putting herself and her children first.

'But, but, we've had such a lovely time. I was going to ask you out for a drink so we could get to know each other better. I wanted to show you how it was to feel special, to be treated as you deserve, but you're…'

'I'm sorry, Henry. I didn't ask you to come here. I don't know what's given you the idea that I would be interested in starting a relationship with you. You're a nice man, but I really don't think of you in that way. I never have, and I never will. I'm sorry if it sounds unkind, but the kids and I have been through a hell of a lot recently, and we just need some time without having to deal with stuff like this. It's not fair on them.' She lifted his coat from the hook by the door and handed it to him. 'Goodbye, Henry.'

His plump cheeks blazed scarlet. 'Well, thank you for your honesty, Kitty. I'm sorry I got it so wrong and made you and the children feel uncomfortable. I'm a clumsy oaf; terrible at this sort of thing – clearly.' He shrugged his coat on. 'I genuinely wish you all the best for the future. You and the children deserve to be happy. Goodbye, Kitty.' He held out his hand, and she shook it.

'Bye, Henry.' She gave a small smile. 'I hope you find someone who truly deserves you.'

He walked past her and out into the cool of the evening.

'Phew!' She leaned against the front door, her thoughts quickly turning to Ollie.

32

'CAN you bake some chocolate squidgy, Mummy?' asked Lily, her curls bouncing as she jumped up and down excitedly. 'For when Bryn comes to tea.'

Lucas sniggered. 'It's chocolate *roulade,* silly. Only babies call it chocolate squidgy.'

'Lukes,' said Kitty, giving his shoulder a squeeze. 'We've always called it chocolate squidgy; ask Uncle Jimby.'

'Yeah, well, Lily's just acting like a big baby.'

'I am not, Lucas. You're just a big meany, isn't he, Mummy?'

Since Dan had left, her wonderful boy had assumed the role of man of the house; bringing in logs from the wood-store, feeding Humph and Ethel and sweeping the path — not that Dan had ever done any of these things. But Kitty guessed that, with Bryn's imminent visit, Lucas might be feeling anxious about his position in the family hierarchy.

'I think he's just teasing, aren't you, Lukes?'

Lucas nodded with a grunt as Kitty folded her arms around him. 'And I know that when Bryn gets to know you two a little bit better, he's going to think you're both totally full of awesome gorgeousness.' She held out her arms for Lily to join them. 'Come on, Lils, group hug!' With an enthusiastic squeal, Lily ran across and squeezed herself between her mum and her brother.

'Ow, Lils, that's my foot you're jumping on.' Lucas's face was flushed, making his freckles all but disappear. 'Can he come on Saturday, Mum?'

'I'll see if he's free.' She kissed the tops of their heads, whispering into Lucas's ear, 'Thanks for being so grown up and lovely about this.'

'The quiff, Mum,' he warned with a smile, pointing to his fringe.

DURING THEIR CHAT in the tea room at Middleton-le-Moors, Kitty had warmed to Bryn. He'd reminded her of Lucas, not just in appearance, but mannerisms, too, like the way he looked up at the ceiling and scratched his forehead when he was thinking about something or searching for the right word. It tapped into her maternal feelings, making her heart ache with sadness for this boy who'd been so badly let down by Dan. He was clearly thrilled at the thought of having a half-brother and half-sister and was eager to get to know them better, to be a part of their lives, with or without Dan.

Kitty had spoken to Karen, his mum, and it was agreed that a good starting point would be if he could come to tea one Saturday afternoon. The conversation had been awkward at first, but nowhere near as uncomfortable as she'd expected; Karen had sounded friendly and warm. For a fleeting moment, Kitty thought about inviting her, too, but quickly shooed the idea away before it had time to take root. That would have been strange on so many levels.

But it still didn't stop her from thinking how weird it was to have the boy, who was the result of her husband's affair with another woman, round for tea. Even putting it into words was complicated.

'Why the bloody hell are you doing that?' asked Vi.

'Because that's the sort of thing Kitty does; you know what she's like,' said Molly. She'd called in at Oak Tree Farm with Vi, one evening.

'You'll be walking on water next,' Vi teased.

'Ha ha. You're so funny, the pair of you. I just felt so sorry for him when Dan said, you know…what he did, and again when I saw him in Middleton. He's a good kid, and desperate for siblings. And the situation's not his fault.'

'True,' agreed Violet. 'And to think, all this time, he was living just a few miles away and you didn't even know he existed.'

'I know, it's weird,' said Kitty.

'What's even weirder is that Dan had been forking out for him for all of these years. That would make my blood boil if it was me. Prat!' Molly shook her head; she no longer bothered to hide her feelings for Dan.

'I'm not about to defend him, but it didn't surprise me that he'd contributed to Bryn's upbringing. He may be many things – prat included – but Dan's not tight. I know he was controlling with me in that department when we were married, but he now makes sure that there's always enough in my account for the kids and me to be okay.'

'Proof that miracles do actually happen,' Vi said. 'Dan Fairfax-Bennett has a redeeming feature.'

'All of that aside, I'm just trying to do the right thing. And I don't want to take on the role of the bitter and twisted ex-wife; it takes up too much energy.' As far as Kitty was concerned, the lad had a right to get to know his half-siblings. Just as Lucas and Lily had a right to get to know him; and she wasn't going to get in the way of that. Of course, Dan would be furious when he found out. But Dan was furious about everything; only the impact of his anger didn't have the power it once had.

BRYN WAS AS EXCITED as his two younger half-siblings and was delighted when Saturday came around so quickly. James was going to be there, too, which pleased him. He was friendly, easy to talk to, and Bryn had felt a bond between them. What would his relationship to James be? Uncle? He wasn't sure. His mum didn't have any siblings, so he'd grown up without any aunts, uncles or cousins. But now he was suddenly being welcomed into the arms of a warm and loving family. He belonged. At last.

33

'I DON'T KNOW what's wrong with Ollie, but he hasn't half seen his arse. It's not like him at all.' Jimby was trying to pick the corner off the freshly baked chocolate squidgy Kitty had just taken out of the Aga. 'Ow, bugger! That's hot!' He sucked his burnt finger.

'That's what you get for trying to pinch it before it's cooled down. Here, run your finger under some cold water.' She smiled, turning on the cold tap. 'Anyway, what were you saying about Ollie? Is he okay?'

'No idea what's up with him, but he's a right grouchy arse.' James shrugged, heading over to the sink. 'He's even talking about there being nothing here for him and Noushka anymore, and how it would be better for them to move away.'

Kitty's heart plummeted. She hadn't seen Ollie since he'd caught Henry holding her hand, and she had the distinct impression he was avoiding her. Just yesterday, she'd been talking to Big Mary outside the village shop when he'd walked by on the other side of the road, head down, hands thrust deep in his pockets; he'd barely acknowledge her. Trapped in conversation, Kitty watched as he'd climbed into his pick-up and driven off out of the village.

Jimby returned to the squidgy armed with a knife. 'Here, let me do it,' she said, taking the knife off him and easing the cake out. She placed a slice on a plate and handed it to him. 'That's rather sudden, not to say drastic. I wonder how Noushka feels about it?'

He popped a piece into his mouth, chewing on it quickly, shifting its heat around. 'Hmm. It'd be bloody tragic if they left this place. It's their home, and there's a lot of people who care about them here. And it would feel like losing my right arm for me. Life in Lytell Stangdale without Ollie Cartwright? Doesn't bear thinking about.' James shook his head. 'This is delicious, by the way.'

'Thanks. I agree – about Ollie, that is.' Her voice was small, and she sensed her brother's eyes on her. Now wasn't the time, but tomorrow she'd bite the bullet and pop over to Ollie's house. If he was thinking along those lines because he'd got the wrong impression the other day, then she needed to get it straightened out. And soon.

THE AFTERNOON with Bryn was a success, and everyone was sorry when it was time for him to head home.

Kitty was impressed with the level of patience he'd shown Lucas and Lily, and how he seemed genuinely keen to hear what they had to say, almost savouring every word. He'd shown Lucas some tricks and cheats on his computer games and listened as Lily introduced him to her collection of soft toys.

In turn, Bryn had found that elusive thing he'd been so desperate to be a part of: a loving family. Granted, his father wasn't involved, but Kitty and the children more than made up for that. James, too, with his school-boyish sense of humour and how he always tried to make a joke out of everything. And when Lily had told him he reminded her of Lucas, he'd beamed with happiness.

34

CHECKING THE TIME AGAIN, Gwyneth paced the hallway. It was almost seven-thirty. Unable to wait a moment longer, she snatched up the phone and speed-dialled Dan's number. The vitriol of what she was so desperate to share with her son had been slowly eroding a hole in her gut, and the sooner she could expel it in a malicious, angry spew the better. She knew there was the risk that her news could upset him, but she felt sure it would just be short-term. What was more important was that he realised he'd been married to a worthless whore. A woman he'd married against her better judgement. And her latest information would prove her right.

Gwyneth counted the rings, cursing as it went to voicemail. She tried his new landline number and could feel her anger boiling as the answer-phone clicked in. 'Daniel, this is your mother! Pick up your phone! Where are you? Why aren't you answering my calls? I need you to call me immediately, I have something urgent to tell you.'

Dan had told her his flight from Thailand was due to land just before midnight, then there was the long drive up the motorway from Manchester to York. But impatience had erased her reasoning, and she was desperate to spill her guts. To tell him that she'd seen his supposed sweet and innocent wife going into Oliver Cartwright's house late one night while he was away. How she'd seen the silhouette of a couple behind the bedroom curtains. She wouldn't mention how she'd seen Kitty leave before anything would have had chance to happen. That was a mere detail.

GROANING, Dan pulled his pillow over his head in an attempt to block out the sound of the landline ringing in the open-plan living area of his city centre apartment. Whoever it was, he thought, they were bloody persistent.

He was knackered. His flight had been delayed by a couple of hours and, thanks to bloody roadworks, there'd been a stream of diversions on the A57 back up to York, adding an extra hour and a half onto his journey time. With barely any sleep the last thing he needed was to be woken by the sodding phone ringing, especially when it would only be chambers calling about work. He was still on holiday time, and they could bloody well wait.

He was also suffering the consequences of a two-day bender and was nursing the mother of all hangovers. At least he'd had the foresight to book the rest of the week out, and the way he felt right now, he'd be sleeping for most of that.

The flat fell silent as whoever had been calling eventually gave up. Dan went to roll onto his back. 'Arghhh!' Prickles of sweat peppered his brow. He was gripped by a spasm of searing hot pain as his skin made contact with the sheet. A grim reminder of a moment of holiday madness. Tentatively, he moved back onto his side, but the pain was unbearable. What the hell had he been thinking? What demon from hell had possessed him to go to the nearest, not to mention shabbiest, tattoo studio down some back street, and allow the equally shabby tattoo artist to needle a gaudy image into his skin? And if the tattoo was in proportion to the pain, the bloody thing would be massive. He could barely remember what he'd asked for, but a vague image of a dragon was swirling around his mind, together with the memory of his travel companion, Chris Naylor, sniggering while he waved a wad of Thai Baht around. He groaned at the thought, running his fingers through his unwashed hair.

CHRIS WAS an old adversary of Dan's from their university days. On the surface, they'd always got on well, but underneath ran a pernicious rivalry that had occasionally manifested itself in nasty spats, particularly when booze or women were involved.

Their paths hadn't crossed for years, until three weeks ago when they'd bumped into each other in a bar in York. Chris was recently divorced and had just moved back to the city after being offered a tenancy at Gallows Hill Chambers. They'd got talking about the evils of women and, after a few bottles of wine, they'd decided that a couple of weeks in the sun would do them both good. Chris had suggested Thailand and the delights it had to offer; he was a regular visitor and didn't need much of an excuse to go back. Dan jumped at the suggestion.

The following morning the pair had sauntered into Cheap Dealz holiday shop and booked flights to Bangkok.

DAN HAD MANAGED to drift back off to sleep when his landline started to ring again. 'Bugger off,' he yelled after the fifth, or was it the sixth, time? The phone obliged.

Lying in the comfort of his bed, he was hoping sleep would reclaim him, but the dull thud of a headache had begun to throb at his forehead, making it impossible. It didn't help that his tongue was so dry it was sticking to the roof of his mouth. Wondering if his breath smelt as bad as it tasted, he cupped his hand over his mouth, huffed into it and sniffed. 'Christ! That could melt eyeballs.' Reluctantly, he threw back the duvet and stumbled his way to the bathroom, his hand against his brow as he searched for any form of analgesic relief he could lay his hands on.

The cabinet offered up a thin strip of paracetamol, containing two tablets. He gulped them down gratefully with a tumbler-full of cold water, wincing at the ensuing brain-freeze it triggered. He peered into the mirror, wondering if it was possible that he could look as bad as he felt. His bloodshot eyes, aching as they struggled to focus, confirmed his fears.

A stab of pain shot across his back, reminding him of the tattoo. He angled himself towards the mirror and peered over his shoulder at the artwork. A wave of nausea washed over him as he took in the large image of a fire-breathing dragon. 'Oh shit!'

KITTY WAS LEAVING the village hall after dropping the children off there. It was Abbie Webster's birthday party, and she was having a bouncy castle followed by a magician, and the place was teeming with excited children. Calling goodbye to Abbie's mum, Rosie, she turned out of the gate to see Aoife and her two children heading towards her. She had a face like thunder and Kitty's heart plummeted. She'd been anxious about bumping into them after the incident at school.

'Morning,' she said, her voice breezy. There was no reply. Instead she received an icy glare from Aoife, whose eyes bulged in a way that reminded Kitty of a highly-strung horse. Evie, true to form, stuck out her tongue and the pair barged past her. This was exactly the situation she'd hoped to avoid. Living in a small community like Lytell Stangdale made it unbearable.

Putting the encounter behind her, she headed towards Ollie's house. She'd been thinking things over and was desperate to clear the air with him. If he was serious about moving away, she wanted to see if there was anything she could say to make him change his mind. Since the Henry situation, their relationship had taken a huge backwards step, and she was keen to pull them back to where they'd been before he'd got the wrong end of the stick.

It was a clear, fresh day and fluffy white clouds scudded across a crisp blue sky, chivvied along by a light breeze. Feeling chilly, Kitty pushed her hands into her pockets and crossed the road, suddenly feeling nervous. Once outside Rose Cottage, her heart began to beat a little faster. Taking a deep breath, she knocked on the door.

She waited a moment. No one came to answer, but she was sure she could hear movement inside. She knocked again, this time a little harder. Within seconds the door was flung open, revealing a heavily made-up woman wearing a sour expression. Kitty took in the shock of harsh blonde hair with its inch of dark roots running down a poker-straight centre parting.

'Yes, what do you want?' she asked in a strong accent, her almond-shaped eyes narrowing as she looked Kitty up and down. 'Well, come on. I don't have all day.'

'Oh, erm. I was looking for Ollie.'

The woman arched a skinny eyebrow. 'He's out with Anoushka. Anything else?'

'Er, no. Could you just tell him Kitty called?'

The woman sneered. 'Hmph. I might. If I remember.' With that, the door was slammed in her face.

What the hell was that all about? Shaken, Kitty stood for a second.

As she headed towards her home a niggle began to develop at the back of her mind; there was something vaguely familiar about that woman, the Slavic eyes…the accent…Kitty racked her brains trying to remember where she knew her from, but the elusive wisp of memory remained just out of reach. A feeling in her gut told her something didn't feel right. She'd mention her to Jimby, see if he was any the wiser.

Spotting Gwyneth fussing over something in her front garden, Kitty put her head down and hurried along the trod. She could do without any confrontation from that one today.

As she continued on her way, her mind leapt between the situation with Ollie and the documents she'd received from Letitia Tickell in the post that morning. She'd planned on making the most of having the house to herself, so she could read through and sign any forms before posting them on the way to collect the kids from the party. It was another step forward in the divorce proceedings, and she was determined to keep the ball rolling.

'Kitts.' A voice broke through her thoughts. 'Kitty, wait up.' She turned to see Molly leaving the village shop, a newspaper wedged under her arm and two double packs of custard creams in her hands.

'Hiya, Moll. How're you diddlin'?' She smiled at her cousin, who was looking flustered.

'Better in health than temper, I can tell you.' She blew a stray strand of hair off her face. 'Have I told you how much I hate my bloody job?'

'Er, once or twice, maybe.' Kitty gave her a sympathetic smile. Molly had been grumbling about her job for as far back as she could remember.

'Well, I really bloody hate it today. I've only gone and been dragged into doing bloody over-time this weekend. They put me on a late shift last night, and I'm on again at two o'clock this afternoon. They seem to have forgotten I'm a part-timer and only supposed to do three days a week, but I've been in every single bloody one for eight days on the trot. I don't know when they expect me to get some sleep, never mind see my family.' Molly took a deep breath and released it noisily. 'Sorry, Kitts, that was a bit of a rant, wasn't it?' Her cheeks were flushed, the tell-tale signs of stress in her eyes.

Kitty rubbed her cousin's arm. 'You look like you could do with a nice cup of tea. Come on, bring those yummy biccies back to mine and I'll stick the kettle on.'

IN THE WARMTH of the kitchen at Oak Tree Farm, Molly visibly relaxed. She slipped her jacket over the back of the chair by the Aga and flopped down wearily. 'Anyway, missus, how's things?'

'Things are good.'

'You look well, actually. Got a bit of colour back in your cheeks. Divorce proceedings clearly suit you.'

Kitty pulled a wry face. 'Not sure that's the expression I'd use, but things are definitely easier. The difference in the kids is just the biggest surprise; they're so upbeat. And I hadn't even realised how they'd crept around the house until they stopped doing it. Poor things were permanently wary of upsetting Dan.'

'Kitty, from where I'm sitting, there's lots of proof it's the right thing to do, and don't, for one second, let anyone – especially him or that toxic old witch of a mother of his – tell you otherwise.' Molly stretched out her legs and rubbed her bare feet across Humph's rotund stomach. 'And it's good to see this lad looking better.'

'It is; he's a special lad,' Kitty said fondly.

'He is, well, apart from his smelly farts. They're getting worse you know, especially with that new food you're giving him. What is it again, "Farter"? Very apt.'

'"Fitter".' Kitty laughed at the face her cousin pulled as she threw a clutch of teabags into the teapot. 'Anyway, wind or no wind, I'm just glad he's okay, and so is Ethel, she'd be lost without him. He's always so upbeat, his tail's always wagging.'

'That right, Eth? You're chuffed your old fella's alright are you?' Ethel wagged her tail at hearing her name mentioned, trotting over to Molly and placing her head in her lap. Molly obliged by rubbing Eth's velvety ears.

'Anyway, how're you doing? Have you told Pip about the baby yet?'

Molly groaned and rubbed her face with the palms of her hands. 'I'm feeling so knackered all the time. Much more so than I did with the twins, and I've been having the maddest craving for custard creams.' She licked her lips at the thought of them. 'I've just bought the last two double-packs from the shop and I'm sure they're getting suspicious. And, no, I haven't told Pip yet. We never seem to have a minute to ourselves to discuss the price of cheese, never mind an unplanned pregnancy.' She fondled Ethel's ears some more.

The kettle began to whistle, Kitty lifted it off the Aga. 'You sound like you've got a lot on at the minute, Moll. Just be careful you don't over-do it.'

Molly sighed. 'And poor old Dad, he's worse than I thought. His medication isn't working so well anymore, and he's been falling over. He didn't want Mum to tell me, but I saw it myself yesterday. He's had an appointment at the hospital, and they prescribed some new tablets, but Mum seemed to think the consultant didn't sound too optimistic. He's giving them a try, but the sooner we get sorted out with the farm, the better. And I just don't know how to break the news about the baby to any of them.' Molly was putting on a brave face and hiding behind her usual tough exterior, but Kitty could see just how upset she was.

'Oh, Moll, I'm so sorry.'

'My head's all over the place what with everything that's going on. And with work being so full-on, I haven't had a minute to think about anything. I just keep wondering how a baby's going to fit in with all of it. Just a mug of boiled water thanks, still can't face tea.'

'It might help if you told Pip about the baby. Maybe relieve a bit of the pressure?' She watched Molly unravel the biscuit wrapper, offering the packet to her. She took a couple. 'Thanks, it's ages since I've had one of these. Sorry, Humph, it's no use sucking your cheeks in and trying to look like you're starving. These aren't for you. Go on, back to your basket.' Kitty turned to Molly. 'I swear he's North Yorkshire's greediest Labrador. Go on. Basket! You too, Eth.' Kitty pointed in the general direction of the dog bed, watching as Humph did the walk of shame across the kitchen, a woeful expression on his face, occasionally turning back to make sure his mum really meant it.

'At least Eth doesn't goz like Humph.' Molly split a biscuit in two, scraping the cream off with her bottom teeth, before popping it into her mouth.

'I'm sure it's only a matter of time. Anyway, what were we saying? Oh, yes, don't you think it would relieve the burden a bit if you told Pip about the baby?'

'That's easier said than done. Whenever I think about telling him, I can't seem to find the right moment or the right words.'

'Well, for what it's worth, I think the sooner you tell him, the better. He loves babies, and he's always wanted a little girl. I honestly think he'll be over the moon.'

'Mmm. But what if it's another boy? Oh, shit a brick, that'll mean even more stinky socks in the house. It's already over-run with them.' Molly sighed, pushing a whole biscuit into her mouth.

35

THE SOUND of a text arriving alerted Dan to the whereabouts of his mobile phone. Snatching it up, he saw that there had been a slew of missed calls, texts and one voicemail message. He half hoped there'd been something from Kitty, begging his forgiveness and asking him to move back home. Fat chance of that though; she'd become far too selfish.

Dan checked his missed calls, groaning when he saw they were all from his mother. He suspected it was her who'd been calling the landline, too; she was nothing if not persistent. Reluctant as he was, he knew that if he didn't call her back, she'd be round, hammering on the door and giving him an ear-bashing, complaining about the state of the flat. He pressed redial and braced himself.

It was the last thing he expected to hear. Kitty and Oliver sodding Cartwright? His brain, swathed in the remnants of an alcohol-induced fug, stumbled over the information his mother had just imparted. Surely, she must have got it wrong?

'Well? What are you going to do about it, Daniel? You can't just take this lying down. The inbred slut needs teaching a lesson. She's made a fool out of you in front of the whole village and must not be allowed to get away with it. Does she know who she's dealing with? She's just a common village girl, and you are Daniel Bennett, and she's disrespected you. How dare she, Daniel? How dare she?' Gwyneth was gasping, such was her outrage.

As Dan's hazy mind began to process his mother's words, he

could feel his anger begin to simmer. He knew Oliver Cartwright had never stopped mooning over Kitty, he could see it in those pathetic puppy dog eyes he made at her. But was it possible that she still felt something for him, even after all these years?

'Daniel! Are you listening to me? What are you going to do about it? You've got to do something! You can't just let her get away with it! I warned you! I warned you about her, but you wouldn't listen.'

Gwyneth's voice was beginning to feel like a sharp knife, the words stabbing into his head. 'That's enough, Mother! I'll deal with it, but you going on at me like that doesn't help. Just back off and let me sort her out.'

Gwyneth smiled; that was all she needed to hear.

KITTY PULLED her woolly hat further onto her head and shivered; the temperature had taken a nose-dive since she'd dropped the kids off at Abbie's party. The wind had changed direction and now carried an icy chill that savaged any exposed areas of skin.

As she hurried along, she passed Gerald,who was sweeping up leaves in his garden. His snug-fitting jumper bore all the hallmarks of Big Mary's knitting skills.

'Hi, Gerald.'

'Hello there, Kitty, pet. It's a bit nippy now what with that north wind whipping up. Think I'm wasting me time here. As fast as I sweep these little buggers up another load gets blown around in their place.' Brushing a straggle of stray hairs from his face, he nodded at the pile of leaves that took off and scurried around the garden.

Kitty laughed, mostly at the new false teeth that he was still getting to grips with. 'I think you're probably right. And it is suddenly so much colder.'

'Aye, it is that, pet. And I can smell snow.' He stuck his nose – red with the cold, and too much cheap wine – into the air and sniffed. 'Oh, aye, mark my words, I wouldn't be surprised if we woke to a canny covering of the white stuff in the morning.'

'The kids would love that.'

'Aye, all bairns love the snow. Never seem to feel the cold, they don't.'

'Unlike the rest of us.' She swallowed a giggle as his top set of teeth slipped forward when he smiled.

With a loud slurp, he sucked them back in, pressing them into place with a set of grubby fingers. 'You're not wrong there, pet.'

'Anyway, Gerald, I'd best be off. Good luck with the leaves and say hi to Mary for me.'

'Will do, petal.'

Drifting back into her own thoughts, Kitty made her way along the trod. She hadn't got far when she heard the harsh tones of a woman's voice carried along on the wind, slicing through the peace of the village. Whoever it was, they didn't sound very happy about something. Pitying whoever was on the receiving end, she rounded the corner, her gaze following the increasing volume of the tirade to the other side of the road.

'Hurry up! What on this earth is wrong with you? Can't you see I'm exhausted, you stupid man? You need to get everything inside before it starts to rain or worse.' Kitty stopped in her tracks. The woman barking out the orders was the blonde woman who'd slammed the door in her face at Ollie's the other day. And there she was again, in the doorway, hands on hips with a face like thunder, ordering Ollie around. He was heading up the garden path with Noushka; both their heads were bowed while their hands were laden with shopping bags in a variety of shapes and sizes. 'And where's the bag with the shoes?' The blonde woman threw her arms up dramatically and stomped down the path. 'If you've lost the bag with the shoes, you'll have to go right back to the shops and find it.'

Kitty's heart went out to Ollie and Noushka, neither of whom looked particularly happy. 'Don't talk to him like that,' she muttered under her breath. But, not wanting to be caught staring, she hurried along the path, hoping to pass by unnoticed. It wasn't to be; she looked up, finding herself fixed by the ice queen's chilly glare.

'What are you looking at?' Nataliya turned on her heel and flounced off into the house.

Kitty looked across at Ollie and Noushka, giving them a small smile. He looked embarrassed, wincing as the woman's voice leapt out of the door with more orders. Noushka looked pleadingly at her, and mouthed, 'Help,' before disappearing up the path behind her dad.

What on earth is going on at Rose Cottage? Feeling worried, she knew she needed to speak to Jimby as soon as possible. Hopefully, he'd be able to shed some light on the weird situation. But it would have to wait until she'd collected Lucas and Lily from Abbie's party.

As she crossed the road, she was treated to one of Aoife's customary scowls. She was leaving the village hall with her children. 'Come on, Evie, hurry up. You too, Teddy.' She was practically pushing them down the path and ignored Kitty's 'hello'.

Kitty's heart sank, she'd never get used to this sort of unpleasantness.

She opened the door to the village hall. Even though the party was over, there was still a gaggle of excitable children running around, screeching as balloons were popped.

As she headed over to Rosie, Lucas ran up to her, his face flushed, his hair saturated with sweat that sat in beads on his brow. 'Hiya, Mum.' He grinned, tipping a load of popping candy into his mouth and sticking his tongue out as it crackled.

'Hiya, Lukes. You look hot.' She went to press a hand to his forehead, laughing as he dodged out of her way.

'Mind the quiff, Mum.'

'Hi, Kitty. You've just missed Aoife.' Rosie gave her a knowing look.

'Not quite, she's just blanked me on my way in here.'

'She's a weird one. If it's any consolation, there are plenty of mums who say she looks down her nose at them. She seems to like me at the moment, but I think that's because I'm married to an architect, which apparently qualifies me as *suitable* friend material.'

'Lucky you. The snotty cow looks at me as if I'm dirt on her shoe.' Lianne, who'd come to collect her daughters, Lacey and Armarni, waded into the conversation, chomping on a glob of chewing gum. 'You should've seen her the other day, she just about elbowed me out of the way so she could catch up with Rosie on her dog walk.' She chewed more vigorously on her gum. 'And that frigging fake posh voice she puts on gets right on my wick.' Her lip curled in disgust while Kitty and Rosie struggled to contain their giggles. She nodded at Kitty. 'Thought she'd be okay with you, like, seeing as though your husband's one of them barristing people.'

'Hmm. She was fine at first, always pushing for the kids to play with each other, even when it wasn't convenient. It felt like she'd decided that they had to be best friends – though my two were never that keen. But something seems to have happened to make her change towards me.' Kitty watched as Lianne pulled her gum out of her mouth and stretched it round her finger.

'She's got the hots for your fella, that's what's happened.' Lianne pushed her gum back inside her mouth.

'Well, he recently left her in no doubt that it's totally unrequited. It was pretty embarrassing actually. And since then, they seem to have had it in for my family, especially poor little Lil.'

Rosie frowned. 'Hmm, I've got a funny feeling she's switched her attentions to my Robbie. She even invited her family to ours for tea on a Sunday. Just turned up on the doorstep.'

'Mmm. I seem to recall her doing that with us once. Dan didn't hang around, though. He sneaked out of the back door, which was a bit awkward when Aoife went hunting for him.'

'Flaming cheek of the woman! If it were me, I'd punch her lights out. I feel like that just looking at her. Stuck up cow acts like she's bloody village royalty.'

Kitty and Rosie exchanged glances; Lianne was clearly not someone you'd want to get on the wrong side of.

36

Gerald's forecast had been right, and the following morning Lytell Stangdale woke up to a light dusting of snow – not enough to make a snowman or go sledging, but enough to get the children of the village bouncing with excitement.

With his coat collar up, Dan huddled against the cold. He'd parked his car on the edge of Lytell Stangdale, out of sight of the residents of the village and, in particular, Kitty. He walked the short distance to the five-bar gate that gave entry to the field next to Oak Tree Farm. He opened it and slipped inside, tucking himself behind an overgrown hawthorn hedge, positioning himself so he could see his former home.

He didn't have long to wait. With an exuberant "whoop" Lucas bolted out of the house, hotly pursued by Lily, calling for him to wait up. Kitty followed, carrying their school bags, smiling as she watched them delight in throwing snowballs at each other, their peals of laughter filling the air. He felt a bristle of anger; how could they be so happy? He wasn't there anymore; wouldn't it be more appropriate for them to be miserable? Selfish little brats. And *she* was no better.

Dan hadn't seen the children since the day he left. He did his bit; making sure they were taken care of financially. Other than that, he wasn't interested, especially after that disrespectful little brat, Lucas, had punched him. And seeing them now failed to stir any dormant paternal feelings, failed to make him realise how much he missed them. Such feelings were extinct in him. If anything, it just reinforced his view that he wasn't cut out for family life.

Once Kitty and the children were out of view, he made his way to the cottage, letting himself in with the key he still had. He glanced around, sniffing as the warmth of the house made his cold nose run. Making his way into the kitchen, he saw the usual breakfast detritus of toast crumbs and half-drunk glasses of smoothie littering the table. Kitty's favourite mug stood by the sink, dregs of tea sitting in the bottom. He pushed it into the basin, watching as it shattered into a dozen pieces.

Ethel barked and jumped up from her bed in the utility room while Humph stayed put, watching him warily. Dan turned to see her pacing across the floor towards him, growling, her hackles bristling. He lunged across the kitchen and kicked the door shut before she could get to him. 'I don't think so.'

After dropping the kids off at school, Kitty snuggled her chin into her scarf and made her way home. It had started to snow again, and large, feathery flakes floated around her, quickly covering any recently made footprints and tyre tracks. If it carried on throughout the day, she'd dig the kids' sledges out of the shed. They'd be desperate to squeeze in a bit of sledging and snowman building before dark.

She passed Ollie's house, which stood tight-lipped and silent; not revealing any secrets. She'd get in touch with Jimby later this morning, see if he fancied coming over for dinner with her and the kids tonight. Hopefully, he'd have managed to find out something about the frosty blonde woman.

As Kitty walked on, her thoughts switched to Violet. She'd mentioned something about a big PR contract she'd landed that was keeping her busy, which was probably why she hadn't heard from her for a few days. There was definitely something of the romantic nature bubbling away between Jimby and her. She smiled to herself as she pushed open the gate, she hadn't really thought about it until now, but they were well matched. She'd have to make sure her brother didn't let Vi slip through his fingers.

Her musings were interrupted by barking coming from inside the cottage. Thinking it was odd for Humph and Ethel to give anything other than a cursory bark at the best of times, Kitty hurried up the path. As she put the key in the door and pushed it open, a feeling of foreboding trickled down her spine.

The kitchen door stood wide open, revealing the closed utility door at the far end. She frowned. She never closed it, it was where the Labrador's beds were, and they were allowed to roam free. The only person who used to close it was Dan, and it couldn't be him.

She glanced along the hallway, but only the metronome-like ticking of the grandfather clock accompanied Humph and Ethel's barking. The feeling of unease intensified, triggering a cold sweat that prickled on the surface of her skin. 'Hello,' she called, her voice wavering.

'Hello.' Dan stepped out from behind the kitchen door. His eyes, cold and unsmiling, were underlined with dark shadows. He was holding the photograph of the children she kept on the kitchen window-sill.

Startled, she dropped her keys. 'Dan. What are you doing here?' Hit by a wave of nausea, her stomach clenched, and her pulse pounded noisily in her ears. She leaned against the coffer to steady herself.

He fixed her with his gaze, his eyes boring into hers. Intimidated, Kitty looked away.

'You. Cheap. Tart.' His words jabbed at her, his tone eerily calm.

He began walking towards her, and she searched her mind frantically, desperate to find something neutral to say, something that would appease him. But the fingers of panic were squeezing tightly, creating a thick fug in her mind. 'Dan, what, I'm, I'm...I mean, I don't understand.'

'Don't play dumb with me, Kitty. You know exactly what I'm talking about.'

'Dan, please...'

'Two words: Oliver Cartwright.' Without missing a beat, he hurled the photograph at her. She gasped, cowering as it smashed into the wall behind her head, showering shards of glass everywhere. Fury blazed in his eyes as he lunged towards her, grabbing her face in his hand and squeezing hard. 'Look at me! I said, look at me! I hear you've been screwing around with that Cartwright loser.' His eyes were wild, his breath so foul Kitty was struggling not to gag.

She shook her head and tried to speak, but his grip was too tight.

'Don't even think about insulting my intelligence by trying to deny it.' He pushed her against the wall.

Her heart was hammering in her chest, her breathing shallow; he was really scaring her. She'd seen him get angry countless times, but this time it felt different. This time it felt dangerous. 'Dan, you're hurting me.' A tear spilled onto her cheek.

'Dan, you're hurting me,' he mimicked. 'You don't know the meaning of the word. I'll tell you what hurts. Finding out that your wife of however many bloody years has been screwing around right under your nose. That's what hurts.' His grip on her face increased.

'Oww! Dan, please listen. I don't know who told you that, but I haven't been doing anything with anyone.'

'Liar! My mother saw you at it with her own eyes.' His expression was wild, spittle gathered at the corners of his mouth. Kitty couldn't remember feeling so frightened of him. She willed herself to stay calm.

'That's not true, Dan. I don't know where she got that from. You know your mother doesn't like me, she never has. Please can we sit down and talk this through properly.' His fingers were digging deep into her face, and she could taste blood as her teeth bit into the inside of her cheek.

'Don't you dare talk about my mother like that. She knows what she saw, and what she saw was you slutting around.'

Tears welled, obscuring her vision. 'I haven't been slutting around. But, Dan, we're separated now, and it's time to move…'

'What?' His face was now inches away from hers. 'You think it's time to move on, do you?' He pushed her shoulder, knocking her off her feet. She fell to the ground, landing on the Persian rug that covered the hard flagstoned floor with a sickening thud. Pain seared through her head.

Dazed, Kitty lay motionless, only aware of the sound of her breathing that came in shallow gasps. She groaned, her head hurt, and her mouth was filled with the ferrous taste of blood. Mingling with the ringing in her ears, she was vaguely aware of Humph and Ethel barking and whining, scratching at the door to be out.

With her eyes tightly shut, she lay still for several seconds, her muscles taut with fear, aware only of her heart thudding in her chest and Dan's feral breathing that hung heavy in the air.

It didn't take long before the chill of the flagstones began seeping into her limbs, the combination of cold and fear making her shiver uncontrollably. Disorientated, she was uncertain for how long she'd been lying on the floor, but it felt like an age. Sensing Dan move towards her, she tensed. 'On your feet.' He yanked her up. 'Time for us to go for a little drive.'

'Ow! Please, no, Dan. Please. I don't want to go anywhere.'

'Whatever makes you think you have any choice in the matter? You've made a fool of me in front of everyone, and you'll never get the chance to do it again.' He pushed her towards the door.

His grip on her arm increased; his fingers nipping cruelly into her flesh. Kitty struggled to break free. 'Please, Dan, no.'

Ignoring her plea, he frogmarched her down the path, just as Little Mary had turned into the open gate.

'Everything alright, my love?' Little Mary's sharp eyes searched Kitty's tear-stained face, taking in the look of fear in her eyes. She slipped the handful of leaflets she'd been delivering for the church into her large handbag and gripped it firmly by the handle.

'She's fine,' said Dan.

Kitty wrenched her arm free and managed to run a few steps down the path before slipping on the snow, crying out as she felt Dan's fingers grab the collar of her coat. 'Dan, please let me go. It doesn't have to be like this.'

'Oh, I think it does. And you can get out of my way and off my property, old woman.' He glared at Little Mary.

'Who do you think you are, you arrogant upstart? Get your filthy hands off Kitty this minute!' Before he had a chance to think, Little Mary had swung her enormous bag at him, hitting him square on the arm and knocking him off balance. 'Get off her!' She hit him again.

Dan cut a pathetic figure as he shielded himself with his arm in defence against the tiny old lady. 'Stop that, you mad old witch! Ouch, that hurt! Ouch,' he yelled. Undeterred, Little Mary rained blow after blow onto him. 'Argghhh!' His face distorted with pain, he let out a high-pitched scream as the shopping bag landed on his newly-tattooed back.

'Can't take you own medicine, eh? What sort of man are you, bullying a woman? You should pick someone your own size, you coward!'

The screech of tyres followed by muffled footsteps thundering along the snow-covered trod caught their attention. Relief flooded Kitty as she saw Jimby, closely followed by Ollie, hurtle through the gate.

Ollie had been returning to the village after measuring up for a new job in Arkleby. On the way back, he'd had to slow down for a huddle of sheep that were loitering on the road and had noticed Dan's car secreted in the gateway of the field next to Kitty's. With a gut feeling telling him things weren't right, he'd driven straight to James's – after he'd stormed out of her house, it didn't feel right to casually call in. Alerted by raised voices coming from the direction of Oak Tree Farm, they'd jumped into his pickup and rushed to help.

'Oh, thank God.' Swamped with relief, tears began pouring down Kitty's face.

'Shit!' Dan was bent double with pain. 'Why do you two always have to be where you're not wanted?'

'You've got a nerve, what the bloody hell are you doing here?' His fists clenched, James glared at Dan, shifting his gaze to the developing bump on his sister's head. 'Has he done this to you?'

Kitty looked at the floor and nodded.

'Yes, he did. Until I started giving him what for with my bag. And there's plenty more where that came from, you brute.' Little Mary shook her fist at Dan.

'Out of my way.' Ollie pushed past Dan and wrapped his arms around Kitty who was pale and on the verge of fainting. 'It's okay, Kitts, I've got you.'

Not caring that Dan was watching, Kitty allowed herself to melt into Ollie's strong embrace, resting her cheek against the warmth of his chest, at last feeling safe.

Grabbing the collar of Dan's coat with one hand, James pushed him with such force he fell back into the wall of the cottage, his free hand balled into a fist. Dan yelped with pain as his tattooed back hit the stone. 'Bastard!' James was poised to deliver a punch.

'Jimby!' Kitty cried. 'He's not worth it.'

James paused, wrestling with every instinct he had to give Dan a thorough pounding. He released his grip on the collar. 'You'd better get your sorry arse out of here before I give you a taste of your own medicine, you spineless piece of shit.'

'Don't worry, I'm going.' Dan shrugged his coat straight and walked away.

Keen for Lucas and Lily not to hear of what had happened, Kitty swore Little Mary, Jimby and Ollie to secrecy. She didn't want her children upset by the situation between herself and Dan any further, especially now they seemed so settled. She'd tell them she'd fallen over in the snow.

◇

ONCE DAN HAD LEFT, Ollie led Kitty into the cottage, followed by James and Little Mary. Jimby let Humph and Ethel out of the utility room, and they made a bee-line for their mum, fussing round, relieved to see her. James filled the kettle, listening carefully as Kitty recounted what had happened before they arrived. 'You were amazing, Mary. And so brave. Thank you for what you did.'

'Oh, it was nothing.' Mary smiled bashfully, her cheeks still flushed from her earlier exertion that had dislodged several of her snowy white curls.

'Yep, Little Mary, the fearless village Ninja, comes to the rescue.' Ollie smiled at her.

'Well, I always knew my big shopping bag would come in handy for something.'

James picked up the bag in question. 'Bloody hell, Mary, what on earth have you got in here, a couple of building bricks?'

'Just my library books and a couple of bars of chocolate. The library bus is due in the village this morning, and I was going to change them, then I'm supposed to be calling in on Aggie for a cup of tea. Not sure I can take any more excitement today, though.'

'Ah,' said Ollie and James in unison, sharing a knowing look. They'd heard about the sort of books Little Mary and Granny Aggie read, with both old ladies apparently favouring spicy novels.

The sound of a woman's high-pitched voice caught their attention, the owner of which appeared to be calling Ollie's name. 'Damn! I'd better go, sorry.' Ollie jumped up, grabbing his coat that was slung across the back of the chair. 'See you later.'

'What was that all about?' James watched his friend disappearing down the garden path.

'I'm not sure.' Kitty looked puzzled but suspected it was something to do with the woman she'd seen at his house. She craned her neck to get a better view out of the window, instantly regretting it as her bruised muscles objected.

'Well, I know exactly what it's about,' said Little Mary, spooning sugar into her tea.

'Come on, Little M, spill the beans.' James folded his arms and leaned against the Aga.

'What's it worth?' She'd always had a mischievous sense of humour.

'A slice of Kitty's homemade chocolate squidgy cake?'

'Done!'

'You have been, I was going to cut you a slice anyway.' James was pleased to see the exchange had made Kitty smile.

Little Mary had recognised Nataliya Shishkin straight away. The arrogance in her demeanour as she'd climbed down from the bus and sauntered over to Ollie's cottage as if she owned the place was a dead giveaway. Mary didn't trust her, never had. Her presence here could only mean one thing: trouble.

Over a pot of tea, she filled James and Kitty in on the comings and goings and how it hadn't taken Ollie and Noushka long before they looked brow-beaten and miserable. Ollie, in particular, looked like he had the weight of the world on his shoulders. Feeling her cheeks flush, Kitty felt she was partly responsible for that.

James scratched his chin. 'I thought he was being cagey. I've hardly seen him recently, says he's too busy to stop and chat, and he hasn't been popping in for his tea break like he'd been doing since he moved his workshop to the spare barn. And when I have seen him, he's had a face like a slapped backside, and hardly uttered two words together.'

'That woman's up to no good, mark my words. Ollie's a lovely boy, and she'll take advantage of him. Just like the last time,' warned Little Mary.

'OLIVER! You're not listening! How many times do I have to tell you that first thing on a morning I only ever drink boiled water with a thin slice of lemon? Not the tea you English people seem to go crazy for. If you want to win me back you need to remember things like this, or it is never going to work.' Her ice-blue eyes flashed with annoyance as she tipped the tea down the sink.

'Talk about high maintenance,' Ollie muttered under his breath, wondering how he'd managed to get himself into this situation. He rubbed the muscles in his back; having given up his bed for Nataliya, they were aching from spending another night on the sofa. Things had definitely taken a turn for the worse when she'd turned up on his doorstep the other night.

OLLIE HAD PLANNED a quiet night in, deciding, for a change, that he wasn't going to work late. His heart hadn't been in it since he'd seen Kitty holding hands with that bloke – if he was honest, his heart hadn't been in anything since then. Tonight, he was going to watch the match and have beans on toast – he might even grate some cheese on them – washed down with a can of beer. Good, blokey fodder. Noushka was at her dance class and wouldn't be dropped off until well after nine o'clock, so he had the house to himself, which meant he could slob out for a good few hours.

He'd just got himself settled on the sofa, England had scored an early goal, and he'd had a couple of forkfuls of food when his evening was interrupted by an impatient knocking at the door. Sighing, he put his tray of food on the coffee table and heaved himself up. The rapping came again, this time harder. 'Alright, alright, keep your hair on,' he muttered.

He opened the door and stood in stunned silence for several seconds, his brain gradually processing the image of the person before him. His eyes ran over the still-familiar, though slightly older, version of a woman he'd hadn't seen for over fifteen years. She still wore her hair tightly scraped back into a smooth ponytail that accentuated her sharp features and Slavic eyes, the same Slavic eyes his daughter had. Beside her on the step was a large, over-stuffed bag. 'Hello, Oliver.' She tipped her head coquettishly to one side. 'Aren't you going to invite me in? Don't you know it's rude to stand there gawping?' Before he had a chance to answer, she'd pushed past him into the hallway. 'Don't forget my bag,' she called as she headed towards the living-room.

'Nataliya, what are you doing here?' He put her bag down by the sofa next to where she was sitting.

'That's not a very warm welcome is it, Oliver?' She pulled at the fingers of her black leather gloves, throwing them on the coffee table.

Ollie rubbed his forehead as his brain re-familiarized itself with her heavy Russian accent. 'Well, it's been a while…'

'I thought you'd be pleased to see me.' She arched a thinly plucked eyebrow at him, before kicking off her five-inch heels and resting her feet on the coffee table. 'Phew! I could murder a vodka coke. Be a darling, go make me one, then we can talk. And make it a strong one,' she called after him as he disappeared into the kitchen.

After a brief rummage through the cupboards, Ollie found a half-empty bottle of cheap vodka that, judging by the dust on it, had been there for quite some time. Doubting it would be up to Nataliya's exacting standards he poured the drink anyway. How, after all these years, did she still have the ability to make him feel rubbish about himself?

'There you go.' He handed her the glass. She took a sip and wrinkled her nose.

'Is this the best you can do?'

37

KITTY LOOKED at her reflection in the bathroom mirror. It had been a week since Dan's visit, and she was relieved to see that the bump on her head had almost disappeared. She'd kept a low profile in the village, hoping to avoid any awkward questions. If anyone had an inkling of what had happened she didn't know, but it would be old news soon; there were always plenty of other things going on to keep the local gossips talking. As long as the kids didn't get wind of it – that was her main concern – but they'd readily accepted her explanation of slipping in the snow.

She was determined to put the experience behind her; she didn't want her relationship with Dan to define her any longer. She was ready for the real Kitty to re-emerge; she'd been hidden away for far too long.

Turning away from the mirror, she headed downstairs and was half-way down when there was a knock at the door. Humph and Ethel, still protective since Dan's visit, started barking and charged along the hallway. 'Shh, you two. Quieten down a bit.' She rubbed the Labradors' ears before taking hold of their collars.

Through the door's small window of warped Georgian glass, Kitty could just about make out the shape of a male figure on the other side which triggered a ripple of anxiety. She pressed down slowly on the sneck. 'Ollie?' The last person she expected to see on her doorstep was standing right in front of her, a sheepish expression troubling his handsome features. Kitty had seen neither hide nor hair of him since Dan's visit. She looked beyond him, expecting to see Nataliya looming not far behind. 'Would you like to come in?' She smiled and stood back, holding the door wide open.

For a moment, he remained rooted to the spot, frowning as his eyes scanned her delicate features, taking in the fading bruise. 'Erm, if that's okay with you, Kitty.'

Without giving her time to answer, Ethel barge passed her and gently took Ollie by the sleeve of his jacket, pulling him into the hallway. 'Well, it's definitely alright with Ethel,' she laughed. 'Come through.' She led the way into the kitchen. Ollie followed her, ducking his head in places to avoid bumping it on the low, uneven beams.

An awkward silence hung in the room. Ollie sighed. 'I feel I owe you an apology. And an explanation.' He pulled out a chair and sat down. 'I'm ashamed to say I've been off-hand with you and haven't treated you very nicely over the last week or so. I'm not very proud of myself. Noushka's not very proud of me either, for that matter, been giving me a right ear-bashing. So, I've come to put things straight – if you'll let me – and hope that you can forgive me, Kitty.'

'Ollie, it's…'

He held up his hands, 'Please, it's important, I want to get this cleared up.'

Sitting down, she could feel her heart begin to race, wondering if she was going to like what she was about to hear. 'Okay.' She rested her hands in her lap, picking at her fingernails.

Ollie explained how he'd felt jealous when he'd seen Henry holding her hand, and how his stubborn male pride had caused him to scurry off and hide while he licked his wounds. Just as he was trying to get his head around what he'd seen, Nataliya had turned up out of the blue, throwing the mother of all spanners into the works.

Ollie rolled his eyes as he repeated how Nataliya had told him that the years away from him and Anoushka had given her time to think. *I'll bet they did*, thought Kitty. How she said that, through no fault of her own, she'd been deprived of any involvement in her daughter's life or of making a success of her relationship with him. And now she felt she deserved the opportunity to put that right. Kitty's eyebrows shot up. She went to speak but couldn't form the right words to say. Ollie lifted his hand, 'Oh, it gets better.' He continued describing how melodramatic Nataliya had become, saying how no one understood the suffering she'd gone through, how hard it had been to have a baby so young, the feelings of being trapped. How it wasn't easy for her to walk away from her new-born baby, but she'd had no choice.

The trilling of the kettle interrupted him. Kitty jumped up and lifted it off the hotplate. 'Blimey, Ollie, I don't know what to say.'

'Well, she reckons she'd spent the years afterwards working her fingers to the bone, so she could save enough money and send for Noushka, but never managed to get enough together to do it.'

'And do you believe her?' Kitty passed him a mug of tea.

'Thanks,' he said before taking a sip.

'Watch out, it'll be red hot.' Kitty's caution was too late. Ollie winced and set the tea back down.

'Would you? Believe her, I mean?' he asked. Kitty shook her head. 'She even said I was selfish for keeping our daughter to myself for all these years. And that she was shocked that I hadn't even bothered to find her. When I told her I'd tried to hundreds of times, but it felt like she didn't want to be found, she just shrugged and said, "So what? That was then." She's unbelievable.'

'Wow!'

'She's even suggested she move back in, and we pick up where we left off.'

'Right.' Kitty's stomach clenched. 'And how about Noushka in all of this? It's a pretty big thing for her, finally getting to meet her mother.'

'Noushka's totally unimpressed. We had a chat last night, and she doesn't want anything to do with her. She actually said meeting Nataliya has made her realise that she hasn't missed out on having a mother at all.'

'Well, that's because you've been such a fantastic dad.'

'Don't know about that.' Ollie smiled bashfully. 'I couldn't have managed without my mother's help. But it's good to know Noushka's been okay all these years. And that she's not expecting her mum to be something she's not, which was my biggest worry.'

'So, what are you going to do?'

'Well, as you can imagine, things have been pretty uncomfortable in our house. Nataliya has managed to take over, kicked me out of my bedroom, hogs the bathroom and leaves her mess everywhere. It's been a bloody nightmare. I feel I've given her a chance, but there's no way on this earth I'm going to let her hurt Noushka.'

'I can understand that.'

'Anyway, turns out Nataliya didn't leave the circus of her own free will like she told me; she was kicked out for stealing and generally causing trouble. Which seems to follow her wherever she goes. She denies everything, of course, blames everyone else, but I don't believe a word she says.' He gave a cynical laugh. 'I told her there was no hope of us getting together again – we weren't sleeping together by the way.'

Kitty shook her head and raised her palms in a gesture that said it was none of her business.

'How did she take it?'

'Well, Noushka…er, Noushk…er, sort of said something…' Kitty watched as a blush crept up his neck and spread across his face. He swallowed and transferred his gaze to the floor. 'She told Nataliya that I'm in love with someone else. Someone who she said is wonderful and kind and a better mother than she could ever wish to be.'

It was Kitty's turn to feel the warmth of a blush colour her face. 'Oh.' She took a quick gulp of tea, hoping to hide her embarrassment before casting a shy glance at Ollie. 'How did she take that?'

'Pretty much as you can imagine. She went ballistic, saying she wasn't going to stay where she wasn't wanted, but how I was a fool to let her go again as I wouldn't get another chance – can't say I'm gutted about that. She stomped upstairs, doors slamming and banging, packed her bag then stormed out, taking all the money she could get her hands on – she even raided Noushka's money box and her wardrobe. Helped herself to a couple of family heirlooms my grandad left me for good measure.'

'What a piece of work. You and Noushka have been having a tough time of it.'

'You could say, but nothing like what you've been through. And I feel terrible that I've contributed to that.' He stood up, looking awkward, not knowing what to do with himself. 'Look, Kitty, I can't tell you how sorry I am for treating you the way I have recently. I know it's no excuse, but I was absolutely gutted when I saw that Henry bloke holding your hand. And I thought … well, I thought … and at the time it just didn't register how uncomfortable you looked. How you clearly didn't want him to be doing that.' He strode across to her. 'Kitty, you know how I feel about you. Nothing's changed there, but I want you to know that whenever – if ever – you're ready, I'll be here, waiting for you.'

Her eyes met Ollie's. He was looking down at her with such love, her heart felt as though it was melting into a warm puddle, pooling somewhere deep inside her. She got to her feet and took his gentle, handsome face into her hands. 'Ollie,' she said softly. 'I'm ready.'

38

CHRISTMAS WAS impatient to get there this year; time elbowed November out of the way. It bounded over the weeks and scurried over the days until, suddenly, it was Christmas Eve.

Kitty had been concerned about how Lucas and Lily would manage their first Christmas without their dad. Dan had sent money with instructions for Kitty to buy presents for them on his behalf, but there'd been no mention of visiting them. The kids had asked a few questions about what he would be doing, and Lucas had seemed subdued for a while. Kitty decided to keep them busy, and they'd spent a lovely afternoon together, baking mince pies and hanging up their stockings on the inglenook fireplace. When Bryn skyped from Austria, where he'd gone skiing with his mum, the kids' excitement levels had rocketed, which was a far cry from their usual state of having to tip-toe around their father. Previous Christmas Eves with Dan had typically involved him spoiling for an argument as he gradually drank himself into a stupor. By early evening he'd usually had such a skinful he'd stagger his way to bed, bleary-eyed, remaining there until late Christmas morning. In retrospect, Kitty realised it wasn't much of a loss for the kids – nor herself, for that matter.

KITTY PEERED out of the living room window. The snow that had been falling steadily all day had finally petered out. Lytell Stangdale had been transformed into a winter wonderland, sparkling in the pale moonlight and the soft glow from the Victorian street lamps that were dotted along the road. She checked the clock: ten to six; time to chivvy the kids to get ready for the carol singing around the Christmas tree on the village green.

Kitty ushered Lucas and Lily out of the door, laughing at their whoops and squeals as they slid along the path, passing the snowman they'd made earlier that afternoon.

As they approached the village green, she saw that there was a good turnout and, as far as she could make out, there was no sign of Gwyneth. She breathed a sigh of relief. She glanced around, looking for Ollie, Jimby or Molly, and made eye contact with Aoife who was wearing her customary scowl. Kitty turned away. There was no way that woman was going to spoil tonight.

She scanned the sea of faces, feeling pleased when she spotted Jimby and Violet in conversation with Ollie and Noushka. Her heart fluttered; Ollie looked so handsome, his dark blond hair ever so slightly ruffled. Stuffing her hands in her pockets, she made her way over to them, her boots crunching as they pressed into the thick snow. She chuckled at Violet who was snuggled up close to Jimby, as if hoping to steal any body heat he had going spare. Seeing how happy they were together, Kitty was pleased that they'd decided to give being a couple a try. It seemed to bring out the best in both of them.

As greetings were exchanged, her eyes met Ollie's, twinkling back at her, a smile playing at his lips. Her heart skipped a beat. Not wanting to antagonise Dan any further, they'd agreed to keep their fledgling relationship under wraps for the time being. Feeling herself flush, she turned to Violet. 'You look frozen, Vi,' she said, rubbing her friend's arm.

'I am absolutely bloody nithered,' Vi said through chattering teeth.

'Well, that's what you get when you dress like a fashion model and not for warmth. I did try to tell her, but would she listen? Nope. Even offered her the use of my spare waxed jacket but she looked at me as if I was mad,' said Jimby. Vi rolled her eyes and snuggled deeper inside his coat, wrapping her arms tightly around his middle. 'Not that I'm complaining, though, if this is what I get.' A wide grin dimpled his cheeks.

'Well, at least you look as drop-dead-gorgeous as ever, Vi.' Kitty took in her friend's lightweight outfit that offered no protection from the evening's snowy conditions.

'Thanks.' Vi's words shivered their way out. 'I turned down the jacket because Jimby said he last wore it at lambing time when he had his hand up a sheep's bum.' She scrunched up her nose, making everyone laugh.

'Nice one, Jimbo,' said Ollie.

'Jimby,' said Kitty, disapproval in her voice.

'I did say I was only joking, but she wouldn't believe me.'

Violet's time was still split between her flat in York and her half-renovated cottage in the village, where she only had a few items of clothing hanging on a clothes rail. Kitty offered to take Vi back to hers so she could change into something warmer, but the offer was declined in favour of cuddling up to Jimby.

'I literally can't wait for tomorrow.' Anoushka beamed. It's gonna be like so cool spending Christmas day at Kitty's with everyone.'

'Me too, Noushkabelle.' Kitty smiled and tugged gently at Noushka's flaxen mermaid plait that was draped across her shoulder. Feeling the warmth of Ollie's gaze on her, she cast a glance in his direction. The look of happiness in his eyes matched her own.

Lucas and Lily ran up to the group, giggling mischievously. 'Hiya, Lukes. Hiya, Lils. Been having fun?' asked Anoushka.

'Lucas has got a present for Uncle Jimby,' sniggered Lily.

'Oh, and what might that be?' James had already spotted Lucas's impish expression and his hand behind his back. 'Could it be one of these?' With lightning speed, James bent down, scooped up a handful of snow and rubbed it in his nephew's face.

'Arghhhh! Uncle Jimby, stop!' Lucas yelled, trying to wriggle free as Lily shrieked with delight.

'You're going to have to move fast if you want to keep up with the master, Lukes,' said James, wiping the snow off his hands.

'Big kid,' said Vi.

James threw his head back to laugh just as Lucas hurled a snow-ball at him, making him cough and splutter as snow filled his mouth.

'Bull's-eye!' Lucas punched the air. 'Was that fast enough for you, Uncle Jimby?'

James replied with a dirty look as he fished out the snow that had sneaked down his scarf.

'Nice one, Lukes. That'll keep him quiet for a while,' laughed Ollie.

'Met your nemesis have you, James? Think you might need one of these to warm you up,' said Jonty, as he walked by with a tray of glasses filled with mulled wine.

THE VILLAGERS WERE in good voice, and everyone had joined in with the Christmas carols wholeheartedly. They were to learn later that their voices had travelled across the yawning expanse of Great Stangdale dale, transported on the chilly night air to be heard in Danskelfe and Arkleby.

Halfway through the final song, it began to snow, falling steadily in huge, fluffy flakes that resembled goose feathers. 'Santa's shaking his pillow again.' Lily held out her hand, allowing some to land on her glove.

'Brrr. I don't think I could get much colder.' Vi shivered. By now the penetrating cold had got to just about everyone. And, just as the villagers were beginning to feel they were frozen to the spot, Bea invited everyone back to the pub for a festive drink.

Kitty was kicking snow off her boots by the door when she was joined by Bea. 'That was fun,' said Bea, her nose red with the cold.

'It was, I haven't done that for years. I'd forgotten how lovely it was.'

Bea gave her a knowing look. 'By the way, I've saved your gang your usual table by the fire.'

'Thank you, Bea, that's so thoughtful.' The thought of sitting next to Ollie by the fire warmed her heart.

Inside, the pub smelled of a traditional Christmas, its usual aroma of wood-smoke mingling with the fragrance of festive scented candles that Bea had dotted around.

Kitty's fingers began to tingle as the warmth set to, thawing their cold nipped ends. She found the others, telling them of the saved table before squeezing her way through the gaggle of people and guiding her children towards it.

'Drinks are on us, folks.' Jonty's plummy tones rang out above the chatter. He was rewarded with a cheer.

Sitting around their table, sipping their warming drinks Ollie leaned in. 'Merry Christmas, everyone.' He held up his glass of mulled wine. 'I've got a feeling this one's going to be a good 'un.' His eyes met Kitty's and it wasn't just her fingers that tingled.

'Merry Christmas!' the friends chorused, chinking glasses.

39

LUCAS WOKE JUST after seven on Christmas morning. Leaping out of bed, he ran into Lily's room and shook her awake before the pair bounded into Kitty's bedroom, jumped onto her bed and dragged the duvet off her. 'It's Christmas, Mummy! Come on, let's see if Santa's been.' Lily's voice was shrill with excitement.

With a head still fuzzy from sleep, Kitty rubbed her eyes. 'Yay, come on, kids, let's go and see if Santa's left some presents and Rudolph's eaten his carrot.'

THE PREVIOUS NIGHT, as soon as Kitty's head had hit the pillow, her mind had taken it as a cue to begin its usual sweep for niggles. Would the kids be okay facing their first Christmas without their dad? Would everything run smoothly for the first Christmas she was having everyone around for dinner? Had she remembered everything for the said dinner? Would there be enough food to go around? Had she invited everyone she was supposed to have done? She'd feel terrible if she'd left anyone out.

Ollie's parents had taken off for the warmer climes of Menorca over the festive period, accompanied by their close friends, Mary and Ken Smith, who were Vi's parents. For Kitty, inviting Ollie and Noushka along with Jimby and Vi had seemed the natural thing to do.

Worries continued to whirl around her mind. It wasn't until the early hours when sleep finally claimed her, allowing little time for her batteries to be recharged in readiness for the big day ahead.

At just after nine o'clock, when every parcel had been opened, wrapping paper banished to the recycling bin, and the children had declared themselves thrilled with their gifts, Kitty set to making breakfast. Standing at the Aga, tending a skillet full of sizzling bacon rashers that were torturing Humph and Ethel, Kitty smiled to herself. She'd never seen the kids so happy and relaxed on a Christmas morning. Her thoughts turned to Dan, and their previous Christmases, bound by the strict rules he'd imposed. Woe betide anyone who got out of bed before nine o'clock. And when they were allowed up, there had to be no loud laughter or noises to irritate him while he recovered from the previous evening's over-indulgence in a heady red wine. But the rule that Kitty found most unreasonable under Dan's regime, was no present opening before his parents arrived. It was the ultimate control over young children. What pleasure could it possibly have given him to stifle the kids' excitement on such a special day? Looking back from the clearer vantage point she had today, Kitty realised it was the behaviour of a man who was deeply unhappy with himself. For a fleeting moment, she felt pity for him. How he would hate that.

She was angry with herself, too. She shouldn't have been so weak; shouldn't have allowed it to happen. She should have stood up for her children. But a memory loomed of last Christmas when she'd let them open the presents their friends had given them before their grandparents arrived. There was no way she could have anticipated the reaction of Dan and his mother, which was completely out of proportion, and cast an unpleasant atmosphere over the rest of the day. Gwyneth had screamed at Kitty, then took every opportunity to lecture the children, making them feel terrible.

Enough! Get a grip, he's not here! She gave herself a shake. Those days were banished to the past; they could do things their way now, the three of them. Since Dan had left, happiness ruled at Oak Tree Farm. And even she was conscious that her once permanently hunched shoulders were more relaxed. They'd disappeared along with the anxious expression she'd previously worn. But what gave Kitty the most pleasure was how Lucas and Lily had blossomed in such a short space of time. The days of tip-toeing around and not daring to make a noise were long gone, and they were free to be happy and behave like children.

Her reverie was interrupted by the muffled sound of snow being kicked off clompy boots at the front door. The Labradors barked as it flew open and a voice boomed. 'Ho! Ho! H…Arghh!' Rushing into the hallway, Kitty and the kids, still in their PJs, were greeted by the sight of James standing in the doorway with his shoulders hunched up around his ears, his hair piled high with clumps of snow. A safe distance behind him Ollie, Anoushka and Violet were bent double, their peals of laughter spilling out into the village. Kicking snow off his boots had triggered a mini-avalanche from the roof which had slid down and landed with an icy thwump on his head and was currently making its way down his neck.

'Oh, Jimby!' giggled Kitty.

'Blimey! That was bloomin' freezing.' He shook the snow from his hair. 'Anyway, what I meant to say was: Ho! Ho! Ho! Merry Christmas, everyone.' He handed Kitty a large Christmas pudding.

'Merry Christmas, Uncle Jimby,' Lucas and Lily chorused.

'Merry Christmas, Jimby. Merry Christmas, everyone, come in out of the cold. I'll just go and fetch a towel for Mr Accident-Prone here,' laughed Kitty.

'Uncle Jimby! You are so funny.' Lily grinned, jumping up and down.

'I do my best.' James bowed.

'There you go, Lucas. Pass that to Uncle Jimby will you?' Kitty handed him a towel.

'Thanks, Lukes.' James took the towel and started rubbing his hair dry.

'Ooh, it's lovely and warm in here.' Vi gave her friend a peck on the cheek. 'There you go.' She handed Kitty a tub of home-made soup for the starter, then hung up her coat and followed Jimby into the living room.

'Noushka, come and see what Santa brought me and Lucas. We got loads.' Lily grabbed hold of her hand and pulled her into the living-room.

'There you go, Kitts. And merry Christmas.' Ollie went to hand Kitty two bottles of Prosecco, laughing when he saw she had her hands full. He leaned across. 'And thanks for inviting us.' He kissed her on the cheek, and she shivered with delight at the touch of his skin against hers.

'Oh, Ollie, you shouldn't have.' Kitty watched as the others disappeared into the living room. 'I'll get these into the fridge straight away.' She spoke loudly for the benefit of the others.

'I'll give you a hand.' Ollie winked at her and followed her into the kitchen. She placed the soup and pudding on the table next to Ollie's Prosecco and turned to him. Standing on her tiptoes she took his face in her hands and kissed him. He responded, running his fingers through her hair, his kisses burning with passion.

'Oh, wow! Like, that is, like literally, totally awesome!' The pair jumped apart and turned to see Anoushka in the doorway; her eyes sparkling with happiness. 'That is, like, literally the best Christmas present I could ever, ever have. You two are, like, totally meant to be together. This is so perfect.' She clapped her hands together.

'Ssshhh!' Ollie put his fingers to his lips while Kitty gave an embarrassed giggle. 'We're keeping things under wraps for now. I promise I was going to tell you, but when the time was right.'

Anoushka responded with a stifled squeal, excitedly jumping up and down.

'What's like, totally awesome?' James peered round the doorway.

'Dad says I can have some Prosecco later on, that's what. Isn't that right, Pops?'

'It is?' Kitty detected the subtle questioning tone in Ollie's response. 'And less of the Pops thank you very much, or I'll change my mind. And it's just the one, very small glass don't forget.'

'Noushka, would you mind going and checking to see if everyone's on for bacon butties?' With a blush still staining her cheeks, Kitty was struggling to make eye contact with her.

'Okay,' Noushka replied. 'But no more snogging,' she whispered, wagging a finger at them playfully.

FULL OF CHRISTMAS DINNER, and with stomachs groaning, everyone had retired to the cosiness of the living-room where they basked, heavy-eyed, in the warm glow of the log burner and the twinkling lights of the Christmas tree. Violet was curled up on the snug two-seater with Jimby. 'Well, I don't know about the rest of you, but I can't remember a more perfect Christmas day.' She sighed, resting her head on his chest.

'Couldn't agree more.' James pressed a kiss onto her glossy hair and closed his eyes.

'Same here.' Ollie glanced across at Kitty and smiled. She was coming back from the kitchen, a tray of coffee in her hands, closely followed by Noushka who'd been helping her while attempting a thinly veiled interrogation about her relationship with Ollie.

'Ooh! Definitely. It's been so totally awesome. I think we should do it every year.' The glass of Prosecco had made Noushka gabbly.

'It's been wonderful. Thank you all for coming and making it so special for the kids and me, we really appreciate it.' Kitty set the tray down on the coffee table and began placing cups onto saucers before pushing the plunger on the cafetiere.

'Yeah, it's been totally mint with everyone here. I've loved it. Me and Lily think it's been the best ever Christmas we can remember, don't we, Lils?'

'Yep, it's been the bestest ever.'

'I think we should be thanking you for putting up with us, Kitts. It's been wonderful. The dinner was absolutely delicious, and you and the kids have made us all feel very welcome.' Vi smiled across at her friend.

'Well, I couldn't think of a better way of spending Christmas.' Kitty cast her eyes around at the scene of contentment playing out in her living-room. Such happiness hadn't seen the light of day in this room since her childhood. It was good to know that the negative energy from Dan's time here wasn't a permanent feature. And today was proof of that. Happiness and positive vibes were doing an excellent job of smothering his legacy.

DAN HAD FLATLY REFUSED his mother's invitation to join her and his father for Christmas dinner. 'I'm not setting foot in that village of half-wits,' he'd spat at her. Her suggestion of the three of them going to a hotel for dinner, or for her to cook it at his flat was met with equal derision. His blood had boiled as she'd persisted with suggestions. Her shrill voice was really grating. 'I'll be fine, Mother. As I've already told you several times, I'm spending the day with friends. It's all planned, and I can't back out now. Look, I've got to go.' When she'd attempted to interrupt him, he'd ended the call abruptly. She was starting to become a meddlesome pain, wanting to know where he was going, what he was doing and who he was doing it with. It reminded him of when he lived at home before he moved in with Kitty. The urge to tell her where to get off was beginning to over-ride the struggle he was having to bite his tongue, which he knew would be a big mistake; she was his greatest ally, and he needed her.

But, despite his protestations, a stark reality was beginning to dawn. Dan would be spending Christmas day in his flat.

Alone.

∾

IN THE WEEKS since his split from Kitty, he'd used a variety of women to distract him, do his washing and, most importantly, share a bed for the night. Though, recently, he appeared to be losing his touch.

When he'd first left the family home, he'd headed straight for Sam, whose sheets had barely had chance to cool down from their previous encounter. But she'd recoiled from the thought of a man living with her full-time. She'd agreed to him staying with her for a couple of days, which he'd managed to stretch into a week and a half before his selfishness had forced her to give him his marching orders.

He'd even tried his luck with Caro Hammondely whom he'd spotted in the Wig and Pen – York's latest gastro-pub and favourite haunt of the legal profession. But he'd lost interest when she'd introduced him to her boyfriend, Sim, a sound engineer, whose sister and brother-in-law owned the pub.

Things weren't looking good.

∾

ON CHRISTMAS MORNING, the already faltering ground beneath Dan's feet became a whole lot shakier. Alone, nursing a hangover and awash with self-pity, he was slumped over the table in the kitchen of his flat, sipping coffee as he flicked through the weekly York Gazette. The paracetamol was taking a while to kick in, and his head was throbbing; the last thing he needed was for his eyes to alight on an article about Dog Daisy Wood. He held his breath as he scanned the report, the words 'antisocial trend for dogging' leaping out at him. 'Oh, shit.' Panic prickled over him as his mind flashed back to his own ill-fated dabble in that very place. His gaze shifted down the page to a smattering of photographs which appeared to show scantily clad people running off into the woods.

Dan banged his mug down on the table, slopping coffee everywhere. He grabbed the paper with both hands as he frantically scrutinised each image, praying that there weren't any incriminating ones of him.

Relief inched up him as he worked his way through the photos. So far, so good. He released his breath, he was on the home straight with only two more pictures to go. How likely was it that there would be one of him? 'Oh, Lord, no!' He pushed his fingers into his tangle of greasy hair. His stomach lurched as he came face to face with a surprisingly clear photo of a man loitering near the woods wearing nothing but a pair of black socks, covering his privates with what appeared to be a bundle of clothing. The photo was a little grainy, he told himself, it could have been of anyone. But anyone who knew him intimately, would recognise the large port-wine birthmark that decorated his backside.

Dan put his head in his hands and groaned. How had his life come to this?

40

'So, Molls, how was Christmas dinner with your parents this year?' Kitty and Molly were sitting at their usual table by the fire in the Sunne, waiting for the others to arrive.

'Not nearly as bad as I expected actually. Well, apart from the usual game of culinary roulette we have with Mum's cooking. Will the gravy be like gnats' pee or so thick you could stand a fork up in it? Will the veggies be a soggy pile of tasteless mush, or as hard as bullets?'

'And?' Kitty giggled. Auntie Annie was lovely, but her cooking was diabolical.

'Well, the gravy could've easily been mistaken for a sample of pee from one of the old dears on my weekly rounds. And the veggies were so rock hard, anyone who was brave enough to eat them was in danger of losing a tooth. But at least the boys managed to sneak in a couple of games of Spit the Sprout, so it wasn't all bad, I suppose.' Molly took a sip of her spring water.

'Ah yes, Christmas wouldn't be the same without it in the Pennock household.' Despite her cousin's joking, Kitty noticed she was still looking washed out. 'So, did you manage to eat anything or is the sickness still as bad?'

Molly fished a packet of mini custard creams from her handbag. 'Well, as you know, I struggle to face Mum's food at the best of times, but this year a mere sniff of her Christmas offerings was enough to make me want to up-chuck. But it did offer me the perfect excuse not to have to suffer it, so I had a quiet word with her and spilled the beans about her latest grand-sprog. But with her nose like a bloodhound for anything like that, she'd already guessed. Said it was something to do with my custard cream consumption, would you believe?'

'Well, she does have a point.' She watched as Molly shovelled a handful of the biscuits into her mouth before waving the packet under Kitty's nose. 'Er, no thanks, Moll, I wouldn't want to deprive you.'

Molly snorted with laughter. 'I hadn't realised how obvious it was that I was wolfing my way through so many packets, and when she told me she already knew, I assumed Pip must've said something. I was livid because I'd sworn him to secrecy – it was different with me telling her because, well, it just was. Anyway, you should've seen Mum's face when I threatened to rip his nuts off if he had told her.'

Kitty swallowed a mouthful of Prosecco and giggled. 'I can just picture her face.'

'It was so funny but, bless her, she was so supportive about us taking over the farm, saying how timing is never right – tell me something I don't know – how the challenge would be good for us, and how it would be the perfect excuse for me to get out of nursing. And, of course, that Pip and the boys would be in their element. Honestly, nothing fazes her.'

'Like mother, like daughter.' Kitty gave her cousin a knowing look. 'And you know she talks a lot of sense. She's spot on saying the challenge would do you good; if anyone can rise to it, Moll, it's you.'

'Rise to what?' Vi plonked herself down onto the chair beside Molly, who popped a handful of the mini biscuits into her mouth.

'I've got a bun in the oven.'

'More like a custard cream,' said Kitty with a giggle.

'Eh?' Vi looked from one to the other. 'Why are you two talking in riddles? Molly's got a custard cream …oh!' The penny dropped with a clatter 'That's good news? Please tell me that's good news.'

'More like bloody unexpected news, but it's grown on me now so, yes, it's good news.' More biscuits disappeared into Molly's mouth.

'Well, I think it's lovely news.' Kitty smiled.

'What's lovely news?' Ollie placed his pint down on the table next to Kitty's Prosecco, unleashing a flurry of butterflies that looped the loop around her stomach. Feeling her face flush, she was thankful for the pub's dim lighting.

'Yep, come on, you three, spill the beans and stop with all your whispering.' James grinned and sat down next to Violet. He turned to Pip. 'Come on Pip, lad, park your bum next to your good lady wife here. This lot reckon they've got some good news and are just about to share, aren't you, ladies?'

'Erm, well … Vi's got a new tattoo.' Molly shifted awkwardly in her seat.

'Have you?' Puzzled, James turned to Vi.

'Have I?' She looked across at Molly who was sending non-verbal messages with her eyes. 'Oh, er, yes, er, well. I'm thinking about getting another one, but I haven't *actually* got it yet.'

'Gobshite.' Pip had rumbled his wife and gave her a knowing look. They'd agreed to keep quiet about the baby for another month, and it had been killing him not to blurt it out. 'Well, if you've told the lasses it's only fair I can tell the lads.'

After hushed congratulations, the conversation moved on. Kitty and Ollie, although tempted to share their news, had agreed to keep their fledgling relationship quiet for the time being. Kitty wanted to make sure the dust had settled after Dan's departure. She didn't want any more trouble from Gwyneth, the last lot had left her wary. Memories of Dan's last visit still had a habit of sneaking up on her, especially in the dark of night.

'I wish I could turn the clock back.' Hidden from view under the table, Ollie rubbed the back of Kitty's hand with his fingers. 'We could've had all those years together, and I would've been Lucas and Lily's dad.'

She gave his fingers a squeeze. 'I believe that everything happens for a reason, Oll. Lucas and Lily wouldn't be the same children if Dan wasn't their dad. And Noushka probably wouldn't even have happened, which is a horrible thought. No, I wouldn't change the three of them for the world. They're the good things that made the bad things worth going through. That's how I see it anyway.'

He nodded. 'When you put it like that…I just wish you hadn't had to go through what you did with…well, you know…'

'I know, but I'm just focussing on moving forward now. The kids and me are in a happy place, and I'm determined not to give regrets the time of day.'

He turned to her, speaking softly. 'Did I ever tell you that you're beautiful, Kitty Fairfax?'

Her eyes met his, twinkling back at her. She was struggling with an overwhelming urge to kiss him. Keeping her voice low, she said, 'Ollie, you're just the loveliest man I've ever met.'

41

THE SECOND THURSDAY in January arrived dull and damp. Fog hung heavy in the dale, curling around the farmsteads that nestled in the hillside, muffling the familiar sounds of rural life. Kitty was dropping down into the village after cutting short a walk with Humph and Ethel. She'd said goodbye to the kids at the school gates, then headed up to the steep rigg that circumnavigated the broad sweep of Great Stangdale. She'd intended to walk the full stretch, but the fog had become too dense, falling as a fine mizzle that got heavier as she scaled the track. Her clothes had become soaked, wicking the cold next to her skin, making her feel chilly. Eventually, the fog had become so thick it limited her visibility, blocking out the vista of the valley and potentially making the walk treacherous. Disappointed, she conceded defeat and made her way back down the path.

As she approached the village, the sound of metal hitting metal rang out from Jimby's forge. Kitty felt a sudden urge to pop in, say a quick hello and make him a mug of tea. And it went without saying that there was also the chance she'd bump into Ollie. The thought made her smile. 'Come on, you two rascals, let's go and see Jimby, he might even have some biscuits for you.'

She was about to take the turn into her brother's yard when she sensed someone watching her. Turning, she glanced across the road and caught Aoife Mellison glaring at her with such naked hostility it stopped her in her tracks. *This is getting ridiculous.* Being on bad terms with anyone made Kitty feel uncomfortable and, as a rule, if she'd had a misunderstanding with someone, she preferred to smooth things over, get them sorted out as soon as possible.

Maybe today would be a good opportunity to do just that with Aoife. She drummed her fingers against her thigh, toying with the idea. She was torn between just ignoring the dirty look and keep on walking to Jimby's or approaching Aoife in the hope that they could put things straight once and for all.

Before she knew it, her legs were carrying her in the woman's direction, a little voice telling her that things couldn't get any worse, so she might as well give it a go. 'Hi, Aoife.' She smiled, giving a small wave as she headed across the road. Aoife looked away, offering no reply, and made to scurry off. 'Aoife, please wait. Can we talk?' Kitty trotted after her, relieved when she stopped. She fixed a fresh smile on her face, hoping it would mask the jumble of nerves that were currently wrestling in her stomach. Aoife turned around with a venomous look in her eyes, and Kitty felt her heart plummet. She took a fortifying breath. 'Look, I'm aware that things are a bit…awkward between us and I'm not really sure why, but I'd like to sort things out if we can. We live in a small community, and it would be so much nicer if things could be okay between us.'

Aoife jutted her jaw, looking down her nose at Kitty.

'We could have a chat over a cup of tea if you like? You're very welcome to come to mine, or if you'd prefer, we could pop over to the tea shop.' She hoped Aoife couldn't hear the shake in her voice.

'I have nothing to say to you, and you couldn't possibly have anything to say that I'd want to hear.' Aoife folded her arms, her top lip curling scornfully.

'Right, well, I'm sorry you feel that way. But, for the sake of the children I was hoping we could at least be civil to one another; set a good example to them.'

'Oh, you do, do you? When you've been bad-mouthing my daughter to other parents and the teachers up at school?'

'I haven't been bad-mouthing Evie, I wouldn't do that. The only time I've mentioned her is when I've been approached by other parents who've voiced concerns about what she's been doing to Lily. And Lily's been upset about it at home; as her mum I had to speak to her teacher. Any parent would — you included if Evie was having trouble with someone. And, anyway, school were already aware of the situation, they'd seen it for themselves. If you ask them, they'll tell you that I was very keen for things to be sorted out amicably.'

'I'm not having that!' Aoife's fake plummy accent slid into its native Teesside. 'You say you want to *smooth things over*, but let me tell you, nothing could ever excuse or explain your behaviour.'

'Aoife, I really don't know what you mean by that.'

'I think you do! Leaving Evie out of Lily's birthday celebrations? That was unforgivable. They were best friends!' Her face was flushed with anger, and Kitty was beginning to feel a little unnerved.

The sudden loud squawking of a cockerel and the whoosh of a cycle whizzing by distracted the two women, creating a brief cease-fire. They looked on in disbelief. 'Get off, you stupid effing chicken!' yelled Lycra Len, a smear of black, as he pedalled past them full pelt, Reg gripping onto the handlebars, his wings flapping furiously.

'Len!' Kitty pressed her hand to her mouth, watching as he managed to loosen the bird's grip with one hand, before casting him down to the ground in a flurry of feathers.

'Little git!' he yelled, before continuing along the twists and turns of the Danskelfe road, leaving a startled Reg to strut back home.

'Well, haven't you got anything to say to that?' said Aoife.

'Sorry?' Kitty dragged her eyes away from Len, suddenly hauled back into the conversation with Aoife.

'I should think you are. I don't see how you can possibly defend yourself.'

'I don't think I need to defend myself. I didn't leave Evie out of any birthday celebration.' Kitty kept her voice low, her tone reasonable; she didn't want to attract attention. 'Lily wanted to go to the cinema for her birthday treat, and we said she could take two friends. She chose Abbie and Maisie, so it wasn't as if Evie was the only child not invited. And Lily has never said that Evie was her best friend, that's always been Abbie, as far back as playgroup. Everyone knows that.'

'Well, you should tell Lily! Tell her that Evie's her best friend. Evie always said Lily was *hers*. You've no right to interfere with that.'

'I didn't interfere with anything, but Lily doesn't feel the same. And Evie certainly hasn't given her any reason to think she's her best friend, so there's been nothing to interfere with – not that I would, anyway.' *This is getting silly.*

Aoife loomed over her, prodding a finger at Kitty. 'This conversation is over. I want to draw a line under this ridiculous situation and

I don't want anything to do with you or your children!' Her eyes bulged.

'Aoife, please, there's really no need for this.' Kitty was keen to calm things down.

'Don't ever speak to me again!' Aoife spun around on her heel and strode back in the direction of her house before turning, hands on hips, to fire the last of her diatribe. 'Oh, and before I forget, Dan's way too good for you. He must've been out of his mind, him an intellectual having anything to do with a little stay-at-home country mouse like you. He should've married someone equal to him, worthy of his status!' Kitty watched, mouth agape, as Aoife flung open her gate and marched up the path, slamming her front door behind her.

Kitty felt sick, and her heart was pounding. Aoife had looked quite terrifying; she'd half-expected a resounding slap to land on her face. Easing out a slow breath, she attempted to steady the thoughts reeling around her mind. She'd always thought Aoife was highly-strung, but this hostility seemed to have mushroomed. Could Rosie be right? Could this behaviour really be explained away by Aoife having an unrequited crush on Dan? Her last mouthful certainly suggested as much. And if it was, what a shame that Lily was suffering because of it. Kitty chewed on the inside of her cheek. Today's confrontation may not have resolved the situation between the two families, but it had made one thing glaringly obvious: Aoife's spiteful behaviour was clearly reflected in that of Evie's. *Like mother, like daughter.* She decided resolutely, it would be the last time she would ever try to build bridges with that woman. She didn't need people like that in her life.

Plastering a smile on her face, Kitty waved at Jonty who tootled by in his old sports car, beeping his horn as he passed her. She watched him disappear down the road. The visit to Jimby's had lost its appeal; he could read her like a book, and she didn't want to foist any more of her problems onto him. She'd go home, make a pot of tea, tackle the mountain of ironing and, hopefully, calm herself down in the process.

With a sigh, Kitty made her way along the trod towards her home, Humph and Ethel walking steadily beside her.

As she was passing the large willow tree by the pond on the village green, she was startled by someone pulling at her arm. She turned to see her mother-in-law's cold, beady eyes glaring at her. 'Gwyneth!'

'I want a word with you.'

'Really?' *Could this day possibly get any worse?* Kitty felt her shoulders slump.

'You ought to be ashamed of yourself. How dare you humiliate my Daniel! How dare you have the nerve to even think about divorcing him! Well, I'll tell you something, he's too good for you and always has been. He's always been an excellent husband and father, and you've never deserved him. Everyone can see he's way out of your league. I tried to tell him, but he was too kind to listen. You're just a pathetic little nothing who got lucky when she married such a high achiever like my son, who excels at everything he does. Working his fingers to the bone to support you and those children who you've turned into spoilt, rude little brats.'

'Just out of interest, Gwyneth, you haven't been talking to Aoife Mellison have you?'

'What? No. Why would I talk to her?'

'No reason.'

'Anyway, as I was saying before I was so rudely interrupted, what exactly have you contributed to your marriage, eh? Nothing! So, if it's true, and you are considering divorcing my Daniel, I want you to know that I'll do everything in my power to make sure that you'll come out of it with nothing!'

'Gwyneth, listen…' Her words were snapped off.

'Well, have you started divorce proceedings? As Daniel's mother, I demand an answer!'

Kitty was in no doubt where Dan got his spiteful streak from, but she wasn't going to be bullied by Gwyneth anymore. 'I'm not sure that this is the time or the place to discuss it.'

'Well, I beg to differ, and I think you should do me the courtesy of answering my question. Have you?'

'Yes, yes I have.' She braced herself.

Gwyneth inched closer, and Kitty felt her nose tingle from the harsh smell of setting-lotion coming from the woman's freshly coiffed hair. She prodded Kitty in the chest. 'How dare you go to a solicitor and bad mouth my son? You've no right! I've a good mind to sue you for slander. What goes on between you and my Daniel is private, and that's exactly how it should remain. I don't know who you think you are, spreading your spiteful rumours about him to other members of the legal profession, making him the subject of cruel gossip with your lies!'

Mesmerised by a gloopy mass of spittle that had collected in the corner of Gwyneth's mouth, Kitty took a moment to answer. Blinking the image away, she drew her shoulders back as realisation rose through her small frame like a rising tide. Dan no longer had a hold on her, she wasn't answerable to Gwyneth, and she didn't have to tolerate this crap anymore. She lowered her voice. 'Listen, Gwyneth, I think it's fair to assume that you'll have had a pretty one-sided story, so I doubt you'll be in full possession of the facts. But I can assure you, after everything that's happened, divorce was the only option for me. And I'm sure if we were talking about somebody else's son – someone from the village – you wouldn't disagree with my reasons. In fact, I know you would love to hear all the sordid little details so you could disapprove in your spiteful, sanctimonious way. But I don't go in for gossip at other people's expense so you won't hear anything about your precious son from me, and neither will anyone else. But if you *were* in possession of all the facts, you'd be very keen to let this drop. Dan and I are getting divorced, and you are just going to have to accept it.' God, it felt good to get that off her chest, thought Kitty. Her heart might be thudding like the clappers, but she felt her courage soar.

With a flick of her tongue, Gwyneth licked the spittle away from the corner of her mouth. 'You conniving trollop. Don't think I don't know what you've been getting up to with that common village boy, Oliver Cartwright. You should feel ashamed of yourself, blaming Daniel for the breakdown of your marriage when you've been throwing yourself at other men. You're nothing more than a cheap tart!' Her mouth pinched into a cruel twist.

Kitty held up her palms to her mother-in-law. 'Actually, Gwyneth, I think you'd better stop there. Let me make this clear, what you've said is well out of order and if you speak to me, or about me, like that again, I will contact my solicitor and make sure she gets you to stop.'

'How dare…'

'And don't think for one minute I won't.' The slight to Ollie had made her blood boil and hurt far more than the personal insults that had been thrown at her.

Further up the village, Molly was leaving a patient's house when she spotted Kitty and Gwyneth. She jumped into her car and headed towards them. Neither had noticed her pull-up beside them.

'Everything alright, Kitty?' Molly asked, climbing out of her vehicle.

Gwyneth started, shocked at being caught speaking to Kitty so savagely. She didn't want news of her behaviour to get back to the doctors at the local surgery who she fawned over and revered so highly. 'Oh, Molly, dear. If you knew the circumstances, you'd be asking me that question and not her. If you could've heard the way she spoke to me and the things she said you'd be appalled.' She placed a bony hand on her chest.

'That's not how things sounded to me.' Molly gave Gwyneth her infamous death stare.

'I suppose it was asking too much to expect anything better of you.'

Molly leaned in to Gwyneth. 'Listen to me, you poisonous, shrivelled old bag. Leave Kitty alone and bugger off back to where you came from. No one around here can stand you, the way you think you're so superior, looking down on everyone with that sour sodding expression of yours, puckering your mouth up like a cat's backside. Trust me, the best thing you could do for everyone is to sod right off.'

Gwyneth set her mouth into a thin line and squared up to Molly. 'How dare you, you, in-bred…' She drew a liver-spotted hand back, ready to deliver a slap to the younger woman's face when a voice stopped her.

'I don't think so.' James loomed behind Gwyneth, grabbing her by the wrist. Ready for a tea break, he'd been making his way down to Kitty's, scan- reading a copy of the previous week's York Gazette he'd picked up in the city. The shrill tone of Gwyneth's voice had pulled him away from the newspaper, which he'd hurriedly folded under his arm once he'd seen who was on the receiving end of her vicious tongue-lashing.

'Get off me, you lout. I'll get my Daniel to prosecute you for assault.'

'Oh, really? Well, there's a rather interesting article in the centre pages of this, with some pretty incriminating photographs you might want to take a look at before you decide to do anything like that.' James opened the newspaper and held it out to Gwyneth, who snatched it out of his hands.

'What do you mean, incriminating photographs?'

Kitty and Molly exchanged glances before looking enquiringly at James who was watching Gwyneth as she scrutinised the images, colour draining from her face.

'Well…well…I'm…I'm, er, sure there's a perfectly plausible explanation for this. It must be trick photography, they can do all sorts these days. My Daniel is a very moral and upstanding member of the community. Not to mention a highly professional person. I can assure you his father will be sending a very strongly worded letter to this newspaper. I'll insist on it. Publishing filth like this. It's an outrage!' She scrunched up the paper and threw it into the gutter where it landed in a puddle. 'You Fairfaxes will be the ruin of my son.' She stormed off towards her home.

Molly was the first to speak. 'Well, she's rattled. You can just about see steam coming out of her lugs. What the hell was in that paper, Jimby?'

James reached down and picked up the gazette, giving it a quick shake before opening out the centre pages. 'Listen, Kitts, I didn't want to do it like this, and I don't want you to get upset, but I'd rather you saw it first-hand than having to hear about it from some vindictive gossip like Aoife Mellison.'

Kitty's heart sank at hearing the woman's name.

'Is it that bad?' Molly glanced across at James. He held the paper open in front of them. 'Oh, shit a brick, it is.'

Kitty stared at the photos in silence, her expression inscrutable. After several seconds she clamped a hand over her mouth and scrunched her eyes tightly together as her shoulders began to shake.

'Oh, God, I'm so sorry, Kitts, that was really thoughtless of me. I hadn't intended for you to find out like this, but I was just so angry at the way that old bag was talking to you that I acted in the heat of the moment. Please don't cry.'

'What the bloody hell have you done to her, Jimby?' asked Molly, concerned.

Kitty glanced at James, her eyes wet with tears. He rubbed his brow; he was clearly feeling terrible. But his guilt was soon chased away when a laugh that his sister had been struggling to hold in finally escaped between her fingers in a noisy splutter. More tumbled out, rendering her unable to speak. Jimby grinned, relieved to see she was crying tears of mirth and not sadness. Swiping them away with her fingers she gasped. 'Oh, Jimby, this is hilarious! Did you see the woman with the enormous rabbit ears?'

'Ha ha! You could hardly miss them.'

'Let's see.' Molly peered over Kitty's shoulder to get a better view. 'Well, I just don't get it. Why the bloody hell would you want to strut about with your bits hanging out and something ridiculous on your head?'

'Good question.' James pursed his lips, nodding in agreement.

'Oh, my face is aching.' Kitty clapped her hands to her cheeks, she was still struggling to keep her giggles under control. 'I would love to have seen Dan scurrying off like that, with his suit covering his privates. He and his mother think he's so bloody perfect.'

'I'd love to have been there armed with a catapult. Or, better, a giant water-pistol, full of cold water. That'd have fettled the lot of them. Imagine the fun you could have taking them by surprise with an icy soaking.' Molly mimed aiming one, making them all giggle.

'I'd be very interested to hear how Dan will explain the photos away to his mother. That birthmark is so distinctive.' Kitty peered at the image again.

'Well, I don't see how he can wriggle out of this one. It's very definitely his arse in the photographs,' added James. Years previously, Kitty had shared details of Dan's birthmark with them.

'Oh, it's him alright. And it's good to see you taking all this so well, and laughing about it with us, but are you really alright about it all, petal? I mean…well, you know?' Molly searched Kitty's face.

'Yeah, you seem really cool about it, but are you okay? Sorry if we've upset you by joking about it.'

Kitty shrugged her shoulders. 'S'alright. I couldn't give a shit. Feel free to joke as much as you like. I've accepted that Dan's a knob-head. Always has been, always will be. And this proves it. Only the people who know about his birthmark will know it's him, so it's not like the kids are going to be embarrassed about it or get teased. I'm just glad I don't have to live with him after the fall-out from this. I can't believe how much better life is without him – for the kids and me. Especially the kids. It's great to see them so relaxed without that spiteful arse coming home and putting a cloud over the house, talking to them like they're dirt. I just wish I'd come to my senses sooner.'

James and Molly looked at one another before bursting into

laughter at hearing her swear. 'Sounds like our Kitts has grown a set of balls bigger than yours, Jimby,' said Molly.

'Enough, Moll!' Kitty grimaced and held up her hand. 'Please don't get started on the testicle chat, especially when it involves my brother.'

'Sorry, Kitts. I just mean it's good to see you standing up for yourself and being all sassy at long last.'

'Moll's right – apart from the bit about the balls – it's good to see you looking so strong and tough. Long may it continue, eh, little sis?' James threw an arm around her and gave her a squeeze.

'Er, yeah, I think my sass might be here to stay – but reserved for those who deserve it. I don't want to be like that all the time,' she added. 'A few minutes before Gwyneth pounced I had an, erm, interesting encounter with Aoife Mellison.'

Molly groaned. 'Really? Well, I hope you gave her what for – if anyone deserves to be put in their place it's that one. I cannot stand that stuck-up cow. If she looks down her nose at me one more time, I swear I'm going to poke my bloody finger right up there.'

'Yeah, she really thinks she's something special, that one. Was she unpleasant?' asked James.

'You could say. That, and what's just happened with Gwyneth has got a lot to do with me suddenly realising that I've got to be more assertive.'

Her experiences that morning had tapped into her new-found resilience. It was half-way through her mother-in-law's toxic tongue lashing that she'd come to the decision that she wasn't going to let either of them get under her skin any longer. Instead of internalising the spiteful words – as she usually did, so she could fret over them, re-live them and beat herself up over them whenever she had a quiet moment – she was going to let them bounce off her like water off a duck's back.

'Oh, and before I forget, Reg has been up to his old tricks again. I think he's traumatised poor old Lycra Len.' Kitty shared the cockerel's latest misdemeanour with Jimby and Molly, who thought it was hilarious. Though James conceded he'd have to deal with him before he inflicted serious injury on someone. As for Len, he'd buy him a couple of pints next time he saw him in the Sunne.

Molly checked her watch. 'Bugger, is that the time? I should've been at my next patient's ten minutes ago. Will you be okay if I head off?' She directed the question at Kitty who nodded with a smile.

'Yep. I was thinking of joining Jimby for a cuppa. Must be around your tea-break time, is it?'

'Sure is. Why don't we head to my workshop and I'll stick the kettle on?'

'Good plan,' said Kitty.

Molly climbed into her four-wheel drive and was fastening her seatbelt when her mobile phone pinged. She rolled her eyes and began furtling around in her bag for it. 'That had bloody better not be work hounding me. Thanks to the ever-increasing pregnancy hormones raging around my body, I'm feeling particularly feisty. Now where the sodding hell's my phone? Ah, here it is.'

Holding back smiles, James and Kitty watched as Molly pulled the phone out of her bag. 'Fabulous! It's a text from Granny Aggie. She never fails to brighten my day, bless her. See if you can work out what she's after.' Doing her best to stifle her laughter, Molly read the message aloud:

"Dear Molly, Hippo your willies are dripping wet. They need some corn plastering? Not Rust. Lots of lovers, Gammy Aggie XOXOXO"

'Any ideas?' Molly raised a questioning eyebrow at her cousins, who were snorting with laughter.

'Ahh, she's hilarious. And what does an old dear like her know about dripping willies?' Jimby sniggered.

'It's all those racy books she reads,' giggled Kitty. 'And I won't ask about the "lots of lovers" part.'

'Well, at least she left the vicar alone in this text. I don't think he could cope with any more of her slander.' Molly threw her phone back in her bag and put her car into gear. 'Right, I'd best be off. Look after your sister, Jimby.'

As she made her way across the yard to the forge with James, Kitty craned her neck, hoping to see Ollie in his workshop, but was disappointed to see there was no sign of him. It gave her a thrill to catch a glimpse of him working, lost in concentration, a pencil tucked behind his ear, and his sleeves rolled up, revealing soft golden hairs on tanned, muscular forearms. Seeing him engrossed in his latest project, magically turning plain planks of wood into something useful was guaranteed to make her stomach flip.

James spotted her looking. 'Oll's gone to a customer's over in Danskelfe to do some measuring up. Won't be back for a while.'

'Oh.' It was hard to keep the disappointment from her voice. Since they'd decided to keep their relationship low-key until her divorce was finalised, any type of contact with Ollie, however small, was like a precious nugget of gold. And it was becoming increasingly hard to keep it secret, especially from her brother.

But there was no fooling him. He opened the door and headed across to the kettle, giving it a shake to make sure it contained sufficient water for two mugs. 'Tea?' He flashed a mischievous smile, telling Kitty he knew.

'Er, yes, please. As long as it's not in one of your obscene mugs.' She batted his grin away.

'I do have some respectable ones, you know. I need them just in case customers call. Though I had to learn my lesson the hard way when the last vicar's sister called round – do you remember her? Eunice, I think she was called, an old spinster, very prim and prudish. Anyway, it was when our Molly's Tom was here doing work experience, and he offered her a cup of tea. I nearly choked when I saw her take a sip out of the mug that Ollie had brought back from his motorbike ride around Scotland. Remember, he stumbled across a village called Tongue? Anyway, the mug Tom had given her had "I Love Tongue" plastered across it. Luckily, I don't think she had a clue what it meant, but Tom was just about peeing himself laughing; little sod. I didn't know what to do first, laugh or cringe.'

'I can imagine.' Kitty giggled, perching herself on a rickety wooden seat.

'Anyway, enough about me. When were you planning on telling me about you and Mr Lover Boy over there?' Grinning, he leaned against his workbench, arms folded across his chest and nodded in the direction of Ollie's workshop. 'Not that you needed to, by the way. There was only ever going to be one reason for the way he's been walking around grinning like the cat that got the cream and whistling his nuts off. I'm half expecting him to do cartwheels across the yard. And the transformation in you, well…'

'Is it that obvious?' She could feel her cheeks burning.

'Yep.'

'And you don't think it's too soon?'

'Too *soon*? Are you mad? The bloke's been in love with you for as long as I can remember. How can that be too soon?'

'It's just, well, you know, with Dan and everything, and him being your best friend. Are you sure you're okay with it?'

'Of course I'm bloody okay with it! It's fantastic. You two were always meant to be together. Go for it, sis. You both deserve to be happy.'

'Thanks, Jimby, it means the world hearing you say that.' Kitty's heart squeezed with happiness.

42

VALENTINE'S DAY

IN THE WEEKS since they'd rekindled their relationship, Kitty and Ollie had managed to snatch a handful of moments alone together. They'd been cautious, not wanting to set tongues wagging, which was difficult, nigh on impossible, when you lived your life under the microscopic eye of village life. And Kitty had to admit to herself that there was something deliciously exquisite about illicit kisses stolen here and there. But there'd been nothing more; Ollie had been the perfect gentleman, not pushing her into anything, allowing her to take her time, happy for her to lead the way.

There was no denying the electricity that fizzed between the pair, and it hadn't gone unnoticed at the smattering of evenings they'd enjoyed at the pub, despite it being in the company of their friends. They always found themselves sitting side-by-side on the banquette, at their usual table, where the meaningful glances they snatched made Kitty's stomach perform somersaults. She was struggling to keep a lid on her newly resurrected passion, which she could feel bubbling with increased fervour beneath the surface. A jolt of lust would shoot right through her whenever the soft hairs of Ollie's arm brushed against her skin. And she could hardly keep her hands to herself when his firm, muscular thigh pressed against hers. And, judging by the look in his eyes, she was in no doubt he felt the same way.

∼

HUGGING a mug of tea to her chest, Kitty gazed out of the kitchen window. She'd just finished slicing a tray of freshly baked chocolate brownies, their mouth-watering aroma filling the room. The sound of Lucas and Lily, calling and giggling, caught her attention and she peered across the misty garden, its hedges and shrubs festooned with dew-laden cobwebs, to where they were bobbing up and down on the see-saw. She chuckled as she watched Lily's bottom lift a good six inches in the air, her thick mop of curls bouncing up and down as though they had a life of their own. Lucas, his head thrown back with laughter, seemed blissfully unaware of the muddy smear running the full length of his jeans, as well as something that looked suspiciously like a rip. The thought of what Dan would make of it crept into her mind, casting a black shadow. If he'd been here to see it, there would have been hell to pay, and Lucas would have been banned from playing in the garden for a week. She gave an involuntary shudder and shoved the thought away. She'd been brought up to believe that it didn't matter if kids got their clothes dirty while they were playing; it showed they'd been having fun. And she was relieved to see that her children appeared to have released themselves from Dan's legacy of bullying and were enjoying the same carefree kind of childhood she'd had.

She smiled and took a sip of her tea as her thoughts meandered to the exciting news Violet had shared when she'd popped round the previous evening. It had set Kitty's mind racing.

'You're doing what?' she'd asked, sure she'd misunderstood or missed part of what Vi had been telling her.

Vi took a deep breath. 'I've – touch wood,' she tapped her fingers against her head, 'sold Purple Diamond PR, I'm renting out my flat in York, and I'm moving back to the village permanently. I'm going to convert that large shed at the bottom of the garden at Sunshine Cottage into a workroom, where I'll be running my new company, Romantique, designing and making vintage-style lingerie. Well, that's the shortened version of events — I'll fill you in on the full version when I don't have to rush off anywhere — but I've been thinking about it for a while now.'

'Wow, Vi. That sounds so exciting!'

'I know. Oh, and I wondered if you'd be my business partner.'

'Say that again.'

'I wondered if you'd be my business partner. We're both a whizz on the sewing machine, and with your artistic flair and my eye for all things vintage, I think we'd make a great team. There's definitely a market for it. I thought we could also design and make costumes for burlesque dancers. There's a huge demand for that, and very few places to get your hands on the right thing — that's why I ended up making mine.'

Kitty's eyes were dancing, her mind racing. 'Oh, Vi, that sounds so exciting. I don't know what to say.'

'Say yes. Simples!' Vi laughed. 'Actually, I want you to think it over for a few days before you agree to anything. Make sure it's what you really want. But if you have any questions, just holler.'

When Kitty had gone to bed that night, her mind had been racing with ideas, Vi's proposition pushing sleep further and further out of reach. The opportunity to flex her creative muscles once more had triggered an excitement she hadn't expected. When she'd awoken early the following morning, there was only one answer she could possibly give Vi: 'Hell, yes!'

THE SOUND of Humphrey snuffling around for crumbs tugged Kitty's thoughts back into the present — the Labrador's twitching nose was getting worryingly close to the wire rack where the brownies were cooling. She was just about to call him away when they were both distracted by the sound of mail being pushed through the letter-box. Ethel gave a half-hearted harrumph as Kitty went to gather it up. There, side-by-side on the coir doormat, lay two white envelopes. One bore the frank of her solicitors, the other a simple first-class stamp. She paused for a moment, before deciding to open them.

The correspondence from her solicitors was in Letitia Tickell's usual breezy, jolly-hockey-sticks tone, confirming that Kitty should be in receipt of her decree absolute within the next six weeks. Her heart jittered at the implications. She took a deep breath and turned her attention to the other envelope. Sliding her finger underneath the seal, she eased it open, her heart pounding. There, looking back at her, was a Valentine's card.

Her gaze lingered over the beautifully understated heart design on the front before she nervously peered inside. She was hoping it would be from Ollie, but a distant niggle in the shape of Henry Wilkinson lurked at the back of her mind. Thankfully, her concerns were unfounded, and happiness surged through her as she read the simple message.

Love you always.
O xxx

She re-read them, this time aloud, a smile in her voice. Fate was talking to her, the letter symbolising the end of her old life, the card, the beginning of her new one.

A loud rapping and Ethel's resultant bark roused Kitty from her thoughts. She opened the door. 'Kitty Fairfax?' A harassed-looking face peered around an enormous hand-tied bouquet of dusky pink roses.

'Erm, yes.' Kitty paused, only locals who'd known her all her life addressed by her maiden name.

'These are for you.' He shoved the bouquet into her arms then pushed an electronic note-pad under her nose. 'I just need you to sign this.'

Kitty took the flowers into the kitchen and set them on the draining board, lifting out the small envelope that was set amongst the foliage, hardly daring to read it. The last time she had been given a bunch of flowers from this particular florist's they'd been unwelcome, and from Henry. She cringed at the thought. But her biggest fear was that they'd be from Dan.

She eased the card out of the envelope.

A rose for every year I've loved you.
O xxx

'Ollie.' She beamed as relief and happiness washed over her. 'Sixteen, seventeen, eighteen!' She counted the rosebuds aloud. Eighteen years? Ollie Cartwright had been in love with her for eighteen years!

Wearing a smile that refused to budge, she dialled his number. He picked up after two rings – he'd been waiting for the call, anxious that she'd be pleased with the flowers. He'd remembered that dusky pink roses were her favourite and had opted for them instead of the usual Valentine red. Ollie had never sent flowers to anyone before, except his mum, and that was only once when she was in hospital having her appendix out. Seeing Kitty's number on his phone made his heart race. 'Hi, Kitty.'

'Hi, Ollie. Thank you for the roses, they're beautiful.' He could hear the smile in her voice, and the tension he'd been holding onto drained away.

'Just like you.' He pulled a face; the words had tripped out before he'd had a chance to think. *Too cheesy?*

She gave a shy giggle. 'You remembered my favourite colour, too.'

'I did.'

'Do you know what a truly lovely man you are, Ollie Cartwright?'

'Well, now you come to mention it…'

'I've just made some chocolate brownies, would you like to come over and try one? If you're not too busy that is.'

'I'm on my way.'

Before Kitty had a chance to check her reflection in the mirror and remove the dusting of flour from the tip of her nose, there was a knock at the door which made her knees turn to jelly. Slinging the tea-towel she was holding over her shoulder, she ran to the door, smoothing her cropped hair with the palms of her hands as she went. She opened it to find Ollie in the doorway. 'I was promised chocolate brownies.' He was leaning against the door jamb, a heart-melting smile on his lips.

'Well, you'd better come in.' She grinned back, opening the door wide so he could step into the hallway. 'They're absolutely lovely,' she said as he followed her into the kitchen.

'Good.'

'The roses, I mean, not the brownies. Look.' Smiling, she gestured to the bouquet she'd placed on the window sill.

Ollie hooked his thumbs through the belt loops of his jeans. 'Well, I'm glad you like them.'

Kitty turned to him, a blush blooming in her cheeks. 'Eighteen?'

'Eighteen.' He nodded. In a moment, he strode across the kitchen, cupped her face in his hands and gently wiped the flour off her nose with his thumb.

'That's a long time.' Her voice came out in a whisper. He was standing so close she could feel the warmth of his body radiating from him, smell his familiar intoxicating scent of fresh moorland air and soap. And it was having a serious effect on her pulse rate. Peering up at him from beneath her lashes, her eyes met his. The intensity in his gaze, darkened with lust, took her breath away.

'Kitty,' he said huskily as he pressed his mouth against hers with a passion that made her lips tingle. She reached up, pushing her hands into his hair, returning his kisses with equal ardour. 'I want you so badly,' he murmured as he trailed burning kisses down her neck.

'I want you too,' she groaned; she could feel his excitement pressing against her.

The back door flew open with a crash, making the pair jump apart like scalded cats. 'Are the brownies ready yet, Mum?' Lucas bellowed as he fell into the hallway. Keen to hide his state of arousal, Ollie hurriedly pulled out a dining chair and sat down.

Kitty swallowed. 'Oh, erm, yes, they should be cool enough to eat now, Lukes.' She smoothed her hair, hoping to smooth away the guilty feeling of almost being caught red-handed by her son.

Oblivious, Lucas hurtled by Ollie in a blast of fresh air. 'Oh, hi, Ollie.'

'Hiya, Lukes. Having fun out there?'

'Yep.' He grabbed a wedge of brownie, eyeing it greedily before taking a bite.

'Take a slice for your sister, too.' Kitty's voice lilted with a faux breeziness, her mouth still tingling with Ollie's kisses.

'Okay. Thanks, Mum.' He swallowed his mouthful and scooped up another slice. 'See ya.' He ran out into the garden without a backwards glance.

Kitty leaned back against the worktop. 'Phew, that was close.'

'Er, just a bit.' Ollie laughed. 'It feels like we're a couple of horny teenagers almost getting caught at it by our parents.'

'I know, but it seems a hundred times worse when it's your kids that almost catch you out, especially when we're trying to keep things quiet.'

'You're telling me.' He paused for a moment. 'Actually, it wasn't just your brownies that tempted me over here. Or your hot kisses for that matter – though they do tempt me more than I care to admit. I was wondering if you'd be willing to go out with me tonight? On a date, but low-key. Well, when I say low-key, it would be at the Sunne for a special Valentine's meal. So, I suppose it wouldn't be low-key at all. Anyway, I've booked a table for two – it's a discreet one, tucked away in a corner – and Anoushka says she's happy to babysit, as you can imagine. But, don't worry, I'll completely understand if you say you'd rather not.' His eyes searched her face.

Kitty was silent for a moment, mulling over the implications of what Ollie had just asked her. He'd taken her by surprise, and the reasons for and against were whirling around her mind, jostling for precedence. But there was one overwhelming feeling that nudged its way forward and finally won out. 'What the hell. I'd love to.'

'Fantastic! I'll pick you up at seven, if that's okay?' He checked his watch. 'But right now, I have to whisk Noushka off to her Street Dance class – whatever that may be – over in Middleton.' He moved over to Kitty and pressed his lips against hers before pulling himself away and grabbing a slice of brownie. 'The things I have to do to get one of these.'

'Cheek!' She giggled, pulling the tea-towel off her shoulder and flicking him with it. 'Here, don't forget to take a piece for Noushka.'

43

LEAVING the brittle cold of the evening at the doorstep, Kitty and Ollie stepped into the warmth of the Sunne. Casting her gaze around the busy pub, she could see that most of the tables were occupied. Ollie gave her a nudge, dispelling the butterflies that were making mischief in her stomach, and nodded in the direction of Gerald and Big Mary who were getting cosy in the corner, sipping what appeared to be exotic cocktails. Both were blissfully unaware that Gerald's false teeth, which were teetering precariously on a beer mat on the edge of their table, were being shown an unusual amount of interest by Scruff and Nomad. 'If Gerald doesn't watch out, Nomad's going to be running around the pub wearing a set of dentures.'

'They'd probably fit him better than they do Gerald,' Kitty said with a giggle.

'Hmm. You've got a point. Did I tell you about the last time he was in here wearing them – Gerald, not Nomad?' Ollie stood aside, letting a couple from Dankselfe go by. He turned to face Kitty and grinned.

'No, I don't think so.'

'We were sitting at the bar – Jimby and me – when Gerald comes in, orders a pint and sits down beside us. He was chatting away, clearly struggling with those teeth, when he started to sneeze. The final one was so hard he actually sneezed his teeth out. Right into Jimby's beer – which went everywhere. You should've seen Jimby's face, it was a picture.' Ollie shook his head, laughing at the memory.

Kitty clamped a hand over her mouth to control her giggles. 'Oh, that must've been so funny. I bet Jimby's face was priceless.'

'It was hilarious and took a good ten minutes before Jonty could stop laughing.'

'Oh, I wish I'd been there.'

Though she hadn't said anything, Ollie knew that Kitty had felt anxious about walking into the pub with him tonight, worried that all eyes would be on them or, worse, George and Gwyneth would be there. He'd deliberately tried to make her laugh, hoping it would help her feel more relaxed. And he was pleased to see that it appeared to be working.

Kitty gave a small shrug of her shoulders, aware that tension was beginning to release its grip, the jitters in her stomach slowly beginning to subside.

'You okay?' He took her hand, giving it a squeeze.

'Yep.' She looked up at him and smiled, the soft light dancing in her eyes.

'THIS IS LOVELY.' Sitting at their table, Kitty cast her eyes appreciatively around the heavily-beamed room, taking in the sumptuous décor. Bea's eclectic flair was evident in every detail. Swathed in soft lighting, with the fire crackling away in the inglenook fireplace and music playing unobtrusively in the background, it would be difficult to feel anything other than romantic in this room tonight. 'And the flowers are just stunning. Bea's good at everything she does,' she said, admiring the artfully rustic display of blood-red roses and dark green foliage which took pride of place on the antique oak table at the far end of the restaurant. There were scaled-down versions on the dining tables, set in squat pewter pots. They contrasted beautifully with the crisp white tablecloths, which were scattered with dried rose petals.

'Yeah, she's got it looking pretty special,' Ollie agreed. 'Anyway, cheers!' Smiling, he clinked his glass against Kitty's.

'Cheers,' she replied, taking a sip of her wine, her taste-buds tingling in response to its citrussy notes. Her eyes met his, triggering the butterflies in her stomach once more – though, this time it wasn't because of the raised eyebrows and knowing smiles as they'd headed to the bar. This variety was purely down to her stampeding feelings for the wonderful man sitting opposite her.

He leaned across the table and took her hand in his, sending a shaft of electricity straight to her core. Pressing it to his lips, he kissed it gently, not caring who could see. 'You look beautiful,' he said huskily.

'Thank you.' She could feel the warmth of a blush colour her cheeks. 'I think it must be something to do with the dim lighting in here.' Still unused to taking compliments, Kitty looked down at the table, thinking of something to say to change the subject.

'It's nothing to do with the lighting, Kitts. You look beautiful because you are beautiful.' Ollie was looking at her intently, his eyes glittering. 'And I'm just really chuffed you agreed to come. I would've been gutted if you hadn't – though I would've completely under-stood. But it's good to spend time together like this, just you and me.'

'I agree, and I'm really glad I came, too.'

'And you look stunning in that dress. It really suits you. You look like you again.' His eyes ran over her appreciatively, and she could feel her blush deepen. The only time Dan had ever commented on what she was wearing was to say something negative. Ollie's compli-ments might take some getting used to.

'Thank you, it's new. I had a shopping trip to York and spent a little bit more than I'd planned on doing, but never mind.'

Kitty had recently emptied her wardrobe of the uniform that Dan had approved for her but had never felt like her. The result was that the clothing recycling bins in Middleton-le-Moors had bulged with black bin bags stuffed with clothes. The dress Ollie was admiring – teal jersey, slightly Bo-Ho, empire-line, finishing mid-calf with exquisite hand-stitched beading around the neckline – had caught her eye in the window of L'Armoire, a small, independent shop in the Shambles. She'd immediately fallen in love with it, and the matching jewelled, soft leather teal ballet pumps, and had dashed into the shop before anyone else could snatch them up.

'Lucas and Lily seemed to accept us going out together as if it was the norm.' He popped a forkful of potato fondant into his mouth.

Kitty swallowed her mouthful before answering. 'They did. I haven't said anything to them either but judging from some of the casual remarks they've made, I get the impression they quite like the idea of us being together. And it helps that they think you're absolutely amazing.'

'Well, that goes without saying,' he joked.

'I'm just so proud of them; how they've coped with everything. And I think that they're aware of the contrast between family life with Dan – or the lack of it – and family life when you and Noushka are around. Everything just seems more…' she tipped her head to one side, looking for the right word. 'It seems more settled.'

'That's good to hear. And I'm sure I don't need to tell you that Noushka is over the moon about us.'

She giggled, 'You're right there. She looks like she's going to burst with excitement every time I see her.'

Ollie reached for his glass, 'Here's to our fabulous kids.'

'To our fabulous kids.' She beamed; she couldn't remember a time when she felt happier.

KITTY POPPED the handmade truffle into her mouth. 'Mmm.' She closed her eyes as the chocolate melted on her tongue followed by a rich, intense flavour of fruit as cherry liqueur flooded her tastebuds.

'That good, eh?'

'Mmhmm.' She rolled the sweet around her mouth, savouring every moment before reluctantly swallowing it. 'Heavenly.'

Ollie laughed as she licked melted chocolate off her fingers.

'Well, if you like it that much, you'd better have mine.' With a lopsided smile, he pushed the dish containing his truffle over to her, insisting that he didn't want it. Kitty grinned and popped it into her mouth. Her sweet tooth, it would seem, was enjoying a renaissance.

'That meal was just perfect. Thank you again for bringing us here, Ollie. I don't think I've ever eaten seared scallops as buttery, and sweet, and delicious as the ones in our starter. I would never have thought of having them with chorizo, but it was a lovely combination. And the beef cheek was so tender it just fell apart as soon as my knife touched it. I don't know how she did it, but Bea certainly succeeded in making Yorkshire portions look delicate and artistic.'

Ollie nodded in agreement. 'Mmm. She's one talented lady. The belly pork was amazing, and whatever she did with the apple-sauce, she even managed to make that taste extra special, too.'

'Yep, and don't get me started on that pudding.'

'There's no fear of that, you were enjoying it so much I thought you were going to have a bit of a moment, if you get my meaning. I don't think the Sunne's ready for that sort of behaviour just yet.'

Kitty giggled into the napkin she was using to dab up any stray traces of chocolate from her mouth.

NOTICING OLLIE HAD FINISHED his wine, Kitty drained the last of hers. As she placed her glass back on the table, he reached across and took her hand, lacing his fingers through hers. 'So, would you like another glass here, or do you fancy having a night-cap at mine?'

Her eyes met his, reading the subtext of his words. 'I think we should go to yours.'

THIS VALENTINE'S night would go down as the worst one Dan could remember. He'd spent the evening in his flat. Alone. The alternative of going out by himself wasn't tempting; the thought of looking like a loser on the, supposedly, most romantic night of the year held little appeal. And, in a rare moment of self-doubt, he was beginning to wonder if he was losing his touch. Earlier that day he'd tried his charm on the young office junior, Laura, but she'd turned him down in favour of a night out with her boyfriend of five minutes. Stupid girl. He'd even found himself on the receiving end of a fierce verbal worrying from Frances for his trouble; she'd overheard him flirting from the junior clerks' room. She never missed a bloody trick, that woman.

Nope, there was no denying it, tonight was totally crap. Instead of enjoying the company of a shapely woman, he'd have to make do with a shapely bottle of red, bought hurriedly from the local supermarket. He cursed at the thought and stalked into the kitchen where he began rummaging through a drawer for a cork-screw. Where was the sodding thing? He could find everything but the one item he was bloody well looking for. What the hell made him think he needed two tin openers? Or so many cocktail sticks? He rooted a bit deeper, his fingers coming into contact with a piece of card. Pulling it out he saw that it was a photo of Kitty and the kids. 'What the hell is that doing in there?' he muttered, throwing it onto the worktop. 'Hiding the bloody corkscrew, that's what,' he grumbled, snatching up the object of his search.

He poured himself a generous glass of wine. Taking a sip, his eyes fell upon the photograph. He picked it up and trudged back into his dimly-lit lounge, flopping wearily into a chair. He gazed at the three faces that smiled out from the photo. 'Shit.' He ran a hand over his face. What had happened to his life over the last few months? It felt like he'd been scooped up by a tornado and dumped somewhere far from where his previous life had existed. Everyone was behaving differently, and he'd lost control of just about everything. He barely recognised his family; he was even struggling to recognise himself.

He picked up his wine, swirling it around the broad curves of the glass, before taking a deep slug. He pulled a face and set it down on the small side table; he didn't even get enjoyment from that anymore. Like everything else in his miserable life, it left a bitter after-taste.

The photo seemed to have magnetic properties, and his eyes were drawn to it again, lingering as he ran his fingers across it. What had happened to the three people who smiled out at him from it? All they'd done was love him. And all he'd given them in return was hurt and heartache until they could take no more. Guilt crept over him as he recalled the last contact he'd had with Kitty, her face distorted by pain. He pushed his fingers into his hair, his knuckles blanched white as he gripped it tightly. 'What the hell have I done to you?' Dan could feel his throat constrict, and the sting of tears burn his eyes. 'Oh, God. I'm sorry. I'm so sorry.'

44

'CHEERS.' Ollie clinked his glass against Kitty's.

'Cheers.' She beamed back at him before taking a sip of rhubarb wine, her taste-buds jangling at its tangy sweetness, quickly followed by a potent kick. 'Wow!' Her eyes widened in surprise. 'I'd forgotten how lethal that is.'

He placed his glass on the sideboard and turned to her, taking her glass, setting it beside his. 'Now, where were we? Oh, yes…'

'Oh! Erm, I was just saying…' Before she could finish he took her face in his hands and brushed his lips against hers. 'Mmm…' She melted into him, her heart responded, pounding wildly in her chest, while her legs turned to jelly. She felt the flick of his tongue, the desire in his lips, that sent a shot of electricity tingling deliciously in her knickers. 'Ollie,' she gasped, kissing him harder and wrapping her arms around him, running her hands over the powerful muscles that rippled across his broad, strong back. Oh, how she wanted him.

'Kitty,' he replied with a moan as he delivered kisses that were fuelled by eighteen years of unspent desire. He ran his hands over her hips, grabbing her pert backside, pulling her into him. Feeling the hardness of his arousal, she pressed her body into his, pushing her fingers through his hair as she kissed him greedily. 'You taste so good,' he breathed.

'Mmm, so do you,' she whispered. 'Take me to bed, Ollie.'

'Thought you'd never ask,' he said huskily as his kisses burnt their way down her neck. 'But I want you to be sure, Kitty.'

'Oh, I'm sure,' she said, kissing him deeply. 'I've never been more sure of anything.' She took his hand and led him slowly upstairs.

In his bedroom, Ollie was glad that he'd had the foresight to make a few preparations – just in case he'd been right about the vibes he'd been picking up from Kitty. He'd filled a jam jar with snow-drops from his garden, tidied his country pursuits magazines away (he'd heard enough times from Molly just what a passion-killer they could be), checked around for any stray smelly socks (or worse) and put a new bulb in the small bedside lamp. As he pushed the door open with his foot, he was relieved to see his efforts had gone a considerable way to soften up the masculine room. Bathed in a warm glow, it looked cosy and inviting.

'God, you're beautiful, Kitty Fairfax,' he said, pulling her close to him, his eyes dark with lust.

'You're not so bad yourself, Ollie Cartwright.' Standing on her tiptoes, she reached up and kissed him, gently tugging at his bottom lip with her teeth.

Suddenly the kisses became more urgent. Before she knew it, Kitty was pulling his shirt out of his trousers, then started on the buttons, all fingers and thumbs in her haste. Seeing her struggle, Ollie pulled the shirt over his head, throwing it to the floor. Without missing a beat, he pressed his lips against hers once more as he began to undo the buttons of her dress. She gasped as it slipped to the floor.

He paused for a moment, drinking in the sight of her as she stood before him in an unbelievably sexy pair of dusky pink polka dot knickers, trimmed with cream lace, her breasts small and pert, like ripe apples. 'Wow! 'You've no idea what you do to me Kitty,' he said with a groan as he pulled off his trousers, closely followed by his boxer shorts.

Emboldened by her passion for him, Kitty's eyes ranged over Ollie's muscular form as he stood before her. He was magnificent. This was a totally different experience to what she'd had with Dan – whom she always seemed to annoy by doing things wrong: being too timid, and not being sexy enough. She'd ended up being a puppet, switching off, detaching herself and performing, until the intimacy, thankfully, fizzled out. But here with Ollie, she'd never felt so sexual, so aroused, so in tune with her body.

As all six-foot-three of him towered over her, his shoulders broad and strong, Kitty was unable to resist the urge to touch him.

Slowly, she ran her fingers over his chest, before tracing them down the length of his arms, over the undulations of his firm muscles, then heading back to the springy curls that covered his chest. *Oh my days!* She was tingling in places she'd didn't know she had.

She shivered with desire as Ollie took her hands and pulled her close, dropping a kiss on her shoulder. 'I've waited a long time for you, Kitty Fairfax,' he said as he laced his fingers through hers and led her to the bed. Throwing back the duvet he gently lay her down and climbed in beside her.

'WELL, that was definitely worth waiting eighteen years for.' Ollie sighed, his arm wrapped around Kitty, her head resting on his chest. He dropped a kiss onto her curls.

'It was amazing.' She snuggled closer. 'I've never felt that way before.'

'Neither have I.' He pulled the duvet around them and hugged her.

Lying in his arms, Kitty was swathed in a blissful feeling of contentment. Tonight, she realised, was the first night she'd actually been made love to.

'I could lie here forever.' She stretched her leg across Ollie's.

'I could let you. In fact, I think we should lie here a bit longer so we can do what we've just done all over again.' Putting his finger under her chin, he tilted her head to him and kissed her.

She wiggled her toes. 'Mmm. That does sound good, but I'm in danger of feeling way too comfy in this bed. And much as I would love to stay in it with you all night, so we can do it all again, there are three children who might have some grumbling to do if I don't head home soon.'

'Yep, you're right, but I just need one more tiny, little kiss.' Before Kitty could answer, he'd rolled on top of her and pressed his lips to hers. 'I never knew you were such a wanton woman.' He grinned as she wrapped her legs around him.'

'WAKEY, WAKEY, SLEEPY-HEAD.' Wrapped in his dressing gown, Ollie placed a mug of tea on the bedside table before kissing Kitty softly on the cheek.

She sighed and rubbed her eyes. 'What time is it?'

'Just gone midnight.'

'What?' She pushed herself up on her elbows.

'Don't panic, it's all fine. I've spoken to Noushka who's been happily texting her friends and watching a film. She says Lucas and Lily have been sound asleep for hours.'

'Phew.' Kitty fell back into her pillow and stretched languorously. 'I've had a really lovely night.' She smiled at him.

'Me, too.' He climbed back into the cosiness of the bed. He still couldn't believe that he'd spent the night having mind-blowing sex with the woman he'd loved from afar for all these years. 'And I know the perfect way to finish it off,' he said, pulling her close to him.

'Mmm. Me too.'

45

MONDAY MORNING ARRIVED full of optimism and cheer, scattering a burst of bright spring sunshine across the moors, some of which was currently poking its fingers through the windows of the kitchen at Oak Tree Farm.

The rosebuds from Ollie's bouquet had started to open out, filling the room with their heady fragrance. Kitty picked up one of the petals that had fallen onto the window sill, smoothing her thumb across its velvety surface.

She cast her mind back to Saturday, and her evening with Ollie. How he'd made her feel sensuous and alive, her skin tingling at his touch, the air rippling with electricity, their bodies so in tune. She blushed at the memory. But it had felt so right, and it came as no surprise that she'd peeled off her usual inhibitions and cast them to one side with her clothes, without giving them a second thought. She'd known instinctively to let her passion take the lead, and it had taken her breath away.

Snapping out of her reverie, Kitty checked her watch; Molly and Violet had said they'd pop in for a cuppa this morning, and they were due any minute. Grabbing the kettle, she filled it then sat it on the Aga and braced herself — there was no way that pair would settle for anything less than a blow-by-blow account of Saturday night. She wondered exactly how long it would take them to start the interrogation and wheedle every tiny little detail out of her. 'Here we go,' she said under her breath at the sound of a car pulling up outside, the slam of two car doors, and the clickety-clack of Violet's heels on the pavement.

'You have, haven't you?' Sitting at the kitchen table, Molly was staring at Kitty intently, her eyes unblinking, a wicked smile spreading across her still-pale face. She nudged Vi. 'Look at her, she so bloody-well has, hasn't she?'

Vi grinned. 'You know what, Moll? There's something about her that's making me think she has, but I can't quite put my finger on it.' She arched an eyebrow.

'I'll bet Ollie put his finger on it.' Molly gave a dirty laugh.

Blushing furiously, Kitty plonked two mugs of tea onto the kitchen table in front of her friends, then slid the biscuit tin across to them, deliberately avoiding eye contact.

'You have and don't deny it. It's written all over your face. It says, "I've had hot, sweaty sex with the hot bloke I've fancied the pants off for donkeys' years".' Molly sat back in her chair, her arms folded across her growing bump while Vi snorted into her mug of tea.

'Well, no one could ever accuse you of not being direct and to the point, Molls.' Kitty was struggling to remember a time when a blush had turned her cheeks this crimson. Busying herself, she added more hot water to the teapot before making a meal of stretching the tea-cosy over it. She was still reluctant to meet her cousin's gaze.

'Molly does have a point, actually.' Vi was watching Kitty's avoidance tactics. 'You suddenly look all glowing and radiant, and relaxed and happy.'

'See, Vi agrees with me.' Molly sniffed, reaching for the biscuit tin. Hearing the familiar pop as the lid was removed, Humph eased himself up from his bed and parked himself next to her as Molly rummaged for custard creams, looking increasingly perplexed. 'Who the sodding hell do I have to screw around here to get a bloody custard cream?'

'Think you've done enough screwing,' Violet said, nodding towards Molly's bump.

Molly batted the comment away. 'Don't tell me you've run out, Kitts.'

Kitty disappeared into the pantry and came out armed with a packet of custard creams. She handed it to her cousin who hurriedly peeled it open and popped a whole biscuit into her mouth.

'Mmmm. You've no idea what a custard cream fix can do for a girl.' She slumped into the chair, and her shoulders sagged as the sugar hit her bloodstream.

'I think we're getting the idea.' Vi rolled her eyes at Kitty, who was glad to have the attention directed away from herself, though she knew it wouldn't last.

'Well, my excuse is that they're the only thing I can keep down.' Molly gazed lovingly at the biscuit between her fingers.

'You've become a custard cream junkie. God forbid we ever have to make you go cold turkey.' Vi took a sip of her tea, eyeing her warily.

'Don't even think about it!' Molly pulled a face.

'If the wind changes, you'll stay like that,' said Vi.

'Talking of wind.' Molly spoke through a mouthful of chomped biscuit, spraying crumbs onto the small swell of her abdomen. She brushed them off and onto the floor, where they were speedily hoovered up by Humph and Ethel. 'Have you seen the state of my stomach? I'm going to have to order some new work trousers; the sprog's already started to show and I'm struggling to fasten these. But I'm not far enough on to look pregnant. I just look like I've either got a massive beer belly or need a bloody good fart.'

Violet curled her lip in disgust. 'Oh, how delightful. Knowing you, it's probably the latter, so if you feel the need to pass wind could you at least step outside?'

'Might do. Not sure what the neighbours'll think, though.' Molly dived into the biscuit tin, glancing over at Kitty who was chuckling into her mug of tea. 'And you needn't think you've got away without telling us all about Saturday night, Little Miss Prim Knickers over there. Get your arse over here and spill the beans. And if you did what I think you did, then I hope you used protection. The last thing you need is to end up in the same condition as me. And the last thing I need is competition for my precious biccies.' Molly split a biscuit in two, scraping off the cream with her bottom teeth.

'God forbid,' muttered Vi.

'There's nothing much to tell, really.' Kitty leaned against the Aga, trying – but failing – to look casual.

'Well, we all know that's not true, so you might as well get yourself over here. You know we won't go until we've heard every last detail. Is it true what they say about the quiet ones?' Molly winked at Kitty.

Knowing when she was beaten, Kitty set the teapot on the table and pulled out a chair. 'Well, I'm not going to give you *all* the details, but Ollie and me did spend some, er, time together.' She smiled happily, feeling the familiar warmth of a blush rise up her cheeks.

'At long last, you finally had sex with Ollie!' Violet's eyes danced as she grinned at Molly.

'Thank heavens for that! It's taken you sodding long enough,' said Molly.

'You're such a potty-mouth these days, Moll. Violet flashed her a disapproving look.

'These days?' Kitty grinned.

'I blame it on the sprog and the bonkers things it's doing to my hormones. Pip's even threatened to get me a swear box.' She puffed a straggle of hair off her face.

'The rate you're going you'll be a millionaire by the end of the year.' Kitty chuckled when Molly stuck her tongue out at her.

'Anyway, what were you saying about your night of passion with Mr Strong and Silent?' Vi waggled her eyebrows.

'Well, I didn't say I'd had a *night* of passion, but we certainly managed a couple of hours of something really special. And I can honestly say that I've never felt like that before. It was amazing.' Kitty's heart began to gallop at the memory, the butterflies in her stomach making a reappearance as her mind suddenly filled with images from Saturday night. *Phew*! She needed a repeat of it, and soon.

'Well, that couple of hours of "something really special" has certainly put a sparkle in your eyes. I'm really happy for you, chuck.' Vi smiled.

'Thanks, I really appreciate how much you both care, and I can't tell you how great it is that we're all seeing more of each other. I honestly didn't know how much I'd missed it.'

'And we're glad we've got you back, aren't we, Moll?'

'Sure are.' Molly popped another custard cream into her mouth. 'By the way,' she said between munches, 'how's things with that Mellison woman and her horrible kids?'

'Better.' Kitty nodded. 'Things seem to have quietened down a bit, and school are on top of the bullying, thankfully. Lil's really happy now, which is such a relief. Aoife gives the odd theatrical performance – clearly for my benefit – when there's a load of other mums around; talking about organising meals out, going for walks and stuff, to which I'm obviously not invited. But that doesn't bother me. She just makes herself look a bit silly, and I wouldn't want to do anything with her anyway.'

'And to think, all that trouble was because Aoife wanted to swap Deadbeat Dave for Dickhead Dan. Silly cow.' Molly groaned as her mobile phone pinged, heralding the arrival of a text. 'Bugger! It's from Pip. Looks like Granny Aggie's been sexting Rev Nev again, and he wants me to sort it out. How come I get all the rubbish jobs? Anyway, another ten minutes won't hurt, I'm finishing my tea before I do anything else.' Picking up her mug, she sat back in her chair.

Relieved that the conversation had moved away from her date with Ollie, Kitty asked Vi how things were progressing with the sale of Purple Diamond. Her friend became animated as she explained that everything should be signed, sealed and delivered within a couple of weeks, freeing her up to concentrate on Romantique. The pair had squeezed in a handful of conversations about their hopes and plans, with Kitty hesitantly showing Vi some of the sketches she'd made of vintage-style underwear. Violet had been blown away. 'They're exquisite, Kitty,' she'd whispered, clearly impressed. 'You shouldn't have been hiding this talent away for so long.'

'They're just a few scribbles.' True to form, Kitty had batted away the compliment.

An experienced business hand, Vi had taken the lead in dealing with the necessary formalities for setting up a new business: registering the company, opening a bank account and making an appointment with an accountant.

Kitty was beyond excited. Thoughts of exquisite fabrics in dusky shades finished with delicate lace trims, and actually doing something worthwhile, filled her head at night, pushing sleep out of reach. Not that she was complaining.

∽

'RIGHT, I s'pose I'd better get cracking.' Molly drained her tea.

'Well, good luck with Granny Aggie and the vicar,' said Kitty.

'Hmmph. I'll need more than bloody luck.'

'Oh, and don't forget my new burlesque class starts next week in the village hall. And as my best friends, I'm expecting you two to support me.' Vi's tone didn't brook any argument.

'On that note, I'm off. See ya.' Molly hurried to the front door.

'Was it something I said?' Violet's eyes twinkled mischievously.

46

THURSDAY AFTERNOON FOUND Dan sitting in chambers flicking through a prosecution brief, knotting its ribbon around his fingers. He was finding it difficult to concentrate. 'Damn it!' he cursed, throwing the brief ribbon across his desk and massaging his temples. He took a sip of his coffee and grimaced; it was stone cold – he must have been poring over the papers for longer than he realised. He sat back heavily in his leather chair and exhaled, rubbing his hands over his face. 'What the hell's wrong with me?' He pushed back his shirt sleeve, checking his watch. 'Christ, quarter to bloody four!' He'd been hunched at his desk for over five hours; no wonder his shoulders ached.

His thoughts were interrupted by a tap at the door and he looked up to see Henry Wilkinson's shiny bald pate poking around it. 'Coffee?'

'Sounds good.' Dan gave a self-pitying smile.

'Two ticks.' Henry smiled back before disappearing downstairs. Dan would have rung down for the latest office junior to bring coffee up to his room, but Henry didn't do things like that. Henry made his own coffee. He even made coffee for others, too, including the lowly office junior. *Fool!*

Within minutes he'd returned armed with two large mugs of steaming coffee, its rich aroma filling the room instantly. He scanned Dan's brief strewn desk, looking for somewhere to sit the mug.

Finding nowhere free, he perched it on a sturdy-looking law book. 'There you go, old boy.'

Dan took a sip, wincing at the heat, the sharp kick of caffeine quickly lifting his mood. 'Thanks,' he added as an after-thought.

It hadn't escaped Henry's notice that Dan hadn't been himself recently. He looked pale and wan and – dare he say it – the edge appeared to have been taken off his infamous aggression. 'So, how are things?' He plonked himself down on one of the tastefully battered leather sofas, adjusting the tweed cushions behind him.

Dan puffed out his cheeks. 'Been better.'

'Oh. Care to talk about it?' Henry crossed his legs as Dan launched into a pull-no-punches character assault on Mitch Turner, a solicitor who was the defence lawyer in a trial that he'd been prosecuting. There was nothing Dan despised more – other than Oliver Cartwright and James Fairfax – than solicitors with higher rights of audience doing the job of barristers in the Crown Court. And, as he perceived it, doing it badly at that.

'If they wanted to practise at the Bar, why the hell didn't they go to Bar School in the first place, instead of training to be bloody solicitors?' Dan repeated one of his regular gripes.

He picked up a pen and began fiddling with it. 'You should've heard his pathetic attempt at examination-in-chief; it was wall-to-wall leading questions. I thought Judge Hastings was going to explode; he had to pull him up about it all the time. It was a joke. In fact, this whole HCA business is a joke. They think that a five-minute training course will equip them with the skills that took us a bloody intensive year at Bar School and a year in pupillage to learn. Turner even had the nerve to show his face in the robing room and start robing up. Can you believe it, a solicitor in barrister's robes? Cheeky sod.' A muscle began to twitch in Dan's cheek.

'That was brave, but Turner's usually a pretty good advocate.'

'Hmmm. I left him in no doubt about what I thought. Haven't seen him in the robing room since. Nor robed and wigged up in court.'

'I can believe that.' Whatever was really niggling Dan, Mitch Turner had picked an unfortunate week to be on the other side in a trial with him.

'It's the only thing Connor O'Dowd and I agree on.'

'Ah, Dowdzilla. Scary bloke.'

'Mmm, he's a pretty formidable opponent. Fights his corner,

though. You always get a decent court-room scrap with him. Got to respect the guy for that.'

'Well, I'd have to agree with you there, but it's not like you to let HCAs get so under your skin.'

'They've always got under my skin, but you're right, I don't usually let them get me feeling like this.' Dan dragged a hand down his face. 'There's something else.'

~

SINCE FINDING the photo of Kitty and the kids, Dan had spent the weekend in an unusually reflective mood, taking a long-overdue look at himself. And, unpalatable as it was, he'd been ashamed of what he'd seen. In a matter of months, he'd found himself without his wife, his children and his home. His self-respect had gone AWOL too.

Determined to put things right, he'd called his father for advice. George had listened intently, confessing that he'd been no saint in his own marriage, adding that Gwyneth hadn't exactly been easy to live with. But Kitty wasn't like his mother, which was exactly what had been so appealing about her when Dan had first set eyes on her in the Sunne all those years ago.

George's advice to his son had been simple: women like Kitty didn't come along often; Dan had been lucky to find someone as kind and sweet as her. And if he loved her as much as he said he did, then he should fight for her. Do all it took to woo her back; flowers, chocolates, romantic dinners, even a trip to Paris.

But Dan wasn't totally convinced. He'd neglected to share the details of how he'd been physical towards her. Would it have sent them too far down the line for recovery?

With Henry in his office, Dan seized the opportunity for a second opinion. 'I've been a bloody fool.' He paused, waiting for his friend to contradict him. He was disappointed. 'I've lost Kitty and screwed up my life in the process. But the weekend gave me a chance to think, and I want to make amends. I want her back.'

'Right.'

Dan repeated what he'd told his father, watching Henry, whose expression remained inscrutable.

'What do you think? Is it too late, or do you think I've got a chance?' He didn't care that he'd been selective in what he'd told

Henry, he just needed him to say the words he wanted to hear – even if it was lip-service. The fact that someone decent like Henry had spoken them would be justification enough for him to put his plans into action.

'I, er, ooh, erm. Gosh, well, I'm not sure. I suppose it's always worth a try. If you really love her, that is.' Henry squirmed uncomfortably, his face burning red as scenes from his visit to Dan's former home ransacked his mind. He hoped Dan hadn't picked up on it.

'You don't sound so sure. D'you think I've left it too late?' He tried to rub away the growing tension in his brow.

The despair in Dan's voice had tugged at Henry's conscience, making him feel uncomfortable, especially when the memory of his clumsy overtures to the man's wife loomed large in his mind. 'Listen, why don't you buy Kitty a bunch of her favourite flowers and a box of chocolates? Take them round, tell her how sorry you are, and ask her if she'd like to go out to dinner with you. Sell it like it would be a date, a fresh start. Woo her back the old-fashioned way.'

Henry's words, echoing his father's, were all the encouragement Dan needed. 'Henry, you're absolutely bloody right.' He snatched up the phone. 'Do you have the number for Bloomz?'

'Er.' He gulped audibly.

AT OAK TREE FARM, the kids had settled down for bed without the usual "just five more minutes…" resistance. A football match over at Danskelfe for Lucas and an afternoon-long dance workshop at school for Lily, followed by their weekly half-hour swimming lessons in Middleton-le-Moors had made for a busy day for the pair. Topped off by a warming dinner and a hot bubble-bath, they'd fallen asleep pretty much as soon as they'd settled down in their beds.

After kissing a sleepy Lily goodnight, Kitty padded along the landing to Lucas's room. Smiling as she saw he looked no more awake than his sister. She walked across the room, picking up a stray sock and throwing it into his washing basket. Bending to kiss him goodnight, she inhaled his warm, clean scent. 'Night, Lukes. Sleep tight.'

'Night.' He smiled sleepily, stretching out his arms and wrapping them around her neck. 'Love you, Mum,' he added, planting a kiss on her cheek.

'Love you too, Lukes.' Her heart surged with love for her gorgeous boy as she kissed his forehead. She smoothed down his hair as she used to before his fondness for male grooming and hair gel kicked in.

'Not the quiff, Mum,' he whispered.

'Sorry, Lukes,' she whispered back.

Downstairs, everything was in place for Kitty's quiet night in. The dishwasher had been emptied, the washing was folded (the ironing could wait until tomorrow) and the Aga and wood-burner were stoked up to the nines, leaving her with the luxury of a peaceful evening ahead. 'Quiet night in for us, eh?' she said to Humph and Ethel, who wagged their tails in response. 'You coming?' Armed with a fresh mug of tea and a box of chocolates, Kitty headed into the soft light of the living-room, the Labradors close behind.

Setting her mug and chocolates down onto the coffee table along-side her notepad of underwear sketches for Romantique and the latest novel she was reading, Kitty curled up on the sofa, plumped up a cushion and squished it behind her back. She popped a choco-late into her mouth then took a sip of tea, the heat of the liquid strip-ping the chocolate off the malted ball, creating a molten pool in her mouth. 'Mmm.' She swirled it around with her tongue before reaching across to the table and picking up her book. *Bliss!* she thought to herself, ignoring Humph's beady eyes that were boring into her.

KITTY HAD BEEN SO ENGROSSED in her book, an hour and a half had passed in the blink of an eye. She was just about to go and make herself a fresh mug of tea when she heard what sounded like car tyres crunching over the gravel of the drive. Ethel lifted her head, her ears twitching, a low growl rumbling in her chest. Thanks to his old ears, Humph didn't stir. 'You heard that, too, Eth?' Kitty paused, listening for a moment. She peered through the curtains of the front window, but it was dark, and the tall yew hedge obstructed the view from the living room, making it impossible to see the driveway. Deciding she must have been hearing things, she headed out of the room and into the kitchen but was stopped in her tracks by a knock at the door. Ethel barked, rousing Humph, and the feeling of relaxed contentment was chased away by a dark, unwelcome one of foreboding. There was only one person, other than herself, who would park on the drive and not on the road in front of the house. Her heart rate accelerated. Another knock at the door, this time louder. 'Shh, you two.' She took the growling Labradors by their collars and led them into the kitchen, closing the door behind her – if it was who she thought it was, Kitty didn't want the children waking up.

Doing her best to ignore the tight clench in her stomach and the anxiety that was creeping up her spine, Kitty swallowed and opened the door. 'Dan!' Her heart plummeted.

'Hi.' He gave the lopsided smile that used to melt her heart.

Her eyes ran over him; despite being a little paler and thinner, he was looking well-groomed in his pin-striped court suit and heavy black overcoat. He'd removed his tie and day collar – as he always did as soon as he was done in court – which gave a contradictorily casual air to his appearance.

His familiar cologne furled around the doorway, suspended on the light mizzle, infiltrating her home again. Her gaze fell to the tired-looking bunch of roses he was clutching. This didn't bode well. She scanned the dimly-lit street, hoping to catch a reassuring glimpse of another person, but there wasn't a soul around, and a muffled quiet hung over the village. Kitty pushed the door to a little, fear from their last encounter creeping into her mind. 'Look, Dan, I…'

He pressed his hand against it, preventing her from closing it further. 'Before you close the door on me, I just want to say I'm sorry. Really sorry. Sorrier than I've ever been about anything in my life.' He was wearing a convincing expression of repentance.

Rooted to the spot, and at a loss for what to say, Kitty was conscious of the rumble of Ethel's growling from the kitchen.

'Look, it's cold out here. And this mizzle is wetting. Can I come in?' Anticipating her agreement, he placed his foot on the doorstep.

'I'm not sure that's such a good idea, Dan. Not now things are this far down the line, and we've both, er…we've both moved on.' She pressed her weight against the door, her heart thudding. Jimby's suggestion of a restraining order after Dan's last visit flashed through her mind, making her wish she'd acted upon it.

He tried one of his winning smiles and, while its effects may have worn thin, she was annoyed at herself that it still managed to tug at a part of her that had long-since been hidden away.

'Kitty, you have no idea how much I regret what I've done, and what I want more than anything else in the world is a chance to put it right. Please, let me come in. I promise I won't stay long, and I promise I won't behave like last time – you have my word.' He was obviously completely oblivious to how little Kitty regarded his "word". 'Come on, Kitty. Wouldn't it be better if we talked inside rather than on the doorstep? And it's bloody freezing out here.' Before she could answer, he'd taken a step across the threshold, giving her no choice but to step back and let him in. 'Thanks.' Grinning, he walked straight past her and into the living room.

Closing the door quietly, she followed him to the room that less than five minutes ago had been her peaceful sanctuary. It felt very different now. The relaxed atmosphere had been extinguished by Dan's domineering presence, and in its place tension loomed. Goosebumps prickled her skin, and she gave an involuntary shiver, hugging her arms tightly across her chest.

'You can't tell me you're cold. It's far too hot in here. The thermostat needs turning down, and there's way too much fuel on that stove.' His voice had the familiar hint of arrogance, moulded by too many years of courtroom theatrics at the Bar. A feeling of resentment rose in her gut; that tone didn't belong here anymore.

Dan marched across the floor. Kitty watched in silence as his gaze swept around the room, no doubt scanning for evidence of male company. Or, more likely, Ollie. His resultant smug smile told her he was pleased to see that she'd been spending a quiet night alone.

Before she knew it, he was standing in front of her, looking down at her intently. 'I bought you these. I know they're your favourites.' He thrust the bunch of wilting roses at her.

'Oh, er…' As she took them her eyes fell onto the remains of a 'reduced' sticker and the name of the petrol station on the outskirts of Middleton-le-Moors. She hoped he didn't go into the kitchen and see the still stunning roses from Ollie. By the time Dan had got to Bloomz they, and every other florist in the city, had closed. In desperation, he'd grabbed the only bunch left in the bucket where he'd gone to re-fuel his car. 'Thank you. But you don't need to…'

He stepped forward and placed his finger on her lips. 'Sshh. Kitty, darling. I do need to. I very much need to. And this is just the start. I've changed. I really have. I've had time to think, and I realise that I was letting the stress of work rule every aspect of my life, but not anymore. I know I've been a bloody idiot and I'm going to make it up to you. I've booked a table for us at Fennel – that fancy new restaurant in York with the celebrity chef, Duncan blahdiblah, whatever his name is – this Saturday. Had to pull a whole load of bloody strings to get it at such short notice. Turns out I represented the chef/owner's brother a couple of years ago – drugs – got him off, and the family think I'm absolutely bloody wonderful.'

'Dan…'

'Let me finish.' He held his hand up to silence her. 'And,' he reached into his inside jacket pocket and produced a travel wallet, 'I've booked us a romantic trip to Paris, the weekend after next. We'll be travelling first class on Eurostar, spending a couple of days there, sight-seeing, wining and dining. Then we'll be hopping on a plane – first class again – to New York. There, I'll be taking you to an exclusive jewellers. What do you think of that?' He looked very pleased with himself.

'Well, I, er…' Lost for words, Kitty could see from his expression the thought that she might not like any of it hadn't troubled his mind.

'Oh, I nearly forgot.' He raised his hand again. 'I want us to renew our vows. At the church here, like you always wanted.' Oblivious to the look of horror on her face, he grabbed her by the shoulders. Her heart froze with fear at his touch.

'Dan, I…I…I…' Panic scurried around her mind.

'Don't tell me that doesn't sound fantastic. How many women do you know have been offered anything like that? I'm trying to prove to you just how serious I am about us, Kitts. Come on, what do you say?' He was feeling jubilant and confident. He'd sold it well. And there was no way that local yokel, Oliver Cartwright, could compete with him. 'Speak to me, Kitty.' Still holding onto her shoulders, he gave them a shake. She tensed, and the look in his eyes told her he'd felt it under his grip.

She felt swamped by his words. They'd gushed over her, knocking the air out of her lungs, making it difficult for her to breathe. How could her peaceful evening be so completely and utterly bulldozed by him? Didn't he realise she could see right through his blatant manipulation? He'd make a good partner for Aoife Mellison; she had a set of skills to match and would give him a run for his money.

She tried to find the words, but her thoughts were being drowned out by the sound of her pulse gushing in her ears. 'I, er, don't know what to say.' In truth, she knew exactly what to say, it was just that she didn't know how to say it without angering him and having a repeat of his last visit, especially as, unlike last time, the children were here.

Thinking quickly, she gestured to the sofa. 'Why don't you sit down while I go and put these roses in water and get you a cup of tea?'

'Sounds good.' He flashed a beatific smile.

She hurried into the kitchen and moved the still growling Labradors into the utility room, closing the door behind her. Snatching up her mobile phone from the dresser, she clumsily bashed out a text to Jimby, hoping he'd pick it up quickly.

In an instant, a text pinged back: *On my way.*

The roses on the windowsill caught her eye, their petals still vibrant and beautiful. They stood in stark contrast to the ones Dan had just pushed at her. It wasn't the only thing, she thought.

Panic had a grip of her. She needed to calm down before she faced him again. Armed with the two mugs of tea, she took a fortifying breath and headed back into the lion's den.

It niggled her to see that he'd made himself so at home, leaning back in the sofa, his arms stretched out, his feet on the coffee table, right beside the notebook of sketches she hoped he hadn't noticed.

With a shaking hand, Kitty gave him his tea. She hated that he still had the ability to make her feel like this. She cleared her throat. 'Look, Dan, this is all very kind of you; the flowers, the meal, the trip to Paris…'

'And New York. Don't forget about New York.'

'Yes, and New York. It all sounds wonderful, really it does, and I appreciate all the thought you've put into it.' Her mouth felt dry. She took a sip of tea, aware of his eyes on her.

'Good.'

'But, for me, it's not about going to expensive restaurants, first-class trips or expensive gifts. I don't need grand gestures. What I'm trying to say is that it's just…well…it's just too late. Too much has happened. I've moved on, and I don't want to go back there again. Especially now the children are settled.' She swallowed nervously.

Dan's expression changed, and his eyes darkened the way they used to moments before he got nasty.

Hurry up, Jimby!

'Let me get this right, are you turning me down?'

'Y… yes.'

'Right.' He nodded, fixing his gaze on her.

'Surely you can understand…'

'You ungrateful little idiot! You know you won't get another chance, don't you?' He leapt to his feet.

'Please, Dan, don't shout, the children are asleep. Please don't wake them. I don't want them to see us arguing, it'll really upset them.'

'Don't tell me what to do.' He loomed over her. 'I don't know why I wasted my time coming here tonight. I might've known you wouldn't know how to appreciate the good things in life. Don't you realise how lucky you were when I chose you all those years ago? I picked you up from the gutter and turned your life around. You silly little girl.'

'I wasn't in the gutter, Dan. I come from a well-respected local family.'

'Really?' he said scornfully.

'And at least we "in-bred idiots" don't make headlines in the local newspaper or get photographed running away naked from a sleazy dogging session, do we, Dan?' James stood in the doorway, watching his words hit their target.

Dan flinched, pinching his lips together as he glared at James.

'I think it's time you left. And let me tell you this, if you come anywhere near this house or my sister again you'll find yourself on the wrong side of an injunction. Then what will your precious mother and work colleagues say?'

Dan turned to Kitty, a vein throbbing in his temple. 'You're making a big mistake.' He strode out of the room and into the night. Seconds later, came the screech of tyres as his car tore out of the village.

'You okay?' Jimby asked, surveying his sister.

'I am now. Thanks for coming, Jimby.' She was visibly shaken.

'No, probs. I get the feeling he won't be troubling you again.'

'Fingers crossed.'

47

IT HAD BEEN six weeks since Dan had turned up on the doorstep, and life at Oak Tree Farm had fallen back into a peaceful, regular rhythm; the kids none the wiser. Kitty was glad of that. She hoped the contents of the letter that had plopped onto her doormat ten minutes earlier wouldn't trigger any unpleasant repercussions to rock their equilibrium. They'd come a long way for them to be unsettled now.

As she gazed out of the window at the swathes of cheerful yellow daffodils, a whisper of crisp, spring air wafted through the window. Kitty inhaled deeply, it smelt of vitality, optimism and new beginnings. She closed her eyes and let the bright spring sunshine wash over her face, squashing down the clutch of nerves that were niggling away in her gut.

The sense she wasn't alone drew her back into the room. Her heart pumping faster, she set her mug down on the granite worktop, rubbing her arms that were suddenly peppered with goose-bumps. She was the only one in the house; the kids were at school, Humph and Ethel were sniffing around the garden and Dan, well…

Nibbling at a hang-nail, she glanced around her, relieved to see that everything seemed as normal, but as she headed towards the door something caught her eye. She looked carefully, squinting, as a small white feather weightlessly zig-zagged its way from the ceiling, landing silently onto the letter.

Kitty stopped worrying her nail as a faint smell of honeysuckle wrapped itself around her. 'Mum,' she said softly, smiling as her eyes prickled and a tear escaped. She swept it away with her fingertips. It wasn't the first time she'd experienced this; there'd been several occasions throughout the bumps and blips of the last six turbulent months. Always appearing at a significant moment, it comforted Kitty to believe that it was a sign from her mum. She'd read about such things, guardian angels sending messages to loved ones from the other side. She liked to think that her mum was watching over her, saying, 'I'm here, looking out for you, my darling. Stay strong, and you'll be fine.'

Taking a deep breath, she picked up the letter. 'If ever there was a time to be strong it's now, Mum,' she whispered. She knew just how easy it would be for a tiny chink in her new-found resolve to grow into a gaping weak spot. Or for her customary self-doubt to start nibbling holes in it, like a moth nibbling holes in a jumper. The proverbial corner had been turned and the black, miserable days of the last few years were forming an orderly queue, ready to be put firmly and resolutely behind her.

She turned the envelope over, her hand shaking as she slowly slid her finger under the flap, easing it open. Nerves rippled in her stomach. *No going back now.*

So, this is what they look like, she thought as her eyes ran over the certificate that declared the end of her marriage to Dan. This one piece of paper that called itself a Decree Absolute was loaded with the power to change people's lives.

She pulled out a chair and sat down, laying the document on the table in front of her, smoothing it out with her fingers. She didn't really know how she should be feeling right now, but her emotions were a jittery mix of happy and sad with a generous hint of relief.

There was no trace of a doubt in her mind that divorcing Dan was the right thing to do, but it still didn't stop her from feeling like something of a failure, that she'd somehow let Lucas and Lily down. She knew these were natural emotions; she wouldn't be the first newly divorced person to feel this way. But guilt was vying for her attention. Guilt for instigating the divorce, guilt for feeling relieved that her unhappy marriage was over. And guilt for the bourgeoning love she had for Ollie. She needed a walk, needed to shake it off along with the headache that was brewing in her temples.

Easing the document back into its envelope, she pushed it into the drawer in the dresser. In the hallway, she shrugged on her coat. 'Fancy a walk, you two?' Ethel leapt from her bed and raced towards the front door. Humph remained where he was, enjoying his nap; he was still taking things easy. 'I'll take that as a yes, shall I, Eth?' Kitty smiled, grabbing the lead as the pair headed out into the bright spring day.

AN HOUR STRETCHING her legs high up on Great Stangdale rigg did the trick. The crisp air had done a thorough job of clearing her mind, and booted out her headache, giving her the clarity she needed. In the process, Kitty had managed to push away the guilt imp that had perched itself on her shoulder. Had she done the right thing, divorcing Dan? *Just take a look at the children*, her conscience answered. *See how they've flourished and lost the shadow of anxiety that had hovered over them when their father was around*. Lucas no longer felt the need to bow and scrape and seek approval from him, no longer had to feel that he didn't quite come up to his father's exacting standards. And he no longer had to be on the receiving end of Dan's cruel put-downs, wearing a look of hurt that ripped at her insides. And little Lily no longer had to feel that she was a nuisance just by her very existence. Now the pair of them were enjoying the blissfully carefree childhood that she and Jimby had shared, having fun without the spectre of Dan's disapproval lurking in the background, taking the edge off their games. They were free to let their imaginations run riot and free to create wonderful memories that would bring happiness again in the future.

'Just a minute, Eth.' Kitty stopped to take in the view. Pip and the other local gamekeepers were burning patches of the moors, filling the air with a sweet, smoky smell. Thankfully, the mild south-westerly was blowing the smoke away from the village where it would sometimes slump heavily, blocking out the sun.

Despite it being chilly, sunlight was splashed all around the broad expanse of the dale, illuminating the land in all its natural beauty. Kitty shielded her eyes, absorbing the verdant signs of spring, cocking an ear to separate all of nature's wonderful sounds, from the plaintive bleating of newborn lambs following their mothers, their skinny pipe-cleaner legs wobbly with unfamiliar use, to the chattering of birds, flitting about, giddy with excitement that the sun was shining. All punctuated by the low baying of Tom Storr's beast in the barn at the other side of the dale. She took a deep breath and smiled.

'Come on, Eth.' She gave the lead a shake and carried on along the path, dodging the deep puddles the previous day's rain had left behind.

As she walked, Kitty mulled over her relationship with Ollie. Did she feel guilty about that? If she was honest, no. And why should she? Dan had shown her no love; his actions had eventually erased any affection she'd had for him.

Her love for Ollie had grown to such a degree its intensity could sometimes take her breath away. She'd never felt anything like it for Dan, and she was in no doubt that he'd never felt like that for her. His tranche of extra-marital dalliances was evidence of that. For a whole variety of reasons, their marriage had become unhealthy and toxic, shrivelling and morphing into nothing but a piece of paper that declared their partnership to be officially over.

Feeling that she'd exorcised every ghost that remained of her marriage, and with a crystal-clear conscience, Kitty made her way back down to the village. It was time to share her news.

As she turned into the shared yard, she heard the hum of voices coming from the barn that was now Ollie's workshop. 'Knock, knock,' she said, tapping lightly on the half-opened stable door. The two men turned to look at her, mugs in hands, greeting her with broad smiles.

'Now then, sis. How's things?' Jimby gave one of his customary smiles.

'Hiya, Kitts.' Ollie's smile crinkled the corners of his eyes and triggered his dimples. Kitty's heart flipped.

'Hi.' She leaned over the lower part of the door, slid the bolt along and nudged it open with her knee. Ethel barged her way through, nearly knocking her off her feet, thrilled to see her friend Mabel who'd been curled up in a basket by the heater. 'Don't mind me, Eth,' she laughed.

'Care to join us for a cuppa?' Ollie held up a mug and cocked a questioning eyebrow.

'Mmm. Please.' Kitty glanced around the workshop, its floor scattered with wood-shavings, the air sweet with the aroma of freshly sawn wood.

'My sister has the amazing ability to sniff out a cup of tea from a mile off,' said Jimby.

'Very true. And it's only yes to a tea if it'll be served in a decent mug. Not any of your usual filth.'

'That do?' Ollie held up a plain white mug. 'And blame your brother for the filth, as you refer to it. It's all his doing.'

'Perfect. And I'm well aware that you two are as bad as each other on that score.' She smiled at Ollie, enjoying the warmth of his gaze upon her. It was enough to turn her knees to jelly.

'So where have you been that's got you all fresh-faced and rosy-cheeked?' Ollie leaned back against his workbench, holding his mug across his chest, waiting for the kettle to boil. The over-head light was glinting off the golden hairs on his muscular forearms, and she longed to smooth her fingers over them. She swallowed, quashing the ache in her body that yearned to feel his skin against hers.

'We've been for a walk up on the rigg. Needed the cobwebs blowing out. It was beautiful.'

'It's not the only thing.' His words made her heart sing.

'Blearghh!' James mimed throwing up, making Kitty and Ollie laugh. 'Thought northern blokes weren't supposed to talk all mushy like that, Oll.'

Ollie replied with a broad smile and a shrug.

'Anyway, I bring news. Thanks.' She took the proffered mug. 'It arrived. This morning. The Decree Absolute. I'm no longer married to Dan.' Her heart stampeded in her chest; it felt funny, saying the words out loud. It was almost as if they had come out of someone else's mouth.

In that moment, Kitty felt the final psychological shackles that had fixed her to Dan slip away. She was free! She was actually bloody free, and it felt amazing. A grin of pure happiness spread across her face.

'Wow!' Ollie let the words sink in.

'Fanbloodytastic, sis!' Grinning from ear to ear, James flung an arm around her shoulders, giving her a squeeze.

'You okay?' Ollie searched her face, not really knowing if it was appropriate that he should show his true feelings.

'I've had chance to process everything – hence the walk – and I'm more than okay. In fact, I'm a really happy mixture of relieved and over-the-moon. I know that might not sound right to some people,' she gave an apologetic shrug, 'but it feels like I've had the heaviest weight lifted off my shoulders.'

'Come here, you.' With his eyes glittering and a wide smile on his face, Ollie strode over to her, scooped her up in his arms and swung her around, sending wood shavings flying. She squealed with delight as he threw his head back and laughed. 'Do you have any idea how much I bloody love you, Kitty Fairfax?' He came to a halt, hugging her close as if he couldn't quite believe his luck, then pressed his lips against hers. They felt deliciously warm as she melted into his kiss, aware of nothing else but the sound of her heart as it thrummed with happiness.

'Would you two please get a room.' James shook his head but his broad smile betrayed his true feelings.

'Sorry, Jimby.' Kitty giggled, unable to wipe the smile off her face.

'Yeah, sorry, mate,' said Ollie before nuzzling Kitty's nose and sneaking another kiss. He wasn't sorry at all.

LEAVING FOR CHAMBERS, Dan had collected his post from his letterbox in the communal area of his apartment. He glowered at the Decree Absolute – the ultimate proof of her rejection of him – his feelings of repentance and declarations of love for Kitty just six weeks earlier forgotten. 'I'll show her I don't give a damn.'

His blood was still boiling when he pushed through the front door of Minster Gate chambers and stormed by the junior clerks' desks, barging past Frances, who was discussing court listing with Laura. His moods had been getting progressively worse, and there was no way she'd tolerate his rudeness. 'Good morning, Mr Fairfax-Bennett. Lovely day,' she said, pointedly.

'Is it?' he called as he took the stairs two at a time, slamming his door like a recalcitrant teenager when he reached his office.

Frances sniffed. 'I'd keep a low profile with that one today if I were you lot.'

Little did he know his day was going to get considerably worse.

IN HIS ROOM, Dan had taken the ribbon off a defence brief in yet another high-profile case. He'd been poring over it for an hour when the phone on his desk rang. 'Yes,' he snapped.

Mr Fairfax-Bennett, there are a couple of police officers here who say they'd like a word with you. In private.' Laura sounded uneasy.

'What? I haven't got any conferences booked. Did they say what case it's to do with?'

'No, they said it was a personal matter.' Dan felt the colour drain from his face. 'Right, well, you'd better send them up.'

As he adjusted the briefs on his desk, he heard a knock at the door. 'Come in,' he called.

'Please, take a seat,' he instructed the two uniformed police officers who entered his room. He recognised the more senior of the two; he'd been the detective in the Campbell murder trial Dan had prosecuted two years ago. 'DC Smithies,' he nodded to him. 'How can I help you?'

The officer cleared his throat. 'Mr Fairfax-Bennet, this is my colleague, PC Grey. This is, er, a little awkward, but we're here to invite you to attend the police station at a mutually convenient time to discuss a rather serious matter.'

'Oh, and what serious matter would that be?' A nerve in Dan's cheek began to twitch.

DC Smithies removed a set of photographs from an envelope and passed them to him. 'It concerns these. And an allegation. You might want to bring your solicitor along with you.'

Oh, shit, thought Dan.

'WE NEED TO CELEBRATE.' Molly's voice boomed down the phone to Kitty who'd just shared the news of her Decree Absolute. 'We need to go to the pub tonight and toast your freedom from that rat. At long last karma has taken a great big bite out of his nasty little arse. Can you get hold of Vi, I know she's in the village? I'd do it myself, but I've got a bit of a full-on day ahead of me.'

'Yep, she's coming here this afternoon to discuss our plans for Romantique. I'll mention it then.'

'Fab! Listen, I've got to dash, but I'm really pleased for you, chick. You're free now, and don't ever think it was the wrong thing to do or beat yourself over it, okay? We're all so proud of you and love you to bits. Anyroad, see you at around half seven, I'll bring my mother, she can babysit.'

'Thanks, Moll. And thank you for all your support.' Kitty felt her happiness bloom.

'No probs, hun, it's what family do. Right, I must go, Mavis Wilson's leg ulcer waits for no man – or woman. See ya.'

She smiled to herself, her cousin didn't often show her softer side.

Unable to wait until the afternoon to tell Vi her news, Kitty called her mobile.

'Yay,' Vi squealed down the phone. 'That's fantastic, Kitty. You're free!'

'That's just what Molly said.'

'Well, it's true. And now nothing can stop you from being with Ollie.'

'I know.' The thought sent butterflies fluttering around her stomach as a huge smile spread across her face.

'You do know you're absolutely perfect for each other, don't you?'

'Yes, Vi, I do. And I can't believe just how much I love him.'

'Aww, babes. That's so lovely.' Vi sounded almost tearful.

As the three women headed to the pub that evening, Kitty paused at the door. 'Before we go inside, I'd just like to ask, can we celebrate discreetly, please? I don't want to attract attention and look like I'm being a heartless cow. And I really don't want it getting back to Lucas and Lily from their friends. Of course, they know Dan and I aren't together, but I don't want to have to go into all the details of the various stages of how I divorced their dad.'

Vi rested a hand on Kitty's arm. 'We totally get it, Kitts. That's why we're going to do this out here, isn't it, Moll?'

'Eh?' Looking puzzled, it took Molly a second before she cottoned on, and copied Vi, who was waving her arms around in the air and wiggling her bottom in a crazy-happy dance. Kitty looked on, laughing and shaking her head.

'Evening, ladies,' called Lycra Len as he rode by on his bike, an amused expression on his face. Vi and Molly froze mid-jig.

'Evening,' the three women chorused, before giggling like school girls.

'Did anyone ever tell you two that you're loonies?' asked Kitty.

'Er, maybe once or twice,' said Molly, her eyes dancing.

'But you're the best friends anyone could ever have.' Kitty wrapped her arms around them and pulled them close.

48

Since their Valentine's meal at the Sunne, Kitty and Ollie hadn't ventured out again as a couple. Instead, they'd opted to socialise in the company of their friendship group, where their budding relationship could be diluted – to onlookers, at least.

Whenever she thought about Valentine's night, Kitty was shocked at their boldness and thought it best not to risk antagonising Gwyneth any further. The woman had been wearing a permanently thunderous expression since their newspaper altercation and would relish any excuse to stir up trouble with Dan. Kitty could really do without that. But it wasn't the only reason, it was also because her conscience wouldn't let her feel completely comfortable being seen in public, flaunting her love for Ollie, until her divorce was properly finalised.

But it hadn't stopped the pair from grabbing the odd, intimate moment and giving the bed sheets a good ruffling whenever the opportunity arose. On one occasion, when Kitty had popped into Ollie's workshop and found him alone, bubbling over with lust, they'd risked a quickie on his workbench. They were lucky not to have been caught by Julie, the post lady. 'Yoo-hoo,' she'd called, pushing at the door and waving a clutch of letters in the air. With a second to spare Kitty had hurriedly scooped up her clothes and sought refuge behind a vast pile of boarding, peering out through a gap between the wood, watching as Ollie kicked at a pile of wood-shavings.

'You can come out now,' he'd said, laughing, when the coast was clear. 'And you might want to check these for splinters.' He scooped a scrap of fabric from the floor, where he'd been toeing the wood-shavings. He'd given it a shake and thrown them at Kitty, who'd giggled when she'd seen that it was her knickers.

The arrival of her Decree Absolute had brought with it a palpable change of atmosphere, assuaging Kitty's guilt and leaving her and Ollie free to go public, though she was still wary of inviting Gwyneth's spite and was keen for them to tread gently. Thrilled at no longer having to hide his feelings for Kitty, Ollie would have happily declared his love from the rooftops for all the world to hear. It had unleashed a more exuberant, care-free side of him and now he found it hard to wipe the smile off his face. But he respected Kitty's wishes, and they took things slowly, starting with a couple of drinks together at the Sunne, before gradually being seen out and about together, walking the dogs and doing things that regular couples did. Unable to hide the fact that they looked deliriously happy, it was obvious to all that the couple were head over heels in love. "At last" was an expression used by many locals, who exchanged knowing smiles when the subject of the love-birds found its way into conversation. 'Her mum and dad would be over the moon,' was another.

Kitty continued to blossom. She'd kept her gamine pixie crop, her soft curves had returned, and her small, elfin face was beginning to fill out, making her look less gaunt. Her once sad eyes now sparkled with happiness, the dark circles that had sat beneath them banished along with Dan.

≈

As the weeks eased their way into early summer, Ollie and Anoushka began spending an increasing amount of time with Kitty and her children. They congregated mostly at Oak Tree Farm, which offered more space. And it wasn't just Kitty and Ollie who were enjoying these new family dynamics; their children were flourishing. Noushka, enjoying being part of a bigger family unit, slipped easily into the role of big sister to Lucas and Lily, while the younger two adored having her around. She watched with admiration as Lucas showed off his footballing skills, or patiently styled Lily's hair like her own. And Ollie's calm, steady presence appeared to make Kitty's children feel more settled and secure.

Noushka secretly prided herself on arranging date nights, keen for her dad and Kitty to spend some quality alone time together. The couple were happy to seize these moments with both hands, cutting short their drinks at the pub and sneaking back to Ollie's for a secret session of passionate love-making.

And Ollie was pleased that Noushka had adapted so easily, particularly since her disappointment of a mother was well out of the picture.

Ollie and Kitty scarcely dared believe that everything was slotting together so easily. 'It's as if it was meant to be,' she'd said to him one night as she lay in his arms, weaving her fingers through his.

'That's because it is.' His hair all mussed up, he'd propped himself up on his elbow, leaned across and kissed her tenderly. She'd moaned and pulled him on top of her. 'And that sweet, innocent exterior of yours does a pretty good job of hiding the racy little vixen that lies beneath, Kitty Fairfax.' He'd pressed his lips against hers, that were still red and plump from their earlier kisses.

'You bring it out in me.' She'd given him an impish smile before clasping her hands around his head, pulling him towards her and kissing him deeply. Who knew it was possible to feel this happy?

∾

OLLIE SMILED SLEEPILY TO HIMSELF; life really couldn't get much better than this. Outside, the birds were unleashing their dawn chorus with unbridled abandon, while the sun was gently nudging away the dark of night. And here he was, with the woman he'd been in love with for years sleeping contentedly in his arms, in the warmth of his bed – a bed they'd made love in twice the previous night. He felt like the luckiest man alive.

It was the second Saturday in May. Noushka was in London on a dance trip, and Lucas and Lily were having a sleep-over at Molly's parents', allowing Kitty and Ollie the luxury of a night alone together. And they'd made the most of it.

He pulled Kitty closer, inhaling her sweet, flowery scent and dropped a kiss onto the top of her head. She murmured and snuggled closer, sliding her arm across his chest.

It was that very moment that Ollie made his decision. There was no way he was going to let the woman he adored slip through his fingers again.

Two days after the officers had called at chambers, Dan attended York police station with his solicitor, Gilbert Froom. He'd explained the circumstances of their visit to Gilbert, who'd drafted a quick statement in readiness for their appointment, advising Dan to make no comment to any questions.

Throughout the interview Dan had remained quiet and sat poker-faced until he was formally charged with the offence of Outraging Public Decency. He'd leapt to his feet, declaring the situation to be ridiculous and flatly denying that it was him in the photographs.

Two days later, he appeared in York Magistrates' Court where he pleaded not guilty and opted for his trial to be heard in the Crown Court. With years of experience working his charm on the twelve members of the public that made up a jury, he reckoned he had a better chance of getting off than if he left his chances to trial by three hard-nosed magistrates. Though the stakes were higher in the Crown Court, the sentences more severe, it was a gamble he was prepared to take.

A meeting of the chambers' Management Committee was quickly scrambled and, just as Dan thought his luck couldn't get any worse, they'd unanimously agreed that it would be best for all concerned if the clerks didn't take on any new instructions for him. He was also advised to take a little time away from chambers.

This was Sam's fault, he'd seethed later in his flat, taking a glug of red wine. And Kitty's.

49

MIDSUMMER'S DAY

OLLIE WAS WOKEN by the warm rays of the midsummer sunshine peeking through the chink in his bedroom curtains. He surrendered to the pull of a yawn, rubbing sleep away from his eyes, as the realisation that today was going to be special dawned in his slumber-fuzzy mind.

He reached for the tiny box on his bedside table, carefully opening its age-worn lid. He smiled sleepily as the contents twinkled back at him, its significance triggering a cocktail of excitement and nervousness that surged through his body, settling in his gut with an audible rumble. 'Wowzers!' he said to himself, pinching one of Noushka's phrases and patting his stomach; he still had a lot to do to make today absolutely perfect.

He threw back the duvet, wafting the sweet smell of Kitty's delicate perfume that lingered in its fabric. He took a deep breath before jumping out of bed, tripping his way along the landing to the bathroom, whistling as he went. Stepping into the shower cubicle, he turned the dial on full and gasped as the icy blast of water bounced off his skin, quickly dispersing the nerves that had begun to pester him.

In no time the warmer water had worked its way through, pummelling his skin, making it tingle. Through the cloud of steam, Ollie reached up to his shower radio and flicked it on, relieved to hear that it was still tuned in to his favourite local station and not one

...e squeezed a blob of
...imself vigorously.

...air, one of his favourite
...t the top of his lungs, ad-
...know with ones he thought
...ways pulling him up about,
...eeded to make him do it all

...ages up from them, was out her
...en she heard Ollie's warbling. She
...m all his life, known he'd always
been ...   ...) knew that love was responsible for
this tuneless .   ... and Kitty had become an unofficial
couple, he'd never b--   ut a smile on his face and a sparkle in
his eye. It warmed her heart.

As Little Mary made her way back up her path, Ollie was tackling the high notes of a song, making her chuckle.

Anoushka was yanked away from a dream and into a morning filled with the sound of someone being hurt. Squinting, she brushed away the stray blonde hairs that had escape her thick plait and straggled rebelliously across her face. She smiled sleepily as realisation dawned; it was *The Day*. And the sound wasn't of someone in pain, it was her dad singing because he was happy; not just an everyday kind of happy, but the happiest he'd ever been. Noushka's smile was quickly banished when her father hit a bum note, and she was forced to pull her pillow over her head in the hope of muffling the sound.

Ten minutes later, she encountered her father on the landing, still singing at the top of his lungs, his eyes tightly shut as he towel-dried his hair. She prodded him in the stomach, making him jump, cutting short some song she didn't recognise. 'Uhh!' He opened his eyes to see her standing in front of him, hands on hips. 'Good morning, Noushka.' He flashed a broad smile.

'Morning, Dad. Can I just say, I can totally think of better ways of being woken up. But OMG, you've got to, literally, promise me you won't sing along like that in front of Kitty tonight. I'm totally serious. If you do, she's totally going to think you've turned into some nutty random and it will, literally, be a total deal-breaker.' Concern troubled her pretty features.

'Literally and totally that bad, eh?'

'Worse.'

As Ollie laughed at his daughter's solemn expression as music floated along the landing. 'Oh, I love this song.' He grinned as he started strutting towards her in his terry-towelling dressing gown that had seen better days. 'No need to ask where you got your dancing skills from, eh?'

'Hmm. I wouldn't be so sure, Dad. Just please promise you literally won't do that tonight.

'Okay, I totally promise. And literally, too.'

'Cool. Oh, and before I forget, I just wanted to say that you're totally the best dad in the whole world ever.' She wrapped her arms around his neck and kissed him on the cheek before skipping off down the stairs in her pink and white striped pyjamas, twirling her plait between her fingers.

'And you're totally the best Noushka anyone could ever have, ever. And literally!' He repeated the line she claimed had worn as thin as some of his socks.

Stopping half-way down she turned and looked up at him. 'Oh, and, Dad, I'll run through everything with you this afternoon as soon as I get back from dancing. It's going to be just perfect. I promise.'

'Thanks, Noushka.' Ollie watched her disappear down the stairs and dance her way into the kitchen, a feeling of pride swelling in his chest. She was a good kid and, even if he did say so himself, he hadn't done such a bad job of bringing her up. It hadn't always been easy, especially when she was little. But, thanks to help from his parents, he'd become adept at juggling work and childcare. He swallowed the lump of emotion that had risen in his throat. His little girl was growing into a kind and thoughtful young woman.

THAT NIGHT, Ollie, Kitty and their friends were going to the Midsummer Music in the Wood event in the grounds of Danskelfe Castle. Caro Hammondely, a reformed character, and enjoying responsibility in her new role as Events Organiser, had surprised everyone and done an outstanding job of organising everything to ensure its smooth running. She'd even managed to book the much-in-demand Gabe Dublin.

At just after six, Pip and a heavily pregnant Molly rumbled up to Oak Tree Farm in their Landie – named Derek. Kitty and Ollie had heard it as it headed down the road towards the cottage and were already making their way down the path. They climbed into the back alongside Jimby and Vi.

'Right, let's get cracking, Pip, lad.' Jimby slapped his knee. 'Should be a bloody good night, this.'

Molly turned to them. 'I'd best warn you, we're in for a bumpy ride; I think Pip left Derek's suspension on some moor top yonks ago.'

'It's not that bad, Moll.' Pip shoved the Landie into gear and set off down the lane.

'Ouch! Bloody hell, Pip!' Violet rubbed her head where it had bumped against Derek's roof as he bounced over a pothole.

'Still soft round the edges from all that city living, are you, Vi?' Pip caught Jimby's eye in the rear-view mirror and winked. He regularly gave Vi a gentle ribbing, saying she'd become even more of a princess during her time away from the village.

He manoeuvred into a pull-in place and let Bill Campion pass by in his tractor, the pair nodding in acknowledgement. 'I maybe should've told you before, but the last passengers I had in the back were a couple of dead ewes. And I haven't had chance to give it a proper swill out, so you'd best mind where you put your feet in case there's any blood and guts lying around.'

Vi quickly lifted her feet off the floor; there was no way she was going to ruin her expensive new pumps. 'Oh, how delightful, Pip.' She wore an expression of disgust.

The others laughed, and Pip received a playful bat on the arm from Molly. 'Don't take any notice Vi, he's teasing. He did give it a tidy, though. I supervised the whole procedure to make sure he didn't cut any corners.

'I can believe that,' said Jimby.

'Me too,' added Kitty.

'Too bloody right, she did. She's got that crazy cleaning thing going on like she had when the lads were about due. She's been cleaning anything and everything that stands still for long enough. The dogs are so clean they squeak when they walk, and the lads have learnt to levitate so they don't have to walk on the carpets.'

'Ooh, that sounds a bit ominous, Moll. You know what the nesting instinct means?'

'Don't remind me, Kitts.' Molly patted her swollen bump. 'But I think we're safe for tonight.'

'Ooh, Vi, you look absolutely gorgeous. I can see why you weren't too keen to travel in the back of Derek,' Molly exclaimed. She turned to Kitty, who looked laid back and pretty in a navy blue tie-dyed maxi dress under a faded denim jacket that had been Ollie's when he was seventeen. Knowing things could turn chilly later, she'd thrown on a pair of navy leggings and tucked her feet into a pair of chunky boots. 'You look lovely too, Kitts. Whereas I look enormous wearing the latest in beached whale chic.'

'Rubbish! You look absolutely gorgeous, Moll.' She hugged her cousin, who she noted was looking ripe and radiant, reminiscent of a juicy peach. Her hair hung in thick, shiny waves, her skin was glowing and clear, while her brown eyes sparkled with vitality.

'Well, I don't bloody feel it. I feel ready to pop.'

'Hmmm.' Kitty thought so, too. She'd keep half an eye on her tonight.

Weighed down with a clutter of picnic baskets, bottles of plonk and fold-down tables and chairs, the group left the already heaving parking area and headed towards the clearing where people were beginning to gather. Pre-recorded music boomed from strategically placed speakers.

Ollie looked at Kitty and grinned. 'You alright?'

'Fab.' She beamed back at him and reached up to kiss his cheek.

'Cut it out, you soppy pair,' joked Pip.

Happy with a spot underneath the branches of an ancient conifer, they threw down their picnic blankets and set up a temporary camp. Molly tipped out a collection of citronella candles and a couple of bottles of body oil which she proceeded to spray liberally over everyone.

'What the bloody hell's that, Moll?' Scrunching his nose up, James gave his arms a sniff. 'You're going to have me stinking like a tart's handbag.'

'It's to keep the midgies away. You'll thank me later when the little buggers leave you alone, Jimbo. You, too.' Molly chuckled at Ollie's expression as he wiped his hand across his arms and sniffed his fingers.

'S'true, lads. It really does work,' agreed Kitty.

'THIS PICNIC IS AMAZING, OLLIE.' Kitty plopped a piece of strawberry into her glass of Prosecco, licking their sweetness off her fingers.

'I wish I could say I had a hand in it, but it's all down to Bea. My only contribution was to go and collect it, which is just as well; I want everything to be perfect for tonight.' His stomach flipped at the reminder.

'You alright, Oll? You've gone a bit pale, me aud mucker.' James nudged him with his elbow and grinned.

'Couldn't be better, mate.' He smiled at Jimby, giving him a pat on the back. 'Don't you worry about me. Hey, Moll, have you seen the custard cream cake Bea made for you?'

'Looks fab. I'll have some later.' She took a sip of her fizzy water, shuffling uncomfortably in her chair. A sickly feeling had started to creep up on her thanks to the greasy smell of fried onions that wafted by on the light breeze courtesy of the burger van a few hundred yards away, mingling with the aroma of freshly silaged fields. She placed a hand over her mouth and retched.

'You okay?' Concerned, Kitty rubbed her cousin's arm.

Molly nodded. 'Fine, thanks. It's just the smell of those bloody onions playing havoc with my guts. Haven't been able to face them all the time I've been pregnant.' She took another sip of water. 'The bubbles in this are doing a good job of calming things down, though.'

'Moll, are you sure you're okay? You've gone a bit green and clammy, chick,' Vi chipped in.

'Mmm. S'just the smell of those.' She nodded in the general direction of the van.

'Yeah, it's not the most tempting of smells,' agreed Vi, wrinkling her nose.

The pre-recorded music stopped, providing a sudden distraction. The crowd held a collective breath as the void was filled by Gabe Dublin's support band who burst on stage in a glare of lights and a blast of lead guitar. It was quickly joined by the rhythmic beat of drums, the low pulsing of the bass and the chirpy arc of a fiddle courtesy of the group's only girl.

'Hello, everyone. We're Tykes! We're from the awesome city of York, and I can't tell you how excited we are at being asked to play support to Gabe,' beamed Jake, the lead singer who didn't look a day over twelve. 'So, the first song we're gonna play is our new single and we want to see you all dance, okay?' The crowd replied, cheering and clapping. Someone behind Kitty pushed a finger and thumb between their lips and gave a shrill whistle, making her jump. She threw her head back and laughed.

Jake bounded around the stage with the energy of a young Labrador. His banter was friendly, his enthusiasm infectious. In no time, the audience were on their feet, dancing and singing along to the band's folk-infused indie music. Their finale was a rousing rendition of their first single which went down a storm, their impressive guitar riffs soaring through the air and up into the outstretched branches of the trees.

Kitty glanced at Ollie, her face breaking into a wide smile. He grinned back, and wrapped his arm around her, hugging her close. 'Love you, beautiful,' he whispered in her ear.

'Love you right back,' she said, snuggling into him.

WITH TYKES! off the stage and the pre-recorded playlist filling the gap before Gabe Dublin's appearance, the evening eased its way into a mellow dusk. Soft shadows stretched out as the sun slipped behind the tall trees of the wood.

The last of the black-clad roadies finished setting up on stage, scurrying off as the low bass-line of Gabe's first hit thrummed out from the speakers. Suddenly, everyone was on their feet, cheering, facing the bright lights of the giant stage that nestled against the now looming shadows of the forest. Gabe sauntered on, singing softly, before breaking into a wide smile. 'Good evening, everyone. How're y'all doin'?' he called out in his soft southern Irish accent. The crowd cheered and whistled.

Ollie glanced down at Kitty, her elfin face bathed in the soft amber light of summer dusk. She'd never looked more beautiful. He still couldn't believe it that this woman, who he'd loved for so long, was finally his. And she was finally free to love him back.

Thoughts of his plans for later in the evening jumped into his mind, making his heart race, setting nerves wriggling in his stomach. He took a deep breath and brushed away the spikes of anxiety. It might be out of character for the shy and retiring Ollie Cartwright, but nothing was going to get in the way of his plans.

Sensing his eyes on her, Kitty met his gaze and smiled, her dark eyes sparkling. He threw his arm around her shoulders, pulled her close and kissed her full on the mouth. He liked the way she responded: wrapping her arms around his middle and snuggling up close. 'Having a good time?' he asked, nuzzling her hair.

'The best.'

Jimby took a swig from his bottle of beer, his eyes meeting Violet's, a conspiratorial smile passing between them.

'WON'T BE A MINUTE.' Ollie gave Kitty's shoulders a squeeze before disappearing into the crowd. It was forty-five minutes into the set, and Gabe had taken a moment off stage, leaving the audience swaying to the mellow tune played by his band.

'You alright, Moll? James asked, giving her a wink as he topped up everyone's glasses.

'Hanging on in there, Jimby.' She massaged her lower back.

Before either of them could say any more a cheer rose up from the audience as Gabe ambled back on stage, his guitar slung across his chest. 'Hello again.' He grinned, fiddling with his mike stand. 'So, tonight's a very special night.' His voice rang around the clearing, punctuated by the odd "whoop" and cheer.

'We love you, Gabe,' a voice called out.

'I love you, too,' he laughed. 'Actually, it's a matter of love that makes tonight so special.'

Backstage, a bolt of nerves shot through Ollie. His palms began to sweat, and his stomach churned. 'You'll do great, man.' Jake, who was in on the secret, placed a hand on his shoulder. 'Me and the band think it's so cool. She must be one special lady.'

Ollie swallowed down the nerves, a picture of Kitty in his mind. 'She is, she's very special.'

On stage, Gabe grinned, brushing back his floppy dark hair with his hand. Zeke, the chisel-jawed bass player, began to strum the base-line of his latest single. 'So, someone contacted me with a pretty special request, and it was such a fantastic request, I just had to say yes – when you hear what it is, you'll understand why.'

The crowd whooped and cheered some more as Kitty leaned across to Molly and Vi. 'Ooh, I wonder what it is?' she said, standing on her tiptoes and craning her neck to get a better view, unaware of Jimby waggling his eyebrows at them.

Gabe laughed and motioned for the crowd to quieten down.

'Okay, folks. For this request to work I need to know do we have a Kitty Fairfax in the audience?' He turned and waved for Ollie to join him on stage. 'Come on pal, it's time,' he said in a stage-whisper.

Kitty watched the vast video screen at the right of the stage, her expression one of utter confusion. There, clear as day, was a man on stage who looked exactly like Ollie. And Gabe Dublin had just asked if someone with the same name as *her* was in the audience.

Things felt suddenly very surreal.

Gabe shielded his eyes with his hands, 'Where are you, Kitty? I've got someone here who wants to ask you something, don't you, Ollie?' He motioned for Ollie to move closer and draped his arm across his shoulder.

She glanced around. Strangely, her group didn't seem to be sharing her feeling of confusion. Jimby was wearing one of his extra wide, extra happy grins. And, totally out of the blue, Vi and Molly had started to jump up and down, screeching 'She's here!' and pointing in her direction.

They were in on this, whatever *this* was. She turned her gaze back to the screen and saw Ollie pointing in her general direction.

'Ahh, that's where you're hiding is it, Kitty? Well, don't be shy now.' Gabe gave the thumbs up. 'Dave, Chris, can we have some cameras on Kitty, please? Thanks, guys.'

Before she had a second to process her thoughts, the gaze of the cameras shifted to her and, amidst more cheering from the crowd, a close-up of her confused face appeared on the giant screens on the stage. Kitty looked askance at Vi and Molly as the pair cheered and whooped, clapping their hands above their head.

Gabe gave a low whistle. 'Wowzers, Kitty, you're gorgeous. Isn't she, folks?' The audience responded with more enthusiastic cheering and whistling. Feeling her cheeks burn, she hid her face in her hands.

'Aww, did I make you blush, Kitty? Well, I'm sorry, but it's true, you're a real babe.' Gabe laughed flirtatiously. 'Okay, folks. Sshhh. Can we have some quiet, please. Ollie here has something he wants to say. Right, then, it's all yours. Go for it, man.' Gabe patted him on the shoulder and took a step back.

Despite being more nervous than he'd ever felt before, the vast-ness of the crowd seemed to make things easier; individual faces being lost in a blurry sea of bodies that appeared to go on forever. Being taller than Gabe, Ollie had to lean down to the microphone. He cleared his throat, the suspense in the audience palpable as they looked on in silence.

'Thanks, Gabe.' He cleared his throat again. 'Erm, I'm not used to this sort of thing, so please forgive me if I sound daft, folks. But well, Kitty, ahem, err, you know how long I've loved you — it's over eighteen years, for all of you who don't actually know.' Feeling braver, Ollie gave a small laugh as the crowd released a collective "ahhh".

Kitty pulled her hands away from her face and clasped them to her chest. What was her shy, quiet Ollie doing up there on that stage? Without warning, she felt the glare of half a dozen spotlights trained on her, forcing her to shrink into the safety of her denim jacket.

Ollie continued. 'And I,' he cleared his throat again. 'I, I wondered if you'd make me the happiest man in the world and do me the honour of becoming my wife?' On the vast screen, Kitty could see his handsome face beaming in her direction. 'Kitty Fairfax, you're the love of my life, will you marry me?'

The audience held a collective breath, and she felt the weight of thousands of eyes upon her as Dave and Chris manoeuvred their cameras into position, zooming in on her face. Ollie wiped his palms down the sides of his jeans and turned to get a clearer look at her expression on the screen behind him.

Tears of happiness sprang from her eyes and trickled down her face. She wiped them away with her fingertips and smiled. 'I love you, Ollie. Of course, I'll marry you.' As soon as the words had left her lips, Molly and Vi pounced on her, squealing with excitement, delivering hugs and kisses.

'Is that a yes?' Gabe strode forward and spoke into the mike. 'She's nodding, Ollie, mate. Congratulations. The beautiful Kitty has just agreed to be your wife.' As the forest filled with the sound of thousands of cheering voices, Gabe began to strum on his guitar, his band following his lead. 'Well done, man, you go and get back to your girl.' He delivered a sound pat on Ollie's back. 'Wasn't it awesome to be part of that, folks? C'mon, let's give the happy couple a huge round of applause.' The crowd needed little encouragement. 'And don't forget to send me an invitation. Actually, now I think about it, I think tonight qualifies me as godfather for your first-born. Oh, and Kitty, if you ever change your mind about Ollie, you know where I am. I wasn't joking when I said you were a babe.' He gave a cheeky wink.

Seeing Ollie emerge from the shadows, Kitty ran to him, a huge grin on her face. 'How did you…? When did…? Who's…?' Laughing, her words were a jumbled mass of happiness.

'Caro Hammondely, believe it or not, and her new fella, Sim.'

'Caro Hammondely?' Her eyes widened.

'Yep, she's a reformed character since she started going out with Sim – he's a good bloke. And having a purpose in life up at the big house seems to have done her the world of good, really calmed her down. Anyway, you know I told you I wanted to shout how much I love you from the rooftops? Well, while I was chatting to them, the idea suddenly crossed my mind, and, well, let's just say they were both fantastic about arranging it for me – he's a sound engineer for Gabe so knows him pretty well.'

'Wow! Ollie Cartwright, you're full of surprises. Shouting it from the rooftops is one thing, but on stage at a Gabe Dublin gig, that must've taken some guts.'

'I just wanted the world to know how I feel about you. And now they do.'

James was the first of the group to offer congratulations. Beaming broadly, he strode over to them and clapped his hand on Ollie's back. 'Bloody well done, mate. You've got some balls going up there and doing what you just did. Congratulations, I couldn't be happier for the pair of you.'

'Toast! Toast!' Vi, who was busy uncorking a bottle of Prosecco, motioned for them to head over to her. 'Here you go,' she said, handing out glasses of fizz. 'Cheers to the best-suited couple ever.'

'Just a little one for me, Vi, as I'm driving,' said Pip.

'Cheers!' the friends chorused, clinking glasses.

'I won't say about bloody time or anything like that.' Molly rubbed away a spasm in her back. Catching Pip watching her, she gave a small shake of her head, mouthing, 'I'm fine.' His concerned expression told her he wasn't convinced.

'No, but I bloody well will.' James gave Ollie a nudge. 'It's about bloody time!'

LATER, with calm restored, Ollie took Kitty's hand and led her away, slipping silently into the shadows of the trees. The temperature had dropped, and the wood was shrouded in a cloak of darkness. The bright cerulean blue of the earlier midsummer sky was replaced by a deep, inky-black, splashed with millions of sparkling stars.

They made their way deeper into the wood, luminescent moon-light reaching through the gaps in the trees illuminating a narrow, winding pathway. With her hand in his, Kitty followed Ollie as he wove his way along, crushing the thick carpet of pine needles under-foot. Eventually, they reached a clearing. Ollie stopped and reached into the front pocket of his jeans, pulling out a small object and clutching it tightly in his hand. He glanced across at her and unfurled his fingers revealing a tiny leather box, slightly faded and worn around the edges.

'And I thought that bulge was because you were just pleased to see me.'

'I'm always pleased to see you, you have me in a constant state of arousal.' He grinned at her before taking hold of her left hand and easing himself down onto one knee. He cleared his throat. 'Kitty, I know what I've just done was very public – I still can't believe I actu-ally did it! – but I wanted to do this bit properly and privately.' He shifted slightly as a pine needle objected to him kneeling on it and dug into his skin. 'Kitty Fairfax, would you make me the happiest man in the world and do me the honour of becoming my wife?' He smiled up at her, his eyes glittering in the moonlight.

She bent forward and cupped his face in her hands. 'Ollie Cartwright, there's nothing I'd like more than to be your wife,' she said before kissing him, her lips lingering for a moment. 'But you look pretty uncomfortable down there, so I think you'd probably better stand up now.'

'I'm so pleased you said that, those pine needles are bloody evil,' he said as he stood up. Carefully opening the small leather box, he lifted out the delicate diamond ring from its seat. 'Well, this makes it official.' He took Kitty's left hand and slid the ring onto her finger. It was a perfect fit. 'It was my Grandma Cartwright's, but if you don't like it, I can take you to a jewellers, and you can choose a different one.'

She held her hand close to her face, admiring the delicate flower of diamonds that twinkled in the soft moonlight. 'Ollie, it's the most beautiful ring I've ever seen. I wouldn't change it for the world.' She threw her arms around him.

Before long she felt the warmth of tears trickling down her neck. 'Oh, Ollie,' she said softly. She'd never seen him cry before.

'Sorry, just ignore me.' He eased his head back and sniffed, swiping an errant tear away. 'I'm just so happy. I never thought this day would come. I've loved you for so long, and there's been such a massive, aching hole in my heart that I never thought would be filled. And now it is, it's taking a bit of getting used to. I love you so much, Kitty, I can't put it into words. And I don't care if I sound soppy, but I never want to lose you again. I promise I'll look after you and love you forever.' He sniffed again and smiled down at her.

Kitty brushed her lips against his, tasting the saltiness of his tears. 'I know you will, Ollie. I've never felt more loved and cherished, and I've never been happier. I've loved you for a very long time, too. For a while, I stupidly hid it away, ignored my true feelings and buried them deep, but you're the love of my life, and now everyone can know about it. In fact, after tonight, I'm pretty certain everyone will.'

'Yep, I guess they will.' He laughed, pressing his forehead against hers.

AS THEY ALL headed back to the Landie, Kitty noticed that Molly seemed uncharacteristically quiet and appeared to be waddling uncomfortably. There was still another three weeks to go before the baby was due, so Kitty put it down to tiredness after Moll's frantic cleaning frenzy. She and Pip had been helping out more with the farm, and it had been full on at work, where she'd been running around like a woman possessed, tying up all the loose ends before she finished for good. But a knowing look from Pip told her he knew what she was thinking.

And their suspicions proved right.

Despite the assistance of Violet, who was pushing her from behind, and Kitty and Pip who were pulling her from inside the Landie, Molly was struggling to climb up into the vehicle. Kitty watched as cold sweat began to prickle her cousin's brow.

'Ooooph!' Molly gasped, her face distorted with pain as a Braxton Hicks contraction gripped, taking her breath away.

'You okay, love?' asked Pip, concerned.

'Just take a minute, Moll, there's no rush,' said Kitty.

'I'm fine. Let's give it another try.' She blew her hair off her face.

'Are you sure?' asked Pip. Molly nodded. 'Right, one, two, three…'

'Stop!' she hollered.

'Eeuuww!' Violet jumped back.

'Oh, shit!' groaned Molly. Her waters had broken, gushing over Vi's prized ballerina pumps.

'Oops,' said Kitty.

AT A QUARTER to three the following morning, 6lb 2oz baby Emelia Annie Pennock arrived into the world.

50

SATURDAY 24TH JULY arrived full of promise. The sky was already a colour–wash of cornflower blue when the pale golden rays of the early morning sun inched over the lofty heights of Great Stangdale rigg. It spilled over into the dale, spreading across the village, its warmth soaking into the rooftops of the sleeping cottages.

The dawn chorus was in full swing, and a solitary cockerel crowed boastfully. Drifting in and out of slumber, Kitty felt herself smile. The bird heralding the day so confidently would be Reg. Up early, he'd be strutting about the village with more swagger than a premiership footballer.

She yawned, stretching her arms above her head. Fingers of sunlight were attempting to prize open the curtains, held at bay by the heavy fabric, suspending the bedroom in a snug semi-darkness. Wiping the remnants of sleep from her eyes, Kitty squinted at the alarm clock on the bedside table. Goodness, it *was* early. She reached her legs out to the cooler end of the bed, giving her toes a wiggle, when a wave of excitement rippled through her.

Today was *the* day.

Lily, who was snuggling beside her, stirred, mumbling a stream of something incomprehensible. Kitty kissed the top of her daughter's head, inhaling her comforting smell. She loved having the children cuddling close beside her. Lily was a regular, Lucas less so — he reckoned he was too cool for babyish stuff like that now. Though, if he wasn't feeling well, or if something was bothering him she would sense him climbing in beside her in the early hours.

Rolling back onto her pillow, she rested a hand on her stomach, hoping to settle the butterflies that were flurrying around in there. The bed felt deliciously comfortable. She sighed, shutting her eyes; she had a long day ahead of her, it'd be good to get some more sleep. But they refused to stay closed, and her mind refused to settle as thoughts skittered about excitedly.

Accepting that sleep was out of her grasp, Kitty slipped out of bed, shrugged on her dressing gown and tiptoed downstairs. Reaching the kitchen, she was greeted by Humph and Ethel, whose tails wagged furiously, delighted at seeing their mum up and about at such an early hour. 'There you go, you two,' she whispered as she unlocked the back door and let them out into the garden.

ARMED WITH A MUG OF TEA, Kitty joined the Labradors outside and followed the twists and turns of the gravel path, the legs of her pyjamas brushing against the dew-wet lavender.

Reaching the bottom of the garden she cradled her mug in her hands, gazing out at the hazy view across the dale. After the warmth of the house, the air seemed cool, but the early morning sunshine was slowly gaining pace, pushing away the flimsy summer mist and filling the valley with an ethereal glow. The sweet smell of summer hay hung in the air, carried across the dale on a barely-there breeze from Bill Campion's newly silaged fields. Kitty took a deep breath; it was a smell so evocative of her childhood; of carefree summers filled with laughter and drenched in sunshine.

In the distance, she could see the Danks's herd of milkers slowly moseying their way to the milking parlour at Tinkel Top Farm. The muffled growl of John's quad bike as he rounded them up mingled with their baying and the cacophony of the dawn chorus that was still in full swing. Reg appeared to be getting increasingly vocal, too. 'Who said the countryside was quiet?' she asked Ethel, who had stopped following a trail of delicious scents around the garden and cocked her head, poised with a front paw lifted off the ground, her nose twitching in the air.

Kitty blew across her tea and took a sip. 'Blearghh.' She pulled a face as a wave of queasiness washed over her. She'd recently lost her knack for making a decent cuppa. Wedding day nerves weren't help-ing, filling her stomach with fluttery butterflies.

A combination of the chilly air and excitement made her shiver, she still struggled to comprehend how different her life was from eighteen months ago. In that time things had settled into a peaceful pattern. Particularly so when, six months ago, and without warning, Dan had moved away. Kitty would have appreciated a little bit of notice, so she could prepare the children. But he hadn't seen fit to get in touch. Instead, she'd found out in passing from George one evening in the Sunne, his face burning crimson as he told her.

AFTER HIS APPEARANCE IN THE MAGISTRATES' court, Dan's case was listed for trial in the Crown Court where the evidence was too damn-ing, and his charm in the witness box had failed to work on the jury, who convicted him for his dogging escapades. As it was his first offence, the judge gave him a suspended sentence and a community service order, which he completed while he awaited the outcome of his fate with the Bar Standards Board, the body to which he'd been reported, and who would decide whether or not he should be disbarred.

Luckily for Dan, a high-profile murder trial was running in the next court to his, which meant all attention was diverted there. His case was small-fry by comparison, and the press had left him alone. Even so, he was eager to get away from the pointing fingers of those that knew, so he'd upped and left for London, leaving no forwarding address.

His abrupt departure, without seeing Lucas and Lily, and his lack of contact since seemed to bother Kitty more than it did them, his name rarely crossing their lips. And since he'd left, she'd been able to enjoy a sense of peace, knowing there was little chance of him turning up on the doorstep. She shuddered as she remembered the last time he had done such a thing.

The appearance of a "For Sale" sign on the Manor House was a welcome sight, too. Unwilling to face up to her precious son's misde-meanours, Gwyneth had been desperate to leave the area. Kitty had heard Cornwall mentioned, which she thought was about as far away as they could go to escape Dan's tarnished reputation.

The dreaded Mellisons seemed to have quietened down too,

which was a blessing. School had been great at keeping an eye on things, pouncing whenever trouble from Evie threatened. And, as a result, Lily was happy and flourishing.

BUT TODAY WASN'T for dwelling on the past. Today she was getting married to the kindest, most decent man she'd ever met. Today was about looking to the future; a future with Ollie.

Kitty glanced around the garden, bending to remove the faded flowerhead from a rose. She couldn't remember a time when it had looked more beautiful or flowered so profusely. Every inch was jam-packed with blowsy flowers in full bloom — the majority planted by her mother. It was almost as if the garden was aware of today's significance.

She'd decided that using flowers from the garden would make her feel her mum was close as she exchanged vows with Ollie. Auntie Annie had been round with Molly the previous evening, snipping away and collecting the best blooms for the church displays. Afterwards, the three of them had decorated the arch around the lychgate at the entrance. It looked stunning, trimmed with roses and carnations in gentle shades of pale pink offset by eucalyptus, sprigs of rosemary and the frothy flower-heads of gypsophila.

Kitty would cut the flowers for the bouquets and wedding yurt later in the morning.

'Mummy, where are you?' Lily called as she skipped barefoot down the path in her pyjamas, Snuggles in her hand. 'When can I put my bridesmaid dress on? I really want to put it on soon. I promise I won't get it dirty.'

'I think it's a bit early yet, sweet pea. In fact, it's very early, and you've got a really long day ahead of you. Why don't you go and snuggle back down in bed for a while?'

'I can't sleep, Mummy. That silly cock-a-doodle-do of Uncle Jimby's is so noisy. He woke me up, and now I can't get back to sleep.' She pouted, rubbing her eyes.

Kitty chuckled. 'Okay, how about I do you some nice breakfast then?' Her stomach curdled at the thought.

'Yep, good idea. Me and Snuggles are starving.'

'Come on then.' Smiling, she took her daughter's hand, and they wove their way down the path to the house. Just as they were about to head inside, they heard a kerfuffle on the road followed by a piercing squawk. Hurrying round to the front garden, they were just in time to see Jimby, resplendent in blue and white striped pyjama bottoms, a crumpled white T-shirt and wellies, tearing down the middle of the road in hot pursuit of Reg.

'Come here, you feathery little shit!'

Kitty clamped her hands over Lily's ears and did her best to stifle a giggle.

'Mummy, Uncle Jimby sweared. He said "sh..."'

Kitty's hands moved swiftly from Lily's ears to her mouth. 'Yes, I heard what he said, and I don't need you to repeat it, thank you.'

With a noisy flap of his wings, Reg changed direction. James made a grab for him but the rooster lurched out of reach with a squawk. Jimby looked furious. 'Little bugger!' He made another lunge for the bird, then, 'Uhhh!' He hit the ground with a thud, face-planting the road as Reg took off down the lane to Danskelfe, complaining vociferously as he went.

Winded, James took a moment before he pulled himself up, noting the holes in his pyjama bottoms. He pressed his fingers against his chin, which was beginning to throb. Spots of blood confirmed his fears: he'd skinned it. 'Bugger! That'll look great for the photos,' he muttered. Sensing he was being watched, he looked around to see Kitty and Lily in fits of giggles. 'I'm fine by the way, in case you were going to ask.'

51

THE WEDDING YURT was everything Kitty had hoped for. Decorated in a country cottage theme of pale pinks, soft greens and cream, it was stunning. Occupying the large field at the back of the Sunne, it was roomy enough to house all their guests, while allowing space in the far corner to accommodate a stage for the band and a small dance floor.

Kitty had joined Molly and Auntie Annie in making the final tweaks and touches to the tables. She'd taken armfuls of freshly cut flowers from her garden, and together they'd arranged them in the squat jam jars that sat in clusters on the gingham-covered tables, complementing the huge displays Auntie Annie had dotted around the yurt.

'Thank you both so much. Everywhere looks wonderful; I couldn't have done any of it without you.' Kitty gazed around the space, a lump forming in her throat, thinking of the one person who would've been in her element amongst the flowers and foliage, arranging and creating.

'We've loved every minute of it, lovie.' Auntie Annie wrapped her arms around her, rubbing her back vigorously. 'And your mum's here in spirit. I can feel her all around us.' She sniffed, brushing away a tear.

'Me, too,' she whispered.

'Come here, you daft pair.' Molly threw her arms around them. 'No tears, we don't want Kitts' eyes to swell up like that porker's that's on the spit out there, do we?' she said of the pig that was currently being roasted for the wedding reception. 'And, of course, I've loved every minute of it. It's got me away from the chaos that's Pip and the kids for a couple of hours. What's not to love?'

KITTY STOOD in front of the full-length mirror of her bedroom, fiddling with the tiny silver locket that sat at her neck – her "something old". It had belonged to her mother and her grandmother before that, each wearing it on their wedding day. She felt her throat tighten at the thought of her lovely mum; what she'd give to have her here today. Her dad, too. 'No tears today,' she reminded herself, patting the locket with her fingertips.

A sudden bright shaft of sunlight slanted through a gap in the branches of the apple tree. A well-timed distraction, it glinted off her earrings and bounced around the room. The earrings that were a present from Ollie. Exquisite diamonds set in the shape of a delicate flower, he'd had them made specially to match her engagement ring and had given them to her yesterday morning. They were her "something new".

Kitty smoothed her hands down the front of her wedding dress. She'd designed it with Vi, and the result was an exquisite ivory silk sheath with shoe-string straps beneath a delicate lace over-dress with three-quarter length sleeves. It was dotted with a thousand tiny pearls and crystals that caught the sunlight, each one painstakingly sewn on by hand. The gown also hid her "something blue": a tiny pale blue money spider, embroidered by Violet into the hem.

Atop her shiny cropped curls sat a delicate silver daisy-chain of pearls and crystals. Her shoes were handmade Mary-Janes in cream leather, trimmed with vintage diamanté buckles that had belonged to Auntie Annie – her "something borrowed".

Kitty made eye contact with her reflection in the mirror and smiled. Eighteen months ago, she wouldn't have recognised the glowing young woman with the happy expression and sparkling eyes who was looking back at her. But now, that same young woman had much to be happy about. And half an hour ago she'd discovered something that made her smile even wider.

Sensing a change in the room, Kitty turned. Her skin prickled, and she gave a shiver; she was alone but had the overwhelming feeling that someone else was there, too. Her pulse quickened, and she looked around her, but the room was revealing nothing. She made to go to the door but stopped in her tracks when the faint scent of honeysuckle wafted under her nose; comforting and familiar. At that moment a white feather drifted silently down from the ceiling. She watched its journey until it stopped, landing on her dress, caught on one of the crystals. 'Mum!' Tears began to sting her eyes, but she blinked them away before they had chance to spill over. 'Pull yourself together, Kitty,' she remonstrated with herself. But it gladdened her heart to know that her beautiful mum was with her, sharing her happy day.

Downstairs, Anoushka was struggling to harness Lily's burgeoning excitement. She'd suggested watching the television, but any attempts at distraction had proved futile, and her patience was wearing thin.

There was a hesitant tap at Kitty's bedroom door. 'Mum, I think it's time I headed over to Ollie's.'

'Okay, Lukes. Come in, let me see how you look.'

He popped his head around the door, his young face serious, his bottom lip quivering. 'Oh, Mum. You look lovely.'

'Thank you. And you look very dapper in that suit, young man.' She smiled at him as he hovered in the doorway, looking endearingly formal in his wedding attire of a mid-blue three-piece suit complete with floral tie and button-hole that matched her bouquet. He scratched his head self-consciously and mustered an embarrassed smile. Kitty walked over to him and kissed his forehead. 'Mind the quiff,' they both said, laughing. He'd grown again she thought, he was as tall as her now. And judging by the heady aroma that was assailing her nose, he'd been rather liberal with Jimby's cologne. 'And you smell very nice, too.'

'Thanks, Mum. I wanted to make an effort for your special day.'

Her throat tightened with emotion; she couldn't be prouder of her son, who'd leapt at the chance of becoming Ollie's best man. 'Thank you, Lukes, that means a lot. And I want everyone to see how handsome you look in your suit, so promise me no football tricks until after the photos. I want you clean and smart for at least an hour, not covered in mud and grass stains. That goes for Ollie, too. Can I leave it to you to keep him in check for me?'

'Yep. But what about Uncle Jimby?'

'Leave him to me, he's under strict instructions, so I think he'll be on his best behaviour.'

'Cool,' he said, before loping downstairs and heading out of the front door.

Hearing the rumble of Jimby's Landie as it trundled up the road, Kitty checked her reflection one last time before slipping on her shoes. Knowing how long she'd be wearing them for today, she was thankful she'd opted for such a butter-soft pair.

As she was fastening them, there was a gentle knock at her bedroom door. 'Come in.' She turned to see Noushka staring at her.

'O.M.G. Kitty you look so, like, totally gorgeous. Your dress! Your shoes! Hashtag delish!' Anoushka ran over to her, giving her a squeeze.

'Thank you, Noushka. And you look absolutely stunning.' She took in the young woman who stood before her, looking heart-stop-pingly beautiful, with her peaches and cream complexion and her glossy hair that fell in long golden waves, cascading over her shoulders, crowned by a circle of fresh flowers.

'Thank you.' Smiling, she gave a quick twirl. Her empire-line bridesmaid dress of cream lace and silk echoed Kitty's. It draped elegantly over her lean, athletic frame, finishing mid-calf. 'And I totally love my shoes.' She gazed at her cream satin Mary-Janes peppered with pearls and crystals that glinted the light. 'Can I really keep them?'

'Of course.'

'My feet had so better not grow anymore.' Her serious expression made Kitty laugh.

'Right then, I think it's time we headed downstairs.' Steadying her nerves, she took a deep breath.

'Before we do, Kitty, I just want to say that I'm so totally happy that you and Dad have finally found each other.'

'Me too, Noushka. Your dad's a very special person, and I love him with all my heart.' She took Anoushka's hands in hers. 'And I want you to know that while I've grown to love your dad, I've grown to love you very much, too. As have Lucas and Lily.'

'And I love you, too. And Lukes and Lils.' Anoushka's bottom lip wobbled as tears threatened.

'Oops, no tears, Noushka. You'll make your mascara run, and we don't want that.' Kitty gave the young girl a squeeze.

'True.' Anoushka wafted her hands in front of her eyes. 'There. All sorted and under control.'

Downstairs in the living room, Lily was twirling around in her dress – a smaller version of Noushka's – while James was trying to pin her down so he could re-fasten the circle of flowers to her curls. With all her excited jumping around, it had worked loose and was hanging off precariously. 'You look like a proper little princess, Lils, but, I think you need to calm down a bit, or you'll make yourself sick. And if I can't fix your flowers properly they might fall off in church, and we don't want that, do we?'

'Nope, Uncle Jimby.' Lily ceased her twirling and stood still.

'There, all done.' He patted her shoulders and headed out into the hallway where he caught sight of Kitty making her way down the stairs, his face breaking into a broad smile. 'By 'eck, sis, you scrub up well.'

'Thanks, Jimby. And talking of scrubs, that's a beauty you've got on your chin.'

'Hmmm. Not my finest hour, I'll grant you.' His hand went to the scrape, his fingers touching it gingerly.

'It's going to look great in the photos. It'll be a talking point for years after.'

'Don't worry, Kitts, I've heard they can do wonderful things with photo software. My scabby chin won't spoil your wedding photos.'

Reaching the foot of the stairs, she rested a hand on her brother's arm. 'Jimby, you wouldn't be you without a scrape, a scrub or a bruise and as long as you're in one piece and not hurting too much, I wouldn't change anything about you for the world. Not even my wedding photos, and I know Ollie will think the same, too.'

'Now don't go getting all mushy on me. It's not every day your little sister gets married to your best mate, and it wouldn't take much to make me a quivering wreck, so I think we should quit with the compliments while we're ahead.' He held his arm out for her to take. 'Ladies, your carriage awaits. That includes you, too, Ethel, and might I add you're looking gorgeous today with that beautiful flower arrangement in your collar.' Ethel, in her capacity of third "bridesmaid", responded with a wag of her tail.

'And you're looking very dapper in your bow-tie, Humph,' Kitty said fondly.

'He certainly is. I bet you can't wait for them to start slicing into hat hog roast, can you, fella?' Jimby chuckled, bending to ruffle Humph's ears.

James's Landie had been given a thorough wedding overhaul. The canvas top had been rolled back and the roof frame wrapped in fresh flowers, greenery and vintage lace – courtesy of Auntie Annie. Pastel coloured bunting hung along the sides, and a chain of blowsy flowers ran from the front centre of the bonnet to the sides. The seats had been covered with a cream damask fabric, which was easier on the eye than the black vinyl, peppered with holes. It did, however, prove to be slippery. And on the short journey to church Lily and Noushka found themselves giggling hysterically as they slid up and down the benches, while Humph and Ethel peered out at the back, barking and wagging their tails.

'Ready, sis?' Kitty and James were standing outside the great oak doors of St. Thomas's church. Behind them, Anoushka was smoothing Lily's dress while Humph and Ethel – who were also accompanying them down the aisle – were waiting patiently, a basket of flowers clamped firmly between Ethel's teeth. Little Mary had been given the nod and struck up the first chords of the wedding march, its melodic notes soaring high up into the rafters.

Kitty took a deep breath, turned to her brother and smiled. 'Ready, Jimby.' She linked her arm through his, and they made their way down the aisle, her eyes fixed firmly on Ollie at the altar, happiness stretching her smile wider with every step.

Sensing his bride getting closer, Ollie turned to look at her, and a beaming smile spread across his face. Kitty's heart flipped at how handsome he looked in his blue suit, his hair combed smooth and his face clean shaven.

How was it possible to feel this happy?

EARLIER THAT MORNING, after a brief rummage in her knicker drawer, Kitty found the package she'd bought in Middleton-le-Moors earlier in the week. With her stomach doing somersaults, she headed for the bathroom. Five minutes later, her suspicions had been confirmed: she was expecting a baby. Ollie's baby. Excitement pounded in her chest; they'd talked about the possibility, though she hadn't expected it to happen so quickly. But she couldn't have picked a more perfect day to find out.

LATER, in the yurt, it was agreed that speeches would be got out of the way first, leaving everyone to enjoy their food and wine without worrying about having to stand up in front of the whole village — the whole village with the exception of Gwyneth and George and the Mellisons.

James relished the opportunity to make a speech, regaling everyone with entertaining stories. At times he had the guests laughing so hard tears were pouring down cheeks, while the bride and groom blushed furiously.

'Thanks for that, funny bloke,' Ollie said grinning. He leaned across to James. 'I'm so glad you felt it necessary to share so much personal information with everyone.'

'Any time, Oll. It's the least I could do. Or should I call you Ambrose? Kept that one quiet, didn't you? Can't think why,' he teased, referring to the revelation of Ollie's middle name during the wedding vows.

Ollie clamped a hand to his forehead and groaned. 'I knew you'd have my life about that one. Blame my mother, it was her grandad's name.'

'Suits you, mate,' James said with a wink.

THE BALMY AFTERNOON melted into a mellow evening, and the trestle tables lining the far side of the yurt were groaning under the weight of plates piled high with slices of pork and stuffing left over from the hog roast. They were accompanied by large pots of tangy apple sauce and mountains of fluffy bread buns.

Kitty felt a tap on her shoulder and turned to see Carolyn Hammondely. 'Caro. Thank you for coming. You too, Sim.' She smiled at the pair.

'You're very welcome and congrats, darling.' Caro air kissed her cheek. 'I hope you've enjoyed your special day half as much as we have. Anyway, I just wanted to say,' she stood back, making a sweeping gesture with her arm, 'we hope you like our gift to you both…' As she spoke the band of young musicians who'd just run in behind Kitty struck up, their familiar blend of rock and folk music filling the yurt to the rafters.

'Is that…? Oh, my god, Caro!' Kitty's mouth fell open.

'Hiya, Kitty, remember me?' asked Gabe Dublin, who'd joined Tykes! on the stage.

The dance floor filled quickly, with no one dancing more enthusiastically than Jonty who twirled a breathless Bea around like his life depended upon it. Soon they were surrounded by a circle of revellers clapping and egging them on. 'Don't encourage him!' she shrieked, laughing as he picked her up and threw her from side to side.

'You look tired. Do you think it's bad if I sneak you home and get you all to myself?' Ollie rubbed Kitty's shoulders.

'Mmm. Sounds good, I'm jiggered. What time is it?'

He checked his watch, 'Half eleven, just gone.' He looked handsomely dishevelled, she thought, with his floral tie askew and his blond hair ruffled. Kitty couldn't think of anything nicer than snuggling up in a soft, cosy bed with him.

As if reading their minds, Molly and Pip sauntered over. 'You look absolutely knackered, Kitts. No one would mind if you headed off now; it's been a long day. And all this can be cleared up in the morning.'

'D'you think? I do feel shattered. I was up with the larks this morning.'

'Yep, I think you should get yourselves off. And you're going to need this.' With a mysterious smile, Molly handed Kitty a key.

'What's this for?' Ollie looked from Pip to Molly.

'It's the key to Withrin Hill Farm Campsite's latest addition, and the place you're going to spend your wedding night.' Pip beamed. 'You remember that vintage train carriage I brought home? Well, it's finally finished, done out in its original glory. I've even wired the old lights up to the electricity. It's en-suite, too. There's been no expense spared, and we want you two to be the first to use it.'

'I don't know what to say.' Kitty placed a hand on her chest.

'You don't need to say anything. Just follow Mum; she's stayed off the booze and is going to drive you up there. We took the liberty of packing an overnight bag for you both – Noushka and your two were very helpful in that department – and everything you could possibly need is waiting for you. All the kids are staying at Mum and Dad's tonight, so you don't need to worry about them.'

'Looks like they've thought of everything.' Ollie smiled at Kitty.

'We have, so go and get yourselves on your honeymoon night, Mr and Mrs Cartwright.' Molly pushed the pair in the direction of Auntie Annie who was waiting by the entrance.

CURLED up in Ollie's arms in freshly laundered white linen, Kitty could think of nowhere else she'd rather be. He'd been overjoyed when she'd told him about the baby and had made love tenderly to her, laying gentle kisses on her stomach, where he now rested his hand protectively.

The pair lay in contented silence, lost in their own thoughts for a while before Ollie propped himself up on his arm. He gazed down at Kitty, running a finger down the side of her face. 'Happy?'

'Very.' She nuzzled into him.

'No regrets?'

'Not one.' She reached up and kissed him.

'Now, where were we?'

SEVEN MONTHS LATER
CARTWRIGHT (NEE FAIRFAX)
Ollie and Kitty are delighted to announce
the arrival of their beautiful daughter
LOTTIE ELIZABETH
Born 21st February
A very welcome little sister for
Anoushka, Lucas, Lily and Bryn

THE END

AFTERWORD

Thank you for reading The Letter – Kitty's Story. If you enjoyed it, I'd be really grateful if you could pop over to Amazon and leave a review. It doesn't have to be long – just a few words would do – but for us new authors it makes a huge difference. Thank you so much.

If you'd like to find out more about what I get up to in my little corner of the North Yorkshire Moors, or if you'd like to get in touch, you can find me in the following places:

Blog: www.elizajscott.com
Twitter: @ElizaJScott1
Facebook: @elizajscottauthor
Instagram: www.instagram.com/elizajscott

ALSO BY THE AUTHOR

The Talisman -Molly's Story (Book 2)

The Secret – Violet's Story (Book 3)

A Christmas Kiss (Book 4)

A Christmas Wedding at the Castle (Book 5)

All are available on Amazon in ebook and paperback format.

ACKNOWLEDGMENTS

First and foremost, I'd like to thank my husband (whose mischievous sense of humour provided much inspiration for the character of Jimby) and my daughters for their unwavering support. If it wasn't for them chasing away my self-doubt I would never have finished writing this book. I must also thank them for putting up with the chaos that surrounded my 'desk' – aka the kitchen table – in the latter weeks as I prepared my manuscript for publication day. Once I move into my little writing room you won't have to put up with it again!

Thank you also to the lovely Berni Stevens for designing such a stunning cover for my book. It's perfect! I can't wait to see what you come up with for Molly's Story. It's been fab getting to know you, and I've enjoyed our email chats, whether it be about goths, music, spooky happenings or the joys of sipping wine in the garden on a sunny evening.

Thank you to Alison Williams for your amazing editing skills and pointing me in the right direction. I've learnt a huge amount from you on this rather steep learning curve! I'm looking forward to working with you on the next book in the series.

I'd also like to thank Rachel Gilbey at Rachel's Random Resources, who worked tirelessly organising the Cover Reveal and Publication Day Blog Tour for this book. I've never known anyone so organised and so calm. In fact, I'm pretty convinced you're Wonder Woman!

I mustn't forget to thank my legal advisor friend for keeping me right with all of the legal references. I owe you a pint!

Finally, a huge thank you to all of the book bloggers who so kindly hosted the Cover Reveal and Blog Tour for this, my first book. I can't put in to words just how much I appreciate it. People often comment on the warmth and friendliness of the book community, and this just proves them right. Your generosity of spirit has blown me away.

ABOUT THE AUTHOR

Eliza lives in a village in the North Yorkshire Moors with her husband, two daughters and two black Labradors. When she's not writing, she can usually be found with her nose in a book/glued to her Kindle or working in her garden. Eliza also enjoys bracing walks in the countryside, rounded off by a visit to a teashop where she can indulge in another two of her favourite things: tea and cake.

Printed in Great Britain
by Amazon

37122577R00199